PILGRIM CITY

TIM MURGATROYD

Cloud Lodge Books
London

First published in 2021 by Cloud Lodge Books (CLB)

All rights reserved. No part of the publication may be reproduced, stored in a database or retrieval system, or transmitted in any form or by any means without the permission in writing of the publisher, nor be otherwise circulated in any form or binding or cover other than that in which it is published and without a similar condition including this condition being imposed on the subsequent purchaser.

Copyright © Tim Murgatroyd 2021

The moral right of the author has been asserted.

A CIP catalogue record for this book is available from the British Library.

All characters and events in this publication, other than those clearly in the public domain, are fictitious and any resemblance to any real person, living or dead, is purely coincidental and not intended by the author.

ISBN 978-1-8380451-6-6

1 3 5 7 9 10 8 6 4 2

Cloud Lodge Books
51 Holland Street, London W8 7JB
www.cloudlodgebooks.com

Heaven and Earth are not kind.
They regard all things as offerings.
.

      Lao Tzu, Tao Te Ching

PROLOGUE

A speck on the ocean, a long, wide cargo ship. Hydrojet engines churned a white wake. Uncountable glints of sunlight on wave crests. Wind buffet and sigh.

As Sri Lanka and the city of Mughalia fell behind, Helen Devereux decided it was safe to explore the ship. Necessary, too, this plasti-steel honeycomb her only home in a world of danger.

Fears of Mughalia lingered. Cloud-swirl images, horrors, sensations. The Grand Autonomy legitimising the creation of new, unnatural life forms. A woman's body gene-sculpted to be forever Beautiful, putrid with gene sickness, so much rotten fruit. Streams of Beautifuls, milling, shoving, trampling, crying out, united solely by a lust to live forever. And always, sickening guilt for a young girl who had trusted her. For Averil Pilgrim. Bonny, innocent Averil Pilgrim, corrupted by the Five Cities . . .

She wandered the ship, aware it was an enormous drone entirely indifferent to her. Crucially, the screen she carried had disabled the vessel's intruder security system. As far as its sensors were concerned, she did not exist.

Torch in hand, Helen travelled corridors intended only as access ways for repair drones or occasional human technicians. The long ship was full of spaces for containers, fusion energy cells, support systems. Though it existed to serve people, it barely needed them.

Towards the stern, a rounded tower rose from the cargo deck. This contained accommodation provided for living passengers, two small cabins with bunks, stores of preserved food, basic equipment for survival.

Steep stairs climbed past softly humming consoles to an old-style bridge, complete with a thick, plastiglass window to survey the foredeck. Waves encircled her like the sky, blue-black with the onset of a sudden tropical twilight.

Her fears subsided. No one back in Mughalia seemed to guess she was here. No one in the Five Cities cared, obsessed with their marvellous new Angels – with enacting brutal change.

Her hand crept to the Baytown Jewel, the golden locket warmed by the top of her breasts. "We might yet see you home," she promised the talisman.

Its single, blue sapphire eye stared back mockingly. Then Helen realised. She had started talking to herself.

* * *

For days, Helen had no idea of the ship's intended route. When she stowed aboard in Mughalia, Synetta's borrowed screen informed her its ultimate destination was Albion. Beyond that, she knew nothing. Just that drone cargo ships crisscrossed the globe, powered by unfailing fusion engines, picking up and delivering supplies to all the Five Cities: Albion, Mitopia, Han City, Mughalia and Neo Rio. And that its progress through the ocean would be slow. What need for hurry, after all?

This particular drone ship showed signs of age. Though plasti-steel could not rust, she detected spots of corrosion upon many metal fittings. Sometimes the engines groaned like grieving whales. The ship vibrated at the edge of hearing.

She dared not risk consulting Synetta's screen, in case someone traced the signal. Yet the device tempted her with the promise of news. On this little island moving through a watery desert, the screen offered significance: confirmation she was connected to a bigger world.

Helen did risk activating the primitive leisure console in her Spartan cabin. An obsolete model, saying much about the pedigree of the ship. As the vessel rolled and grumbled, she flicked from holocast to holocast. Each of the Five Cities ran its own information service; it soon became clear the news from all five was grim.

For hours she watched, aware much of what she saw must be censored by the Ruling Council – or what remained of it, after the Brubachers' purges. These, it seemed, were on-going. Anyone foolish enough to oppose their new Life Perfected, let alone the creation of original, sentient life forms, was subjected to a brief show trial. Then stripped naked, and banished beyond City limits, to feed hungry Primitives or other beasts.

Nor were malcontents the only victims. Health alerts indicated the gene-infection Helen had witnessed in Mughalia was now a pandemic. Those afflicted found organs could mutate in a matter of days. Bladders morphed into kidneys, hands to strange, bird-like claws. Treatment meant instant sterilisation, one's precious body reduced to hygienic ash.

Holocast followed holocast. Several Cities demanded secession from the Ruling Council. That the technology for gene renewal should be made public, not hoarded and controlled by a tiny group of Founders, especially the Brubachers. A rebel leader in Mitopia threatened civil war. He vanished mid-holocast.

At night – though night and day blurred in the cabin – Helen dreamt of her nose growing pointy as a witch's from children's books. Then her heart burst inside her, flooding her lungs with blood until she choked – and woke, gasping for air.

Just another bad dream. Since the Great Dyings began when she was young, genuinely young, nightmares had evolved into normality.

Synetta had linked gene-infection to visiting Honeycomb in Albion, the sole place on earth where cell renewal was permitted. It was many years now since Helen had gone there. Hence, the wrinkles on her hands and face. Sagging neck, breasts and thighs. Streaks of grey in her hair. The miracle that kept her body forever youthful was dissipating like spring blossom drifting from the tree.

One day, Helen watched a bizarre holocast of Marvin and Merle Brubacher admonishing any who spoke of independence from the Five Cities. They wore suits of thinly beaten gold. Courtiers and the new creatures dubbed Angels surrounded them. Near the back, Helen glimpsed a pale, familiar face: Averil!

So she was alive, in the dubious protection of the Brubachers.

Helen shut down the leisure console, grieving for her lost friend. She mounted the stairs to the ship's bridge and looked ahead to the line where sky met sea. A dark horizon awaited.

* * *

Helen examined the Baytown Jewel, hung at all times on a chain round her neck. She had grown superstitious about its safety.

The Medieval locket was diamond-shaped, pure Indian gold. A mother and child engraved on the front. In the centre, a flawless blue sapphire. On its back, a hideous, grinning skeleton, the fate awaiting mother and child.

But the Jewel was more than just a reminder of mortality. A hidden catch opened the locket to reveal a small compartment for prayers on tiny pieces of parchment, magic spells to defy death.

It was a long time since Helen had released the catch. She gently eased open the locket, expecting it to be empty. What she found made her gasp.

No bigger than a fat pea. In shape and colour, a pearl. She recognised it instantly: a device for storing dense networks of information, code upon layered code.

Long discarded memories stirred. How long ago, ten, fifteen years? Back then her protector and lover, Blair Gover, had adopted the name Bertrand Du Guesclin, complying with a fashion for playing the role of French medieval chevalier, shepherd, troubadour, or prince. They attended a masked ball along with other Founders of the Five Cities, including Marvin and Merle Brubacher. Also, Blair's old colleague, Dr Guy Price, then using the name Guy de Prie-Dieu. All evening, Blair maintained a tense conversation with Guy. After the ball, they returned to their palatial home in the centre of Albion, where Blair paced in the bedroom, unable to sleep.

"What's wrong?" she asked, from beneath the quilt.

"I am afraid, Helen."

"What of?"

"Guy. Yes, him. And others I cannot seem to identify, however hard I try. They are tampering with all we have achieved here. They do not seem to understand the Beautiful Life is fragile as an egg. Once cracked, its essence could rot. Nobody understands DNA completely. It is always evolving, adapting. Sometimes in ways one abhors."

"Is this *tampering* to do with Guy? You spoke with him all night."

She noticed two info-pearls on a side table. Blair's eyes followed her gaze. He laughed harshly.

"They think me a fool," he said. "But in those two little seeds I have implanted codes capable of controlling every networked system in the Five Cities. Indeed, *every* important system we possess. All are designed to be interconnected. Every drone and essential device, however small. Thus, the Ruling Council guarantees itself complete power, should the need arise. It is a secret known only to myself and Guy. We devised the master codes when the Five Cities were first created. But we never told a soul. Each of us agreed to store the codes on two of these info-pearls. These we would hide where no one could find them."

"Doesn't that mean you could shut down all Five Cities? That is impossible!"

He sniffed. "Never mind, my love. Let us pray that I am never forced to run the codes."

Touching the info-pearl in the locket, Helen remembered something else. She had caught Blair hanging round the display case of the jewel, just before he disappeared. Then she understood: he must have hidden it where no one in the City would suspect, a haunt of primitives. Doubtless, he had expected to send a drone to reclaim it when needed.

Helen guessed something else. Though Blair might be dead, this nugget of power might be turned against the Five Cities. Her heart beat quickly.

"My God," she whispered. "My God."

She must deliver it to Michael Pilgrim. Above all, to the City-exile in York known as Lady Veil. That tortured, abused rebel against the Beautiful Life might know how to turn it against the Five Cities. To their absolute ruin.

* * *

The ship entered the South China Sea. Soon the weather changed.

High winds piled up waves; a constant spray of sea and rain blew against the portholes. From the bridge she witnessed titanic battles of thunder, lightning and black cloud. Swells washed over the hull of the ship. It creaked and groaned in response, eerie protests magnified by the vessel's many hollow spaces. Fusion engines chuntered. Helen dreaded the silence of them failing, of becoming flotsam for a pitiless storm.

PROLOGUE

For two days they passed along the edge of the typhoon. Now the ship rolled and bucked, tossed by gale and deep canyons of water, its prow climbing waves then falling with a resounding crash that shook the vessel. Rain and troughs swilled over the deck and superstructure.

No clambering out onto the observation platform now. Not unless she wanted to be whipped away into the void. Helen retreated to her cabin, vomiting from seasickness, white with hunger and exhaustion. No sleep, just clinging to a bunk that tilted and span like her stomach and head.

Then the typhoon lapsed into a tropical storm, showers and mere wind. She risked standing in a doorway that gave onto the deck. Sea and sky were grey as restless slate.

* * *

When the ship reached the island of Taiwan, Helen had recovered a little strength. Han City lay on the west coast, built upon an earlier city, its compacted rubble a twenty-foot layer of earth and bone, plastic and concrete.

Helen had never cared for Han City. Perhaps its precarious position alarmed her, at the far limits of the Five Cities' influence, facing out across a hundred miles of ocean to a dark, hostile continent.

The people of Han City were less inclined to whimsical, feckless pleasures than most Beautifuls, more focussed on the systematic management of ur-humanity's scattered remnants. Blair Gover once explained it this way: "Before the plagues, my dear, the leaders of Han City ruled China and the other states in the region. Billionaires a thousand times over, generalissimos, little gods and goddesses. They feared their own people then, and clearly still do. Actually, that is prudent. If the peoples of South East Asia recover, they will pose a threat to us all. Besides, culling the Asian primitives – who are notoriously fecund – keeps the Beautifuls of Han City active and spry."

Helen had not argued. In those days, to her shame, she had approved warily of efficient heartlessness. How *spry* to hunt down every last human on the island of Taiwan, as once mankind expunged the dodo. How *active* to devise horrible new diseases to infect the primitives.

As they approached Han City, Helen checked the gun given to her by Synetta. Better to take her own life than surrender.

The cargo ship dutifully took its place among a small queue of drone vessels outside the port; automatic onshore systems guided it to a berth. Drones trundled from warehouses to extract rectangular containers from the hold. Others prepared cargo destined for Neo Rio, Albion or Mitopia.

Helen watched through a porthole. Little sign of life in Han City other than the dock drones. A few aircars floated between skyscrapers, stray birds where once flocks flew. Lights burned all over the city, indicating people.

Then she noticed a sprawled body on the dockside. To her disgust, a small creature climbed out of a drain. Rearing on back legs, it sniffed the air. The rat scurried to the body. Burying its snout in an eye socket, it commenced feeding. Soon dozens of its kind were crawling over the corpse, wriggling beneath clothes for better access.

Shaking, Helen sat on the bed, pistol on her lap. So the holocasts did not lie: gene sickness was out of control in all the Five Cities.

With a surge of hydrojets, the ship backed away from the docks and turned once more for open ocean.

* * *

The ship sailed on, heading deep into the Pacific. Lonely days piled up. Helen talked to herself more and more. Odd exclamations, passionate monologues – often railing against Blair Gover – fits of hysterical laughter.

I'm going mad, she told the mirror in her cabin. The haggard face it contained did not contradict her.

A fine place for insanity, this drone cargo vessel. Because she did not exist it treated her like a ghost, a spectre carried by the ocean, a message in a bottle.

From the deck, she saw vast islands of rotting plastic, weed-tangled fishing lines. Yet birds were plentiful – petrel and albatross, sheerwater and fulmar – shadowing the silvery shoals, dipping and diving.

Yes, nature would outlast foolish, wicked mankind. There must be hope in that. Helen wept for joy at a passing school of humpback whales, hundreds strong, spouts like fountains. Dolphins weaved between the great, labouring beasts, lithe needles sewing the sea's cloth.

Two weeks passed. The preserved food she depended on had to be rationed. Sometimes she panicked at the thought of the water purifier breaking down and hurried to fill every available container with drinkable water.

At times the rumble of the vessel's hydro-engines altered pitch. The changes worried her more than running out of food. If the ship broke down mid-ocean, the Five Cities would most likely abandon it as unsalvageable, given their current crisis.

They entered the stormy Drake Passage between the foot of South America and Antarctica. Waves ran high, wind buffeted, straining the engines yet further. Though it was hard to judge speed on a featureless ocean, Helen sensed their pace slow.

Then the ship changed course. On the control bridge, red lights flashed a silent alarm.

More interminable days and nights. Pale from inadequate food, exhausted by her fears, Helen at first dismissed the line of craggy cliffs on the northern horizon as a mirage. But no, land! Was this why the ship had changed direction, for landfall?

Still the hydro-engines rumbled and juddered. They drew near a bare, wind-blasted moorland with mountains in the distance. Rounding a cape, Helen spied buildings from the Before Times, scores of houses with collapsed roofs, the decaying remains of a township.

The ship headed for a squat, grey compound with reinforced concrete walls, high as ten tall men, its steel gates open like a black, gaping mouth,

Helen realised the limping ship had made for the nearest source of repairs. Indeed, an enclosed dock lined with cranes and gantries provided such a facility.

Her elation turned to tense anticipation. Such a compound might have a technician stationed there, supervising drones to repair damaged ships, before they headed up the coast of South America, bound for Neo Rio and the Atlantic crossing to Albion and Mitopia. Maybe more than one technician. One would be enough to activate any resident security drones.

"The Falkland Islands," she told herself, remembering maps of the world. "I must have sailed all the way to the Falkland Islands."

Helen hurried down the steep stairs from the bridge to find her pistol. As she did so, the ship crept into dock. With a final groan of protest, the hydrojets switched off. Silence descended. The ship creaked. She could hear gulls out on the sound.

Her hand crept to the Baytown Jewel. Its precious cargo was possibly the last chance to vanquish the Five Cities, and the dark future for humanity they had planned.

ONE

Seth and Hurdy-Gurdy trailed through the streets of York. Both stepped carefully in case the mud concealed animal or human waste. Spring leaned over winter. Birds squabbled in the eaves of shops and houses. York was fast becoming a safe centre for industry of all kinds, from papermaking to gunpowder manufacture.

"It's right good to see you," Seth said. "You're always so busy these days."

Gurdy paused from singing softly to himself. "Young Nuncle is bored in York? Eh?"

"Aye. They've told me if I step beyond the City Walls before my trial, I'll be condemned as easy meat."

"Easy meat?"

"It means anyone in the Commonwealth of the North can kill me on sight without penalty."

"And you assume I am a vegetarian?"

Seth had no idea what such a creature might be. "No one's turned their hand against me here. I'm under the protection of Lady Veil. But no one speaks to me either. I'm pointed out on the street as Big Jacko's toy."

"A simplistic appellation," mused Gurdy. "Hey, the silly-o!"

"They say I'm destined to swing. I reckon they're not far wrong."

"Perhaps. Perhaps."

"Have you heard whether a date has been set for my trial, Gurdy?"

With an abrupt shift of mood Seth took for granted, Hurdy-Gurdy reverted to a favourite persona: that of mad clown. He sang in an operatic tenor, while walking on his hands:

Let the punishment fit the crime!
The punishment fit the crime!
Ee aye addio,
The world is shit and grime.

The young man laughed, despite his worries. He liked his humour coarse. A fluid movement later, Hurdy-Gurdy was back on his feet.

"Poor, lonely Young Nuncle," he purred. "Let us visit the Other Young Nuncle, and talk a while. Yes, let us. He is lonelier than we two, eh?"

The mismatched pair reached a former park overlooking the River Ouse. Within it, the ruins of a medieval abbey housed a cemetery. As Seth led the way between trees to a fresh mound of earth, he sensed eyes upon them.

"Bella!" he called. "Bella! Show yourself. Gurdy's here."

No one appeared. Branches with opening buds stirred above them. He looked round for Bella and her fellow strangelings, genetically altered to be half hare, half human, monstrous experiments in new, hybrid life forms conducted by the City. For what possible reason, he could not conceive.

"Bella comes here, you know," said Seth. "To visit her brother's grave. Other strangelings come with her. And they're not all hares either. I've seen half-dogs and cats, the size of small people, walking on two legs. And once, a strangeling owl that could fly. Sometimes Bella comes up to me and sniffs. I can tell she does not trust me. She and her companions run free in the countryside and I'm sure they will be hunted. Lady Veil can only guarantee their safety in York."

ONE

"Ah," said Gurdy. "So she is drawn to Jojo's grave. Proof of residual memory. A lingering capacity to love. The City would not like that. If she is a prototype life form, as I believe she and her fellows most certainly are, they would class her as a dangerous failure."

"There's still a soul inside her," said Seth, "if that's what you mean. She seems more human than the others. Like she remembers who she was. I think that's why she's a kind of leader amongst them."

Tenderly, he led Gurdy to the grave mound. Around it, daffodils and bluebells sprouted like a gaily dressed crowd of young courtiers. Grass shoots had found root space on the bare soil of the grave.

"Strange to think of Jojo in there," said Seth. "He'll never see the summer flowers this year. Or feel a warm breeze. So strong and handsome and fine as he was." His voice rose. "It is I who should rot there! Food for worms and beetles. Not Jojo. He were too damn good."

Tears started to his eyes. *Cheap as tears at a funeral*, people said of weeping back in Baytown. And Seth agreed. All his life, he had watched people wail and cry then laugh fit to burst a moment later. How else was the world to be understood? Or endured.

Just then a clang of bells sounded an alarm. Seth started from his gloomy contemplation of the grave; yet the old holotainer seemed to be listening out for the summons.

"Come Young Nuncle," he said, gently. "Let us see who the Minster bells bring to York."

* * *

Hundreds were gathering at the Minster when Hurdy-Gurdy and Seth arrived.

"This way," said Gurdy, leading Seth up the ancient cathedral's stone steps to join Lady Veil and her entourage. As ever, a tightly bound scarf round her lower face concealed the hideous wrongs done to her by the City. But hiding is not the same as forgetting – or forgiving.

"Is it him?" Hurdy asked her.

Lady Veil's hands moved in rapid sign language. Her interpreter spoke up, "He comes."

"Then the wheels on fortune's bus go round and round," he replied.

Seth knew that Lady Veil and Gurdy had known each other in the City, fellow rebels, before their banishment among the primitives. He thought of his father's old stories about angels rebelling against God – their calamitous tumble from Paradise to Hell.

Again, her hands moved.

"You are right, as always," declared the City-man, who had taught himself her sign language. "Rely on me to twitch his reins."

He uttered a loud, disconcerting whinny. Horsemen appeared on the road. At their head, Michael Pilgrim, known as the Protector of the North. Seth shrank further.

Beside Michael rode Tom Higginbottom and others Seth remembered from his troubled boyhood in Baytown. Folk with long memories – and grievances towards him – of their own. New faces, too, soldiers and leaders of communities from York to the borders of Geordieland. Among them, a face concealed by a deep hood and wide umbrella. He seemed to wish avoiding recognition from above, not below.

At the sight of Michael Pilgrim, the crowd cheered and clapped. Here was the victor of Pickering, of Lindisfarne, vanquisher of the hated Big Jacko, a leader advocating progress and education, laws to protect strong and weak alike. He nodded in reply but did not smile.

As for the cowled man beneath his bobbing umbrella, Seth noticed Tom Higginbottom stayed close beside him. A thin chain was attached to the man's wrist.

* * *

ONE

They formed a semicircle of chairs: Lady Veil, Michael Pilgrim, Hurdy-Gurdy, Tom Higginbottom and Mister Priestman. A sixth person sat in shadows. A faded plastic mask from the Before Times concealed his face. It depicted a smirking clown.

The long room was in York's ancient Guildhall, where Lady Veil dwelt and based her administration. High windows overlooked the river; the banter of boatmen could be heard outside. Rats scratched beneath the floorboards.

A man and woman in leather-patched clothes entered. They slouched like folk accustomed to long miles afoot. Lady Veil, through her interpreter, who stood beside her chair, introduced them as scouts sent south to spy on Albion.

"For we know," she said, 'things are changing behind their high walls and guardian drones. Why else have we been ignored for so long?"

The spies had ridden south with a score of others, all heavily armed, down a great deserted road from the Before Times haunted with ghosts, a long week's travel.

"We found Albion is an island," declared the woman.

Well-endowed with brawn, she reminded Michael of his ex-Crusader comrade, Aggie Brown. He hoped she did not share Aggie's cruel pleasure in another's pain.

"South of the city are woodlands, wet and boggy. We saw a few patrol drones there. Not many. Even fewer drones watch the northern border of Albion."

"Why fewer drones?" asked Michael. "What lies directly north of Albion?"

A landscape, it turned out, of fens and meres, stretching for fifty miles to the sea. Mud bound together by young willow and alder woods formed islands. A desolate, eerie land, yet full of green life.

"There we concealed ourselves," she concluded.

"Is it less dangerous than the southern approach to Albion?" asked Michael.

This point seemed important. Perhaps the City, in its arrogance, had a soft underbelly.

"North, south, east and west," said the woman, "a high concrete wall stops entry to Albion."

"But drones and walls aren't the only danger," broke in her companion, a grizzled fellow. "Swamp-devils dwell in the shadow of that place. And plenty of 'em."

Mister Priestman nodded sagely. "Hobs, pixies, goblins and fays love a marsh right well," he informed the others. "They send forth will'o'wisps to snare souls and suck out their spirit. Aye, as you or I might the yoke of an egg."

"We saw none of that," replied the man. "Fen Men, we saw, dressed in green like toads. They didn't take kindly to us."

"Fen Men?" probed Michael.

"Dwellers in the swamps, slippery as eels."

"Our guns scared them off," added the woman. "Still, we didn't try their patience by hanging round. We were only there two days when we came upon the prisoner."

All waited.

"He were naked as a babe fresh from the womb," said the woman. "And almost as bloody, scratched by briar and thorn. He begged us not to eat him. He jabbered about things turning rotten in Albion. Fighting like rats in a cage."

Again Michael heard the scratch of tiny claws beneath the floorboards.

"Anyway," said the woman, concluding their tale. "That's why we hurried him back here for questioning."

Mister Priestman stood suddenly, his arms raised to the stars. His

ONE

battered top hat decorated with gull feathers, shark teeth, semi-precious stones, dried willow and thyme, hung askew.

"I have a far-sight!" he declared, the Nuagers' term for a cosmic vision. "I see the fens! A queen o' faeries dwells there in a palace woven of reeds. Her faeries are lifting their wands, ready for battle. *Come*, she says, *come and set the world right. Come brave mortals and set the world aright. Faery shall be your friend if you set the world right.*"

An awkward silence followed.

A snort escaped the cowled, masked man in the corner. "Must I really endure such drivel, Pilgrim?" he complained. "I insist you take this *witch doctor* away. He is insufferable."

"Be quiet, Gover," warned Michael. "Only a fool ignores Priestman's far-sights."

Or someone willing to offend the sizable community of Nuagers in the Commonwealth of the North. Which he was not.

"Remember, not all wisdom is measured by cold reason," he added.

Tom Higginbottom rubbed the knuckles of his right hand, big and obdurate as a bull's hoof.

"Shall I take the bugger outside?" he offered.

"No," said Michael, "Gover's knowledge of the Five Cities might be useful to us. Let's question this naked City-man next."

The last time he and Tom interrogated a man – or youth, as it happened – the torture they practised for quick results stained their souls another shade darker.

* * *

A tall, handsome young man was prodded in, hands bound tight. He wore filthy sackcloth and plastic flip-flops from the Before Times. Bruises and cuts coloured his skin. Terrified eyes flickered. At Lady Veil, he paused in bemusement; but at Hurdy-Gurdy, his eyes opened wide.

"Y-you?" he spluttered. "Here? Declan O'Hara! It *is* you. Do not let them eat me! I am innocent."

The gnarled holotainer's grin resembled a gargoyle's. He rose and bowed. "It seems Declan has found a fan. Declany-poos *loves* a fan."

Michael Pilgrim was less delighted.

"How is it the prisoner knows you, Master Gurdy?"

Michael's deep voice echoed in the big room.

"Aye," added Tom Higginbottom. "I were wondering the same thing."

"Everyone knew Declan once," said Hurdy-Gurdy. "Oh lordy, yes!" His voice took on a sycophantic edge. "*Declan O'Hara, TV superstar then holotainer supreme. Declan could do anything, juggle, sing, act, play any instrument you gave him, hypnoshows, dance extravaganzas, anything!*"

"Except modesty," offered the masked man in the shadows.

"Ah, fame," mused Gurdy. "I clung to that trembling bubble for more years than you can imagine. Didn't I, fan?"

"Oh *yes*, Declan." The prisoner had found a powerful friend. "Help me, I beg you!"

A complex snort escaped the man in the corner.

Lady Veil's hands moved. Her interpreter spoke: "She says, 'Best leave the interrogation to Hurdy-Gurdy. He has ways with weak minds.'"

Michael exchanged doubtful glances with Tom.

Hurdy-Gurdy sat the prisoner on a comfortable chair, loosening his bindings.

"See, my friend," he hummed, "you are perfectly safe now. No chopping you up for stew. Look me in the eye. Yes, that's right. Poor, poor fellow. Relax. You are safe now. Quite safe."

The City-man blinked.

ONE

"In my eye. Quite safe. Look. Quite safe. Lo-ok."

The prisoner's gaze fixed on Hurdy-Gurdy's bloodshot brown eyes. Slowly, his tension slackened. The guileless smile of a reassured child lifted the corners of his bruised mouth. His eyelids quivered. He exhaled slowly.

"Aaargh," he sighed, "Declan O'Hara."

His eyelids fluttered, and closed.

As if on cue, clouds covered the sun outside; the high-ceilinged room fell into shadow.

"What's he doing?" whispered Michael.

Black magic, surely. Not that he held with superstition. Still, you could never be too careful.

"Yon Hurdy-Gurdy is of the goblin-folk. " explained Mister Priestman. "They pluck men's souls like buttercups."

Lady Veil's hands moved and her interpreter whispered, "Hush, please. Do not wake him. Trust us."

"If you answer dear Decky-wecky's questions, how free you will feel, how happy."

"Yes, Declan."

His strange, remote voice set Michael on edge. Perhaps Mister Priestman was right: Hurdy-Gurdy *was* stealing his soul.

The next hour brought a tale Michael Pilgrim had waited his whole life to hear. As it unfolded, he recollected Lady Veil's predecessor as leader in York, the Modified Man. He had told Michael: *They are monstrously arrogant in the Five Cities, utterly sure of their power. One day that hubris might bring their test tubes and beloved devices crashing down on their heads.*

Rain spattered against the windows; candles were lit for the scribe recording the prisoner's testimony. The City-man's voice droned, thoughts and memories guided gently by Hurdy-Gurdy. Some of what

Michael heard seemed too farfetched for truth. Much revolted him.

An episode unfolded of the prisoner's former position in some far off place, Mughalia, how he had borne the title, Supervisor of Animals, preparing every beast imaginable for monstrous gladiatorial fights to entertain bored Beautifuls. Some of those animals walked on two legs, men and women from all over the globe, including Britain, hacking one another to death for sport.

Then came the man's account of the current situation in the Five Cities. At first, Michael judged he was lying. Could so great a power be brought so low, so quickly? The masked man left his corner. His hood fell back, the clown mask cast aside in anguish. Blair Gover clutched his upper chest, where a bullet almost felled him at Lindisfarne. It still gave constant pain.

"I warned them," he groaned. "Over and over. They would not listen! All my life's labours come to this."

"Gurdy, ask the prisoner about Averil, my niece," urged Michael. "The City stole her away, we believe."

Hurdy-Gurdy obliged.

"There was a primitive in Mughalia," agreed the Supervisor of Animals. "A guest of powerful people . . . She was servant to a powerful lady, the former lover of a great man . . . The lady addressed her as Averil."

"So she is alive!" cried Michael. "That must mean Helen is, as well."

Blair Gover pointed feverishly at the prisoner. "Intensify his unconscious state," he commanded. "Was the lady he mentions, Helen Devereux? If so, did she wear an antique gold locket? One with a blue gem."

"You refer to the Baytown Jewel," said Michael.

The moment they returned to Baytown from Lindisfarne, Blair Gover had asked after it. He had cried with despair to find it gone from its display case in the Museum.

ONE

"Why is it so important to you?"

Gover ignored the question.

"Damn you, O'Hara. Ask the fool about the locket. If need be, deepen his hypnosis. Did he see the gold locket with the blue sapphire?"

Lady Veil's hands moved urgently.

"Very well," said Hurdy-Gurdy. Hitherto he had listened to Gover with ill-disguised contempt.

When the prisoner spoke, his voice was like that of a dead soul.

They come to visit my colonia in a fancy aircar, one bearing the Brubachers' insignia . . . Oho, I tell myself, here are people to be flattered . . . The girl has a slight bump, pregnant, no point making her fight . . . They gawp at the primitives in their cages . . . Helen Devereux, yes, I recognise her from the newscasts, draped on Blair Gover's arm at galas . . . And yes, Blair Gover's paramour wears . . . Oh, be wary of her! Blair Gover is a devil . . . Yes, she wears a gold locket with a blue gem on a chain round her neck. I see it. I see it.

Suddenly the man's eyes widened.

After the parade, after the Angels . . . I meet her again. We are all afraid now. It is her! Heading for the port, Negombo. To find a ship, yes, that thought crosses my mind, to flee Mughalia in a ship from the port. Why else would she be on that monorail? It goes nowhere but the docks at Negombo. She is hiding her face with a holomask of the Mona Lisa but I recognise her . . .

Terror broke his trance. He cried out. His eyes opened wide. He found himself staring not into the face of his new friend, Declan O'Hara, but the great Blair Gover, Founder of the Five Cities.

"My God," stammered the Supervisor of Animals. "You are here, as well."

Gover folded his arms. "I have learned enough. I conclude Helen Devereux has boarded a ship bound for Albion. Already she may be drawing near the British coast. What she carries *must* be given to me."

Hurdy-Gurdy touched the quivering prisoner's arm.

"You sang well, little canary," he said. He turned to the guards. "Take him away."

Gover raised an imperious hand. "Not so fast, O'Hara. That wretch has seen me. He knows I am alive. His knowledge puts me in danger. Kill him."

"No!" Michael Pilgrim's voice had commanded armies. The entire room froze. "Is there always to be more blood? Whatever this man's crimes, he has earned mercy. And there may be more to learn from him."

His cold blue eyes met Gover's: the latter glanced away.

"We must consider this news at leisure," said Michael. "Me? I'm for some fine York ale, a ripe cheese, fresh-baked bread, butter, and a decent beef pie, if such is to be had."

"None of you understand," moaned Gover. "Final extinction threatens, and you talk of pies! Do not believe for a moment that what you heard is good news."

"A decent pie is always good news," said Tom Higginbottom.

The room emptied. Twilight brought more shadows. The rats beneath the floorboards emerged, one by one.

TWO

Averil Pilgrim sat in the first real sunshine of spring. Her hands rested on the swollen bump of her stomach, an image of fertility as ancient and persistent as intelligent apes. But not here, not in Albion. Here, no one fell pregnant, no womb brought new life to the world save through artificial incubators. The Beautifuls she lived among had traded fertility for eternal life.

That much of the mysterious process by which her new friends renewed their bodies, Averil understood. Somehow, she was special. Marvin and Merle seemed to think so. And whatever they thought, the Beautifuls surrounding them echoed.

"Dora," said Averil, languidly.

Dora was her first proper servant; and striking the right tone was proving hard. It would have horrified Averil had she realised, but her model was a woman buried alive beneath a former radar station on the North Yorkshire Moors, in Fylingdales, a Cold War tomb as obsolete as Queen Nefertiti's pyramid. Pharaoh Jacko's consort, Queen Morrighan, had known how to keep servants in line. Then it had been Averil who tasted fist and whip. Though the scars on her body had been healed miraculously by the magic of City-medicine, her soul stayed raw.

"Dora, tell me why that pyramid over there was built?"

The woman she addressed, a buxom, black-skinned matron more than twice her age, wore the drab uniform of an unBeautiful technician.

After it became clear the gene sickness did not affect them – only Beautifuls who had visited Honeycomb for cell renewal were at risk of the disease – superfluous technicians were retired early by triggering a chip planted in their skulls. As a skilled nurse, Dora had been spared, mainly at the insistence of a certain Dr Wakuki.

Dora squinted up at the three-sided pyramid. It rose hundreds of feet from a marble-paved square. Buildings towered all around, lined with high windows so their occupants could be seen and admired. Beautifuls compared themselves constantly, lest they lose face or position. Averil was trying hard to acquire the same habit.

"It's a monument, Miss," said Dora, in her timid way, a natural subservience which perhaps explained why her head stayed on its neck. "It celebrates the Crusades. You know against the primitives. Three Beautifuls from Albion died culling Locusts."

Averil frowned. "Locusts?"

"That was what the primitives were called, Miss."

"I see."

It occurred to Averil that Dora might be mocking her. What was she but a primitive herself? Even the favour of the Brubachers, Joint-Presidents of the Ruling Council, could not change that.

Yet Dora's expression was guileless. Averil watched the sides of the pyramid project holograms of smiling young men and women in duraplastic battledress, heroic Crusaders, along with hordes of savages rounded up by drones for cleansing, the slaughter cloaked by desert dust clouds, billowing smoke. Uncle Michael had been conscripted to fight in that war, along with dozens of Baytown lads and lasses, only a handful of whom came home. Always, Averil had accepted their view of the Crusades as genocidal horror. In the heaven of Albion, she was less certain.

"I want to go for a fly," she declared. "Dora, summon an aircar for me."

TWO

Her servant produced a screen. Unexpectedly, Averil recalled her estranged husband, Amar, father of the child in her womb. Amar had longed to fly, treasuring every scrap of science the City allowed their community. A hardness entered her soul at the thought of him.

"Yes, I need a nice long fly round the City. Do hurry up, Dora."

* * *

Averil knew she would never take flying for granted. To be like a bird! When she was a girl, she had sometimes lain on her back on the cliffs of Baytown as a drone flew overhead. Shielding her eyes with a palm, she tracked it across the sky, wondering how the world looked from up there, how powerful it must feel, an eagle circling a field.

And now, she could be that eagle whenever she chose. True, Marvin and Merle allowed her to fly no further than Albion's limits – proof they wished to keep her safe – but that was wonderful enough.

Up the aircar rose, her stomach gripped by pleasurable tension as the earth fell away. The low buzz of the four rotors delighted her, along with the sterile aroma of the freshly sanitised cabin. Everything germless in the City. None of Baytown's filth and disease. The child in her womb would be safe here, not join the others in darkness, lost, tiny souls, never given a chance for life. Yes, Albion was life, *her* life now.

So it was with pride, mingled with fear that her precious new existence might be taken away in an instant, Averil sat back on the soft seat, gazing down at Albion.

The city had been built by demolishing every last structure from the town of Huntingdon and the surrounding area. Only a medieval, six-arched bridge over the River Great Ouse survived the pointless eras before the Great Dyings, a tiny nod at continuity.

Albion lay within a broad circle, twenty or so miles in diameter. Each of the Five Cities was designed for no more than a hundred thousand resident Beautifuls (too many people playing the Beautiful Life forever would turn ugly indeed). Beyond Albion's compact residential and entertainment hub lay industrial and agricultural facilities, sufficient to maintain the small population.

Averil's aircar angled round as it reached the fortified boundary wall.

"Fly lower," she instructed the drone. Its obedience delighted her. Sometimes she still had nightmares about the random drone attack on Hob Hall, ancestral home of the Pilgrim family. She had been little older than a girl. That was before she understood the City better. Before the world's harshness made her understand power.

Slowing, the machine skimmed the high concrete barrier bounded by a deep moat. Every couple of miles, a watchtower had been constructed, monitoring the deserted woodlands and fens for primitives foolish enough to pose a threat. None ever did.

Round the circle she flew, passing huge warehouses where exotic vegetables and fruit grew in artificial conditions, warmed by suns that never dimmed. Over factories where autonomous drones designed, manufactured and repaired other drones, over bio-facilities for incubating and growing original life forms, so-called Angels, to serve the new vision of Life Perfected. Many hundreds had already been shipped to Albion from laboratories where they had hatched in secret for years. Now they could serve openly, alongside conventional machines.

Marvin had explained it one day when asking about her pregnancy: "Some machines are made of metal and plastic, even wood, others of flesh and blood. The point, my dear, is who they serve. And how well."

On she flew, bypassing a large airfield and travel hub lined with flying machines of all kinds, sufficient to connect Albion with the other Cities and their colonia scattered round the world. On, over lakes for pleasure and fish production, parks for strolling amidst nibbling, Arcadian sheep, right round the circle until she came to a large, deep

TWO

manmade lake connecting the widened and dredged River Great Ouse to the sea, fifty miles north.

"Stay here," she commanded.

The aircar hovered.

In the pool, a cargo barge was arriving, laden with containers delivered to Kings Lynn by ocean-going craft from all over the world, and then ferried along a great canal through the wild fenlands to Albion.

Averil gazed north as the aircar hovered. Beyond that morass of reed and mud and willow, lands human ingenuity and toil had once drained for agriculture, far up the east coast of Britain, lay Baytown. Momentarily, she longed to see old friends and companions, even if for one last time. Then bitterness, long brewed, washed her weakness away. She clasped her bulging belly. She must be determined for Baby's sake. The only way she would return was as a Beautiful, blessed with eternal life, all ugliness smoothed away by surgery, a healthy, strong child at her side, along with Angels to serve and guard her, a small fleet of drones at her command. Yes, only then would she return to Baytown.

Yet that glorious vision soon wavered. She must get back. Marvin and Merle might ask for her. Even now, the hangers-on around them might be whispering against her.

"Back to my apartment," she ordered the aircar. "Quickly."

Dora, who perched on a small seat beside the luggage rack, met Averil's eye and seemed about to speak. Then she looked away.

* * *

Of course, everything was necessarily strange in Albion. To Averil Pilgrim, strangest of all were its citizens. Some seemed beyond human, like the Greek and Norse gods and demi-gods that featured in Uncle

Michael's lessons when she and Seth were small. She could almost hear his voice now, parroting the legendary Reverend Oliver Pilgrim: *Preserve, preserve, preserve.*

Preserve the few mouldy crumbs of a failed civilisation lingering in the dirt? Pecks of knowledge fit only for birds or hungry mice. Oh yes, the City had taught Averil what was worth preserving.

Still, not every Beautiful seemed divine. Especially, Dr Wakuki.

After her circuit of Albion in the aircar, Averil flew to Dr Wakuki's laboratory. When not treating her, the doctor worked obsessively on a cure for the new gene sickness. Before that, he had spent decades in Han City, designing what he once called "cures' for the primitives on mainland China and beyond.

Dora was present when Dr Wakuki said this. Averil noticed he avoided the large, motherly woman's eye.

Averil submitted gladly whenever Dr Wakuki told her she needed to go into deep sedation for scans and treatment. More than once she awoke to find a whole day had passed. She would lie naked apart from a sheet, her vagina and womb aching.

Later that afternoon, following another period of sedation, she opened her eyes to find him gazing down with peculiar intensity.

"Is Baby sick?" she cried, with a premonition of disaster. "Is everything alright?"

Dr Wakuki smiled reassuringly. He was short, his face reminiscent of folk back home, in that his features were unimproved. Averil supposed he was too obsessed with his work to bother about his appearance. When he spoke, his voice was gentle, calm.

"Baby's progress is satisfactory. Do not distress yourself. However, the birth may be delayed by a month, or even longer. That's perfectly normal in the circumstances."

At this news, Averil pulled the sheet closer to her chin. Was such a thing possible? Surely, Baby would grow too big for her womb. But anything was possible in the City.

Dr Wakuki's forehead creased. "Whatever happens, I shall ensure you are fine."

"Thank you, doctor," she murmured.

Yes, Averil knew she was lucky. Everything would be fine. Just fine. An image of the wild, dark fenlands she had seen from the aircar entered her mind. Imagine giving birth out there, among the savagery and mire!

* * *

Marvin and Merle Brubacher had transplanted their entire household to Albion, along with hundreds of hangers-on, courtiers, place-seekers, squads of Angels, drones and human technicians. The move had come soon after the Grand Autonomy where the couple became, in effect, absolute rulers of the Five Cities through pre-eminence on the Ruling Council. Averil knew enough of City politics to comprehend these things. One thing baffled her. Why choose rainy, cold Albion for their home instead of fragrant Mughalia in the Sri Lankan Highlands?

One grey morning, she stood by the living room window of her tenth-floor apartment, watching steady rain. Dora entered the large suite of high-ceilinged rooms in her usual quiet way: it was time for the hourly tests Dr Wakuki insisted on.

"Marvin and Merle could have easily delayed coming here until spring *really* warms up," said Averil, pettishly.

She enjoyed referring to the mighty Presidents of the Ruling Council by their first names in front of Dora. It showed that she was important, particularly when she felt lost and helpless.

"Spring always comes, Miss," said Dora.

"How long have we been here now? Over three months already."

Dora summoned a small drone with the testing equipment. She shot Averil a quick look.

"Of course, you know about the gene-infection, Miss," she said.

"Of course I do. I'm not stupid. Marvin and Merle will soon have it under control."

Averil hugged her arms as she watched the rain.

"Last week I saw a man being taken away by security drones. He had tried to hide a misshapen ear beneath a hat. It got exposed and, well, everyone in the café scattered to get away from him. I wonder what happened to him? He probably only needs a little surgery to make himself better."

Dora stopped preparing the test. "Do you really not know?"

"What?"

"What will have happened to him?"

"Why, should I? He was a total stranger, nobody important." Averil laughed. "The funny thing is, an ugly ear like that would be nothing back in Baytown. Everyone is ugly there. I was ugly until Marvin and Merle gave me an operation to look nice. They are so very kind to me."

"That man . . ." began Dora.

"Yes?"

"He will have been sterilised."

"Good. Once the germs are dead, the poor man will surely get better. I told you, Marvin and Merle will soon have it under control."

For a long moment, Dora examined Averil, as though judging her in some way. The kind of look Averil had always hated from Uncle Michael or Father. To her surprise, the technician indicated she should sit down.

"I feel that I should explain," said Dora. "You see, the Presidents came to Albion simply because it is the nearest City to Honeycomb. Indeed, it is the gateway to Honeycomb. Without first being processed in Albion, no one is allowed to take the shuttle there. By settling

TWO

here, the Presidents can keep stricter control of the problem's source. Perhaps, of what is going wrong."

Averil laughed, though less lightly than before. "Going wrong? I see nothing wrong. Albion is perfect in every way. Apart from the weather, of course."

"I meant the gene infection," said Dora.

"But the City can cure anything," protested Averil, determined not be alarmed. "Oh, Dora, you can't scare me! I worked as a nurse in a Little Dying we had in Baytown. You should have seen the buboes on the people's armpits and necks and groins, the vile stench when they burst, and how death came as a relief from their pain. No, we are quite safe here, Baby and I."

Dora looked at her with new respect. "You were brave to nurse people with the plague," she said. "I would not have expected that."

"I was reckless," said Averil. "But I really don't want to think about Baytown. I want to forget it forever. Tell me more about this gene sickness."

"No one really knows the precise cause. Even Dr Wakuki and the other great scientists. Though it is not reported on the newscasts, every week hundreds die of it across the Five Cities. Han City and Mitopia are said to be worst hit."

Averil leaned away from her. Could Dora be infected? Perhaps Baby could catch it through breathing.

"Do not fear," said the older woman with a smile. "You and I cannot catch gene sickness. Only Beautifuls can. That much *is* understood. They think it originated in Honeycomb, a mutation of cell renewal no one anticipated."

"I still do not..."

"It is a sickness of essence in the altered cells of some Beautifuls. It is transmitted – so I have heard – by a new kind of virus. An entirely novel life form. Some think the virus was created by accident when making Angels or hybrid life forms from jumbled DNA."

Averil understood little of what Dora said. But it seemed very unkind to deliberately alarm her in this way.

"How do you know all this?"

The technician smiled. "Servants always know more than their masters imagine. Now, it is time for your tests."

"First, tell me more about Honeycomb. *That* I would like to hear about. It sounds a miraculous place. I would love to go there."

Again, Dora hesitated. "The science is miraculous. Honeycomb lies on an island to the west, called Anglesey. Naturally, being only a technician, I have never been there. Nor will I. Once that was a grief for me, for it meant I am only allowed a little life. Now, I'm not so sure. Lift your arm, Miss."

Obediently, Averil held up her arm for Dora to apply a broad, pulsing band. A sensor on the equipment scanned her. Small needles pricked her skin; Averil's arm tingled. Outside, rain spattered on the window, running in small rivulets like tears.

* * *

Marvin Brubacher had always loved toys, animal, human, or mechanical. Nor was he inclined to allow novel diseases or uproar in the Five Cities to curtail his pleasures.

One morning, Averil received an invitation on a stiff piece of coloured plastic. It depicted a strange machine with eight wheels beneath the slogan, *Old-fashioned Fun!* Guests were instructed, *Dress: Nineteenth Century.*

When Averil asked Dora about such clothing, she was guided to one of Albion's numerous attire-facilities, where all styles of garment since the bearskin loincloth could be borrowed.

"You mean, like a library for dressing up?" asked Averil.

Dora smiled. "Yes, Miss. Everyone looks more important if you dress them up. I'll help you choose something nice."

At the appointed time, Averil found herself queuing with hundreds of Beautifuls. Her sky blue silk gown shimmered and made a gratifying rustle as she moved, parasol in hand.

Marvin Brubacher's *Old-fashioned Fun* was taking place at a facility on the outskirts of Albion's travel hub. Monorail tracks ran alongside platforms normally busy with Beautifuls heading across England to Honeycomb for cell renewal. All journeys in the special armoured train had been cancelled by the gene sickness. Indeed, a strange stillness lay over the vast travel hub, where hundreds of aircraft stood stranded – which perhaps explained why the irrepressible Marvin had found a new use for the monorail station.

Averil's invitation funnelled her into a select gathering of a few score Beautifuls on a platform at the edge of the terminus. Hundreds more, lesser in status, watched from tiered seating. All spectators wore antique costume: top hats vied with bonnets, tailcoats with hooped skirts, parasols with ornate walking sticks.

Averil felt her spirits lift at the splendid show. *Here* was what made the City such fun, life a game of make-believe so that dreary, grimy, greasy reality could be forgotten, and not just for an hour like in horrible Baytown – if you were lucky – but forever and ever.

Angels bearing trays of drinks circulated among the favoured guests. A functional design of Angel, with two arms on each side of its body to carry a double load of trays. The creatures' faces were blank, expressionless. Yet Averil wasn't sure she liked the way their eyes moved.

No one spoke to her. The courtiers and influential people summoned by Marvin talked in discreet huddles. Averil positioned herself behind a pillar to be less conspicuous. Two Beautifuls conferred on the other side, unaware of her presence.

"I hear it is only getting worse," murmured one, "although they say the Brubachers and Wakuki have a partial cure. Doses of the original, untainted elixir seem to have an effect. There's just so little of the stuff. And they can't seem to manufacture any more that's one hundred per cent pure."

"Still, there's enough for themselves."

"Oh, yes." The voice added, cautiously, "Thank goodness."

None of this meant a thing to Averil. She knew only that the pair of gossiping women referred to the gene sickness.

"Wakuki will find a cure," predicted one.

"Let us hope it comes soon. I hear the other Cities are arming themselves, to put pressure on the Ruling Council."

"Whatever for?"

"For control of Honeycomb to be taken from the Ruling Council. They want a committee running the facility with an equal number of representatives from each City."

"That is sheer Discordia!"

"Of course. The Presidents believe it better for everyone if they retain a complete monopoly on any cures for the sickness that come from Honeycomb."

"Who can blame them?"

"Not I. I am loyal."

An uncomfortable silence followed. The pair lapsed to a favourite conversation among the courtiers around Marvin and Merle Brubacher: what to do when the Life Perfected realised its full glory. All aspired to their own mini-kingdoms served by Angels and drones. Averil learned that rivalries for who should be apportioned the choicest, most scenic parcels of land were already intense, with petitions to the Ruling Council piling up.

"Obviously, people of genuine vision should be favoured," declared one of the pair. "Personally, I have been designing whole new animals and birds in support of my claim."

Her friend affected a yawn. "Oh, we're all doing *that*, my darling. Why else are we here?"

They laughed conspiratorially. Averil coughed and the laughter ceased. A young woman's face in a Victorian bonnet popped round the pillar. At the sight of Averil, it paled and withdrew.

"It's the experiment," came a whisper. "Hush. She's been listening."

Further talk was halted by a piercing shriek that made Averil jump.

* * *

A long shed stood a hundred feet or so from the platform. With a loud drum roll and blare of synth-trumpets, its doors swung open onto the monorail track. Another piercing whistle was preceded by billows of steam. Slowly, an extraordinary vehicle emerged from the shed.

It consisted of a long cylindrical body and open driver's cab resting on eight wheels; half a dozen carriages were dragged after it. In short, a steam locomotive adapted to run on standard mono-track.

Smoke and sparks rose from a tall funnel, the fire fed by a team of dwarf Angels fresh from the incubator. Their strong arms shovelled coal as if their lives depended on it — as, indeed, they did. One might say they had only been allowed life for that purpose. And should they prove unsatisfactory, their remains would be composted.

Driving the train was Marvin Brubacher, peaked cap jaunty on his bouffant black and grey hair.

The crowd broke into applause and cheers.

How very Marvin, they cried, hands stinging to clap the loudest. He designed it all himself, you know. Or told the programme what to do. Such ingenuity! Do you know, there isn't a single part that is electrical or digital in the whole machine. Not one. It's entirely mechanical. Trust Marvin to start a new fashion at a time like this! Others chuckled admiringly. *Even in the middle of a pandemic he is all gaiety and chutzpah!*

The steam train huffed up to the platform, propelled by wheels gripping the track's sides.

"All aboard!" cried a familiar voice, amplified over the hissing whoosh of the train by a loudspeaker.

Averil gawped. Could that be Merle Brubacher in an antique ticket collector's uniform? Something about her expression suggested she was not entirely happy with the role. Nor was Averil. She had learned only too well from the reign of Pharaoh Jacko and his Queen that power must never lower itself. Perhaps that was why she hurried to join her patroness.

"Let me do that, ma'am," she cried. "Please! It is beneath you."

Merle blinked at her, unsure whether to be angry or grateful for the girl's heartfelt outburst.

"Good girl," she murmured. "You do mean well. It is a shame Marv gets so silly about his toys sometimes. But boys will be boys. You may sit beside me in the carriage when we set off."

Averil flushed with pleasure. She sensed envious eyes all around her.

After the excitement and bustle of boarding the train's antique-style carriages, she sipped delicate wine and nibbled exquisite taste-wafers with the President of the Ruling Council. Dr Wakuki, she noticed, had absented himself.

The train huffed to the borders of Albion then took the monorail leading – if one crossed England and travelled round the north coast of Wales to Anglesey – all the way to Honeycomb. On either side of the track, vegetation formed tangles of variegated green, choking ruined towns and villages. It was all such fun.

Merle's screen beeped an urgent warning. Activating it, she rose in horror.

"We must go back!" she cried. "Tell him. We must go back."

"Who?" said Averil. "Tell who?"

"Marvin, of course, you ridiculous creature. Someone stop this train!"

Soon everyone's screen was bleeping or chiming. News spread through the packed carriage faster than any contagion. News no one had ever expected. All the Five Cities except Albion – Mitopia, Neo Rio, Han City and Mughalia – had done the unthinkable. They had declared independence. The federation of the Five Cities was over, unless – or so the separatist Cities threatened – the secrets of Honeycomb were shared equally. How else, they argued, could a quick cure for the gene sickness be found and administered fairly?

"Spies have told them we have a cure," whispered Merle Brubacher. "We must defend ourselves."

Averil shrank back in her seat, afraid of being noticed. Could the Cities really be so foolish as to turn on one another? While the occupants of the carriage jabbered, she felt baby kick hard in her womb.

THREE

"Young Nuncle is a bat," declared Hurdy-Gurdy, throwing open the door and striking a pose. "Bats love shadows and twilight. During the day they hang upside down, like pheasants when their meat turns dark and sweet."

He strode into Seth's room. It overlooked St Helen's Square, formerly the manager's office of a grand restaurant. Seth stored what few clothes he possessed in a rusty filing cabinet; his bed lay on a long, broad desk. An elevated bunk meant the mice had a longer climb to annoy him, likewise the resident beetles and snails.

"Gurdy," said Seth, closing a book he'd found, *The Rough Guide to Paris*. "You're my first visitor since the last time you called."

Hurdy-Gurdy leaned over the book's cover.

"*Ah, la belle France! Mon dieu! Et Pare-e-e. Paradis pour l'âme et le coeur.*"

Seth looked at the tattered book dubiously.

"Was it true?"

"*Comment, mon pote?*"

"It sounds too good to be true. Were people ever that friendly with each other? Millions of folk living in peace. You need a fuck of a lot of trust and goodwill for *that*."

"Nothing is too good to be true when humanity is true to its best," declared Hurdy.

"Which doesn't happen round here very often."

"In the case of France, it happened with its cheeses. *Ah, si magnifique!* All gone. Are not men cheese, from a certain perspective?" He paused for effect. "Shat out by time."

That was more Seth's style of humour, as Gurdy knew well.

"Now, Young Nuncle, busk! Busk! Away we go!"

"Where to?"

"The future."

"I haven't got a future."

"Come now."

"Gurdy, I'm going to swing."

Gloom settled on Seth's face. Still, he allowed Hurdy-Gurdy to chivvy him into the sunshine. Their route took them by the river, along a flood-crumbled concrete embankment. The ex-holotainer capered to lift his young companion's spirits.

Knots of folk were drifting in the direction of the Knavesmire, a large, open field to the south of the city, once a racecourse. No one insulted Seth in the company of Lady Veil's close companion: to offend her invited swift expulsion from York. It was an irony of Lady Veil's rule that she employed similar methods to the City when it came to disunity.

On the Knavesmire, hundreds of men and women conducted a weekly drill. Lady Veil rode a large horse, inspecting each unit carefully. Every citizen between the ages of fourteen and fifty (few enough lived beyond their fifth decade in any case), were required to bear arms in some capacity.

Prominent among them were companies wearing black uniforms. Lady Veil had established a new cult in York, the Grow People. Their creed was simple: mankind must eradicate every last trace of the Five Cities. Only then might humanity renew itself.

As they drilled, hundreds of voices joined to chant the Growers' litany:

City men are not men.

City women are not women.

Cleanse and burn, cleanse and burn.

Grow, grow again!

"Them Growers scare me," Seth said. "They're mad as rabies."

"They are as much the City's creation as drones," said Gurdy. "Who is to say they are not sane to be mad? That only madness will cure madness?"

Well-designed single shot rifles blasted targets daubed with the slogan: *NO MERCY FROM THE PURIFYING FIRE.* Some squads of soldiers seemed to be practising how to start blazes quickly. Plumes of acrid black smoke rose. Others drilled with swords and halberds.

Seth and Gurdy mounted a stand of terraced seats originally meant for race-goers. From here they could watch the manoeuvres below.

"What use is all their hate against a single drone?" demanded Seth. "Crazy fuckers."

Below, Lady Veil admonished a halberdier not displaying sufficient enthusiasm when stabbing a straw dummy.

"They say she'd gut every last one of 'em. Then drink their blood in a pint glass," said Seth.

Hurdy-Gurdy showed his rotten teeth. "She has reasons."

"The City did turn her mouth into a smelly cunt," conceded Seth. "Anyone would want revenge for that."

Below, a fresh volley boomed, sulphurous smoke rising in a cloud.

"To business," said Gurdy. "In a few days it will be your trial."

"Don't I fucking know it?"

"It is time you took counsel. Now, tell me about your past misdeeds. Hold nothing back. Sing, ragged robin, sing!"

Seth felt inclined to refuse. What was the point? But Hurdy-Gurdy might help him to a less painful end, if nothing else. As they watched

Lady Veil's army drill, he began. The City-man interrupted and probed. When the tale was told, his friend's frown was grave.

"See now why I'll swing?" demanded Seth. "There's no changing the past."

In reply, the old holotainer crooned:
When remedies are past, the griefs are ended
By seeing the worst, which late on hope depended.
To mourn a mischief that is past and gone
Is the next way to bring new mischief on.

Seth shook his head. "You're hopeless as mud, Hurdy. That's what I like about you."

* * *

The Council of the North met in a large hall attached to what had once been the Yorkshire Museum. Michael Pilgrim wandered the dusty galleries before the conclave. He fingered shards of pottery, tarnished weapons and ornaments, bones and shreds of rotted fabric – talismans from layers of civilisation.

His own people's layer had contributed nothing new. No great monuments. Or art. Or inventions. Their sole achievement was clinging to life. Now, like the barbarians who burned Rome, he and his allies schemed to extinguish the one remaining source of scientific progress, namely, the Five Cities.

The Council consisted of representatives from all important communities within the Commonwealth. Folk from far afield: Lancashire and Geordieland, Cumberland and South Yorkshire, Derbyshire and Scouseland. The flimsy ties binding them were laws of a rudimentary kind, guaranteeing peace, liberty and safety, freedom of belief and assembly, unbriganded travel, and the right to trade freely. Laws

Michael Pilgrim played no small part in drafting.

Many tens of thousands were represented by the men and women seated in a great circle. This weight of numbers gave Michael hope. As did the fact disputes between the communities were rare. What was there to quarrel over? Free land was abundant, likewise access to fish and forest.

A smattering of knowledge about human nature suggested such unity could not last – yet another reason to strike soon.

"Friends," he said, addressing ranks of expectant faces. "We are here to debate hope."

The word echoed in the room.

"Hope, where we have persuaded ourselves there is none. And not without good reason. Hitherto, only a maniac would fight the Five Cities. But just as the sun rises, everything changes. Friends, the world we have known and hated is like a house collapsing. Therein is our hope of winning a better life."

Michael Pilgrim had prepared his arguments carefully, consulting old allies and new: not alone did he propose what seemed madness. Lady Veil pledged the considerable resources of York and the Grow People; Mister Priestman promised the support of Nuagers, populous communities all over the North. As for Yorkshire, Michael did not doubt hundreds, perhaps thousands would rally to this cause.

"The spirits judge it a righteous crusade," announced Mister Priestman to the assembly. "Let nature reign supreme, they say. Let sun and moon be once more the world's king and queen."

Others spoke in support of the proposal: Tom Higginbottom for Baytown and the East Coast; Aggie Brown for the populous and thriving Yorkshire Vale; Cuthbert of Lindisfarne promised hundreds of seasoned veterans from the North East; the folk of Hull and the Yorkshire Wolds pledged likewise.

THREE

Finally, Michael and his allies fell silent. For long moments no one spoke. Then a grey-haired man took the podium. He hailed from the West Riding, where folk were naturally canny – and blunt.

"It's all very well promising victory," he said, scornfully. "What with? Bare hands? Musket? Sword? Bow and arrow? When did such weapons daunt a drone? We all hate the City, lad, but death comes soon enough as it is. I'll not rush me and mine over *that* cliff."

Others rose to protest the same thing. Here was no straight fight, but suicide.

Michael bided his time. At last, no more naysayers stepped forward to argue. He paused to scan the room.

"Friends, let me answer this objection. First, I have a witness. Bring him in, Hurdy."

A smooth-cheeked prisoner was summoned, instantly recognisable as from the City. Perfect teeth, hair, skin, more divine than human. He walked as in a dream, led by the hand like a child. He appeared not to notice the many primitives assembled in the hall.

It was the former Director of Animals, mastered by a deep, hypnotic trance.

"This man has a tale of astounding change," said Michael Pilgrim. "Hurdy, persuade our friend to tell us about the situation in the Five Cities..."

Shadows lengthened as the prisoner talked. His mere presence made some look round for vengeful drones. A few of the representatives asked questions, but there could be no doubting the significance of the City-man's account. Their enemy was divided, self-absorbed, afflicted by plague, weaker than ever before.

Once the Director of Animals had been led away, the same West Yorkshireman as before rose.

"HBut how does all that make them less powerful? A single, big-bastard battle drone, just one, would scatter an army ten thousand strong."

A murmur of approval greeted these words. Michael took the podium. "Friends, I agree," he said. "We are mice to drones. But what if there were no drones. What then?"

A voice jeered, "What if the Christmas faery was true? What then?"

At the implications of this blasphemous suggestion, Mister Priestman and the Nuagers muttered angrily.

Michael held up a hand for silence. "Let's hear from another Cityman. Bring him in."

A very different figure to the smiling, guileless Director of Animals entered. No question of leading this man by the hand. All sensed his inner power. He walked awkwardly, left shoulder lowered as if by a painful wound. Though he shared the eternal youth of all City-folk, his was a face lined by pain, anger, and cold, calculating resolve. A face with little use for common kindness.

He looked round the assembly of representatives, and laughed. "Will they understand me, Pilgrim?"

"Just tell your tale," Michael said.

"It seems I have no alternative."

"Seems not."

For ten minutes the City-man spoke. First, he explained the source of his knowledge and expertise in this matter. Indeed, proclaimed his genius. "Just think of me as an all-powerful wizard," he advised, 'though my magic is in fact science." Then he explained how, if he deigned to help them, he was offering a chance to oppose the City without inevitable slaughter from drones.

A sea of doubtful faces greeted this statement. Some laughed at the notion.

"Bollocks!" shouted one.

"You're trying to trick us," called out another.

The City-scientist quivered with outrage. It seemed he might withdraw in pique.

"Friends, hear him out," called Michael Pilgrim. "Go on, Gover."

"Very well. If I must."

In an impatient voice, he claimed to have the means to shut down not just the defensive systems of Albion, but *all* the Five Cities' systems.

When he finished, his audience was more confused than enlightened. What were these *master codes* he described? It fell to Lady Veil, through her interpreter, to explain in terms all could comprehend, exactly what the mysterious stranger was suggesting. And how, with terrible danger and no great certainty of success, she was certain his knowledge might dismay the Five Cities. How this unique chance could never come again.

"Let me second Lady Veil," called out Michael. "I believe the City-renegade before us has the means to deliver exactly what he promises. It won't be easy. It might even prove impossible. But it's our only way to kick them while they're down. And kick 'em so damn hard, they never get up again."

There was no laughter in the big room now. All eyes were upon Gover; his lips rose mirthlessly in reply.

"That's enough for today," declared Michael. "I ask that each delegate goes away tonight and decides whether they can support this proposal. We'll meet again tomorrow."

So the first session of the Council of the North concluded.

"Pleased with my little performance, Pilgrim?" asked Gover, as the representatives filed out.

"You did well."

"I wouldn't entertain your crackpot scheme if other options existed. But one must evolve."

Michael examined him closely. Months of unwelcome proximity had taught him when Gover was up to something.

* * *

The Strangelings chose a deserted place a few miles east of York. Perhaps it chose them: much of what they did flowed from instinct.

Deep silence lay across the former suburb, rows of semi-detached houses with trees poking through roofs, cars accumulating earth and moss to form humps. Animals rustled through undergrowth, bird and fox and feral cat. Badgers expanded their sets beneath fallen garages and deer stepped nervously under lamp posts without light.

Nearby, lay a confusion of large buildings, the old university, built around small lakes swollen by annual floods. Young woodland besieged the campus. Its walkways and bridges haunted by young, excited voices, lost intrigues and passions, life's adventure just beginning. Lecture halls hosted debates between mould and wood-munching beetles.

Into the former university, lolloped and hopped a line of creatures unanticipated by evolution. Unless, that is, evolution encompassed the wilful caprices of City gene-splicers. Their creators not even human, artificial minds programmed to design and engineer new life.

Yet every loaf needs yeast to rise. Nothing comes of nothing. The creatures were not entirely new.

At the head of the line came a half hare, half girl who could still recall her former name: Bella Lyons. She led a dozen fellow upright demi-hares to a lake outside a large round hall, and settled. Some scratched fleas with muscular legs. Others stared up at the fat moon. They were hungry. A few leapt upon ducks roosting amidst the reeds; wings clattered and the birds scattered in alarm. Yet raw meat sat badly in their modified stomachs, just as raw vegetables were hard to digest.

Above them, the moon moved across the sky. Its light glinted on the lake. The demi-hares groomed each other's short fur. Then warning snorts and cheeps broke the silence. Though the hares might have arrived first, others were anticipated.

A pack of man-dogs prowled their way up to the lake. One might have expected the hares to flee. But the different species mingled, sniffing and recognising, bound by an essential sameness. Likewise, a flock of grotesque, humanoid owls flew down to the lakeside, legs terminating in clawed, five-toed feet, their faces something from a Medieval bestiary.

More creatures arrived, experiments dropped all over the North by a City no longer interested enough to monitor them. Obsolete models. Natural wastage.

By midnight, the strangelings were assembled, drawn by compulsion, scents, improvised language, social urges expanding almost daily. Ah, the exhilaration of being understood! Of affirming selfhood! To devise a gesture and agree, this means *food* or *tree* or *friend*. The heady sense of unity communication engendered, even between apparently incompatible species. The strangelings were growing far beyond their creators' imaginations.

They recognised in one another the kernel of humanity. Upon this, animal bodies had been cultured. They sensed their own and others' souls. Awareness stirred memories rising like bubbles of lost self; and remembering stirred rage. They recalled themselves – tortured glimpses – impossible longings – as they had been. And conceived vengeance.

Demi-rabbits mingled with foxes and enormous man-rats, homo-cats with dogs, plus a few *jeux d'esprits* from the gene architects. Once the biological template had proved viable, endless variations were possible. Here, an amusing human otter. There, a man-bear sculpted to resemble a toy panda from its creator's suburban childhood. Other flying creatures, too, bat-people, crow-men.

They sat or perched, sniffing, fidgeting, scratching, waiting.

The moon washed fur and feather with wan light. Wind stirred the trees. Then the leader of the man-dogs threw back his short muzzle, howling at the cold, indifferent stars. His fellows leapt up, baying and barking. Those capable of flight flapped heavily into the air, circling the lake. Other strangelings added their cries until the buildings echoed, not with alarm but purpose.

At last, they fell silent. As if with one will, they turned in one direction. With a determination that would have astounded and appalled their creators, the strangelings headed south. They headed for the nearest City: Albion.

* * *

In York, revels had commenced with the coming of darkness; the representatives attending the Council drank and dined well. Many a bed creaked.

Seth Pilgrim hurried after Hurdy-Gurdy through the darkness.

"Hey! Slow down."

The former City-man showed no signs of slowing.

Seth had been woken by knocking to find Hurdy-Gurdy, rechargeable torch in hand. The tireless holotainer led him down muddy Stonegate, round the looming mass of the Minster, to a big old house near the city walls.

"What's this all about?" Seth asked.

No answer. They entered an orchard, apple blossom eerie in the moonlight, and climbed ancient stone steps onto the medieval city walls. On a corner tower was a platform. Here, a fire burned in an old metal litterbin. Beside it, sat a man in a thick coat, smoking his pipe. A black and white collie lay at his feet.

Now Seth understood why Hurdy-Gurdy had kept their destination quiet. If he'd known it was to meet this man, he would have never come.

"Fuck," he breathed.

The dark figure's face was pale in the moonlight.

"Sit yourself, Seth." Michael Pilgrim waved at a much-repaired park bench. "Warm yourself by the fire."

Seth hesitated and perched on the edge of the bench. His throat had gone dry.

"Well then," said Michael, with a small, sad smile. "Who would have expected this? We all thought you were dead."

Seth's old defiance flared. "No, Uncle, I didn't die. Maybe it would have been less inconvenient if I had."

Sparks rose from the glowing log in the brazier into the star-strewn night.

"We could all say that, lad. After I came home from the Crusades, I felt . . . Well, simply wrong to still be alive. I had a choice. Live in shame, or prove myself better than I thought."

Seth looked round for Hurdy-Gurdy, but he was gone.

Michael offered his tobacco pouch.

"Smoke?"

Seth rummaged in his pocket. The little pipe he used to smoke weed was there. When he took a pinch from the pouch, the tobacco smelt familiar. A variety grown in Hob Hall. Michael held out a glowing twig; they puffed the pipes alight.

"Your Dad, rest his soul," said Michael, "considered tobacco the devil's weed, along with many another pleasure. Sometimes he considered me a bad lot, too. I bet you didn't know that."

"No."

It occurred to Seth he knew almost nothing about his own father's feelings. Too selfish to care at the time; too late to ask now.

"Me and him wasted years when we could have been the best of friends," said Michael.

They drew on their pipes.

"Why did you want to see me, Uncle? Is the trial due?"

"Yes. As soon as the Council of the North decides what to do about the City. I wanted to see you before the hearing." He hesitated. "Your weird pal tells me you're a reformed character."

Seth felt a stir of pride. To possess such a loyal friend as Hurdy-Gurdy was something.

"I'm just what you see."

"I doubt that. We don't even see ourselves clearly, let alone others."

"In case you wondered, I don't expect mercy from the court," said Seth, proudly. "I've thought it all through. I'll be pleading guilty if anyone cares to ask."

Michael nodded. For a while they puffed at their pipes.

"I was given a second chance to set right my mistakes," he said. "And I would like to see the same for you. Not least because I promised your father on his deathbed I would save you."

Seth felt a stab of hope. Would his Uncle Michael misuse his high position to up-end justice?

"But I cannot protect you from the law," continued Michael, his eyes mournful. "Laws I helped to write. Or there is no law. I'm sorry, right sorry. Though no doubt you think me flint-hearted. Prepare yourself for the worst, lad."

The tension in Seth's gut melted a little. All was settled.

"Don't you worry, Uncle, I've been preparing myself for the worst since I came here." He was defiant once more. "I'm begging no man for favours. I could have run away from York, you know. But this time I'm running no further."

Above them, ribbons of stars unrolled across the night; the fat moon discarded its mantle of clouds behind York Minster.

* * *

The Council of the North reconvened next morning. A blearier gathering than yesterday: the alehouses of York had done brisk trade. Perhaps lingering drunkenness emboldened a few who would otherwise have inclined towards caution. Perhaps it was the testimony of the two City-men: only fools believed the Five Cities' current disinterest in primitives was anything but temporary. All now knew of the half-human, half-animal strangelings and hybrids the City was breeding to replace humanity. Now was the time, lest there be no more time.

Also decisive were feelings beyond reason. Lives trapped in backwardness, dreams of progress crushed. Were their children and grandchildren to hide in the woods and swamps and ruins until harried off the face of the earth?

When the following proposals were put to the vote, each gained a sizable majority.

Firstly, that an army gather at York, comprising all available men and women able to fight. Led by Lady Veil, it would march south towards Albion, as soon as possible.

Second, a smaller force led by Michael Pilgrim would seek to gain entry into Albion and disable the systems there, using the expertise of the City-renegade, Blair Gover. Everything depended on that. If they failed, the main army would disperse and return home. If they succeeded, Lady Veil would rush in to attack.

Third, a small naval expedition would sail down the east coast to The Wash, in the hope of encountering a vessel bearing another City-exile, a woman this time, Helen Devereux. It was believed she, too, might hold the means of defeating the City promised to them by Blair Gover. A hopeless expedition – ugly stories of the Fen Men abounded – yet even the slimmest hope must be pursued.

After the votes were declared and recorded, a few younger folk cheered. Older, wiser heads were subdued. Still, casks of ale were breached in honour of the decision.

"Let us call our army, the Crusade of Star Seekers," declared Mister Priestman.

At which, Tom Higginbottom shouted out: "Nay, let's not forget our general, Michael Pilgrim."

The suggestion raised applause: the Protector of the North had not failed as a war leader yet. And the ale was strong and plentiful.

"No," shouted the querulous West Yorkshireman, who had no intention of joining the expedition but was happy to toast its success at another man's expense. "If you wish to honour Michael Pilgrim, call it the Pilgrimage of Fools."

His joke earned a laugh and cheer, yet the name stuck. Nor was it inappropriate.

That same afternoon, riders dispersed across the Commonwealth of the North, bearing appeals freshly printed on a hand-press, the ink still damp, to gather with food and arms at York. A great stir of excitement gripped the ancient city.

One young man, however, kept to his dismal room and thoughts. Seth Pilgrim had been informed that despite the intense preparations to march south, time would be found for swift trials – and, he did not doubt, equally swift hangings.

FOUR

One morning, Averil stood on her balcony and realised spring was settling across the land. She smelt it in the cool breeze blowing south from the fens adjoining Albion's borders. A walk among blossom would do Baby good: it might even help Baby's exhausted mother, who found herself waking in the middle of the night, shaken by bad dreams.

Without telling Dora, Averil dressed and rode the lift down to the ground floor of her vast apartment tower. Nearby was a stand of call-cabs, one of Albion's many free amenities.

Out on the wide boulevard – usually dotted with Beautifuls, drones and technicians hurrying about their duties – no one moved. A single aircar swished overhead.

Strict quarantine prohibitions confined Beautifuls to their own lavish quarters, though the exact means of the gene sickness's transmission was unproven. Holocasts from the other Cities showed similar measures in place. Mitopia and Han City were especially vigilant, testing the entire population weekly. The roll call of those sterilised included names familiar in all the Five Cities: entertainers, scientists, fashion-setters.

None of that seemed important as Averil sniffed the scent-laden air. A long chevron of ducks overflew the City, heading for wetlands to the north. The sky was a few shades paler than summer blue.

She noticed a woman, her face concealed beneath a gaudy carnival mask, leaving a neighbouring apartment-tower. The woman glanced around guiltily. Then she hurried in the direction of the Double Helix monument at the heart of Albion.

At once, there came a hoot of alarms. Averil clutched at her swollen belly. A long drone airbulance descended, a new kind she had noticed from her window.

It settled with a pneumatic hiss, rotors slowing to a chunter. Doors opened and a security drone on caterpillar tracks rolled out.

Please co-operate fully, it urged. The drone's soothing tone was at variance with its grab-claws.

The woman, pretending she had not heard, turned back towards her apartment-tower.

Please co-operate, repeated the drone, rolling forward to cut her off. *There is no need for alarm. Please step over to the testing facility.*

Trembling, the woman pulled off her mask. "I was going to visit a friend," she pleaded. "He is very depressed. He begged me to help him. We are both pure, I tell you!"

Please co-operate fully.

Averil watched the terrified woman enter the airbulance. A door slid shut behind her.

With the incident seemingly over, she stepped once more towards the line of call-cabs. Abruptly, the security drone trundled her way.

Please co-operate fully. We are just going to conduct a little test.

Averil's dread of drones, primordial in primitives, paralysed her. Her palms sweated, heart beat frantically. She battled with a desire to flee.

"I can't catch it, I tell you! Baby and me are immune! We've never even been near Honeycomb!"

The drone's claw-like arms extended towards her.

There is no need for alarm. Please step over to the testing facility.

"Don't come closer!" she shrieked. "Okay. Okay."

FOUR

Half-fainting, Averil approached the airbulance, fumbling for her screen. A message must be sent to Dora, Dr Wakuki . . . But when she reached into her screen pouch, it was empty.

"The Presidents of the Ruling Council are my friends! I need to send them a message."

This is for your benefit. There is no need for alarm.

The airbulance door slid open. The woman, clutching her carnival mask, stepped out. Her expression of deep relief turned to outrage at the sight of Averil so close.

"Get away from me! I'm pure. You might infect me. Get away!"

Averil backed off, bumping into the claws of the drone. The woman ran back into her apartment-tower.

Please enter for a simple test, the drone urged Averil.

A cloud of scented disinfectant billowed from the doorway.

Inside the vehicle, a cubicle was equipped with deep-scanning devices. The door closed behind her.

Please remove all items of clothing, commanded the airbulance. *This test is for your benefit.*

With shaking hands, Averil tugged off her clothes, including the underwear that had so astonished her when she first came to the Five Cities. Her naked body was revealed in three mirrors, the big bump of her pregnancy and swollen breasts exposed.

She tried to cover herself with her arms.

"I must speak to Dr Wakuki! He is my doctor."

Your personal purity test will now commence, advised the airbulance. *There is no need for alarm.*

A pulsing glow filled the cubicle, pierced by crisscrossing blue beams. For long minutes, she quivered. When the glow faded, the voice spoke more reassuringly than before.

We are pleased to inform you. You require further testing.

"But I can't catch it!"

Re-robe. You require further testing.

After she had dressed, the exterior door opened. Averil squawked: a flying cage had positioned itself directly outside.

Now it was the cage that spoke. No attempt to comfort had been programmed into its synthvoice. It was all business. *You have failed your purity test. Your internal organs are abnormal. You must be sterilised for your own benefit.*

"That's not poss—"

An electric shock cut her short and she stumbled into the wire mesh cage. She fell to the floor as its door clanged shut.

Then earth fell away. The cage rose, propellers whirling and clattering. Air buffeted her face, hair blowing wildly. Mechanical arms extended from the cage, pinning her tight. As she drew in breath to scream a bitter taste filled her nose and mouth. The world went dark.

* * *

Averil woke with a start. She lay in a bed familiar from numerous examinations and probings. The room was bright with sunshine pouring through floor-to-ceiling windows.

Dr Wakuki's laboratory! Then Averil remembered the terror of the airbulance and flying cage. How near she had come to sterilisation.

Three people entered: Dr Wakuki then Marvin and Merle Brubacher. The latter wore visors and gloves to prevent infection, airborne or otherwise. As so often these days, Averil grew anxious at the coldness of their manner. How changed they were from the kindly uncle and aunt who adopted her in Mughalia.

Averil struggled to sit up.

"Rest," urged Dr Wakuki. "You've had quite the shock."

"Silly girl!" scolded Merle. "What on earth possessed you? Is this really the time to gallivant around Albion? After all we have invested in you."

"If Dora had not alerted me," said Dr Wakuki, gravely, "you might not be here now."

"Let's not be *too* hard on her," said Marvin Brubacher, looking up from his screen. "No harm done."

"But there could have been," snapped Merle.

She turned to Wakuki. "*Has* harm been done?"

"None detected."

"You have assured us this experiment has distinct possibilities, and I expect results. In fact, to avoid further nonsense, she should be incarcerated."

"I really cannot allow that," snapped Dr Wakuki.

Merle's laugh of reply was icy; the diminutive doctor flinched.

"Allow? It is I who allows you. Do not overestimate your usefulness to us."

"Hush," urged Marvin. "Really! You'll frighten the girl. And I agree with Wakuki. I can't imagine what you propose is good for the child."

"The test said I wasn't pure!" burst in Averil. "But I can't catch gene sickness. Why did it say I wasn't pure?"

Marvin and Merle exchanged glances.

"The machine made a mistake," said Dr Wakuki. "All machines are limited by the confines of their programming. They lack imagination. They see only what they have been constructed to see. Entirely new phenomena would be misinterpreted."

His mysterious explanation was directed at the Brubachers, not her.

All three examined her. Their appraisal reminded Averil of the annual Baytown Beast Fair, where livestock was bartered.

Then she noticed a rumble. Faint, swelling, coming nearer.

"Why," she said, "how strange. That sounds a lot like drone-thunder."

* * *

They came in low. How many? Thirty, forty. Nor were these small drones. Big weapon carriers, many of which last saw service in the Crusade against the Locusts. Their unmuted engines roared like raging dragons, designed to instil terror. Sirens pulsed, assailing the citizens of Albion with waves of percussion. Averil covered her ears and screamed.

How could this be? Only the other Cities had such might. Mughalia, Han City, Mitopia and Neo Rio must be striking against them, desperate to gain access to Honeycomb and a cure for the gene sickness.

She turned to Marvin and Merle. Surely they would know what to do. But the all-powerful Presidents of the Ruling Council cowered.

"They must not detect us!" wailed Merle. "They have come to kill us."

Marvin was talking into his screen: Averil caught a few snatches... *Don't initiate firing. Under no circumstances initiate firing...*

The high windows of Wakuki's penthouse laboratory offered a panoramic view of Albion. A huge battle-carrier, bristling with rockets, jets making the floor tremble, floated slowly past, scarcely a hundred feet away.

Dr Wakuki edged over to the tall pane of plasti-glass for a better view.

"We must give them access to Honeycomb," said Marvin. "Unless someone can think of an alternative."

"They must be punished!" shrieked Merle. "Sterilised! Every last one of them."

With a shaking hand, she sprayed soother-chemicals into her mouth; if her expression was any guide, they had little effect.

Drones hovered all over the city, the message plain: *Next time, Albion will be reduced to burning buildings, storms of rocket and cannon fire.* The exact threat that kept generations of primitives obedient.

Averil watched Marvin and Merle in astonishment. Were they so easily intimidated? Did they not have drones of their own? If the couple fell, no one would care about Baby or her. She would be carted off in a cage.

Pharaoh Jacko and Queen Morrighan came to mind. *They* had never given up, right to the end. A cruel ruse would have been their response, a ruthless counter-stroke.

"Merle is right," Averil called out, above the calamitous thunder of the drones' engines. "Strike back quickly while you have the power. Or all your authority will blow away like dust in drought-time."

She met Marvin and Merle's startled eyes.

"They must be got rid of before they can do it again. Or it will be too late for you."

Averil clutched her swollen stomach. Was that what she truly wanted? War and suffering? For Baby she would sacrifice anything – and for her own sake, yes, for herself.

"Perhaps the savage is right," said Merle.

She turned to Marvin. "You know how clean it could be. How simple. Remember what I told you."

He looked at her with something like horror. "Are things so . . . so *final?*"

"Do you think they will let you and I survive if they win?" she asked. "Think how they must hate us. The girl is right."

"But we would have to rebuild everything," said Marvin. "The work of a hundred years."

Merle Brubacher did not reply: she was watching the drones depart, their point well made. She wrung her hands convulsively, as though washing them.

By the window, Dr Wakuki spoke softly. "How frightened they must be. Frightened people will do anything."

* * *

What separates a god from a humble human? Averil once overheard her Uncle Michael and his Nuager friend, Mister Priestman, debate the question over frothing flagons of ale.

The god – or goddess – in question had been the Faery of Hob Vale. Priestman insisted this lady ruled the valley where the Pilgrims lived and farmed, an immortal expression of its inner energy, the force of its earth and transitory, living things.

"The Faery o' the Vale, Pilgrim? She is yon stream's bubble and flow. The sap in that oak and heat rising from that pile of rotting leaves. She has her caprices, Pilgrim. I read 'em right enough. I sense 'em."

Her uncle had asked, what purpose has a goddess without morals? It was merely nature Priestman described.

But the crazy Nuager had laughed. "The Faery of the Vale favours thee, Michael Pilgrim. Hers is the power to give or take."

Power. Yes, that was all that mattered in the end.

A few hours after the drones withdrew from Albion, the Ruling Council summoned the entire populations of the Five Cities to a mass holo-announcement. Its purport was widely anticipated. After the display of determination and unity from Mughalia, Han City, Neo Rio and Mitopia, little choice remained but capitulation. Access to Honeycomb would no longer be determined by the Ruling Council, but a committee of representatives from each of the Five Cities. Marvin and Merle Brubacher would be brutally deposed. Along with all who had supported their coup at the Grand Autonomy in Mughalia. Such was the general wisdom.

At the appointed hour, Averil sat in her apartment's leisure room – a large, open space meant for parties and gatherings to fill long, idle days. Dora hovered near the door. The holoset activated automatically, proof, if any were needed, every piece of communication equipment, from the humblest screen or domestic control device, could be accessed via central systems available to the Ruling Council.

A hologram expanded to fill half the room.

Marvin and Merle Brubacher sat on splendid thrones upon a dais. The golden suits they wore glowered like an angry dawn. At their feet, on low stools, perched the remaining members of the Ruling Council, a handful of wary men and women dressed in black. Around the Brubachers stood craggy, muscular Angels, naked save for long swords, heralds of the new Life Perfected. A revolving statue of the double helix, symbol of the Five Cities, turned near their thrones.

Averil shielded her eyes to block the light pouring from the Brubachers' robes.

"What is given can be taken away," announced Marvin. His voice was solemn, deepened by a synth programme. His sweating brows contracted sternly. Those with knowledge of toxicology might have detected symptoms of chemically induced elation, utter self-certainty, associated with megalomania-cocktails.

"Privileges lent can be reclaimed," added Merle. Her own voice sounded thin and twittery. Her pupils were dilated, feverish.

"Long ago, the Ruling Council anticipated this moment," said Marvin. "When the Five Cities were founded we foresaw the possibility of rebellion against the Beautiful Life."

"Traitors!" cried Merle. "Fools!"

Marvin frowned at her interruption.

"Yes, we anticipated and built in fail safes," he continued, "never expecting to use them. That we would be forced to need them."

Merle was shaking, wiping away tears of self-pity. Her dilated eyes rolled. "You made us do this," she sniffed.

"It is our duty now to protect the Beautiful Life," ploughed on Marvin. Was that a shadow of doubt on his implacable face? If so, it passed quickly. A bead of sweat formed on his forehead. "You have given us no choice."

Merle's bizarrely youthful face contorted. It was then Averil realised she was insane. The Presidents of the Ruling Council – and the tamed courtiers at their feet – were ruled only by selfish fear – and would stop at nothing to outlive this crisis.

"Blame your own selves," said Marvin, his synthesised voice booming. "We are gods today – the world's only gods, born to rule forever. You have proved yourselves unworthy of us. Unworthy of immortality. Mere mortals, who must perish through our apotheosis."

"We gave you every chance," screeched Merle. "Fools!"

"So we say, regretfully now," said Marvin, ignoring her, "farewell to old friends and colleagues across the Five Cities. Your sacrifice is not in vain. For you led to our divinity. Farewell."

With that, he held out a small control box to Merle, so that his thumb hovered over the switch. She reached over to place her own thumb on his. For long moments both hesitated. Silence mounted. A few courtiers and members of the Ruling Council hid their faces. Several sobbed aloud.

It seemed to Averil the Joint-Presidents dared not activate the switch. Then Merle Brubacher's face twisted. Her wild eyes strained. With a shriek, she forced down Marvin's thumb. The hologram folded in on itself and vanished.

* * *

Helen Devereux chafed at the slow progress of the cargo ship. Its bow rose and fell through wind-churned seas, a world of huge horizons oppressing her with motion.

Albion, it seemed, was still far off. A delay compounded by long weeks at the drone ship repair facility in the Falkland Islands. A place deserted by humanity – for some reason its resident technicians had

FOUR

been withdrawn – yet still serving its function, until the engines of the vessel revived. On a morning of wind-driven rain, they had edged back out into the North Atlantic.

Helen was convinced they were heading north, parallel to the coast of South America to Neo Rio, originally a small, gated science-town dedicated to gene-technology and advanced robotics. She could not risk using Synetta's old screen to pinpoint her position, in case it was being monitored. The ship must be trusted as her gaoler, master, feeder and, if her plan worked out, ultimate liberator.

She took to sitting and sleeping in the vessel's old-style control bridge; that way, she would get early warning of a place she remembered well – but not fondly.

Most futuristic of the Five Cities, Neo Rio mingled wide parklands with intricate white buildings linked by elevated highways, all set on low hills round a picturesque harbour. Tolerant of primitives – only so long as they stayed on the level of Stone Age hunter gatherers in the vast rainforests inland – Neo Rio's vigilance had been focused north, to the badlands of America, an irradiated, poisoned continent, yet full of resources. There, the primitives were monitored rigorously by satellite and surveillance drones designed to circle enormous territories. Attack fleets had been dispatched on several occasions to snuff out nascent population clusters and forbidden technology. A heavy hand was found most efficient in such cases: tactical fusion bombs could obliterate areas scores of miles wide, eliminating the need for tedious levels of accuracy. Where primitive populations were too scattered for such tactics, individuals were kidnapped and infected with new strains of plague to de-fertilise their savage tribes.

Neo Rio was famed among the Five Cities for its exuberant nightlife, priding itself on less chemically inspired pleasures than one sought, say, in Mughalia. Decorous delights Helen hoped very much to avoid. Unless her cargo ship changed destination, the final stop would be the seaport of Kings Lynn on the far side of the Atlantic. First, she must escape detection when her vessel docked in Neo Rio to load and unload.

*　*　*

At last, land was sighted. Helen reasoned they must be passing what had been a great nation in her youth, Brazilia, a deforested country re-greening in the absence of humanity. A thousand miles further north lay Neo Rio.

That night, she slept in a huddle of blankets on the floor of the bridge as it tilted and fell. The next daybreak, Helen stared through the thick plasti-glass window over the long, forward portion of the vessel. A few containers were magnetised onto the deck but most lay within the hold. The sea was transitioning from dawn's black-blue to grey in mimicry of the sky. She descended to her quarters and made coffee, carrying a flask and cup up the steep stairwell back to the bridge.

There, a prolonged series of vibrations startled her – as though invisible forces were passing through her body. The big ship itself seemed to shudder.

Puzzled, Helen sipped the coffee. Far in the distance, to the north, a smudge of black cloud was rising, spreading. A storm perhaps.

Out of nowhere, a huge wind buffeted the ship, slewing its course. Objects clanged against the vessel, earth, stones, was that a bush? For several minutes the gale blew, whipping up the sea. Then it had rushed past.

Onward the vessel ploughed. They had left the ocean depths, sailing over shallower waters, a continental shelf, towards the coast. Helen rubbed her tired eyes. The black cloud was still rising, stretching out dark wings. Below it, an optical illusion: the entire northern horizon was edged with white. A terrible suspicion gripped her.

In the ship's lockers were electro-binoculars. Helen activated the screen. And gasped. A towering wave rushed towards her, rearing as it went. The screen zoomed on wild, frothing foam, objects borne along by the force of the water.

Helen looked round: no help was possible. But the drone vessel had sensed the tsunami rushing its way. Hitherto untried programs responded. With a surge of its fusion engines, the vessel turned at a steep angle, so the wave would not hit it broadside but head-on. All over the ship, storm hatches locked into place. Compartments sealed themselves in case the hull breached. The few containers on top of the main hold were de-magnetised, drones rushing forward to cast them overboard.

Still the tsunami rushed on. Helen could hear it distinctly now. Deep rumbling and growling like an earthquake. When would it strike? Five minutes, ten? She hurried over to a large control chair bolted to the deck. Strapping herself in, Helen clutched the Baytown Jewel for reassurance.

On, on came the wall of water. A high cliff, its force unstoppable. In response, the freshly repaired fusion engine picked up speed, heading straight for the tsunami, the vessel's bow rising as it gained momentum.

The roaring was unbearable now. Helen could not close her eyes. She screamed in terror. Any moment, any moment . . . Then the great wave smashed down and the windows went black.

The world sank beneath her. The ship was being forced underwater by the weight of the wave. She closed her eyes, clutching the arms of the chair to block out the sound of plasti-steel and glass straining.

Surely they had capsized. The deck became a ceiling that her chair clung to, so that she was elevated above the floor, until a caprice of the tsunami spun the vessel upright once more. Like a cork, it popped back out into air. The wave thundered onward, leaving the vessel bobbing, floundering from side to side, buoyancy programs using the hydro-engines to stabilise. After carrying the ship forward for many miles, the great wave loosened its grip, rushing on towards what used to be Brazil.

For an hour the ship floated listlessly. It was assessing damage: despatching repair drones. Helen stayed in the seat, too numb to move. The high, swirling wind that preceded the tsunami died back into stray gusts.

With a grumble, dutiful hydro-engines restarted, guiding the ship back on course to Neo Rio.

* * *

Dusk when they approached Neo Rio. A slow, cautious journey. Helen did not doubt the container vessel had suffered internal damage from being shaken like a doll by an enraged child. Still, it was proving a doughty fighter.

At first, Helen wondered what had happened to the small city on its line of pleasant hills round the bay. A dark cloud of smoke and dust concealed it. As the ship drew near, Neo Rio's intricate network of high white buildings connected by lofty road and walkways had vanished. Even the hills had become mounds of earth and smoking rubble. As for the port area, it lay underwater or in piles of wreckage along with the beach zone, where sand glittered oddly, fused into jagged lumps of glass. Glowing fires attested to momentous energy unleashed.

Helen gawped. What could do this? No earthquake or act of nature. Only a fusion bomb – and a large one – caused so much destruction. Hence the tsunami that nearly broke her ship.

Someone deranged and wicked had destroyed this place, and all its citizens. For tens of miles inland there would be only blackened earth and tree stumps.

The cargo vessel waited outside the bay for codes summoning it to the docking area. Codes cancelled forever.

At last, it turned and limped on its pre-set course north. Within an hour, the ruins of Neo Rio lay behind. Yet the plume of smoke was visible until shrouded by night.

* * *

For days deep gloom smothered Albion. For many, it was a stupefying despair. Even the most abject and craven courtiers of the Ruling Council refrained from public celebration. The Presidents set the tone: now was a time for necessary grief, mourning the betrayal of the Beautiful Life by those destiny had returned to dust.

Averil kept to her apartment, afraid of punishment. She was the one who had suggested they strike back hard for the drones flying over Albion. What if Marvin and Merle regretted their actions, and sought someone to blame?

Dora could be heard weeping in her room at night. The entertainment channels that so entranced the girl from Baytown displayed only abstract, swirling shapes accompanied by eerie, funereal music. No one dared contact friends or acquaintances, lest it breach some unspoken edict.

Yet spring did not cease its work. When Averil stood on her balcony, she noted more flocks of water birds flying north to the fenlands. That must be a fecund land, she reasoned. A longing for meadows and woodlands coloured by wildflowers and blossom touched her. Ah, to be home and walking through the orchards of Hob Vale . . .

Guiltily, she activated her wonderful screen, reminding herself its marvels still existed, even if the other Cities were no more. The Five Cities would grow again, only better than any stupid flower that returns to earth when winter comes: Marvin and Merle Brubacher would see to that. And she had other powerful friends.

"Send message," she instructed the screen.

***

A drone opened Dr Wakuki's door for her. It led her past the examination rooms and laboratories to a sealed entrance in his private quarters, a place previously barred to her.

Averil knocked nervously. When no reply came, she activated the control and it slid aside.

Within, Dr Wakuki sat cross-legged. The cube-shaped room was windowless, bare of any furniture, its walls, ceiling and floor pure white. One wall served as a holoscreen, depicting images of utter ruin – piles of smoking rubble round a crater a mile in radius.

Averil stepped closer to the wall. "Is that . . . is that what happened?" she asked. "What Mughalia looks like now?"

Her voice was unsteady. When she first went to Mughalia it seemed the closest to Heaven possible on this earth.

Wakuki did not stop staring at the image.

"That is Han City." His voice was lifeless. "A surveillance drone recorded it. Everything was destroyed within a radius of fifty miles. I hear the Ruling Council have sent out battle drones to hunt down and finish off survivors. How fragile it all was in the end."

Fresh tears started to his eyes. To Averil, his seemed an odd grief: no sobs, his face blank, expressionless, yet lines of tears glistened on his smooth cheeks.

"Was Han City your home?"

"Yes. I was brought up there to be a technician. Then, because of my work, I was elevated to the status of a Beautiful. All my friends lived in Han City. Everyone who cared for me."

"I did not . . ."

"Know? Why should you? Your part is not to know anything. I would advise you to stick to that role. For your own safety."

She looked for the door. It had vanished in the illusion of entirely blank walls. She gestured at the destroyed city.

"I still don't understand how they did this."

"The Ruling Council ensured fusion bombs were planted beneath all the Cities and their major resorts," said Wakuki. "Secret weapons never really intended for use. Indeed, only a criminal lunatic would consider using them."

He seemed not to care whether the Ruling Council's spy devices were monitoring this blatant Discordia. Perhaps that was the point of the blank room: a refuge beyond detection.

"I'm sorry," said Averil.

"The fusion bombs must have been hidden beneath places I walked over a thousand times. And none of us guessed."

She knelt beside him, struggling to sit with her big swollen belly. The images on the wall shifted from death to life.

Now came faces, mostly oriental like Wakuki's, some three-dimensional, others projections of ancient 2D photographs. There were old men and women, grandparents, perhaps, a smiling young mother with her son – a child Averil recognised as Wakuki himself, long ago, another Wakuki – and still more: friends laughing round a table covered with plates and glasses, individual images of earnest girls and studious-looking boys.

Averil did not ask these people's names, or who he had lost. It could only make his pain worse. She reached out to take his slender hand. He flinched at the contact. But Averil gripped tight. Then he ceased to pull away, allowing her fingers to close round his until the holoshow played itself out.

FIVE

York. Clouds dousing the light of stars and moon. The city's ancient streets, trodden by conquerors and pilgrims for millennia, await dawn.

Some are busy already, as though impatient for daybreak. To the south of the city walls, hand-cranked rechargeable electric lamps join a flicker of burning torches to illuminate justice.

Grow People wearing Lady Veil's blood-red armbands and black uniforms shove six men and women stripped naked for ejection from the Commonwealth of the North. Their crimes? The old litany: theft, rape, unlicensed violence. Two road-murderers sway in the breeze from a gallows attached to the Minster. With the Council of the North in session, justice has been busy.

Others are also busy in the darkness. Fires redden the sweating faces of smiths at work on weapons, harness, armour, accoutrements to kill a man. Tired city officials prepare quarters for the thousands expected to arrive in York over the coming weeks. Already squads of volunteers have marched and ridden in from communities nearby. The young predominate, gay as if for a May Day holiday.

Common wisdom calls the Pilgrimage of Fools the end-time voyage foretold by the Nuagers. Preachers and prophesiers of all faiths proclaim the portents.

Where are the drones now? Where the impregnable Deregulators' compounds so recently ringing the coast? All gone or abandoned. Why so many City-folk found wandering, expelled from Albion, bearing tales of bitter division in their paradise? Regard the strangelings that appeared last year then vanished from the Commonwealth in their hundreds, a small army heading south. Everyone knows of them. One thing is sure: the strangelings have no love for the City. My enemy's enemy is my friend.

Yes, folk declare, the City is failing, and will topple with one push. So they say. So they dream all over the North. Dreams can set whole worlds ablaze.

In a chamber lit by candles and glow-lamps, others explore hazardous possibilities – and probabilities. Blair Gover sits before sheets of handmade paper, drawing detailed maps of Albion from memory. His companions watch, question and learn: Michael Pilgrim, Tom Higginbottom, Mister Priestman. They need the City-man, humour his mockery. Without Gover's co-operation, their slender hope vanishes.

Other folk await the coming dawn without hope. Seth Pilgrim lies on a bare bed, his cellmates rats and beetles. His small basement prison beneath the medieval Guild Hall was once a storeroom for documents, long since devoured by vermin.

No one comes to visit on this last night before his trial. No family. No friend. Their absence condemns Seth more than any judge.

* * *

Seth sat in a small anteroom, watched over by two guards armed with clubs. On the other side of the door, a thuggish gang was condemned for robbery, violence, sheep and crop stealing. The guilty verdict raised a loud cheer from a community risking threats and reprisals to bring the accused here in chains. A sign of new order, of progress. Off to the gallows the brigands went.

Me next, thought Seth.

Taking a deep breath, he stepped into what had once been a large council chamber, complete with worm-riddled oak panelling and throne-like chairs for local dignitaries. These were occupied by a jury of nine men and women.

To one side sat the Commonwealth of the North's leaders, including his Uncle Michael, Lady Veil and Tom Higginbottom. Mister Priestman had lit a candle scented with hemp to counter psychic impurities.

Many faces in the crowd were all too familiar. A single, startled glance revealed his accusers.

Charlie Gudwallah's widow and her children, still mourning their father. Beside them, Armitage the Baytown blacksmith. His beloved eldest daughter, Miriam, had been lost to Big Jacko, and the burly man had never forgiven Seth Pilgrim's part in her seduction. Dozens of other Baytown folk jostled, murmuring at the sight of him. They had travelled far to see justice well and truly done.

Be calm, Seth urged himself, *imagine Jojo is watching*. As indeed his ghost might well be: waiting for Seth to join him.

Yet when he risked another glance round the room his spirits sank further. His one friend, Hurdy-Gurdy, had stayed away. He was alone. Not a single ally left on earth.

The guards prodded him to a raised dock. He stood with head lowered while the charges were stated. All predictable enough.

First, murder, as part of the gang that killed the wandering tinker, Old Marley, and the rogue, Johnny Sawdon. Murder, too, while warring for Big Jacko and enabling his cruel rule as a trusted aide.

Next, a charge of treason for betraying his home community. All knew Seth Pilgrim guided the deposed Pharaoh's surprise attack on Baytown. Here, calls of outrage and hate among the spectators grew so loud the hearing was halted. Girls and women wept to recall violations they endured; many had loved ones to mourn, lost in the looting and havoc.

When order resumed, Seth looked over at his uncle. Michael Pilgrim's face, always haunted by melancholy, looked bleak as winter moorland.

When the charges were concluded and witnesses heard, the judge, none other than the irascible West Yorkshireman, banged a pistol butt on the table. He had been selected for his lack of connections to the Pilgrim family and its widespread influence.

"A-reet then," he declared. "There's two sides to every story. What's yours, lad?"

* * *

Mouth and throat dry as a coffin, Seth lowered his eyes. Feelings crowded up. What *was* his side? On whose side had he ever truly been? Not his own, if this was the consequence of the choices he made when sixteen-year-old. Perhaps that should be his plea. That he had been young, stupid. That he'd understood nothing much. And probably didn't understand a great deal more now.

An image of Jojo Lyons' brave, honest face filled his mind. He clutched at the memory. Instead of confusing him, it made him stand a little straighter. Yes, Jojo *had* been a friend. For his sake, for the love between them, brief as it had been, he would act as his friend would have desired.

"Speak up, lad," said the West Yorkshireman. "This is your chance."

Seth licked his dry lips. Shrugged. "I'm grateful to see so many folk here who I did wrong to."

Some in the crowd called out at his lack of shame.

"I'm grateful," he said, "for a chance to tell them I'm sorry. Mrs Gudwallah, Mr Armitage, and all the rest. I don't expect you to hate me the less for that apology. But I offer it anyhow."

He paused. His head swam with tension.

"As for the charges, well, they are true. All of them. I did those things – and more you haven't mentioned. It was just, you see . . ." He struggled for words. "When I think of it, there was another me back then. You know, with Jacko and the rest. A stranger to me now. A *me* I find hard to recognise six years on."

"I recognise you!" roared Armitage the blacksmith. "Yer little shit!"

A rotten apple flew from the crowd and struck Seth in the chest.

"Enough of that!" shouted the West Yorkshireman.

Best to get it over with. Get *himself* over with. Seth ploughed on. "Do you know what I'm grateful for an' all? That I got a chance to fall into good company. Better company than I deserved. It helped me become a better man. While I still had time. That's it. I've nowt more to say."

The court waited for the judge's verdict. None doubted what must come next. The only question: what form should the execution take?

Then a wiry figure segued through the crowd. Wild-haired with bulging eyes, his age indeterminable. He wore a strange white wig and long, flowing black robes. He carried a tottering pile of thick, hardback books, four feet high. These he dropped onto the judge's table with a resounding thump. Dust flew from the ancient pages.

"What the fuck," muttered Seth.

It was Hurdy-Gurdy.

* * *

"Oh, it's you again, is it?" remarked the West Yorkshireman. Wary respect mollified his usual bluff manner. The crowd watched Hurdy-Gurdy in silence.

"Indeed, your most honourables," he declared. "It is I. I have come! Like a knight of yore to protect something precious yet frail, delicate yet strong as hill-roots. In short . . ." He brandished a finger at the courtroom. "Justice."

"Bloody "ell," muttered the West Yorkshireman. "Well, say your piece."

Hurdy-Gurdy commenced.

"Who here has not committed acts of folly when young? And not just when young." He looked from face to face for long moments. Many turned away guiltily. Others were fascinated by his eyes' intensity. "Do we punish children for their crimes? Were *you* punished?"

"There's my Miriam's blood on that little bastard's hands!" called out Armitage.

Hurdy-Gurdy ignored the interruption.

"Hear me! Hear me!"

There was something uncannily suggestive about Hurdy-Gurdy's voice. Something with the power to lull one's own thoughts and pay particular weight to his words.

"I say to the Judge this. Yes, he is guilty. Plain as a wart."

Mutters of approval from his accusers.

"Yes," continued Gurdy, seizing one of the law books from his pile and brandishing it to the heavens. "This courageous lad tells the world as much. For – note this! – he is here to make amends for his mistakes as a silly boy. To find a way he can sacrifice his life for the good of all, and so make some amends."

Seth wondered what sacrifice Gurdy had in mind. He hoped it wouldn't be too painful.

"And I ask you this. Do not people who truly regret their actions deserve a second chance? Especially when so many guilty wretches, aye, who in no way regret their deeds, fly free as birds?"

Gurdy's hands fluttered like bird wings: many an eye found the movements oddly beguiling. His tone softened. Tender concern replaced bombast.

"I appeal to the mothers here today. Imagine your children's bonny, innocent faces. You reprove them, yes, then help them learn through their mistakes. Ah, a mother's love!"

Mrs Gudwallah wiped a tear from her eye.

"And as for fathers," Hurdy-Gurdy pinned down Armitage with his gaze. "I say to you, punish this young man with something far worse than a swift hanging. Hardly a punishment at all." His voice sank to a whisper, somehow audible at the back of the big room. "I have a far worse punishment in mind."

Seth sagged, faint with despair. Even Gurdy, the one person on earth he trusted, was against him.

"Now yer talking," mumbled Armitage, who could not take his eyes from Hurdy's own. "Make the little bastard suffer."

"Just so," said Hurdy-Gurdy. "Seeing all that remains is his punishment, I beg leave of the Judge to confer with him in private. Let the guilty man bear the harshest woe, I say."

He looked deep into the Judge's eyes. "Don't you agree, sir?"

The West Yorkshireman blinked. "Well, I'm not right sure..."

"Surely, you agree?"

Hurdy-Gurdy leaned forward and said softly, "I think you do agree."

Despite his bluff nature, the Judge appeared bemused. He blinked slowly.

"Aye, I suppose I do," he said. "We'll decide what to do with the lad in private. That's it for the day."

Seth Pilgrim was led back to his cell, staring at the floor.

* * *

"Do you really believe we can win this battle?" asked Tom Higginbottom.

He nodded at the force training on the former racecourse south of the city. An army unprecedented in size, swelling every day. Fresh

FIVE

tactics were being drilled into the enthusiastic, but largely unblooded volunteers. Rather than tight, disciplined formations effective against massed ranks armed with pike, musket and bow, Lady Veil had divided the army into small companies of no more than fifty. Each was intended to be self-sufficient, carrying its own supplies, spare ammunition, powder, arrows and crossbow bolts, as well as edged weapons for close up killing, Each company was designed to operate with a high level of independence from a central command, much like guerrilla bands. The battle plan could hardly be simpler: get in close enough then hit and run. At the first sight of drones, scatter and scarper.

Michael and Tom watched with the other commanders.

"If Gover delivers what he has promised we can win," said Michael. "And I do believe him capable of such a miracle. Why, I have seen him set the ocean ablaze and create lightning storms and clouds of poison gas with his infernal science. We must risk trusting him. Or send everyone home with their tails between their legs. But then, surely as time passes, the City will recover like a waxing moon. And our future wane."

Lady Veil waved her hands vehemently.

"She says," reported the interpreter, "'Do not blame me if Blair Gover proves a treacherous liar.'"

"Even liars can speak true," pointed out Michael. "Besides, what choice do we have?"

"In the circumstances, none," replied Lady Veil. "For all we know, they may have already found a cure for whatever sickness afflicts them. Temporary madness is one thing, but our enemy is the master of self-preservation. We are already almost out of time. As for Gover, he is your responsibility, Michael Pilgrim."

"I'll keep a beady eye on Mister Gover," said Michael. "And don't forget, he is as desperate as the rest of us. For him, too, this is a last chance."

"But for what?"

"That remains to be seen."

A hairy man rode up on a rusting, two-wheeled contraption constructed of salvaged parts. Michael Pilgrim recognised it as a bicycle. The tyres might be solid plastic hoops but they allowed the rider to spin on one wheel and balance on the saddle with his arms outstretched like aeroplane wings.

"Mr Gurdy," said Michael. "Good day to you. It's arranged then?"

The old clown dismounted with a flourish that turned into a somersault. Yet for once his acrobatics failed. He landed awkwardly, stumbling and falling to his knees.

"You alright?" asked Tom Higginbottom.

The City-man attempted a smile. "I am a fond old man. And must fall before I rise."

Michael felt awkward in Hurdy-Gurdy's company. He owed him too much. Whilst deeply relieved at the miracle that had occurred, he felt uneasy. The court's unexpected clemency towards Seth had stirred much anger. Many believed justice had been trampled upon, the fledgeling law abused to favour the powerful. What hope for the law if no one trusted it? The accusation piqued both Michael Pilgrim's conscience and vanity. It was, after all, largely true. Yet it had been none of his doing when Hurdy-Gurdy took the judge aside at the trial. What exactly went on between them in the private chamber at the back of the courtroom no one knew for certain. The judge's own recollection was oddly hazy. Michael suspected it involved the same magic of the mind that turned their City-prisoner into Gurdy's obedient toy. If so, an outrage against justice had occurred. One he was only too happy to ignore.

"You have everything you need, Hurdy-Gurdy?" he asked. "There'll be no help for you down there. They say it is a barren, haunted region.

And the drones will be watchful as hawks."

Lady Veil's hands grew agitated. "I still oppose sending Hurdy-Gurdy on this foolish, madcap mission. Its chances of success are nil. His unique skills and knowledge belong with the main force."

Hurdy-Gurdy bowed. Restless eyes glittering, he crooned in a voice sweet and lilting.

Heigh-ho! sing, heigh-ho! unto the green holly:
Most friendship is feigning, most loving mere folly...
This life is most jolly.

As the refrain died away, he remounted the outlandish bicycle. Singing as he pedalled, Hurdy-Gurdy departed in the direction of the river.

After he had gone, Tom Higginbottom snorted. "Mad as a wren caught by lime."

"Mad or sane, he has my gratitude," said Michael. "That stranger fulfilled a deathbed promise when I chose not to. I swore to my poor brother, James, I'd save Seth. Yet I failed him all over again. My nephew will be lucky to survive long down there."

"We'll all be departing the same way soon," predicted Tom, gloomy as ever.

* * *

The first departure from York took place in haste. A flat-bottomed coble, crewed by a dozen fishermen from Hull waited at the wharf of King's Staith. They had been chosen because the coastline south of Humber was familiar to them.

Supplies, weapons, tents, equipment were piled into the hold. Light rain fell. Hurdy-Gurdy cycled up, and regretfully passed his machine to one of the soldiers protecting the ex-prisoner from lynch mobs.

"Tend my trusty steed," he said. "It prefers oil to oats."

"I'll give you this piece of shit in exchange," said the soldier. "I reckon I've got the better half of the bargain."

He pushed forward, none too gently, a young man in clean new clothes and boots. He had been provided with a knife, carbine, pistols and cutlass. On his head was a sailor's leather cap.

Seth Pilgrim clasped Hurdy-Gurdy's hands.

"You saved me," he said, in wonder.

"Look what the cat brought home," purred Hurdy. "Meow!"

"I expected to be dangling from the Minster by now." Seth's elation dimmed. "Maybe it's what I'll get if we make it back. How did you do it?"

"If all received their just deserts this world would be deserted."

"I mean it. How did you do it?"

The answer came in a confidential whisper. "Once upon a time, Hurdy-poos had his own hypno show. Wildly popular! Such ratings! Sheer genius! Weak minds can be *so* persuadable. This tomcat has ways of making rat catchers fill his bowl with cream."

Seth laughed. "Well, I'm a relieved rat, alright. I still don't get why you stuck your neck out for me. Helping me has earned you mortal enemies, I'm told."

He glanced uneasily at the guards.

Hurdy-Gurdy's smile grew wistful. "Perhaps a foolish old man sees a boy he once was. Perhaps he wishes someone had steered him a little when he needed it. Gurdy has not always been nice."

Seth squeezed the jaded holotainer's wiry fingers.

"Don't talk crap! I know no one kinder. And I hear you're to come with me. A suicide mission, they called it."

"True. Indeed, I must accompany you at all times. I am, Young Nuncle, your oath-bound guarantor. And you are my bonder, until your sentence is expunged. Or you die. The latter seems more likely. Such is the generosity of the court. Now, busk! Busk! Every moment's

FIVE

delay makes our journey more pointless than it already is."

They boarded the coble and sat at the stern. Strong, skilful oars drove her out into the tidal current. Soon, the boat vanished round a bend in the river.

The second departure from York occurred two weeks later.

An army thousands strong drew up in a long line of companies. Mules and horses laden with food accompanied the soldiers, along with droves of sheep and cattle. There would be little chance of foraging until they reached their destination, two hundred miles south.

At the head rode Lady Veil and the Protector of the North; beside them, a man with hands bound to the pommel of his horse, face concealed beneath hood and clown mask lest aerial drones recognise him. A large contingent of Nuagers broke into their master-hymn as the Pilgrimage of Fools moved off. Drums beat the time. Many an unbeliever sang with them, and the streets of York echoed to lusty, determined voices:

Swing low, sweet universe,
Coming for to carry us home.
Swing low, sweet sun and stars,
Coming for to carry us home.

SIX

Seth Pilgrim wondered how it all went wrong so suddenly. Their journey down the Ouse to the Humber, swollen by spring rains draining from the land, had been swift. Likewise, passage round the towering wreck of the Humber Bridge. Its central section had long ago fallen into the river, blocking its middle channel, so they were forced to hug the shore. Seth ducked as they sailed beneath what remained of the huge vault of steel.

"What did they not dare to do in the Before Time?" he exclaimed.

Words addressed to Hurdy-Gurdy. He received no reply. The old holotainer had covered himself in a blanket, sweat shiny on his broad brow. Seth had never seen him sick before. With his miraculous skills, he seemed more than mortal.

"You alright, Gurdy? You looked a bit peeky in York. Maybe you caught a fever when we camped in Goole last night. Place was such a crap hole, probably gave us all the plague."

His concern was genuine. Like every one of his generation, Seth had seen folk rise fit as frogs and be dead by dusk.

"Declan is tired, that is all," said Hurdy-Gurdy, "a bad penny, old and worn."

Seth wrapped his own blanket round him.

"Get some sleep, Gurdy. And drink this ale. You'll need all your strength soon."

SIX

Yet strength proved elusive. Gurdy, the leader of the expedition, was in a high fever when they reached The Wash, a day's sail south from the Humber.

During the journey, Seth had been able to size up his new companions. The fishermen were masters of their craft, no question, but he wouldn't rate their chances in a fight. Not if surrender was an option.

* * *

As a Baytown lad, Seth Pilgrim thought he knew the sea. But he'd never known a coast quite like this.

Mile upon mile of mudflats interspersed with deep channels, gave way to dreary salt and silt marshes braided with streams and rivers. What flooded at high tide was exposed at low. A land of unbroken horizons: sea, sky, cloud; rims of darker green inland where salt marsh became brackish swamp, surrounding rare islands of higher ground.

Few landmarks gave definition to the coast. Houses and buildings poked from the marsh, sited on lost fields once drained by dike and pump and sea-wall. Rising sea levels laughed at millennia of human attempts to tame the ocean. Walls and roofs washed away by tidal surges like children's sandcastles.

Some buildings endured better than others: which is what guided Seth to the big old church tower. It rose not far from the sea channel running from The Wash to the City's compact port, a high walled facility built upon the ruins of King's Lynn.

"Is this a good base?" he had whispered to Hurdy-Gurdy, suddenly insecure, conscious the fishermen lacked a natural leader. Most were no older than him, and when it came to camping within sight of a port swarming with drones, no bolder.

Hurdy slumped in the boat, bloodshot eyes closed.

"We'll chance it," decided Seth. "But keep the guns handy, lads, just in case. I can't imagine anyone crazy enough to live in this cesspit, but you never know."

High tide floated them right up to the medieval tower, which stood beside the long stone church. Close up, it became clear other folk used its thick stone walls as a safe island. A jetty of scavenged bricks had been piled to allow entry onto the first floor. Logs driven into the mud served as mooring posts. There were traces of fires, too, on the slab floor: none smelt recent.

"We'll camp here," said Seth.

To his surprise, no one argued. With Hurdy-Gurdy so feeble, the fishermen's fears made them accept his authority – temporarily, at least. The novelty, and irony, of such a situation did not escape Seth.

"Keep weapons handy," he told his companions. "Whoever made that fire might come calling."

* * *

The village houses were laid out in neat lines of piled brick, glass and concrete. These narrow islands supported a few spindly shrubs but mostly the vegetation consisted of salt-loving grass, growing round creeks and pools. Birds brought colour and welcome voices to the dreary scene: gulls, geese, ducks of every variety. A few wild horses and deer grazed, ready to retreat inland when the tide was high.

Seth observed these things from the very top of the church tower, through binoculars from the Before Times. His attention, however, was focussed out to sea. Prior to lapsing into his fever, Hurdy had told him their task was to intercept all City ships entering King's Lynn. Any vessel might carry a person important to their cause, the former curator of the Baytown Museum, along with something of inestimable value in her possession. What could be so precious, Hurdy did not reveal.

SIX

"You mean, Miss Devereux?" Seth had asked, aghast. Of the many, many people he wished to avoid in this world, she ranked high.

She had been Big Jacko's wretched prisoner the last time Seth saw her – indeed, he was the one who bundled her into a wooden box for transportation to the abandoned radar station, out on Fylingdales Moor. Not to mention serving as her gaoler. Nor had he been a kindly one.

"I'll leave her to you, Hurdy."

That was before Hurdy's sickness meant Seth must manage her – in the improbable event she turned up – along with everything else. The mission. Fresh water supply. Food. Firewood. Spies out in the marsh. Watch rota. All required decisions.

Seth scanned the sea for ships approaching King's Lynn. The coble stood ready to sail at any time.

No ships came. The unscalable concrete walls of the port winked with lights as dusk fell. Seth dared not go close. Days passed and Hurdy-Gurdy's condition worsened.

When not on watch, Seth sat by his friend, bathing his hot forehead with a damp cloth. Midges floated in clouds and flies were drawn to their salty sweat. The church tower rustled at night with bats and mice; it was impossible not to feel a trespasser in their world.

Seth could tell his companions were losing courage. As leader, he knew he should reassure them. Somehow the right words would not come. His Uncle Michael would have known exactly how to raise their spirits and instil confidence. He would be out on The Wash each day, learning the layout of the channels, seeking advantage. The only other style of leadership Seth knew, Big Jacko's free-fisted bullying and bribes, appealed to him more with each day that passed.

Sometimes he overheard the fishermen whispering to one another of devils and cannibals lurking in the marsh. If they decided to scarper, Seth knew he was done for. The terms of his parole meant desertion would cost his neck.

One night, he climbed the stone stairs to the tower's flat roof and looked out to sea. Stars glittered in ribbons across the immensity of the night sky. Then he noticed a rhythmic flashing. A City ship was coming.

* * *

As dawn lit the eastern horizon, Seth balanced on the prow of the coble. Its crew used their oars to steady the boat against the incoming tide. The mast was up, sail ready for unfurling.

All night the City-ship had stood out to sea, lights flashing, waiting for high tide to provide maximum draft through the channel leading to King's Lynn. In the half-light, Seth ordered the fishermen to row nearer. Firearms stood ready in waterproof leather tubes: a feeble reassurance against drones.

Could the large vessel truly require no crew? It seemed impossible, but Hurdy-Gurdy had whispered hoarse instructions from his nest of blankets . . . "Don't go too close. Or wake the dragon. If you do, use the thing I showed you." For a moment he fainted. Then he mustered a sickly grin. "And die well."

This reassuring speech over – Seth was glad none of the fishermen heard it – Hurdy-Gurdy lapsed into unconsciousness.

Out at sea, he raised his binoculars.

"Keep her steady, lads. Let's see if she's aboard."

He focussed the binoculars. Christ, it was big. Its lines sleek, with extendable arms for fishing nets.

"That bugger's caught more cod than you ever will," he joked.

The wide-eyed fishermen from Hull did not laugh. Seth's own heart beat with painful expectation. *Think of Jojo*, he told himself. *Think how Hurdy-Gurdy trusted you. Prove those fuckers back in Baytown wrong.*

SIX

The fishing vessel's engines grumbled as it slowly angled towards the channel.

"Get a bit closer," he urged. "If you spot a certain lady, shout."

"Fuck this!" cried the youngest fisher-lad, his voice trembling. "Have you seen that thing?"

Seth placed a hand on his pistol butt. "Fucking do it! Or you'll answer to Lady Veil herself."

They might have chucked him overboard; but one fear mastered another. Cursing, the fishermen took up their oars.

Closer, closer. They were still half a mile off, having just entered the channel, when the tillerman bellowed a warning, "Behind us! Behind us!"

All turned. An aerial drone had risen from the high concrete walls of the City-port. Without apparent haste, it drifted towards them. The dragon had woken.

"Turn!" screeched Seth.

The aerial drone paused, hovered, surveying the ants in their nutshell craft. Any moment it might decide to breathe fire.

"Break your backs, lad!" shouted the tillerman.

Seth fumbled with the lid of a leather tube. It contained Hurdy's secret weapon meant for drones. Then something caught his eye. A big puff of smoke from the marsh, followed by a low boom rolling across the water. The drone veered, swivelling to scan the salt-marsh.

In the time this took, their boat left the channel behind. Perhaps they passed an invisible line for the security drone paid them no more attention. Circling over the sea-marsh, it returned to the port.

Seth trained his binoculars on the area where the puff of smoke rose. Slightly higher ground. Then he spotted movement. Plastic from the Before Times, floating inland with the rising tide? He could not tell.

* * *

Back in the church tower, Seth climbed to the roof for a clear view of the port.

How it functioned was obvious enough. A large, deep pool into which ocean-going ships sailed, docking beside a huge processing facility. Whether people lived there was moot. Certainly, he saw no one. He watched drones unload containers from the fishing vessel. These were then transported along the docks to a second, smaller basin lined with drone barges to traverse the broad canal connecting King's Lynn to Albion.

Something *had* distracted the aerial drone sent to intercept them. A midge bite, perhaps, but it had won them time to escape. Perhaps they were not quite alone out here.

More days passed. No new vessel bearing Helen Devereux arrived. When relieved from watch, Seth nursed Hurdy-Gurdy or explored.

The church's foundations lay deep in the slime of the marsh. When the tide was out, Seth perched on a marble tomb of a knight and his lady, side by side for eternity. He thought mournfully of his Father's longing to preserve the faith he loved. Then, as now, time washed the firmest faiths away.

What had Father always said at the end of his stupid prayers?

Amen, he told the long, empty building. *Forgive me, Father, I never meant to turn out this way. A fuck-up for a son. Thanks be to God. Amen.*

Seth returned to the small chamber where Hurdy-Gurdy shivered. The City-exile was still delirious. His breath reeked of infection.

"You knew all along it was bollocks for me to hope for a new life in the City," Seth said. "You just went along with it to humour me. Maybe to learn me better."

"Honeycomb," muttered Gurdy. "Destroy honeycomb or they can rebuild."

Seth ignored his talk of bees. Fat chance of a buzzy bee out on this stinking marsh.

SIX

"Thanks to you, Hurdy, I did learn better. There *is* hope for me now. If life is hope, as they say. What the fuck I'm meant to do with it, who knows?"

"Honeycomb," gasped Hurdy-Gurdy.

A cry came from the lookout at the top of the tower.

"Ship! Ship!"

* * *

Days of frustration galvanised the small band. They scrambled with reckless will into the coble, rowing towards the distant ship.

The tide was rising and would allow the vessel direct access to King's Lynn. Once more, Seth stood in the prow with his binoculars.

This was even bigger than the drone fishing boat, a container vessel with a large, rounded tower ringed with tall observation windows. If folk were on board, that's where they'd gather. Dents in the hull spoke of fierce battering.

Could it carry Helen Devereux? There was only one way to find out.

"Bugger this!" Seth cried. "Cut her off, lads."

If the drone from King's Lynn flew up, they might not get lucky a second time. He took up a signal rocket. The coble swayed in the fast-flowing tide.

Soon the prow of the cargo vessel loomed, cutting a white wake. Through the binoculars, Seth thought he saw a dark silhouette behind the windows of the control tower.

"Here goes!"

Seth lit the fuse of the signal rocket in its tube. With a whoosh it flew, exploding a hundred yards from the oncoming ship in a puff of coloured smoke and an echoing bang. He grabbed a second rocket. Up it went.

Then Seth waited. Whether for death or delivery, he could not say.

* * *

For days, Helen Devereux had watched the coastline of Southern England pass by, a green land of rolling hills between abandoned towns. At night, flickers of light beaconed the remnants of humanity.

Such realisations led her to ponder the burden she carried. Daily, Helen opened the locket and examined the info-pearl. Her only answers were questions. What codes did it store? Why was it so important that Blair took the trouble to hide it where no one in the City would look?

One thing she knew: the deranged, megalomaniac Brubachers must not get hold of it. Before she reached King's Lynn and commenced her final, hopeless task on this earth – extracting Averil from the pit of Albion – that info-pearl would go overboard, to vanish forever.

Other preparations were necessary. As the ship passed the Thames Estuary, Helen packed a small bag of clothes and pocketed Synetta's pistol. She examined Synetta's old screen. At King's Lynn, there would be no more point in discretion: the screen could be fully activated. Its signals might even deter the port's security drones from assuming she was a primitive.

Helen stood on the ship's bridge. They entered a bay she recognised as The Wash from former pleasure trips with Blair Gover. One year he had ordered the construction of a jaunty yacht painted blue and white, a crew of drones tending the sails. Helen's role had been to serve refreshments. But he soon tired of playing skipper. Ocean horizons, endless and uncontrollable, made him nervous.

Still, here was The Wash and no Blair Gover in sight. She had contrived to cross the entire world to get here. Helen marvelled at the success of her improbable gamble. It gave her confidence.

With a judder, the ship's hydro-engines slowed; it inched up the

SIX

channel towards King's Lynn, a few miles distant. Sensors would be scanning for underwater obstructions or unexpected sandbanks.

Helen donned a thick coat. Taking up the electro-binoculars, she focussed on the port ahead. Then something caught her eye.

At the edge of the channel bobbed a small boat. Its mast was raised, sail furled. A craft she recognised from years of watching the Baytown fishing fleet: an East Yorkshire coble. Her heart leapt.

Close up on the boat, she instructed the binoculars.

The crew appeared full face on her screen. Helen gasped. Looked again.

A face she had hoped to never see again. Older, true, but unmistakable. A face associated with the most miserable months of her life, when she and Averil languished as prisoners in the basement of Fylingdales Radar Station. A face summoning other loathed faces: Big Jacko, Queen Morrighan, his leering confederates. The face belonged to none other than Michael Pilgrim's turncoat, treacherous, cruel runt of a nephew, Seth Pilgrim.

Could he have been sent to meet her? Had Big Jacko survived? That seemed impossible. Other explanations were as bizarre.

She focussed the electro-binoculars on his face. The young man was panicking, that she could tell. He laughed wildly, calling out to the crew at their oars. Pointed at the ship. Issued a command. Oars dipped, the boat advanced.

What could he be about? The height of the ship's hull made boarding impossible, even if there had been no security drones.

Intuition nudged her towards the truth. Perhaps he had reconciled with his uncle. Somehow, they must have guessed she was coming. Why else would he loiter here, waiting for her ship to arrive?

Seth Pilgrim took out a flint lighter and set off a signal rocket trailing red smoke. Then another. Both exploded with a puff.

Then Helen was in motion. Grabbing her bag, she clambered down the steep stairs from the bridge onto the long forward deck.

Outside, cold wind whipped her face and hair. Sea-scents filled her nostrils.

Helen ran along the deck, dodging round cranes, until she reached the high prow. From up here, she could see the flimsy wooden coble two hundred yards off. With clumsy fingers, Helen pulled out Synetta's powerful screen.

Activate voice amplifier and image projector to maximum, she directed. *Identify target. Yes, the boat. Project a hologram of me. Five metres from the young man at the front. Yes, him. Magnify me three times life size.... Project!*

A huge image of herself unwrapped before the boat. Though she could not hear from this distance, she saw Seth's mouth open to scream.

Her voice boomed across the placid water, amplified until the screen's speaker rattled.

What are you doing here, Seth Pilgrim?

The crew cowered, oars in disarray. Though the youth was terrified, he spoke urgently to the hologram hovering over the waves.

Lip read what he's saying, she instructed the screen. A suave, smug voice replied with a distinctly North American accent: *We've come for you. The Council of the North sent me. Uncle Michael. Jump when we come close.*

Helen recoiled from such a drop.

Jump? she asked, her voice booming. *Are you mad?*

Jump, replied the unflappable American synthvoice. *We'll take you back to my Uncle, back to York. There's no time.*

Helen saw he was right. Time was up. An aerial drone had risen from the port of King's Lynn.

* * *

SIX

Helen Devereux watched in horror as the drone hovered, assessing threat levels. It was in no hurry.

The fishing coble's sail unfurled and, helped by oars and skilful seacraft, it sped towards the container ship. Helen judged she had just a few minutes before it arrived – and passed by – then it would be too late.

Her eye fell on an emergency locker. A muster station had been positioned at the front of the vessel in the inconceivable event the ship sank with a crew on board. Rushing over, she activated the locker, dragging out a life jacket. This, she inflated. While it puffed up, Helen pulled the Baytown Jewel from round her neck. No time to extract the info-pearl as she had hoped. The precious Jewel must leave her. In the life jacket was a zipped up, waterproof, survival pouch. She opened it, thrusting in the Jewel, before sealing it again.

Helen ran back to the prow. Just in time! The coble was almost directly below, the faces of the crew upturned, backs bent as they rowed, struggling to steady their boat in the churn of the great ship's wash.

Listen, her amplified voice resounded. *Take this life jacket to Michael Pilgrim. Tell him to look inside the Jewel. Do you understand? What it contains could change everything. Tell him Blair Gover hid it there. Do you understand?*

Seth's mouth moved and the lip-reading synthvoice replied. *Yes. I'll give it to him. Now jump. Jump. Jump.*

Helen leaned over the ship's rail, tossing down the life jacket. It bounced a few yards in front of the coble. Seth leaned over the foaming sea, dragging it aboard.

Then the coble was passing along the hull. Too late for her to escape now. Too late to risk her life to regain a life. To meet friends and neighbours in Baytown once more. Oh, for her neat quarters in the Museum on the cliff! A harsh doubt crossed Helen's mind: Averil better be worth this sacrifice.

She looked towards King's Lynn. The drone was moving. It had decided to act.

* * *

Like all sensible primitives, Seth Pilgrim regarded drones with instinctive terror. Trickles of sweat streamed down the sides of his face at the sight of an aerial security drone heading their way.

The enormous bulk of the cargo vessel and its churning hydro-engines threatened to suck them under. Now he panicked. Nor was he alone.

"Veer starboard!" called out the tillerman. "Come on, boys. Out of the channel."

They rowed with swift, deep strokes, the coble shooting back towards the marsh.

Seth glanced at the ship. The drone circled over the prow of the great vessel, as though scanning Helen Devereux. An unworthy part of him rejoiced. Yes, concentrate on that snooty bitch. Rip her arms off not mine. Forget us insects in our little tub.

Then they were out of the channel, heading for an inlet where a small river merged with the sea. A cluster of ruined buildings jutted from the ocean to form a manmade island.

The drone rose again. Turned. Whatever business it had with the City-woman was over. It floated their way.

"Fuck!" cried Seth. "Row faster, you cunts! Faster!"

Despite his frenzy, Seth recalled Hurdy-Gurdy pointing out a leather case useful against drones. He dragged out a long bundle of metal tubes welded together, each two inches across, terminating in the stock of a rifle, along with trigger and heavy hammer. Was he meant to wave this slingshot at a fucking drone?

SIX

"Pull! Pull!" urged the tillerman.

They were near the ruined buildings now, a former warehouse. The mounds of concrete offered some shelter. Seth pulled on the life jacket Helen Devereux had thrown down. By some City-sorcery it clicked tight round his chest.

He squinted up at the drone. Its rotors chuntered lazily. A hundred yards off. Why didn't it fire? Perhaps they weren't worth a rocket.

At fifty yards, he shouldered the strange gun, aimed.

"Keep fucking rowing!" he moaned.

His finger curled round the trigger. *Bang*. The hammer detonated a percussion cap. Hurdy's contraption quaked in his hands. Rockets whooshed out, not flying straight but somersaulting, dipping, wheeling like crazed fireflies or bats, silver sparks of magnesium drifting in the air.

Instantly, the drone diverted course. It sprayed fire at the midge dance of rockets. Tracer streaked. Cannon shells exploded. Water and mud spurted. Shots raked the ruined buildings poking from the sea.

But the coble was unharmed. With a grinding groan, it struck the concrete island. Seth, at the prow, scrambled across breeze blocks covered with limpets that cut his hands and knees. Behind him, an explosion. The force tossed him into a cleft in the rubble filled with water and weed.

The drone hovered over the coble, then a cannon shot broke the hull in two. Of the crew, most were already dead. For the rest, horribly exact, the drone used single shells. Heads protected by feeble, imploring, outspread fingers exploded. With each crump, gobbets of brain, blood and bone spattered as Seth grovelled, pretending to be dead.

The drone's rotors chuntered. Perhaps it did not sense his heart beating. Perhaps it considered its work fulfilled. He must not open his eyes. *Do it quick, you fucker*, he thought. Then – its command codes appeased – the drone flew off. The noise of its rotors faded. Gull cry and lapping waves became the dominant sounds.

If Seth had poked up his head, he could have watched the drone escort the cargo vessel safely to King's Lynn. And seen, too, how a slight, female figure stood defiantly at the prow, having taken out a pistol she emptied into her screen, the smoking remnants going overboard. Instead, bleeding and quivering, he wept.

* * *

Seth had to wait long hours for the tide to turn. He lay low on the island of old buildings while the waters slowly receded. None of it noticed him. Sky or clouds. Tiny crabs in the pool where he hid. A seemingly endless procession of gulls, carried by the wind out to sea, directed by lazy wing beats.

At last, he left his meagre shelter, hugging himself against cold and wet, astonished by the scarcity of his injuries. Nothing more than bad grazes on hands and knees from the limpets; it hardly seemed fair. When he climbed down to what remained of the coble, he was confronted with headless corpses and severed limbs. These he kicked into the sea as a kind of burial. Better the fish ate them than hordes of screaming gulls. What fools they had been to trust his leadership. Yet Seth was glad to be alive.

With low tide, the salt marsh emerged as broad ribbons of sandbanks held together by tough, reed-like grass. Wind-rippled creeks formed a maze of water. A broader channel, quarter of a mile wide, lay between his current sanctuary and the nearest patch of elevated ground.

Seth surveyed the sky. A few hours of daylight left. The church tower lay miles to the east. Unless he wished to spend the night on this miserable heap of rubble, he must move fast.

One advantage had been given: the City life jacket tossed by Helen Devereux. It was tight and snug. Given the wondrous nature of all

SIX

things connected to Albion, he did not doubt its effectiveness in water.

The sea numbed him as he waded in. But Seth had known much physical hardship in his short life, not least as a field-bonder up in Lake Country. When his feet no longer felt sand and silt beneath, he launched himself forward in a dog-paddle, breath heaving, battling against the residual pull of the retreating tide until, lowering his legs, he felt solid ground once more. Soon he was wading out, boots sinking in mud.

This reminded him of a real danger: quicksand or quagmire might swallow him yet – and there were no helping hands to drag him free.

Seabirds rose in a cloud as he cautiously advanced, using a piece of driftwood to test for patches of liquid sand. Behind him, the sun descended into the flat earth. Through creeks and over mini-islands, he threaded his way, passing roofs and walls devoured by the sea, rusting heaps of vehicles exposed by low tide. Sea-tilth filled some creeks with dense, tangled plastic.

It was almost dark when Seth reached the ancient church tower. Never had he felt so exhausted – or amazed to be alive. One thought obsessed him, to find Hurdy-Gurdy, and get them both from this hell.

"Hurdy!" he called, dragging up the stairs to the tower's highest chamber, where the City-man recuperated. "Hurdy! I found her. But it all went wrong . . ."

His voice died. A short, wiry young man in waxed cloth trousers and jacket lolled against the wall, picking his teeth with a splinter. His other hand pointed a crossbow at Seth's chest. He grinned. An impish twist of mouth, possibly cruel, possibly not.

Seth's startled glance revealed two other men in similar garb, all armed. Hurdy-Gurdy lay in his blankets. Ignoring the strangers, Seth staggered over to the prone figure. Felt his forehead. Still burning hot. Still alive. The fuckers hadn't murdered him yet.

The young crossbowman's grin widened to reveal an absence of teeth.

In an accent strange to Seth, he said. "So what's gooin' on 'ere, 'bor? Yo-oo put on quite a show out there today."

Nobody spoke. The young man, clearly the leader, stopped grinning.

"A damn nuisance of a chap like you needs to come with us, I reckon." A sly, cocky smile flickered. "An' we shan't be taking no for an answer."

SEVEN

Averil was in Dr Wakuki's aircar, on the way home from a tedious function where she had been displayed to a group of curious doctors. He sat beside her, fidgeting as usual. Night lay heavy across the land, heavy as Baby in Averil's womb. Up-spilling light from Albion tinted low clouds a sickly yellow.

Wakuki's screen bleeped. After checking it, he stiffened. "I am needed. As, apparently, are you, Averil. I'm afraid you must accompany me. A team is already there, scanning for traps."

What kind of traps, he did not explain. A short journey brought them to the rooftop of an enormous tower. Dora had once pointed it out as the former palace of Blair Gover. Here, they found medi-techs and security drones. Also present was Merle Brubacher, along with Angel bodyguards. Due to losses from gene sickness, many Beautifuls were undertaking tasks for which they had little expertise or aptitude. The nervous man cringing before Merle Brubacher was clearly such a one. Her frown expressed dangerous displeasure.

"Madame President, the probe discovered a hidden access way from Blair Gover's private study," he reported. "The first drone we sent in was disabled by a security system. As was a second. We think it's safe now..."

"Think?" broke in Merle. "I never rely on *think* for my safety."

"Of course, Madame President. But I've been in there myself. I believe it is safe."

A gravity-chute cunningly concealed within one of the tower block's huge supporting pillars whisked them down to a complex of underground rooms. This maze spread beneath Blair Gover's former palace. Its secret construction was clearly the work of many decades.

Laboratories led to storage facilities and research centres. Workshops contained prototype drones and machines. Screens of many kinds lay inert.

"By blundering in here, I suspect you triggered a general shutdown," pointed out Dr Wakuki, mildly. "The systems will only restart with codes known to their deviser."

"Idiots!" Merle hissed. Her hands clenched.

The Beautiful in charge of the surveillance team retreated a step.

"Forgive me, Madame President! But look, we found this!"

He led them to a cabinet of temperature-controlled flasks. They bore symbols Dr Wakuki recognised instantly.

"My goodness, I do believe . . . Yes, it is the original serum that Gover devised! Just think, more than a century ago. These compounds must be entirely uncontaminated. See here, the dates on the flasks prove that. They represent knowledge Blair Gover always refused to share. It is early to say but, yes, with this I might develop a vaccine for the gene sickness. And sooner than we hoped possible."

Merle sank into a chair, clutching her side. "Do it soon, Wakuki. Do it very soon."

"That's not all we discovered," continued their guide.

He was sweating visibly. Two bare-chested Angels stood directly behind him.

"We found a passageway from here that leads several miles. Indeed, to a long-abandoned underground railway station, dating back to the founding of Albion. Blair Gover connected this complex to that station. He even had his own tunnelling machine. We believe he dug the tunnel as some kind of access way. Why, is unclear."

Merle Brubacher frowned. "Strange. Do you know, I remember that old railway station."

Dr Wakuki raised an eyebrow. "I do not recollect it."

"You would have been a boy in Han City. It was built when Albion was still Huntingdon, a gated science town. I had forgotten. We and the other Investors would ride an elevated shuttle here from our private airport at Cambridge."

Her face darkened. Yet anxiety haunted the recollection.

"Even then, stuffed with free food and holotainment and narco-pleasures, those ungrateful wretches were rebellious. There were riots. One Investor was lynched before his security team could intervene. And now the descendants of those scum are out there, breeding like rabbits again."

The Beautiful bowed. "We found something else, Madame President, almost by accident. When our second drone was destroyed, a section of floor cracked. It revealed a cavity. This was concealed there. It must be important."

He held up a small box. Inside, nestled a fat info-pearl. Though none of them could know, the pearl exactly resembled its counterpart, currently secreted in the Baytown Jewel.

"Fetch the prisoner," ordered Merle. "She might know something useful about this place and its secrets."

Merle glanced over at Averil. "That is why you are here. Persuade your former mistress to co-operate."

* * *

Helen Devereux's windowless cell was not uncomfortable. Its floor carpeted, walls padded, bed and quilt soft. Even the toilet and wash facilities that emerged from the floor on command were insanely luxurious by Baytown standards. Yet her mind ached: and the world within a skull is its whole world.

Was she a fool to come here? The arrival at King's Lynn had been followed by a short hour's wait, overseen by security drones, before an aircar arrived from Albion. More drones processed her: forcing her to strip for intimate scanning. Wrist bracelets had been attached, locking into place. If they chose, Helen could be monitored, tortured, or merely have her arms blown off. Finally, she had been given new clothes and flown to this cell. No sign of Averil. No sign of anyone, other than distant, hurrying figures on the street. Albion, never seething with people even before the Five Cities' recent disasters, seemed deserted.

A day passed. So she guessed. Without the sky, time blurred. Then the door swished open to reveal two security drones.

Twenty minutes later, Helen stepped back a decade. The aircar delivered her to a building poignantly familiar: Blair Gover's palace with its aircar-port on the flat roof. The mansion they shared for a century.

Was bringing her here a cruel joke? Perhaps they had found Blair, and wished to torment them both. But when Helen was led to a concealed gravity-chute and whisked down to an underground complex, it wasn't Blair waiting.

"Averil! Thank God, you're safe!"

The girl, dressed in glittering silks and laden with jewels from the Before Times, sat heavily on a chair, hands resting on an immense stomach. Flanking her were two figures with intent, assessing eyes: Merle Brubacher and an oriental man. Security drones and two half-naked warrior-Angels bearing razor-sharp halberds stood guard.

"Averil," said Helen, "what have they done to you?"

*　*　*

SEVEN

Merle Brubacher waved an imperious hand. "You may only speak when permitted. What you say will determine whether you leave here intact."

Never before had Helen seen so clearly the madness lurking behind Merle's eyes. Yet it had always been there. And Helen had always suspected it. The Beautiful Life depended on selective blindness.

"Averil!" she cried. "How can you still be pregnant? Your due time was months ago. Has something gone wrong?"

Pain engulfed her. She fell, spasming on the floor. Agony twisted her gut. When it subsided, she realised Merle was toying with her screen.

"Playing stupid will force me to play harder," she cautioned.

Through tears, Helen looked for Averil. The girl's face, tense and pale, remained neutral.

Questions began. The world shrank to three realities: question, answer, pain.

Why did you come here?

"To save Averil. Averil! You must not trust them . . ."

Pain.

We have established that you stowed aboard a ship from Mughalia and somehow avoided detection. That does not matter now. What interests us is this secret place. When did you last visit here?

"Never. Blair kept its existence from me . . ."

Pain.

"He only told me what he deemed necessary. I was his lover, not confidante. Sometimes a mere decoration on his arm. You must understand him. He only ever shared small compartments of himself with anyone . . ."

Pain.

"I don't know what he did down here. You must believe me. I really don't. He used to vanish from our apartment sometimes. Then reappear unexpectedly. Perhaps he came here. He may have had other secret places. I never asked . . ."

Pain.

"He was always busy with schemes. It was what kept him interested in life. I stopped asking, even wondering. For years I just wanted to please him."

No pain.

A gentle finger felt her pulse. Helen dared to unscrew her eyes. It was the oriental man. He stared down at her. A shadow passed over his face.

"She has suffered enough, I think," he said. "I believe she is telling the truth."

"More pain is needed!" shrilled Merle Brubacher.

"I don't think so."

Merle ordered him to stand back. She held up the perfect, translucent info-pearl.

"What about this? When did you last see this?"

Perhaps knowledge betrayed itself in Helen's eyes.

"I . . . never saw . . ."

Pain.

Wakuki sighed. "Please," he urged. "Do not play stupid."

"Yes! Yes! I saw it," sobbed Helen. "Briefly, by accident. He never meant me to see it, I'm sure. Years ago. Blair told me it contained codes."

"Of course. That's what info-pearls are for. But what codes?"

"He didn't say."

Pain.

"Codes to do what?"

"He didn't say. Codes to control things."

"Do not play stupid. That is what all codes do. Control what?"

"I don't . . ."

Pain.

"He never trusted me the way you think! Never trusted anyone."

Helen shook uncontrollably. "He never really loved me. He just got used to having me around. He never loved anyone properly. Just his dead wife. Oh, why did I come back here?"

Pain. Pain. Pain.

At last, Helen blacked out.

* * *

Despite her best intentions, Averil Pilgrim could not help weeping. A drone aircar was summoned to take her home and she found herself left alone in its rear seat.

After Helen Devereux passed out on the floor of the secret laboratory, Averil had almost implored them to stop their questioning. She had wanted to, but didn't dare. Despite all that Helen had done for her, she did not dare.

Why had Helen come here! No one asked her to come. It was not as if they had been *real* friends. Averil knew how friends let you down. Miriam Armitage back in horrible Baytown had taught her all about *that*.

Helen had always been selfish. Jealous now, as well. Stirring up trouble could only harm Baby. Even Helen's blurted question – apparently well-meant, whether the extended pregnancy was normal – what a question – was designed to scare her. Miracles *were* normal in this astonishing place.

Thoughts came, provoking more tears. How quickly she had forgotten Baby's father, her husband, Amar. She had loved him once with fervent gratitude. Did Amar miss her, and wonder if she was safe? Her heart knew the answers.

Dora was waiting when the aircar landed. Up in her spacious apartment, Averil ordered the older woman to sit. She perched on the edge of a seat.

"Dora," she asked, "is something not right with baby? The birth has been delayed by months now. Someone tonight – I won't say who – suggested, well, it is not *natural*."

Dora looked away. Touched her mouth. Licked plump lips.

"You must ask Dr Wakuki, not me."

"I am asking you!"

Unexpectedly, Dora's reserve fractured. She glanced round as though terrified of spies.

"After it is born," she whispered, "you must get away. Return to your own people. You still have people. They will care for you. I will help if I can."

Averil shrank back. Was this Discordia? It must be. Yet she had to know more.

"Why should I leave Albion? I'll be needed here to breastfeed Baby."

"You are not a bad girl," said Dora, tugging nervously at the control-bracelet all technicians were obliged to wear. "Surely you see they have grown wicked. Deranged! You will not know this, but the gene sickness is abating. Those that survived have some kind of immunity. So it is believed. Just as with the plagues."

Averil gaped at this news. If true, it had been unnecessary to destroy the other Cities, along with hundreds of thousands of people. Unnecessary to reduce miraculous Mughalia and Mitopia, Han City and Neo Rio to mounds of smoking rubble and dust. Unless, of course, the Ruling Council had struck first to ensure its own survival, sacrificing the rest.

"Stop this." Averil tried to sound like Merle. "I will not hear another word. I am loyal."

The medi-tech dabbed her eyes, and rose. "To what?" she asked, bitterly.

A moment later she had gone.

SEVEN

* * *

The next day, Averil insisted on a consultation with Dr Wakuki. She flew alone to his surgery and laboratory. Dora claimed sickness, and that suited her mistress. As for Helen Devereux, Averil tried not to think of her.

A series of tests were carried out with Averil under deep sedation. She woke on the usual bed. As she had come to expect, her female parts ached. Dr Wakuki appeared a few minutes later. His eyes suggested tension and strain.

Averil asked anxiously, "Is Baby alright?"

A tiny, nervous tic appeared on his forehead.

"It is more complicated than I expected," he said. "There must be one final period of delay before the birth."

Averil struggled to rise.

"Why is it so complicated? You promised everything would be fine. I don't understand."

Doubts she could not read showed in his frown.

"It will be fine."

"Can the birth not happen sooner?"

"No."

"Baby's so big he hurts me. All the time. I can't bear it much longer."

"I shall give you something to manage the pain."

He walked over to the tall window, looked out over Albion. A light summer rain was falling. The city was quiet. With Albion's population much-reduced, Beautifuls accustomed to idleness found themselves training for essential tasks. All were expected to play their part: the reward for this labour would be mini-kingdoms assigned by the Ruling Council. First, production of drones and Angels must resume in earnest. Food supplies and raw materials, including from distant *colonia*, must be restored.

"Always I have urgent business thrust upon me," said Wakuki. "Demands. Demands. Absurdly, I have been instructed to oversee uncovering the codes for Blair Gover's control systems. A labour for which I am unqualified, and so must delegate. Actually, there is hardly anyone left in Albion who *is* qualified. Then, of course, there is the little question of using Dr Gover's stock of renewal serum to cure gene sickness. If *that* were not enough, I have been tasked with settling the primitives. Once and for all. You didn't understand a word of that, did you?"

He regarded her intently, his odd smile twitching. "The primitives are the trickiest problem. How to cure them without infecting other species."

"Cure?" said Averil, uneasily.

Everyone in Baytown suffered from some malady or other. With dogged loyalty, she said, "If anyone can cure people bred from dirt and ignorance and ugliness, it's you, Doctor. You can do anything, I'm sure."

Dr Wakuki's face softened. "I promise you, this will be the final delay before Baby's birth. Then you will be set free. Indeed, I shall insist upon it."

He nodded stiffly, leaving her alone to dress. A serving-drone appeared with her clothes and jewellery. Averil took deep puffs from her soother-spray.

* * *

Helen Devereux was transferred to a new windowless cell beneath the Palace of the Presidents, as the Brubachers' mansion in Albion had been renamed. When led out to perform duties, she passed lines of identical cells in a maze of corridors. Not all doors were locked. Some stood open, sleeping and feeding quarters for Angels, empty until their long shifts exhausted them. In this regard, Angels were inferior to drones. Indeed, she noted her own special guardian was always a security drone. Clearly, much development work remained in perfecting the functionality of Angels – a journey no doubt considered part of their novelty. As she soon learned, the quest for novelty obsessed Marvin Brubacher and his circle.

Helen was astounded she had not been sterilised, her remains composted. What other usefulness did she possess?

But it suited the Brubachers to flaunt a link with their vanquished enemy, Blair Gover. She served as a living symbol of their triumph. At banquets and balls – events projected into the sky via immense holograms, visible for miles in all directions – she was forced to perform acts of contrition and obeisance. Sometimes she was instructed to play the violin, as once she had performed to entertain Blair Gover. The slightest reluctance on her part triggered jolts of agony from the wrist-bracelets.

Whenever it seemed safe, Helen tried to catch Averil Pilgrim's eye. The girl's swollen stomach was grotesque, as though she might explode. If not for powerful drugs, the pregnancy would have caused constant misery. Averil sat through the Brubachers' fiestas in a daze, barely moving, an object of curiosity referred to as *The Experiment*.

Some days Helen was not called upon. Then she brooded in her cell, imagining the progress of the Baytown Jewel, out there, somewhere in the green wilderness beyond Albion's walls. Somewhere freedom still breathed. The info-pearl with its master codes concealed in the Jewel, still offered the slimmest of imaginable hopes.

EIGHT

Better to march towards hope than arrival. Michael Pilgrim remembered this saying as the army made slow progress.

His own decisions had not helped. Rather than take the most direct route, through Selby then Lincolnshire, he advised using wide ghost roads from the Before Times. Lesser roads often petered into quagmires. Dragging several thousand men, women, horses, mules, wagons, flocks of sheep and droves of cattle through uncharted bogs held no appeal.

They marched west towards Leeds along the old dual carriageway. After two days, a motorway, known in local legend as the Hey One Em, came in sight.

Consulting maps from the Before Time, Michael Pilgrim identified the tangle of elevated roadways and young woodland, choked with the decaying carcasses of vehicles, as Junction 44. The army scattered to encamp, seeking streams for washing and fuel for cooking. Smoke plumes rose. A haze of voices and song joined the soft twilight.

Outside his tent, Michael Pilgrim watched in frustration. This army – the sum of their hopes, perhaps mankind's last hope – behaved more like a wandering summer fair than a disciplined force set on victory. Lady Veil made it clear she believed swift, ruthless, efficient slaughter – thereby giving their enemy no chance to regroup – offered their only chance of victory. A slim enough chance at that.

EIGHT

Michael watched a lad and lass not yet twenty walk past, arm-in-arm; they might as well have been strolling down Lovers Lane. Paradoxically, so many diverse folk from all over the North sharing food and fellowship proclaimed the best of human nature. How sad, then, humanity's ultimate triumph could only be won through violence.

Blair Gover sat on the bonnet of a nearby car. Inside, a family of skeletons grinned.

"Well, well, Pilgrim," he said. "Do you even hope to reach Albion with this ragtag circus of bumpkins?"

"We'll get there."

Gover sank into gloom.

"You have no idea what risks I am taking. What a desperate throw of the dice this is."

He grimaced in an attempt at humour, "Not that I am foolish enough to expect gratitude. It is my fate to be a pearl cast into an unspeakable pile of ordure."

Michael listened uneasily. Being utterly reliant on Gover troubled him: the instant their interests diverged, the City-man would betray them, that he did not doubt. Nor did he doubt Gover concealed some ulterior scheme. But what choice did they have, other than abandon the expedition and await the City's inevitable recovery?

"I would be grateful for some straight answers," he said. "I'm puzzled, Gover. You know full well we intend to rid ourselves of Albion for good. Yet you offer to lead us into its very heart. I gather you were a chief founder of that place. Do you really not care we intend to destroy it?"

Gover's eyes flashed in the firelight.

"Enough will be left for me afterwards," he said.

"To do what?"

"Live forever, Pilgrim. What else?"

What else indeed, thought Michael. Above them, in the clear sky of early summer, stars were emerging. He pointed up at them.

"Have a care," he said. "My Grandfather taught me many stars we think brightest are dead by the time their light reaches us on earth."

He let the implication dangle. When he looked down from the ribbons of galaxies, Gover had withdrawn into his tent.

* * *

The long, straggling column proceeded down the great road. One by one, its numerous companies from all over the North ceased singing. No more wild tattoos on the drum or choruses of ribald ditties mocking the City. A realisation of the perilous nature of their expedition was spreading: with it came quiet resolve.

Michael Pilgrim ordered riders to scout ahead and spread word of the Pilgrimage's coming. Any wishing to join were welcome, so long as they were ready to fight and die. Groups of recruits waited by the roadside all through South Yorkshire, some well-armed, others with improvised weapons.

A week passed before they reached the Midlands. Green lands, well-wooded, fallow earth supporting a growing number of farms and hamlets. Anxious folk drove cattle and pigs into the woods, hiding until the army passed; yet a steady stream joined the column, young people mostly, reckless of life and with a future to win. Nuagers were common in this region and their preachers galloped between homesteads, proclaiming a prophecy that the fall of Albion would open fresh gateways for cosmic journeys to the stars.

"I told you," Mister Priestman chuckled to Michael, as they watched a company of Midlander Nuagers embrace fellow believers from up North. "The Faery o' the Vale has flown ahead of us. She's spread the word to all her fay kin. It would not surprise me if a regiment of boggles and pixies joined us. Their wands might yet spray forth musket balls!"

Gover's sneer, increasingly fixed as they approached Albion, grew weary.

So many new recruits slowed progress further. Michael Pilgrim felt it wise to order a rest for marshalling, numbering and training while the weather continued dry. Command structures were established that he suspected would fall apart the moment they gained entry into Albion – assuming Gover's scheme worked as promised. Perhaps a little havoc was necessary, so long as the companies of fifty did not fragment into smaller bands. According to the map of Albion drawn by Gover, the City covered a large circular area, ten miles in radius from a compact central zone. Roaming units might best fulfil Lady Veil and the Grow People's dark project.

Michael scanned the skies more anxiously. Nor was he alone. Surely, so large a force would be noticed by surveillance drones. Yet none flew overhead. It seemed the City-prisoners were correct: Albion was preoccupied with its own woes, indifferent to the world beyond its borders.

Finally, Peterborough came in sight – or what remained of that city. Shattered buildings protruded from young woodlands; numerous deep bomb craters were filled with water and huge, fly buzzed lily pads.

"So far so good," Michael remarked to Lady Veil. "This is a better place for skulking than open country. Ruins and trees provide lots of cover to hide from drones, especially if we spread out. Plenty of water and firewood, too. Once you've established a camp, I'll depart with Gover."

The former City-woman's delicate brown eyes hardened.

"Remember," she said, through her interpreter, "at the first sign of treachery, eliminate him."

Tom Higginbottom snorted, "I'm game."

"We must trust Gover a little," insisted Michael. "We'll find out his true loyalties soon enough."

Maybe too late for all these people, he thought, watching the army enter Peterborough.

* * *

Seth Pilgrim wondered if it was his fate to be a prisoner. In York, confined within the ancient city walls on pain of death; here, ordered to remain on the Isle of Ely or face unspecified consequences. Not that *here* was so bad. No one hated him for past misdeeds. Indeed, he was accorded a kind of awe. Seth Pilgrim, the fucker crazy enough to take on a drone – and survive.

Ely even felt oddly familiar. Piles of ruins overrun with vegetation. Hens pecking industriously. Gardens where the town's inhabitants tended crops round the shattered remains of a monumental church.

Cutty Smart, his captor and leader of the Fen Men, told him the City demolished Ely Cathedral, jealous of rival towers on the horizon.

"You see, bor." His smile hovered halfway between sly grin and smirk. "Albion don't like being reminded there are people out here clever as 'emselves."

"Are you Fen Men that clever?" Seth asked.

"Smart by name, smart by nature. Mostly. Being daft in the Fens means you drown, like as not. Or starve when winter blows in."

When Cutty Smart rescued them from the saltmarsh near King's Lynn, he had placed the inert Hurdy-Gurdy in the bottom of a long, shallow barge, cocooned in blankets. Water, Seth soon realised, was the dominant element. A country of bogs, meres and labyrinthine streams.

Still, both he and Hurdy-Gurdy had dry enough feet. Their open prison consisted of mildew-scented rooms above a former jeweller's on the high street. Rusting watches with plastic straps littered the

EIGHT

display window.

Twice a day, they received rations. Simple fare: coarse, gritty bread and inevitable fish or eel and vegetable stew, which Seth mushed before spooning it into Hurdy's mouth. It seemed his friend would never recover.

Days passed. Then Seth received a summons via one of Cutty Smart's pals, Ell, who was tasked with keeping an eye on the drylanders.

"Make sure you're at the Marina-moot come sundown," she muttered. Wiry as an eel, Ell was a girl of few words.

* * *

By the River Great Ouse, a swathe of meadow had been cleared. Goats and sheep owned in common and destined for public feasts nibbled its grass and wildflowers. Willows offered shelter against showers. Nearby, was the town's former marina, a manmade basin slowly silting, littered with the hulks of abandoned pleasure cruisers.

Seth made his way there at dusk. He had left Hurdy-Gurdy in a profound stupor, muttering about honeycombs. So obsessed with honey was his friend, Seth begged a small jar, feeding him spoonfuls dissolved in hot water.

As he walked, Seth listened to wind-murmur in the leaf-laden trees, punctuated by diverse bird voices. The Fen Country was a land at peace, save for strange flashes of light leaking from nearby Albion.

Several hundred folk had gathered in the pleasant summer twilight, young and old. A band of fiddle, guitar, pipe and percussion banged out a circle dance he remembered from Baytown. As they shuffled and hopped, the people sang the same ancient words: *She loves you yeah yeah yeah* . . .

Leading the line, gay ribbons round strong limbs and long hair, was Cutty Smart, nimble as a rabbit, roaring with mischievous enjoyment.

Seth felt a hot stirring at the sight of the young man. A stir once provoked by Jojo Lyons. Instantly, he felt ashamed. Jojo had been noble and earnest, a hundred times worthier than a cheeky fen slodger.

After the dance, folk took food from communal tables, using their own bowls and cutlery. Big rounds of bread and ladlefuls of eel and lentil stew. River fish fried until charred and crispy on huge flat pans, flavoured with handfuls of herbs and chervils.

Once the business of eating was done, Seth realised eyes were upon him. A familiar lurch tightened his full stomach. Time, yet again, to be judged.

* * *

The Fen Folk conducted business without over-fondness for ceremony. Seth was led to an area of tables and benches. Pitchers of tart, heady cider were passed round.

"Give the drylander some an' all," said Cutty.

His bright eyes suggested a few mugs had already come his way.

Seth stood warily. His judges, men and women bedecked like Cutty with plenty of bright ribbons, looked him over.

"Well then," began their leader, 'seems we must decide wha' to do with you and your bothersome friend."

Dancing resumed on the meadow to the flickering light of several bonfires. The flames cast a red, devilish tint to Cutty's eyes.

Seth said nothing.

"Thing is, bor, we've already had scores o' City-folk wanderin' in the Fens, naked as babbies. Bootiful as faeries, they were. Trouble would come of 'em being among us, so we gave 'em old clothes and took 'em to the fen edge. Where they went from there's none of our concern."

Still Seth kept his peace.

EIGHT

"As for you, you're a different kind of bother. Instead of wanting to get away from Albion, you seem dead set on stirring 'em up. In fact, it wouldn't surprise me if you was looking for a way to get inside there."

The shrewdness of this guess made Seth blink.

"Damn brave of you to fight a drone though," grinned Cutty. "Daft as coots, but damn brave. Only we don't need no trouble with Albion. We don't want 'em to notice us at all, thank you."

At last, Seth found his voice. "My friend is much too sick to travel. He's near enough dying, I reckon."

"I knows that," said Cutty.

A medicine woman visited Hurdy each day to check his breath and feed him broths of healing herbs.

"So, this is how it must be," said Cutty. "You ain't going nowhere for now. Fine. But we don't feed nobody for free here, bor. Can't afford to."

A peculiar tale followed. News had travelled the twenty miles of swamp and waterways separating Ely from another Fen Men community, Wisbech. It seemed the people there – never numerous due to a scarcity of reliably dry land for crops – had vanished. Travellers reported a ghost town. Yet upright shapes had been seen moving among the trees and buildings. Shapes neither quite human nor animal.

"We don't like none of it," concluded Cutty. "That's why we think it best to take a look. And seein' we have a fearless fighter an' warrior as our guest, it seems best you come along too."

Seth hesitated. Perhaps he should reveal he was no soldier, brave or otherwise.

"Well . . ." he began.

The faces watching him wore expressions of respect. The novelty of the situation made him add in a gruff voice. "So long as my friend is tended while I'm away."

"That's settled then," said Cutty.

They set off in a shallow-drafted wherry, raising its single sail and following broader waterways than usual. Cutty Smart took the rudder while Ell – silent as usual – tended the sail. Seth sat near the prow loading, priming and checking various guns from a small arsenal maintained by the Ely community.

The Fen Country in summer was a tangle of fertility. Streams formed patterns like braided veins on a leaf, interspersed with hollows and meres, small islands where dense copses grew, spurs of river terminating in reed bog. Buildings and structures poked through the greenery and water, including lines of rusty electricity pylons and street lamps draped with ivy.

Most of the day passed in travelling. They entered the heart of the Fens, crossing wide lakes lined by reeds beds. The remains of former villages and farmhouses were rare out here. Horizons were huge: billowing white clouds glowed silver beneath the slanting sun. Everywhere, water beetles, butterflies, dragonflies haunted the wetlands. Snakes rippled in the water; beaver lodges were common.

Seth scrambled from the prow to join Cutty.

"Is this Wisbech safe?" he asked.

"Nowhere's quite safe out here, bor. Not unless you know nature's little ways. See that grass verge on the side of the stream? Suck you under soon as step foot on it. An' the more you struggled, the quicker you'd disappear. Wisbech is an island in the bog, so it's safe enough underfoot. Question is, who else might be wanderin' round there."

* * *

They neared Wisbech as the long, slow midsummer's day dwindled. Cutty sniffed the wind. His puckish face grew thoughtful.

EIGHT

"You'd expect to see an' smell smoke from cooking fires round about this time."

"P'raps it's true all the people have gone," said Ell.

Seth shared their foreboding. He noticed sweat on his palms.

Wisbech must once have been a grand country town. Streets of big, three-storey houses lined the riverbank, their roofs collapsing. Mills and warehouses were sinking into the swamp. The low-lying parts of the town, which was most of it, suffered high floods in winter. And the water hung around for the rest of the year.

An area of ground rose to the east of the town centre. It was here the resourceful fen slodgers had settled, occupying a big hospital. To Seth, it felt like visiting the end of the world.

He realised Cutty and Ell were waiting for the bold warrior to take command.

"This is what we'll do," he said. "Ell, you stay in the boat with that blunderbuss. First sign of trouble, fire in the air. We'll come running. Meantime, me and Cutty will look around."

The boat crept up to a dockside empty of tethered craft; proof, perhaps, the Wisbechers had fled en masse. Only boats under repair remained.

"I don't like it much," grumbled Ell. "I'm thinking they've had plague here."

"Maybe," said Seth.

A good dying led to communities scattering in haste. Why hang around when there was so much empty land for the taking? But it crossed his mind there are many kinds of plague.

* * *

Bella Lyons scratched her armpit with a modified leg. The Fen Land was poor country for a demi-hare. Too much water. And mosquitos, proboscises sucking rich, enhanced blood. Her travelling companions on the long journey south from York also scratched constantly.

Some had fallen on the way, victims of frightened villagers whose territory they passed through. A few man-dogs went feral, devouring a fat homo-cat and demi-rabbit. Their own pack leader led the mob of vengeful strangelings to surround the offenders, biting, clawing, tearing with owl-beak, kicking out frenzied hind legs strong enough to break a man's neck. Barely conscious why, or how, the assembly of strangelings knew this much: they belonged to one another. Those fashioned from random flesh were bound together until their flesh withered away. Freaks granted a brief spell on earth by two-legged gods. Perpetual outcasts, unable to breed, allowed no family but each other.

Consciousness was the light that flickered; borrowed instinct the darkness driving animal functions. Yet consciousness allowed glimpses, tortured snatches of self-sight. Consciousness tormented former selves lingering in their brains, residual memories, fogs of understanding. It mocked and taught hatred. For being made monster, for being unmade from who and what they were meant to be. Consciousness taught a destiny: revenge.

Bella Lyons – oh, she remembered her name, repeated the wondrous syllables as goad and charm – and she remembered Jojo and a former heaven called Fountains – Bella Lyons retained more shreds of buried self than most strangelings. Perhaps that brief time with beloved Jojo unlocked her soul treasures. Though she was feeble in a fight compared to demi-fox or homo-cat, man-bear or hungry humanoid owl, Bella had reinforced her pre-eminence among her kind on the long journey towards Albion.

It was she who saw clearest how to avoid the settlements they passed through. How to steal what sheep or other meat they needed without provoking the man-people. How the Fens provided cover from prying

EIGHT

eyes and a safe route to Albion, as well as abundant food. It was Bella Lyons who urged the winged stranglings to fly south and spy on their enemy, the City drawing them home, its glow sinister on the horizon.

It was Bella, indeed, who realised they must rest before the final trial. She led them lolloping onto the island of Wisbech, whereupon its population fled.

Although the stranglings preferred to sleep in undergrowth or simple shelters of their own making, sometimes Bella was drawn to a complex of hospital buildings where the Fen-people lived. There, amidst relics abandoned to hasty flight — a rag doll or child's carved toy, pots, pans, bedding — Bella quivered with anguish, her lost self welling up through a murk of grafted instincts. To remember love and being loved: unbearable. Then she would hurry outside. Run free as a hare. Feed as a hare. But each heady draught of the lost Bella sharpened her craving for more self.

Which is why, when she saw them approaching from the river, Bella did not summon the fanged man-dogs, clawed homo-cats, sharp-toothed fox-men and man-rats, to drive the intruders away — or feast on fresh meat. Bella did not summon them because she knew the lost Bella would not have done so.

* * *

Cutty clutched a wide-bored shotgun. Seth held his own musket looser, but already cocked.

The path from the landing stage where Ell guarded their boat passed through a dense copse of willow and alder coppicing. Cutty knelt to examine a pile of dung. Sniffing, he poked the mess with a twig.

"Queer quantity of bones in here," he said. "It's fresh enough."

Even Seth's untrained nose recognised that much.

"Funny thing is," continued Cutty, "I haven't no clue what kind o' beast dropped it. Whatever it was, it liked meat an' fish an' birds. An' plenty of 'em."

"Where's this old hospital you mentioned?"

"That way yonder." Cutty hung back. "You go first."

The copse terminated in strips of fields cleared from a public park and planted with scraggy crops. Behind a rusting fence spread ramshackle one and two-storey concrete buildings: some showed signs of repairs. Seth looked for movement. Again, Cutty's nose wrinkled.

"Funny smell round here, too," he remarked. "Bit like a badger's arse, if you know what I mean."

"At least we know it's got empty bowels," said Seth.

Cutty did not laugh: but the joke emboldened him. Seth recollected how his uncle had a knack for using humour to steady wobbling nerves. Unbidden embers of lore burned into his reluctant brain as a child glowed. This spark belonging to Shakespeare: *A coward dies a thousand times before his death, but the valiant taste of death but once.*

"Let's take a closer look," he said.

They advanced up the path towards the hospital, guns raised. Wind rustled the trees and grass. With each step, Seth's sense of danger intensified. They were being watched, he felt it. Some primaeval instinct assured him of peril. Twilight was thickening fast. They should get the hell out, sail back to Ely under the stars and moon and count themselves lucky.

Near the ancient hospital entrance, more strange turds lay around.

"These come from a lot of different kinds of animals," said Cutty. "None of it is natural or right. I've seen enough."

Seth touched his arm for silence. Compelled by courage or recklessness, he called out. "Anyone here?"

His voice died. Nothing. Wind blowing east across the flatlands. He sighed with relief, turning to retrace their steps. Then he froze.

"Don't move," he whispered.

EIGHT

Despite the warning, Cutty slowly turned.

* * *

This is what Cutty saw.

The light was dimming but clear. Behind them, a dozen creatures emerged from bushes and undergrowth, mostly upright as a man moves, but not like a man. They were not men: not as he understood the term.

He cried out as he recognised features that should never be: a fox's snout protruding from a round, human face, a fox's ears poking from a tousle of red hair, and at the rear, a big, bushy tail. Was that a cat on two legs, clawed hands reaching out, back legs ready to pounce?

Shapes the size of large children flapped up from roosting in the hospital eaves. Cutty screeched. They were circling! A teenage girl with a bat's leathery wings; a man-crow with huge, glinting eyes. His head grew dizzy. He lifted his shotgun as though in a dream. A hand gently lowered the barrel.

"Take your finger off the trigger, Cutty, that's it. Put the gun on the floor. Do it now."

Seth seemed unafraid, not half so terrified as reason demanded. Cutty did as ordered then covered his eyes with a hand, peering out through splayed fingers.

More were-creatures – there seemed no other explanation for them – came round the corner of the hospital. These resembled human hares, along with a pug-nosed man-dog.

Seth Pilgrim called out. "Bella! It's you."

For long moments the hare-girl, for Cutty recognised a girl in *it*, twitched its nose. A powerful leg scraped dust, as though uncertain whether to attack.

"Bella! Remember, I was Jojo's friend. He asked you to trust me."

Death seemed certain to Cutty.

"Remember, I put myself between Jojo and the knife. I tried to die for Jojo."

Lifting his shirt, Seth turned, revealing a deep scar on his back, livid among older scars of whip marks. The creature's face showed no emotion.

"I need to talk to you," said Seth. "About the City. That's why we're all here, isn't it? Why you strangelings gathered. Because of what the City has done."

The she-hare waved a clawed hand to summon Seth over. Cutty watched in horror.

"Don't go!" he cried. His voice quavered. "It'll eat you, Seth."

"Wait here. Don't move."

Cutty stood paralysed. One by one, man-fox and man-cat crept closer, examining him, silent, speechless. He fell to his knees, awaiting the end. He buried his eyes into his sleeve like a quivering child.

In this way, Cutty did not see Seth Pilgrim's reunion with the hideous hare-girl. Nor did he want to.

NINE

"What the hell happened here?" Tom Higginbottom gave a low whistle. "No, don't tell me, Mister Gover. Same as the other towns."

Blair Gover peeped through the eyeholes of his clown mask. This close to Albion, the City-renegade's fear of facial recognition from surveillance drones had grown obsessive.

"Cambridge was not used for weapons testing, Higginbottom," he replied, emphasising the last two syllables of the name.

"Oh, aye? You could have fooled me."

Journeying south from Peterborough, they had swung west. The route included several flattened towns. Gover explained it had been Albion's policy to test military toys on all major settlements within fifty miles of its borders. Thus, as he put it, *killing two birds with one stone*.

"How was Cambridge different?" asked Michael Pilgrim.

The city's buildings and streets were rubble; indeed, their column of cavalry had been forced to dismount and lead the horses. Gover pointed at the twisted metal corpse of a battle tank draped with ivy.

"There is your evidence," he said. "What do you deduce from it, Pilgrim?"

"War."

"Very good. What a rational fellow you are becoming under my influence."

The nearer they drew to Albion, the more insufferable Gover grew.

The column had approached the remnants of Cambridge from the south-west. According to the battle plan agreed with Lady Veil, the main army would advance rapidly from Peterborough as soon as word reached her Michael was in position. Everything depended on exact timing – and luck. But really, Michael had to concede, everything depended on Gover.

Rain and drizzle fell as they picked a careful way through the overgrown rubble of colleges, shops and houses, reaching their destination at twilight.

The airport, though grim and silent, was surprisingly intact. It lay to the northeast of the city on what must have been agricultural land. Its high metal fences had rusted or fallen. Nearby, stretched a reed bog Gover said marked the borders of a great area of wild, untamed fen, stretching north to the sea, surrounding most of Albion's eastern half. Impassable terrain for horsemen, that was certain.

Beyond the fences, a few large buildings rose from the big field. Ancient aeroplanes stood on the runways.

"I want to be away from here at first light tomorrow," said Michael. He turned to Gover. "Do you think that's possible?"

The City-man frowned at the airport; Michael sensed he was remembering it before the Great Dyings.

Tom Higginbottom met his eye. "Cat's walked over someone's grave," he muttered.

* * *

They trotted into the airport in lines of ten. The horses' hooves thudded dully on the permaplastic surface of the runways. A squad led by

NINE

Tom Higginbottom galloped ahead to the main buildings. These were quickly searched, revealing no obvious threat, just mounds of rotted furniture and telescreens. A wide lounge and bar area overlooked the runways, its reinforced plate glass windows unbroken. To the side were hangars and fuel storage facilities.

Gover took off his mask as he was led into the lounge.

"Ah," he said.

"Familiar?" asked Michael.

"If you refer to a world long gone, yes. Glorious days of hope, Pilgrim, when this facility was first constructed. Yes, I remember coming here then."

"Tell me about those days."

"You would not understand."

"Sharing a little knowledge might save our necks tomorrow."

Gover settled in a corner, hugging his chest.

Tom Higginbottom allowed one large fire for cooking. He spread the men out across the lounge, having set a guard rota for the horses stabled in a large, echoing baggage collection hall. With the coming of night, the rain cleared; stars appeared. It seemed unlikely they would be troubled. Cambridge and the lands around had been abandoned by humanity. Few wished to build their lives a mere ten miles from the borders of Albion.

As they ate hot, salty stew, Michael sat beside Gover. The City-man was morose. The anticipation in Michael Pilgrim's gut tightened.

"Time for that history lesson," he said.

"Very well."

By the dancing light of the cooking fire, and the glow of a small lantern – for Gover hated the dark, fearing it like a small child, just as he grew uneasy in big open spaces – he told his story.

* * *

The airport, Michael learned, dated back to the decade before the Great Dyings. At that time, over a dozen so-called 'science cities' had been established. A close-connected network spread across the globe. Their shared endeavour: mankind's ultimate Promethean prize, to become gods, to unshackle the great enslaver of human genius, to conquer mortality.

By then, most of the world's wealth was controlled by a tiny international elite, fabulously powerful. Yet what use were riches when one faced inevitable extinction? Little surprise the more visionary among the multi-trillionaires, co-ordinated by a mother and son team with a vast worldwide media empire, saw the possibilities as soon as cell-renewal became a reality. They convened a secret conference, dubbing themselves The Investors. Each pledged their entire resources would flow into The Project, as the quest for immortality became known.

Most governments were already under their control, granting whatever was necessary. In England – Scotland and Wales had effectively gone their own way by then – the ruling party happily granted them an entire town and surrounding district, in exchange for free supplies of drugs and holotainment to keep the nation pacified. The area's residents were extravagantly bribed or, where necessary, coerced to leave.

Fences were erected to seal off a ten mile radius round Huntingdon. This depopulated zone was renamed Albion, with all access strictly controlled. Within its electric fence, The Project leapt forward. All over the world, other science cities made similar strides, walling themselves off from stupefied, divided populations, increasingly herded into overcrowded cities for maximum control.

"Did not people rebel against this tyranny?" asked Michael.

Gover smiled. "You misunderstand human nature. You are childishly idealistic. Given limitless free food and mood-adjusting substances, along with free reality-headsets and constantly evolving holo-facilities, most created their own numbed cocoons. Add to that, conditioning from birth to distrust and fear their own neighbours, along with a cult of ignorance founded on the worship of trivia, and, believe me, they did not rebel. Most could not conceive of it. Those that did were quickly identified and neutralised."

"Neutralised?"

"One way or another. There were many ways."

"What happened next?"

What happened was triumph. Glory. The hitherto unimaginable made real. A decade before the first Dying, a small team led by Gover and his colleague, Dr Guy Price, discovered a serum to enable fully regulated cell renewal in humans. Death died that day. At once, The Investors threw their entire energies and resources into The Project. A race against the clock of their own mortality.

This airport was constructed to avoid interference when landing private aircraft, along with an elevated monorail straight into Albion.

Gover's examined the pulsing embers of the fire.

"You will not like the rest of my story."

Yet it was broadly familiar to Michael Pilgrim, dark legends passed on by survivors like his Grandfather. How the plagues came in annual waves; how cultures all over the world, intricate and thriving as ancient rainforests, vanished in a few, calamitous years. Of the original twelve science cities, only five survived the chaos: Albion, Mitopia, Mughalia, Han City and Neo Rio. Those in North America fell quickly to rampaging armies and nuclear weapons detonated by zealots proclaiming the End of Days. Albion itself was threatened by what little remained of the plague-devastated English army. A fierce battle took place in Cambridge. Fortunately for them, The Investors had spent as lavishly on weaponry as on every other aspect of The Project. Victory was achieved, and with it, the securing of the Beautiful Life.

"For several years, pathetic hordes appeared at our fences and walls," said Gover, "starving, scrofulous, begging to be allowed entry. To be allowed to live. No doubt they hoped to resume a pointless existence of gaping at holotainment while gorging themselves on whatever intoxicants they were allowed."

He hesitated. "Their weeping and terror was something to see, Pilgrim. Something not easily forgotten."

"Why did you not help them? You had the means."

"Because . . ." The smooth, youthful skin on his forehead wrinkled. A sudden weariness aged his face in the yellow glow of the lamp. "Because we saw no use for them. Actually, we did let some enter, those who could prove they possessed skills we required. Very few, but some. You knew such a one, Helen Devereux, and her sister, who you knew as Dr Mhairi Macdonald, musician and doctor, respectively. You see, we were never irrational."

"Just cruel. Heartless."

"Cruelty implies pleasure in another's misfortunes. We were simply practical. Anyway, after a few years, no more came. As for those that survived . . ."

"Yes?"

"They were busy adapting to their new environment, evolving, you might say. Into people like you, Pilgrim. In that sense, we – I – created you." His face twisted with anger. "And now, to think that I – the guiding genius behind Albion, and so much more – must sneak like a thief into *my* creation!"

Michael Pilgrim's expression grew hard to read.

"I'm looking forward to seeing Albion for myself," he said, quietly. "Tomorrow, before dawn, we leave."

* * *

NINE

As the sun rose over the flat eastern horizon, a parade gathered on the runway of the old airport. Of the hundred men and women present, ten stood to one side without horses, armed and bearing backpacks of equipment and supplies. The remainder stood by their mounts, led by Tom Higginbottom.

Michael clasped his friend's hand.

"Well, this is it," he said. "If we meet again, it'll be inside a place we never wanted to see."

"Reckon we'll meet again?" asked Tom, glancing over at Gover, who shivered in the chilly dawn despite layers of clothes and his mask.

Michael followed his look. Both stood silent.

"Best be going," said Tom, never one for a long farewell. Risking the sea's unpredictable moods to feed his large family had inclined him to confront danger head-on. "But count on one thing, Mikey. I'll be where I promised if it all goes arse over tit in there."

He nodded at a row of wicker baskets.

"Time?"

"Why not?"

The baskets were gently carried forward. From within came low cooing and wing flutters. Straps were loosed and lids lifted. One by one, allowing a few minutes between each bird so they did not gather and flock, pigeons were released with a clatter of wings. One by one, they circled then vanished into the grey dawn, heading northwest. Their destination – it was prayed – being a mobile pigeon coop on a wagon currently with Lady Veil's waiting army in Peterborough. Messages tied to their legs would trigger an immediate advance on Albion.

"Think they'll make it?" asked Tom.

Michael could only shrug in reply. Everything depended on the signal getting through. Previous experiments had worked – mostly. Watching the last bird fly, he felt a compulsion to get moving. *The clock starts now*, he told himself.

* * *

The troop of cavalry trotted from the airport back towards Cambridge. Michael rejoined the small squad of foot soldiers. All were veterans of numerous bloody scraps, selected for their courage and a certain ruthless streak, but none was a match for the enemy awaiting them. Victory, as Michael had emphasised, depended on avoiding any fighting at all.

They tramped down the long runway to a monorail track beside a station platform. The track climbed at a low angle to the outskirts of the airfield, where it levelled out as an elevated railway line heading northwest, thirty feet above ground level. Gover had explained this monorail had been the safest way between the airport and Huntingdon, too robust for quick sabotage (it rested on thick permasteel columns), too high for easy access by rebels.

So began a precarious journey. The monorail was narrow and cloaked with vegetation: they were obliged to walk single file, conscious there was no safety rail should they slip. Gover was roped to burly men before and behind, lest he topple.

Bushes and shrubs found root space in surprising crevices. If Michael had not used his absurdly sharp City-sword as a machete, progress would have been impossible in places.

Within half a mile of the airfield, the pylons on which the track rested were surrounded by boggy ground; another mile, and they were passing over true fenland, reed beds, swamp and braided streams, along with small patches of woodland. From this elevated position, the fens stretched far away. Birds roosting on the track rose in alarm as they shuffled along.

Mid-morning brought Michael's first proper glimpse of Albion. He ordered a rest. The rain at last stopped. Blue sky appeared through grey banks of cloud. Taking out his binoculars, he gazed in wonder

NINE

and awe.

So close to Albion's borders – four or five miles as the monorail ran – he could pick out individual features. An array of immense towers rising above the plain. A darker line, nearer to their current position: the security wall, enclosing a twenty-mile diameter circle. What surprised him for such flat country, were various cone-like hills jutting up from within the enclosed area of the City. They were almost symmetrical, reminiscent of fairy-tale hills in books from the Before Times. Everything about Albion seemed magical and unreal, even its hills.

Michael turned to Gover. The City-man cowered beneath a pungent shrub, scanning the sky for drones.

"Yon hills," said Michael, "they don't look natural to me."

Gover followed the direction of his pointing finger and laughed.

"Natural? I see you have been an inattentive pupil. *Natural* is a conceit, a self-delusion. Let me tell you the names of those hills. That one is St Ives Hill, and those two round peaks, to the southwest, are St Neots' Hills."

The names meant nothing to Michael, though they sounded familiar from his study of ancient roadmaps.

"You see," said Gover, "after their inhabitants were, let us say, *rehoused*, we used drones working day and night to demolish the towns of St Ives and St Neots, and sculpted the rubble into those – as you term them – *unnatural* hills, along with a vast quantity of earth removed to form pleasure lakes."

"Oh," said Michael, as the immensity of such an undertaking struck him. "Oh."

"*Oh*, indeed. Do you begin to comprehend what you are setting yourself against now, Pilgrim."

"I do."

"Good."

"Except, like it or not, Gover, it's *we* not *you*."

The City-man did not respond.

Soon they set off again, eager to reach the borders of Albion before dark. Yet the nature that Gover derided mocked their littleness. Rain fell in earnest, adding a cold drenching to the exhaustion of groping along a narrow path, one slip from plunging thirty feet into the morass below. Sometimes they passed through dense copses, alder and willow obstructing their route, forcing them to wriggle under branches or clamber over. Sometimes they looked down on bleak, quaking bogs where to walk would be to drown in silty mud. Step by step, they neared the boundary walls of Albion.

* * *

Michael had been wise to leave the abandoned airport at first light. Despite the fact it was near the summer solstice, the long day was barely sufficient to reach their destination.

The first warning came when the track began a shallow-angled descent. For some time they had been hacking a path through a thick wood, their vision reduced to ten or so feet. As they emerged from the trees, Michael called out a warning. Startlingly close, less than a mile distant, the security walls of Albion rose from a steep earthen back. Four tall men high, the thick walls were constructed of concrete and debris from vanished settlements. A ditch lay at its feet, cleared of vegetation by drones. To the north, a surveillance tower rested on the walls, lights flashing on top. Beyond, the city centre itself appeared close – frighteningly so – though still six or seven miles away. Its skyscrapers and towers formed the hub of Albion's great wheel.

Michael lowered himself to the ground.

"Everyone down. No one must stand upright."

A shuffling behind him; Gover crawled up.

NINE

"Can you see it?" he hissed.

"What? The City?"

"No. The tunnel mouth."

Michael risked rising with his binoculars. Yes, there it was, just as Gover had predicted. The monorail descended to ground level then dipped into an abandoned railway cutting. A tiny dot of black, concealed by shrubs, indicated a tunnel mouth. Not too far either. Half a mile, at most, then another half mile to the border wall – although by then they would be safely out of sight underground. With one last effort, they should reach the shelter of the tunnel by nightfall.

"Thank goodness," said Gover. His laugh of triumph held an edge of hysteria. "This crackpot plan of mine might yet come good. I was afraid they had blocked or sealed the entrance in my absence. You see, I always made sure it was left undisturbed."

Michael wriggled forward on his belly.

"No time for talk. We're exposed up here. Remember, stay flat." He called over his shoulder, dryly. "Like worms."

Or like the Serpent that crawled into Eden to banish Adam and Eve.

TEN

Averil Pilgrim lay on the same bed in Dr Wakuki's clinic where she had so often woken, her womb aching after tests. Waking was different now, scarcely waking at all. Her womb was raw and heavy, groaning with active, kicking life.

Averil's intake of sedatives and pain-suppressants clouded all rational thought. Her mind dreamed murkily. Rest was impossible, she lay gasping from hour to hour, a fish drowning in air.

Occasionally, the numbing cloud dispersed enough for awareness. Then she would cry out. What was happening? Baby was wrong. Something was wrong. Dr Wakuki could not save her son. For all his miracles, he did not know how to save anyone. If Baby died, Averil knew she must go with him. Her presence in Albion depended on the child. Where else did she have? Certainly not Baytown, filthy, bestial Baytown.

Awareness included faces. Dora hovered anxiously, tight-lipped and silent. Though Averil moaned and begged to know when it would be over, the medi-tech could do no more than hold her hot fingers, cool her brow with a spray. Averil hated Dora then, even as she was grateful for her presence. Dora was her only visitor, only friend, apart from Dr Wakuki.

The latter came to see her whenever she awoke, promising that soon, sooner than she imagined, it would all be over for good. His words

TEN

flowed through her without sticking: a date had been set. Soon, sooner than she imagined . . .

Averil's dreams formed tormenting pictures. Not a moment's peace was possible. Baby must come soon. Or she would die.

* * *

The next day brought excitement to Albion. Holocasts flashed every few minutes, reminding that – thanks to the vision and genius of the Presidents of the Ruling Council – leaps forward in the Life Perfected were to be announced that evening.

Speculation was necessarily fervent among ambitious Beautifuls: failing to demonstrate enthusiasm might taint one with Discordia. Others, still grieving for the destruction of lost Cities and vanished friends, stayed unobtrusive. As for those blessed enough to inhabit the Brubachers' inner circle, they already knew what was coming.

All day, Helen Devereux curled on the bed of her cell, sick at heart. The Presidents' announcement did not interest her. No doubt it would be as grotesque as Marvin and Merle's other pet projects.

Her windowless cell possessed no holo-facilities, and so she did not hear the proclamation released by Albion's rulers. How Marvin Brubacher gravely reminded his audience that, hitherto, no effective way of recreating one's genes through biological children had been discovered; how the process of gene-renewal rendered its beneficiaries infertile. Or hear of the Presidents' great breakthrough, assisted by the much-lauded Dr Wakuki, so that – for the first time in a century – a new kind of dynasty was possible. One requiring surrogate mothers, true, but still a wonderful marker of progress.

"Behold," he declared, "I have become a father and my spouse a mother. Through adapting foetuses already in brood-primitives, we, the Perfect, the Beautiful, may once more have children partially our own. Think of it!"

He paused to let the implications sink in. Thousands of hearts beat eagerly. Not only might they be granted small kingdoms of their own, but a family to share the pleasure of ruling.

Marvin's voice grew stern. "Yet know this, dear friends, the number of such descendants will be strictly controlled. A rare privilege, to be granted only to those judged worthy by the Ruling Council."

All over Albion, Beautifuls burst into spontaneous gasps of approval – just in case their reaction to the announcement was being monitored.

Marvin Brubacher smiled benignly. "Better still," he said, "Wakuki's method means the characteristics of the child can be determined as it grows – imperfectly, at this stage – but to an astonishing extent."

Locked in her cell, Helen did not witness the images that followed. How an unconscious Averil Pilgrim was cut open by an operating drone's precision blades and a swift Caesarean conducted. How the child made Albion's population gasp with a mixture of revulsion, amazement and admiration as it was held up, still bloody and trailing its umbilical cord. For that small mercy, Helen should have been glad.

ELEVEN

Lady Veil listened gravely, along with Mister Priestman and other leaders from the Council of the North.

A drone had circled low over Peterborough the day before. Impossible to believe it had not detected the ragtag army scattered across the ruined city. It had not attacked, and Lady Veil's knowledge of drone programming suggested they were not perceived as a threat – yet.

"Well then," said Mister Priestman, removing his top hat to scratch his bald pate, "the Faery Queen must be masking us beneath her silver cloud."

Lady Veil's hands moved. Her interpreter spoke. "She says, 'We must assume they do not imagine our purpose. If they guessed that, the sky would be full of drones. They will simply have detected scattered groups of harmless primitives. Let us stick to the plan."

As if on cue, there came a sound of rapid footsteps along the corridor of the old hotel chosen as the small army's headquarters. A man in the uniform of the Grow People entered, bearing a small wicker cage. Inside, cooed a pigeon.

The room grew still and intent at the sight of the bird.

"This is the first," said the soldier. "A second arrived just now."

Lady Veil was handed a tiny, rolled up piece of parchment. On it written: *Tuesday. Dawn.* She passed the message to Mister Priestman, who grunted.

All eyes turned her way. As general of the Pilgrimage, the decision whether to proceed rested with her.

Should they ignore the possibility of annihilation by drones and advance? Or stick to the plan, defying the new danger? Michael Pilgrim and Blair Gover might be on the outskirts of Albion by now, if not penetrating the underbelly of the city. Gover had promised a secure, hidden way in. Should the raiders succeed, and the army not be in position to seize the moment, all would have been in vain.

Her hands moved; the translator spoke. Round the room, heads bowed at the implications of her choice.

* * *

After crawling and inching along the elevated monorail, Michael Pilgrim's small party was too exhausted to advance further. A fire would have been welcome, but they could not risk one, even some way down the tunnel. Drones possessed sensors only fools underestimated.

The dozen men and women slept in a huddle, wrapped in blankets, taking turns to keep watch. Not that there was much to see in the deep dark. Even the mouth of the tunnel, shrouded by vegetation, was midnight blue. Michael's awareness of smell and sound intensified. Both senses told tales of water: drips, mould, decay, damp soil.

"Hard to believe this tunnel goes all the way beneath Albion's walls to the centre," he whispered. "Surely that is nigh on ten miles from here."

Beside him, Gover stirred. "It does not go miles underground. Let me try to explain it again. Do listen carefully. After a single mile or so – which takes us safely under the perimeter defences – we shall reach a disused station. Due to my foresight, a quite ordinary tunnelling drone spent several years connecting that station to a private facility constructed beneath my home. Understand now?"

Michael hoped so. "I still don't get why it's not guarded."

"I told you, Pilgrim, because I made sure it was my little secret. Even rabbits maintain escape tunnels from their warrens."

"Except we're not trying to escape. Breaking in is different."

"Doors swing both ways."

"Let us hope so."

Michael longed for a pipe of well-cured Baytown tobacco; he dared not risk even that.

"I'm going back to the tunnel mouth to check the sky."

When Michael reached the exit, grey light peeked through leaves and branches; a chorus of birds anticipated dawn. He made rapid calculations. Almost exactly twenty-four hours since the carrier pigeons were released. Though a few would lose their way or fall prey to hawks, some would reach Peterborough. Lady Veil had agreed to be ready to march at a moment's notice. As Peterborough lay only a few miles from the northwestern border of Albion's great circle, it seemed likely she was already in position. Not too close, he hoped, but close enough to swarm in when the lights went out. If Gover's plan played out – and so far all had gone remarkably well – Albion would wake to its final day within a few hours.

Victory seemed scarcely credible to Michael, however ardently he longed for it. Still, Gover's resourcefulness during their perilous journey through the Highlands of Scotland had taught him one thing: never underestimate the City-scientist.

Michael remembered, too, how Pharaoh Jacko's final bolthole at Fylingdales had been penetrated through an abandoned tunnel from the Before Times. What worked once might work again. Surprise can be the deadliest of weapons.

He crept back along the monorail track to rejoin the raiding party. There, he switched on his rechargeable torch. Time to risk a little light.

* * *

The tunnel was wide enough for just one track. Water dripped through slimy cracks in the plasti-concrete walls. Gover explained that it formed a loop like the eye of a needle, so trains could deposit passengers at an underground platform before circling round to return to the airport.

Talk of trains made Michael Pilgrim realise they had only encountered a single one so far, back at the airport station. Where were the others? He decided it did not matter.

"Keep close to me," he told Gover.

The City-man's eyes glittered in the yellow beam of the hand-cranked torch. Even down here, he kept his face covered. Michael noticed the hands of the man on whom their fate depended trembled uncontrollably.

He split the raiding party. One group to proceed further into Albion, led by himself, the other to linger near the tunnel entrance.

"If the lights still shine on the security wall, you'll know we've failed. Go then straight to the rendezvous with Tom Higginbottom. He'll be waiting with horses. You'll need to get word to the main army fast."

Nothing more need be said. Private orders had been agreed with the five men accompanying Michael and Gover. Orders concerning Gover's fate if he proved treacherous. Not that vengeance would solve anything. Michael suspected it might even worsen their situation, in ways no one could anticipate.

Adjusting the torch beam, he took the lead. The tunnel sloped gently down; soon they were wading through water. The air tasted dank and fetid. Nothing seemed to live down there, not even rats. Michael was about to question Gover when they came upon a fork in the track. Playing the torch beam down both tunnels offered no clue which to choose.

"What lies beyond this fork? Does it matter which tunnel we take?"

Gover sighed. "The tunnel loops round to a station. Its entrance to the surface was long ago filled in and grassed over. Therefore, it is irrelevant which tunnel we take."

Michael sniffed left and right. Neither offered a clue.

"We'll go left," he said.

A decision that possibly saved his life.

* * *

Minutes later, the tunnel began to climb. He held up a fist to indicate a halt.

"From now on, we go silently," he murmured to Gover, directly behind him. "Pass it down. Ear to ear."

For once, Gover did as instructed. What good stealth might do against a drone's sensors was unclear.

The tunnel curved round and up. The water was left behind. Michael stooped to lay his hand on the narrow strip of sandy ground running beside the monorail. Quite dry. A little further brought another change. His torch revealed the rear of a train carriage, almost circular in shape. It had come off the track, effectively blocking the tunnel.

Michael gave Gover a quizzical look. The City-man shrugged. No help there.

A door hung ajar at the rear of the train, no doubt designed – and used as such, long ago – as an escape hatch. Michael pushed it wider, playing his torch over the carriage. Rotted seats. A skeleton in foetal position on the floor. At the far end, another door, also ajar. His beam could not illuminate what lay beyond.

Michael passed over his shotgun and backpack to a soldier, retaining only his City-sword, which he slung across his back, and a pistol.

"Do not come after me, whatever happens," he breathed into the soldier's ear.

Wide, frightened eyes blinked acknowledgement.

Then Michael dragged himself up into the carriage. Nothing jumped out of the shadows. Dust and debris crunched beneath his wet boots as he brushed aside a veil of cobwebs. The next carriage was much like the first, except several skeletons formed a jumbled heap over the chairs, as though bodies had been piled there. Rusted guns from the Before Times littered the floor. Although the dead men's clothes had rotted, strips of plastic bearing insignia remained, along with sturdy plastic boots.

Another carriage: more warriors sleeping away eternity, this forgotten train their Valhalla. In the final carriage, Michael realised how the train came to be jammed into the curved tunnel. The front section, including the driver's cab, was a tangle of scorched metal and plastic. A rocket or grenade? Maybe a mine? Either way, the explosion had been followed by a crash, causing the concrete casing round the tunnel to collapse.

Michael listened in the dark, his torch off. Not even a faint sound of wind. If the tunnel looped back to the fork, you might expect wind. Perhaps that way was blocked, too, maybe more completely than this.

He eased open a buckled door, gratified by deep darkness beyond. A bent, twisted monorail track slanted, still curving round. More skeletons here, many bones scattered. More abandoned weaponry.

With elaborate stealth, Michael lowered his legs down to the track. He froze. Tomb-like silence prevailed.

Michael checked his crude, three-chambered revolver. One of Lady Veil's designs, brutally effective at short range. His mind reached out to the woman who must be waiting avidly for the lights to go out all over Albion. Then the pitiless work she craved could begin.

Yet killing with the pistol was not on his mind. Warning shots would alert the raiding party to flee like startled deer. The best he could do for those who trusted him.

*　*　*

A few minutes later, Michael sensed change. Although the way was still cavern-black, an echo behind his shuffling feet suggested a large space ahead.

By now, he had adjusted the shutter of his torch to a mere glow worm. Could he chance proper light? Surely, this must be the station. Were sensors in place? Light, sound and movement detectors? For all Gover's braggadocio, it seemed impossible the City would allow rats a way in.

He breathed slowly to calm himself.

"Fuck it," he muttered and turned the torch to full beam.

What it revealed made him grunt with relief. A long platform occupied one side of the tunnel. It was deserted. Thoroughly deserted. A lifetime of searching ruins had taught him an instinct for such questions, on which your life might depend. The platform littered with dust and yet more skeletons, told him no one had trod here in a long, long while.

According to Gover, somewhere along the platform was a door to the tunnel dug by his own personal machines. Michael imagined drone-moles, tireless claws burrowing through the earth, day after day, year after year if need be, until their work was complete. Perhaps Gover's tunnel did indeed lead back into Albion to his private lair. Nothing seemed too grand or improbable for Dr Blair Gover.

Hope prickled. This same hideaway might yet conceal the key to turn off all power within Albion, including its defences and drones.

Bolder now, Michael followed the track, playing his torch beam over the platform and walls. At the exit, he paused. This wide passage must lead up to the surface, a way sealed by tons of earth and rubble.

Further down the platform, a small, rectangular plasti-steel door had been set into the wall. A hatch clearly built after the station had fallen into decay. So Gover had not lied. Utterly secure in his power and cleverness, the City-man had not even bothered concealing the door.

Pulling himself onto the platform, Michael warily approached the hatch. It was entirely smooth, without a keyhole. Maybe it only opened from the inside. He suspected forcing it from the outside might trigger a booby trap.

Then Michael heard faint voices. The voices were coming from behind the door, from behind Gover's supposedly secret tunnel. Any moment the hatch might open, revealing him, open-mouthed, torch in hand.

* * *

Michael Pilgrim always remembered his grandfather's deathbed. To the last, the old man – by then in his nineties, an absurdly long life for the times – had shown little weakness. He lay in the old library of Hob Hall, surrounded by his beloved books, a room of wonders Michael would inherit and explore himself.

Although his eyesight was fading, old Oliver Pilgrim spotted a mouse near the fire, whiskers twitching. When Michael, just a lad, stirred to scare it off, his grandfather breathed, "No, no, let it be."

For a while he watched the rodent, then turned to his grandson.

"Even if you had tried to catch her, she would have escaped."

Michael wondered how he knew the mouse was a *she*. But Grandfather knew everything.

"I've tried to teach you as much as I can in the time allowed."

Oh yes, Michael had thought, words burned across his soul: *duty . . . responsibility . . . justice . . . the quality of mercy is not strained . . .*

preserve, preserve, preserve.

"Here's the last thing," gasped the old man. "Only be a lion when necessary, Michael. You are too apt to take risks. There's no shame in playing mouse."

The memory flashed across Michael's mind as he heard the voices behind the plasti-steel hatch. Then, swift as a scurrying mouse seeking its hole, he jumped lightly onto the monorail track and ran for the tunnel entrance. He had just reached there when a grating hiss of trapped air alerted him the hatch was opening. Michael deftly laid himself flat on the far side of the monorail to the platform; in this prone position, the raised flange of the track concealed him from anyone on the platform. Then he waited, still as a mouse.

A loud, drawly voice echoed in the silent station.

"Imagine such a place. Beneath us all the time."

Bright lights danced over the walls.

"We'll need to fetch a drone to go up these tunnels," came a second voice.

"Whatever we do, it better be good. You can bet *she* will have us composted if we miss something important."

An uncomfortable silence. Michael wondered who *she* might be.

"No one's come here for years," said the first man. "Look at those skeletons."

Boots crunched up and down the platform. Good, thought Michael, they are covering any footprints I left in the dust. He suspected they would never think to look for footprints, or other hunters' clues. Too blind to notice their quarry's shit if they trod in it.

"Got your pistol?" asked Voice One.

"Of course. But don't you think we should bring up a security drone?"

"Why? Let's take a look up this tunnel."

"I'm not sure . . ."

"If we find something it might give us credit. Remember, they will be apportioning estates as soon as the primitive problem has been settled."

"True. I'll send a message to Control. Tell them what we're doing."

Michael knew he had to act: move or murder. Right now. The men were still conferring, pre-occupied, distant enough not to see him. His hand brushed the hilt of his sword. But the City-man had a pistol.

He started crawling along the tunnel, each movement an agony lest it betray him. No one called out. No gun boomed. Then he turned a corner and the station was out of sight. He adjusted his torch to a faint glimmer. Rising, he hurried on tiptoes towards the wrecked train. He glanced back. Lights had appeared behind him. Voices echoed.

Suddenly, the train came into view. With a last scurry, Michael made it to the tangle of burned metal blocking the tunnel. Dare he risk more light to find the narrow way he'd squeezed through when leaving the train? There seemed no alternative.

He tentatively widened the shutter for a stronger beam, locating the buckled metal door. It was still ajar, as he had left it. He wriggled through, pulling it back into position – it creaked alarmingly – then he doused his light.

A minute passed. Another. The City-men could be heard, the clump of their boots echoing. Glowing light filtered through a gash above the door. Michael scarcely breathed.

"I'm sure I saw a light," said Voice Two, nervously. "We should have waited for a drone."

"It's just the reflection of our flashlights."

"And I heard a noise. A definite scrape."

"You are imagining things, my friend. But this place does give me the creeps. It reminds me of the Crusades, somehow."

"You were in the Crusades?"

"God, yes. Damn Locusts! Just when you thought you'd cleaned the devils out, another swarm would pop up."

"I hear the primitives are on the Presidents' sensor-grid now. Poor devils."

"Good riddance, I say. If you'd seen those animals the way I did in the Crusades, well, you can imagine . . . Let's go back, this way is blocked."

Michael waited. The light seeping through the crack faded. Footsteps receded. He permitted himself to breathe.

* * *

Five minutes later, they were wading through fetid water, aware every delay brought drones nearer. At the tunnel fork, Michael glanced back towards the station. No light. No pursuit. Not yet. He decided to risk a little more noise.

"Pelt for it!" he hissed.

His comrades needed no encouragement. The tunnel echoed with splashing and laboured breath. Even as he prepared to run, Michael realised Gover stood paralysed in the water, shaking uncontrollably. He seized the City-man's hand. Shone the torch into his eyes. For once, the mask had been removed, as though facial recognition no longer mattered to him. Despair haunted Gover's youthful face. He stared sightlessly into the darkness.

"We must go," said Michael, gripping his arm.

"Why?" Like his expression, Gover's voice was gaunt.

"There's still time."

"Not for me."

"Gover!"

"That tunnel was my last hope. I am defeated."

Michael hesitated. Simply abandon him? But then Gover would put the City on their trail – a dreadful prospect.

"I've wanted to do this for a long time," he muttered.

Michael slapped Gover hard across the cheek. His head snapped back. A light appeared in his eyes. Michael shook him like a rag doll.

"I thought you wanted to live forever, you heartless bastard," he hissed. "Now fucking move!"

To his amazement, Gover did. Their feet echoed in the tunnel as they ran. Then silence resumed, the water grew still, as though it had never been disturbed.

* * *

An hour later, two men in perma-plastic overalls, machine pistols at the ready, stepped from the entrance of the tunnel and surveyed the monorail rising to its elevated track over the swamps. With them came two security drones on caterpillar tracks.

"So this is where it ends," said the first. "I really had not the slightest idea it was here at all."

"Blair Gover must have known about this," remarked his companion.

"Little good it did him. Do you know, he was such a big cheese for so long I find it hard to believe he could be removed so easily. Makes you think."

Out of habit, both men glanced round for monitoring devices. But there were none in this uncivilised wilderness of nature.

"You don't think his death was an accident?"

"Ha! We're both too old for that fairy tale, my friend."

Indeed they were. Far, far older than appearances possibly suggested.

"Let's go back and make our report. Not that there's much to say. The place has been deserted for decades, I'd say. Seal it off and have done with it."

As he turned to go, his nose wrinkled. Looking down, he noticed something in the bushes by the tunnel entrance. Brown and still moist: a human stool, as though someone had used the bush as a toilet.

He took out his pistol suspiciously. "That's from no animal. Don't you think? Good lord! People must come here. Primitives."

His companion peered down at the turd. When he looked up, his face brightened. "We can get it analysed. At last we have something juicy to report."

TWELVE

Lady Veil was accustomed to nurturing her ruthless streak. Before the Great Dyings, she excelled at suppressing protests by terrorists – as anyone opposing the interests of the elite was classified. A high-ranking officer in the English Peace Force, her speciality had been autonomous drone attacks against unarmed crowds. Drones, she found, worked best: immune to compassion, empathy, uncompromised by community ties or folk memories, ethical niceties or solidarity. Above all, they were untroubled by conscience. Facts she had been fond of explaining to squeamish politicians. In short, military drones transcended morality.

That same ruthlessness proved essential in the precarious early days of the Five Cities. Terrorists had been replaced by hordes of starving, diseased primitives desperate for sanctuary in Albion. Her efficiency in culling them had been rewarded with the position of Commander, one rung lower than the Ruling Council.

With such a pedigree, it had surprised everyone – not least herself – when she sickened of genocide towards primitives. The Crusades against the Locusts of Africa proved her moral tipping point. Naively, she had banded with other Beautifuls suffering a late onset of guilt. Her grotesque punishment for this Discordia, followed by banishment, served as a model warning. If an earlier rebel against the Five Cities, known to the primitives as the Modified Man, had not harboured her in York, she would have perished.

Now the Modified Man was dead; and Lady Veil barely remembered her own name. Death itself seemed a blessing. She might well be called mad. Except her cold-hearted gifts as a tactician remained intact.

Mustering the Pilgrimage of Fools for its assault on Albion, Lady Veil did not hesitate to make necessary decisions. Sat on her horse, she ordered each company of fifty to march past. A casual point of her finger decided their fate, like souls queuing before the respective gates of Heaven and Hell. Some were directed to gather on the old ghost road leading to the borders of Albion. Others to take a different route, dispersing across the densely wooded ridges west of Peterborough.

Mister Priestman and the other leaders watched the division in bemusement. By the end, hundreds of troops waited on the ghost road, while many times that number had vanished into the woods.

"We all trust your judgement, I'm sure," said Priestman, "but if I'm not mistaken, that column on the road is far weaker than them up on the hills. Not just in numbers, but not so handy in a fight. Some only carry spears and clubs and bows."

Lady Veil's hands moved. Her interpreter spoke.

"She says, 'Correct'."

"Well then," pressed Priestman, "it don't make no sense."

Lady Veil replied. "She says, 'It is not meant to make sense to you.'"

"Oh, aye?"

"She says, 'You are not a drone, I believe.'"

"Not the last time I looked."

"She says, 'Then leave thinking like a drone to me.'"

Priestman was scarcely reassured by what happened next. Grow People fanatically loyal to Lady Veil emerged from hidey holes in Peterborough, handing out dozens of symbols he recognised as religious. Big wooden crosses, even Nuager star and planet totem poles. In addition, they instructed the people to cut leafy branches. These, they announced, would serve as camouflage against drones.

"What's all this about?" demanded Priestman.

Lady Veil's hands moved impatiently.

"She says, 'This is a pilgrimage, is it not, Priestman? A Pilgrimage of Fools?'"

He couldn't argue with that.

* * *

It was noon before they advanced on Albion. The scattered bands in the oak and birch woods spread out, picking routes south. The far smaller force waited nervously on the old motorway.

Before joining the companies up on the ridge, Lady Veil rode to inspect the men and women in their loose column. For several minutes she assessed them. Her hands did not move to disclose her thoughts. A small company of Grow People took up positions front and rear.

A herald rode up the line to deliver a simple message. "Good folk, you have been chosen to act as a reserve force. You will only be ordered to advance when the walls of Albion are breached. Be ready! All must play their allotted part!"

Lady Veil turned her horse and cantered off without a backward glance, her entourage disappearing beneath the trees.

Hours passed on the motorway. The afternoon was humid. No rain for a change. The relief force on the road laid down weapons and sat. The sun came out, warming their faces. A few cooking fires were lit. Most counted themselves lucky to have avoided the worst of the battle ahead. Yet no sounds of fighting could be heard from the direction of Albion. They had been promised evening would make everything clear: night would douse the bright lights of Albion forever. Soon a new age would commence.

Children ran and played or climbed trees. Older folk talked in groups or lay with heads propped on knapsacks, watching clouds float west. A few sat up, alerted by a perceptible rumble. Were those circling black dots birds? Or surveillance drones?

Mister Priestman had insisted on staying with the relief column. He was troubled by a far-sight all was not as it seemed. On the one hand, it made military sense to hold the weaker folk back. Kinder, too, though he knew well enough kindness had little place in war. If Michael Pilgrim and Gover were successful then the peaceable folk around him would be forced to spill barrels of blood. It was that simple. And ugly.

Priestman recalled his home in Baytown. Several wives waited for him back there, along with a dozen children. What he would give to walk the stony beach beneath Baytown cliffs now! On such a windless evening, the waves would be calm, lapping on the stony beach. If the tides were right, he might take a stroll along the foreshore to the village, supping a few pints at the Puzzle Well Inn. Then the stars would rise over the ocean. Up would come the moon, its pale face gazing down on troubled humanity. As an orthodox Nuager, Mister Priestman knew well how the moon transmitted regular reports to the Happy Planets concerning one's fitness for the Cosmic Voyage.

Priestman was not a man for sustained hating. Maybe he should hate all City-folk more. Yet when he considered the state of this world, it was with sadness rather than anger. If folk could just treat one another kinder, why then, the stars would bless one and all! That simple truth was self-evident.

He looked over the Nuager totem poles, the green branches and tall wooden crosses. What was Lady Veil's game? Why these symbols?

The first hint of twilight brought a new rumble from the south. People clambered to their feet. Most reacted from an instinct stained deep into their souls by a lifetime's terror. They looked round for somewhere to hide: the deepest hole possible.

Lady Veil's Grow People ran down the column, shouting out commands. "Raise your branches! Raise your branches!"

Absurdly, many did, cowering beneath shelters thick as an oak leaf. The rumble of drones grew loud. The earth seemed to vibrate.

* * *

Mister Priestman looked round for cover. Saplings surrounded the eight lanes of the ghost road, along with brambles and low bushes. A few abandoned cars and lorries, shrouded in ivy, dotted the churned up tarmac. To the northeast lay the scorched ruins of Peterborough. Plenty of crannies to hide in there. Nearer, on the opposite carriageway, the land climbed to the remains of a motorway service station among trees.

Louder, louder, grew the jet engines. Surely, he told himself, not for them. The City no longer even sent out regular patrols. Why should they care if a horde of primitives gathered, doing no apparent harm?

Priestman had not survived to the venerable age of fifty by relying entirely on the goodwill of the stars. Common sense had its place. When young, he had been granted a memorable far-sight by the Faery Queen whilst under the influence of mushrooms, indicating – though the memory was vague – reason is faith, faith reason, except when faith is faith and reason loses reason, all at the same time.

"Run! Run!" he bellowed. "We're buggered!"

He grabbed the arm of a Grower officer. "Order the column to scatter, damn you!"

The young man in the Grow People's black uniform shook him off. With a cry, he mounted his horse, galloping along the length of the column. "Form up! Close up! Raise high the crosses! Cover yourself with the leaves of your branch!"

Paralysed folk from all over the North and Midlands stirred. Friends

TWELVE

and neighbours who had joined this crusade as pals, huddled together. Most threw aside weapons and fled. Closer, closer roared the drones, recognisable now as two large gunships.

* * *

Here is what the drones saw, if complex banks of sensors may be likened to eyes. Here is what they thought, if electronic impulses may be termed intelligence. Enough data for their offensive systems to identify viable targets.

Earlier that day, a report had been sent to the Defence Centre concerning primitives in a disused railway tunnel close to Albion's perimeter wall. A chemical analysis of fresh faecal matter confirmed some had even penetrated the defences, albeit harmlessly. Given that a large gathering of primitives had been detected the previous day, lurking in the rubble formerly called Peterborough, it seemed possible both incursions were connected. The Defence Centre's artificial intelligence accordingly launched a couple of drones.

After first conducting a routine surveillance sweep over the bogs and wetlands north of the mother city, the two gunships closed in.

Holo-images of numerous primitives cowering beneath tree branches and wooden crosses were flashed back to the Defence Centre. A list of predictions and analysis glowed beside the holo-images:

Religious and/or fertility gathering – 51.4% probability
Ritual battle between rival tribes – 43% probability
Economic activity – 5.4% probability
Hostile gathering – 0.2% probability

The holoscript began to flash. *Awaiting instructions. Awaiting instructions.*

These promptly arrived. The holoscript stopped flashing.

* * *

Fifteen miles north, the pair of hawks in the sky adjusted their engines. Side by side, they hovered. Each as long as one of the articulated lorries rotting below. Short, stubby wings were equipped with weapon pods, as were turrets on the main fuselage. One drone was painted pastel blue and pink, the other metallic silver and gold. No camouflage was necessary. Nothing could stand against them save a comparable machine.

For a full minute they mapped the terrain, recording dispositions, immediate threat-levels (0.00001%) and probable behaviour patterns of selected targets. Sensors concentrated on the primary command. They detected more primitives widely dispersed out on the wooded ridge a few miles to the west but this did not concern them. Only large concentrations of primitives concerned them, as Lady Veil knew well.

Surveillance complete, weapons systems activated, the drones sent a final request for confirmation. It came back promptly. Their work commenced.

Mister Priestman rushed over to a knot of Nuagers, older folk mainly, drawn to the Pilgrimage of Fools by duty and hope. Also, to keep a more experienced eye on the young 'uns. They stared up from the old motorway, gawping.

In his time, Priestman had seen rabbits paralysed by the menace of stoat or weasel. The two drones hovering above the column created the same frozen panic. Priestman did not even have time to urge his people to find a hole – any hole. Before he could speak, it began.

Spurts of fire from the gunships. Small rockets curved down, trailing smoke and sparks. A series of dry harrumphs followed by ear-splitting bangs as the missiles exploded. Earth, tarmac, plants, rusting cars and trucks rose in the air. Amidst the debris, soft flesh, limbs, smouldering tatters of skin and clothes.

A second salvo followed. Rings of fire crumped outward wherever the missiles struck, setting ablaze grovelling survivors and melting the leaves off shrub and bush. Even above the uproar, screams rose.

Then the drones were descending, gun turrets spitting cannon at selected targets fleeing in all directions. Bellies burst apart, limbs and heads were torn away, blood and organs spilt. Still people ran, attracting fresh bursts of cannon. The wisest played dead, though the need for air amidst so much smoke and cordite fumes gave many away. The gunships flew low patterns over the target area, belching out balls of napalm until the young woodlands were ablaze for hundreds of yards around.

With a surge of engines, the drones rose and began to circle, one clockwise, the other anti-clockwise, seeking survivors. Within a few minutes they halted, hanging in the air a thousand feet above fire and black smoke and carnage.

Finally, like dark fates, or dragons depicted in old books from the Before Times, wicked serpents it was said good men like St George could vanquish through courage and strength of arms alone, the drones flew south towards Albion, and were gone.

* * *

Mister Priestman lay at the edge of a smoking crater. Around him, bellows and moans and cries from a tiny number of survivors. So few, so few. Of the people like a field of wheat on the motorway, only chaff remained.

He coughed, retched. A gaping hole in his side shrieked with pain. His time had come. The time of truth anticipated all his life. With it came a far-sight. Not, as he had hoped, a blessed vision of his spirit rising gleefully, winging to the Happy Planets, soul-havens worshipped on clear nights. Priestman was not granted that last relief.

As his eyes closed, a far-sight horrible in its implications unrolled. York burning, drones releasing bomb after bomb until the ancient streets collapsed in heaps, sparks and smoke filling the sky, its citizens rushing helplessly to throw themselves in the river rather than roast alive. Then people known and loved, Baytown folk who accompanied his journey through the long, hard years, crawling wretchedly in the mud of Hob Vale, begging for the mercy of a bullet in the brain, anything to stop the agony of the disease Priestman's far-sight revealed had been spread by Albion to render all that remained of humanity into bones...

"No," he prayed, "let those things never be. Hear me!"

Perhaps the stars heard. Perhaps the Faery o' the Vale heard. Perhaps they did not. Mister Priestman's consciousness faded, and he died.

THIRTEEN

When Cutty Smart talked to Seth Pilgrim about life in the Fenlands, winter hunger featured often. That life was hard and starvation a constant menace, Seth needed no telling. But for the Fen Folk, dwelling as they did upon precarious margins, amidst flood and sucking bog, oneness with nature meant more than mere sustenance. Nature was their necessary faith, sustainer of soul, as much as body. Which was how Seth got involved with Cutty's eggs.

They punted from Ely as the sun rose fair. A lulling breeze carried floating white seeds, as did the slow currents of the stream. The blue sky a vast, cloudless ring of horizons, so clear Seth could glimpse Albion in the distance, its towers small from this perspective, glass walls glittering faintly.

The sight stirred guilt. He should be wading through the mire to find Uncle Michael. Helen Devereux had said, when throwing him the Baytown Jewel: "What it contains could change everything. Tell him, Blair Gover hid it there."

What this mysterious *it* might be, Seth had no idea. Rather than rush to fulfil his duty, he preferred biding with Cutty and his pals, drinking ale and cider, larking about amidst the peace of fen and waterway. And he had a fine excuse for staying put: no way would he abandon Hurdy.

Seth realised other boats were converging on a flooded village, ivy-covered roofs poking through trees.

"Who are all these people?" he asked.

"They come from miles around. There's more of us slodgers than you'd think. And beyond the edges of the Fens, there's big communities we trade with."

"What the fuck are we here for?"

"For luck," replied Cutty.

It was an egg ceremony, held late in the breeding season so a fresh generation of ducklings and young waterfowl was already on the water. The flooded village formed an island in the miles-wide mere of reeds and merging streams. Perfect feeding grounds for mallards, gathering in thousands. The old houses and buildings provided concealed nest spaces for large late clutches. Hence this gathering, the game simple: the more eggs you collected for pickling over winter – and devouring at the Winter Solstice with mulled apple and pear cider – the luckier you and your family would be.

Cutty poled his punt between half-submerged houses, rooting out nests invisible to Seth's eye. All around, other egg-seekers could be heard calling and blaring horns. The air filled with clattering wings, honking, hooting fowl. Then Seth froze. Listened hard.

"Hear that?"

On cue, two huge battle drones came in low and fast from the direction of Albion, unmuted engines roaring. If the machines noticed the wooden boats and their crews, no sign was given. While the Fen Folk cowered, the drones swept on, circling round to the northwest.

Slowly, the engine rumble lessened.

"What lies in that direction?" asked Seth.

"Peterborough. Or what's left of it. Though I have heard tell . . . Idle talk, mind."

Seth climbed a high mound of bricks for a better view. He examined the direction taken by the drones.

Minutes passed. A mutter of explosions rolled across the still flatlands. Seth's sharp young eyes detected smudges of smoke. Bright flashes. Was the Pilgrimage of Fools the drones' target? Why else unleash such powerful machines?

He climbed down to rejoin Cutty.

"We need to find out what the hell's going on over Peterborough way," he said.

Lucky eggs forgotten, Cutty gathered a couple of his friends, including Ell, the wiry girl who had accompanied them to Wisbech. While they conferred, Seth tasted familiar poisons. Inadequacy. Self-contempt. He had lingered here too long. He was letting down those who had trusted him, beginning with Helen Devereux; and not least those who gave him a second chance when by rights he deserved the gallows. Time to get moving. But when he left, he was determined not to go alone.

* * *

Back in Ely, Seth hurried away from the town to a large wood of oak and alder, its roots easing apart buildings, trunks bursting through the engines of cars.

In his hand, a laden basket, the contents covered with straw. A memory came to him, long cast aside. His mother telling a bedside story. A girl in a red cloak, alone in a dark wood, taking a basket to her grandmother's cottage. Averil must have been listening, too, they had been young enough to still share a room when Mother was alive. Tears started to Seth's eyes; he brushed them away angrily. *Stupid cunt*, he warned himself. He had broken the golden rule. Never think of Mother. Of all the doors to his losses and failures, her early death brought the deepest pain. And this was no time for tears.

Seth passed beneath a canopy of branches heavy with summer leaves. Eyes were upon him. None of them friendly to mankind. Good. Scared whispers in Ely spoke of more and more strangelings gathering. No one came to forage here now.

With the reluctant agreement of Cutty, Seth had led Bella and her fellow outcasts to this old suburb by the River Great Ouse. They might prove useful allies if the Pilgrimage of Fools attacked Albion – albeit unpredictable ones. Certainly the strangelings kept a baleful watch on the City. Why Albion obsessed them, no one knew for certain. Except Seth had an inkling. Oh, he knew what it was to hate so hard your guts twisted into strangling knots. The creatures must surely crave revenge against those who turned them into monsters.

Deeper into the wood he pushed, until a clearing surrounded by fallen houses appeared. Goalposts tottered like forlorn totems.

"Bella!"

His call faded. The leaves murmured in the breeze. Even birds shunned this clearing. Perhaps they'd all been eaten. Seth walked to a goalpost and waited, aware his every movement was scrutinised.

"Bella!"

Out she lolloped, from the midst of a huge honeysuckle. Others followed. A pug-nosed man-dog and creature mingling cat and teenage girl. Something about the strangelings had changed in the short time since Seth encountered them at Wisbech. They seemed shabbier, fur or feathers less sleek and glossy, eyes duller. The gift of long life had evidently not been part of the magic that created them.

Seth realised the rectangular lumps beneath their skin – City tracking devices, according to Gurdy – had been torn out, leaving open wounds or deep scars. How that could be, he did not understand. Hurdy-Gurdy had said the lumps would explode if cut out. Perhaps the strangelings were of no further interest to their makers, the tracking devices switched off.

THIRTEEN

"Bella, we must talk urgently!"

Well, he must talk. All the hare-girl could manage were cheeps and strangled syllables. On the whole, Seth preferred the cheeps.

"You must get ready for war, Bella. We must all be ready. You and your . . ." He wasn't quite sure how to describe the other freaks, and settled lamely for, "You and your friends."

Seth displayed the basket to the monsters forming a circle around him.

"Look! A gift from the people of Ely. Lucky eggs. Each a promise of new life. To give you strength. We need to be strong against the City now."

Bella's nose twitched. The girl-cat scratched furry breasts.

"And I've brought something else to show you."

Seth fumbled in his pocket for the Baytown Jewel. It glinted in the sunlight.

"This locket is like another kind of egg. It contains something to bring Albion low as dust."

Now, he really had their attention. Seth wondered how many other strangelings, apart from Bella, retained some mastery of human language. If so, the torment in their minds did not bear thinking about.

"You must come with me soon. All of you. The time to fight is coming. You must trust me."

Good luck with that, he told himself. Fat good trusting him had done Jojo Lyons. The memory of kind, handsome Jojo made Seth flush.

Perhaps Bella's thoughts strayed in the same direction. Suddenly she spoke a name, her voice barely human, a cheeping screech of anger and despair: "Jooo-jooo-ooo!"

Seth stepped back.

"Jojo would want you to join me against Albion," he said. "Tonight I'm going to take a closer look at the City. Tomorrow I'll return. You need to be ready to leave then."

He pushed through the circle of clawed and fanged monsters, his heart labouring. None took a swipe or bite. He glanced back just once. Bella raised her head and cried out, the name echoing in the glade littered with rotting playthings for children turned to dust and moss.

"Jooo-jooo-ooo!"

* * *

Seth went straight to find Cutty Smart.

"I've something to tell you."

"No need, 'bor, I can see you're about set to go against Albion again." He added airily, "A good pal knows when a friend's wadin' in so deep he might drown. Might not like it, but he knows."

Seth realised Cutty was right. They had become good friends in the time he'd stayed in Ely. In fact, each sought the other's company every day.

"So when you goin'?"

"Tomorrow. Though I don't think Hurdy'll ever wake up. There's something strange about his illness, like it's coming from deep inside. Sometimes he stirs and talks, but only to himself. It's like he's arguing with himself, if you see what I mean. He's worn out, I reckon. Lived too long. Longer than you can imagine, Cutty. Nothing about him is natural."

Losing Gurdy would be no easier for that.

"All I ask is that you keep Old Meggie looking after him."

A long silence followed.

"I'm thinking I should take a closer look at the City before I head for Peterborough," said Seth. "Seeing it's so near."

"Well then," said Cutty, "I'll take you to see their lights tonight, just me and you."

THIRTEEN

Dusk found the two young men in a sailing dinghy on the River Great Ouse. They had followed the meandering stream through the islets of Ely then Sutton. Year by year, more folk were clearing the land to host swelling families. Some cottagers waved or called out greetings. Cutty was much-respected; his youth belied a deep authority, based on a talent for consensus. In that, he reminded Seth of Uncle Michael. Where they differed was in the battles they fought. The only blood on Cutty's hands ran from creatures he caught to eat. One sought peace through war; the other avoided war for the sake of peace.

As he tended the sail, Cutty sank into silence, a habit of withdrawal Seth found comforting. It was one he shared. Many Fen Folk possessed the same reticence of speech, an expression of independence and isolation, maybe, or sheer pig-headedness. They were a stubborn lot. Yet he sensed other currents in the Fen Folk's make up: a profound acceptance of nature's rules, and a deep instinct for liberty.

As darkness fell, Cutty tied the skiff to a willow growing on a small island in the marsh. For some miles the towers of Albion had loomed like dark shadows above the trees. Finally, the high boundary wall came in sight. Any nearer, Cutty declared, it was unsafe to venture.

The island was obscured by shrubs. They found an elevated dry patch with a good view. Cutty produced food and drink, as well as weed and pipes.

The fens settled. Dew fell. Day's scents turned to night's muddy aromas; birdsong died back, throat by throat. For a while they spoke only of small, practical things. A growing sense of anticipation tightened Seth's loins, along with a sharpening awareness of the warm body beside his own.

***

Darkness brought lights to the high boundary walls, dimming the stars.

Simultaneously, countless fusion-powered lights activated all over Albion. Seth cried out in astonishment. Such harsh power! How dare the Pilgrimage of Fools challenge the makers of such brightness.

Then came coloured beams, piercing the sky. Seth watched, mesmerised.

"Has anyone ever got in there?" he asked, puffing on a pipe of weed. "I suppose that's impossible. How could they?"

Cutty leaned back on his elbows to admire the shifting lights, and laughed.

"Not quite true, 'bor."

"You're having me on."

"No, there *is* some among us who've found ways in. Crazy fuckers like yourself, nat'rally."

"In there?"

"They even brought back City things to prove it. Old Badger got in there, just two year past. With his daughter."

"What's she called? Young Ferret?"

"No, it's Ell, of course. She can get in anywhere."

They laughed.

"Look, Seth!"

Huge holograms projected up into the darkness. Scenes from Olympus, or wherever the gods resided. For half an hour, a triumphal parade of vehicles and gaudily costumed young men and women processed through canyon-like streets between tower blocks. No sound accompanied the images, making them eerier still. Just the creak of grasshoppers and occasional cry of a night bird, the ceaseless rustle of reeds.

The holograms condensed to faces transported by ecstasy. Two faces, in particular, a slightly older man with swept back hair and a gamine young woman. Thousands of perfect people bowed to the King and Queen of Albion. Seth remembered Pharaoh Jacko and his murderous

THIRTEEN

bitch Queen Morrighan. But they were long dead. Why should he fear ghosts when the world was one enormous graveyard?

Then his mouth opened in surprise. In the background, a floating face he recognised. Helen Devereux. She wore dirty rags like a beggar. Her expression was far from happy. Then she had gone.

"Pass me that cider," he muttered.

The procession entered a vast banqueting hall. Drones and odd-looking creatures, like pictures from fairy tale books printed in the Before Times, bore laden platters to the beautiful people.

"My God!" cried Seth.

Could it be? He recalled Uncle Michael saying that Averil had been spirited away to the City. His own twin sister sat there, near the table occupied by the king and queen. Or someone hauntingly alike to her. Except the nose was straighter, face more regular. Somehow, Averil had been magically changed to resemble all the other City people. At last, the hologram shrank, and died.

"Their feast must be over," said Seth, troubled by thoughts of his sister.

"Maybe it's time for our feast then 'bor."

What happened in the warm, dark hours belonged to them alone. Many lures led Seth into Cutty's arms – and they were strong arms, as indeed, were his own, grown stronger than he had ever imagined possible – and softer, too, if the occasion required. Just then, the occasion did.

* * *

Back in Ely, Seth hurried to the old jeweller's shop shared with Hurdy-Gurdy. As he climbed the rickety stairs, a familiar voice rose in thunderous protest.

"Fie! Be gone, foul crone, with your noxious ministrations! I'll drink no more sludge. Show me the mirror. I wish to see how your potions have undone my beauty."

Moments later, the same voice cooed with admiration. "Why, Declan, you handsome old rogue, you!"

Seth clattered up the stairs, splintering a rotten floorboard, until Hurdy-Gurdy stood before him, no longer on a bed of sweat-stained blankets, but upright – though terribly grey and gaunt.

An ancient woman in homespun clothes, Old Meggie, was trying to angle a bowl of pea-green medicine to his mouth. Hurdy flapped her away. Tears started to Seth's eyes.

"You're awake! You're fucking awake!"

Hurdy-Gurdy examined his young friend sadly. "Am I awake, *mon ami*? It has been said, 'We are such stuff as dreams are made on, and our little lives are rounded with a sleep.' I wonder if I am still dreaming the same dream I did when just a little child."

"Sod that crap!" Seth gave him a tight hug.

"Oh, he's warm!" declared Gurdy. "If this be magic, let it be an art beautiful as eating."

Seth noticed something glinting on the table. The Baytown Jewel. He had left it there for safekeeping.

"There is much to talk about," said Gurdy.

While they breakfasted, Hurdy-Gurdy listened to all that had occurred since he fell ill. When Seth asked what malady had laid him low, the City-man grimaced.

"All live on borrowed time, Young Nuncle, but some are more in debt than others. My body is fading collateral."

Hurdy broke into a keening, mournful song:
"A great while ago the world begun,
With hey, ho, the wind and the rain,
But that's all one, our play is done,

THIRTEEN

And we'll strive to please you every day."

Seth could say little to that. Nor did he wish to provoke another verse. Hurdy's attention, however, had drifted to the Baytown Jewel. After questioning Seth about Helen Devereux's gift and message, he scavenged a jeweller's kit of tools from the shop below. With these, he worked at the tiny catch on the talisman's side.

"Naturally, I remember Helen Devereux, Blair Gover's consort," he said. "She had a small reputation as a violinist before the plagues. Nothing compared to my own fame, of course."

"Of course," said Seth.

"It says little for her taste that she stuck with that heartless monster for nigh on a century. Mind you, people do change. And sometimes for the better."

He examined Seth with a raised eyebrow. Then he returned to tinkering with a screwdriver.

"Still, she is the very last person I would have expected to . . . Ah!" The catch clicked. Easing up the lid, Hurdy-Gurdy looked inside. "Behold!"

"Anything useful?" Seth doubted so small a container as the Baytown Jewel could conceal a weapon capable of harming almighty Albion.

"A pearl of great price," said Hurdy.

He extracted what indeed looked like a pearl – or an ivory, translucent pea.

Seth snorted. "I risked my life for *that*?"

"You risked well."

Hurdy's affable face assumed an intensity that made Seth sit up. The City-man rose, and began to throw their few possessions in a travel sack.

* * *

They hurried to Cutty's cottage. The young Fen Man sat in the garden, weaving eel traps from strips of split willow. As the two young men greeted each other, both looked away, uncertain of last night's intimacies.

When Seth blushed, Hurdy smiled, his glance darting between their faces.

"Hey ho," he said. "You have been busy during my little siesta, I divine. In and out we go!"

Seth tried to sound gruff. "Cutty, we was wondering if there's news from the scouts you sent to Peterborough?"

They had returned that morning with news. None of it pretty. Hundreds slaughtered by drones though many times that number survived. It seemed the Pilgrimage of Fools had failed before it even began.

Hurdy conferred with Cutty, their voices low and urgent. They seemed to be arguing. The Fen Man was being asked to help against the City.

Seth could have told Gurdy not to waste his breath. The Fen Folk were the opposite of warriors. He watched Hurdy open the locket and explain to Cutty what it contained.

A long pause. Cutty scratched his mop of curly hair.

"Ah," he said in his expressive way. Then he nodded. Just once.

Hurdy beckoned for Seth to join them.

"Well, well, well," said the City-man. "I have convinced your young friend to take us to Peterborough. And perhaps further, eh, Mister Smart?"

He leered. "Why not keep each other company on the way. Though they say two's company and three's a crowd. Hey ho!"

Cutty met Seth's eye with a bold grin. "You thought you was the only crazed hero round here, didn't you, 'bor? Your pal here assures me the City won't ignore us forever. And I'm reckoning he's right. So I'll go as far as Peterborough. Find out, as we like to say, how the reeds are bending."

"You'll join us, Cutty! I'm glad."

The young man laughed. "I can't help feeling sort of responsible for you, I do. Wouldn't want some na-asty bog sucking you drylanders under now, would we?"

FOURTEEN

"Don't lose heart, friends," urged Michael Pilgrim.

Twenty or so folk stood ready to leave Peterborough, bags on their shoulders. The only thing still marking them out as soldiers were their weapons.

"It's a long walk home," he continued. "If we do return, it is safer to travel together. Bide a few more days. Everything will be decided soon."

An angry debate followed amongst the people. Though they were deeply afraid, his argument about safety in numbers won through. Michael comforted himself he retained some authority, even after the failed incursion into Albion and disaster on the old ghost road. Not that he would blame anyone for heading home. Hope, his grandfather had been fond of saying, is the thing with feathers. If so, the wild flock that led them here had almost flown.

He did not mention his suspicion Lady Veil knew very well how drones think when she lined up the column on the motorway. Nor did it escape his notice all their best fighters, including the fanatical Grow People, miraculously survived, concealed in deep woods. If Lady Veil's plan had been to distract the drones from attacking the main force, it worked. Mostly, the slaughter revealed how small a threat they were to the City.

Among those lost, an old friend and ally. Michael had known Mister

FOURTEEN

Priestman all his life. Yet if they fled now, Priestman's sacrifice would be for nothing. Thankfully, Iona was safe with their unborn child back in the North. New life gifted to the world was always the best kind of hope.

* * *

The summer was blithely indifferent to human hope or despair. After days of rain, the weather turned, lulling Michael's fears with soft blue skies. Pleasant breezes cooled the midday sun. The vice constricting his gut and heart since fleeing from the black railway tunnel beneath Albion loosened.

He found himself longing for summer in Baytown, the sea changing colour from blue to green to grey with the moods of the sky. Longing, too, for his son, George, who had been badly neglected by his harried father. That would change for good if he ever made it home.

So what, if abandoning the Pilgrimage of Fools meant the end of hope when it came to vanquishing the City? The Five Cities had been omnipotent as gods since their foundation. Well then, so they would remain. All he possessed was a brief life. It was time to harvest as much happiness as he could garner.

A day after rejoining the army, Michael rode off to inspect the drones' work on the old ghost road. Tom Higginbottom accompanied him, along with Lady Veil and Gover. Surly silence lay between the leaders. That morning, Michael had intervened forcibly when Lady Veil tried to hang a few deserters. Her black-uniformed zealots had already tied the nooses when Michael stopped them. If folk fled – he argued – so be it. Already, several companies had departed in the night. He had been relieved when Lady Veil bowed to his demands, though the rage in her eyes boded trouble. The closer she drew to Albion, the more he doubted her sanity.

Out on the motorway, no one spoke. Bodies and burned weapons lay scattered.

They stayed on their horses, surveying the carnage. The beasts nickered nervously. Gover, concealed in his deep hood and mask, stirred first.

"Well, Pilgrim," he said, "what is to be done?"

They had discussed their dilemmas the night before. Firstly, finding another means of entering Albion to reach Gover's hidden laboratory. No solution to that. Then came the question whether his laboratory, and codes hidden within it, would even be unguarded. It seemed improbable. The City had discovered his access tunnel to the abandoned underground station. They were probably scouring the laboratory right now to discover the rest of his secrets. Without Gover's precious codes all prospect of success was lost.

Lady Veil's hands moved. Her interpreter spoke.

"She says, 'If this army is allowed to disperse, it will never form again. To retreat now is to surrender forever.'"

"What is your alternative?" asked Michael. "We cannot risk another massacre like this."

"She says, 'We should conduct a thorough examination of the full circuit of Albion's perimeter. Perhaps they have grown careless. As for this renegade.'" Lady Veil indicated Gover. "'It is certain he knows more than he is letting on. I suggest you allow me to question him. In my own way.'"

For once, Gover did not sneer in reply. Michael could tell the modified woman disturbed him. Even a few crumbs of revenge against Gover would taste sweet to Lady Veil. Whatever usefulness he once possessed was vanishing fast.

"What do you reckon we should do, Tom?" asked Michael.

Tom Higginbottom was staring up the road with a frown. He took out his binoculars, and grunted.

FOURTEEN

"I reckon we'll have to stay a few days whatever happens. Out of good manners, if nothing else. We've got company. And they won't take kindly to turning tail the moment they arrive."

He passed Michael the binoculars. What they revealed tightened the vice in his gut another notch.

A large column of soldiers, some mounted, most on foot, along with wagons for supplies, advanced like a centipede down the old ghost road. Flags at the front fluttered bravely: entwined white and red roses for Yorkshire and Lancashire, a popular symbol in the Commonwealth of the North; Nuager standards, too, depicting star, flower and moon.

Other standards he recognised with amazement. They belonged to enemies he and Tom fought on Lindisfarne, just six months earlier. One was deep blue with three white stars: the Kingdom of Buchan's banner. The second, that of Adair, King of Fife, a red lion rearing across two bands of yellow and sky blue.

"There's a load of fucking Jocks with them!" cried Michael.

He focused the binoculars and was rewarded with another unpleasant surprise. Riding a white mare at the front was the last person on Earth, apart from his son, he wanted within twenty miles of Albion. The person with whom he hoped to build a future. The woman whose image haunted the best, and softest, part of his soul. The lady he had learned to honour deeply for her courage, grace and compassion. Iona of Skye, wearing the many-coloured robes of a Nuager Priestess, had joined the Pilgrimage of Fools.

"Best if I ride ahead before they stumble on this little lot," said Tom Higginbottom, nodding at the corpses surrounding them. "Otherwise, they might just head back the way they came."

An event Michael would have welcomed, so long as Iona led the retreat.

* * *

That night, Iona sat late with Michael Pilgrim in a tumbled down supermarket, along with scores of Lindisfarne Nuager volunteers, including many of her own people from Skye. For several miles around, ribbons of smoke dispersed into a hazy twilight. The army's leaders had struggled to limit fires except for communal cooking. Demoralised hearts craved light and comfort. Michael feared that if drones came to investigate, the night would truly blaze.

Still, their own fire cast a dancing glow. A stew of salt pork, lentils and vegetables warmed their stomachs. The reinforcements had brought much needed provisions.

Iona lay with her head cradled in Michael's arms. His hand rested on her stomach where the baby swelled imperceptibly, hour by hour. Iona was gifted with the art of companionable silence; another of her qualities he was learning to appreciate.

"I do wish you had not come," he sighed.

"That you have made clear."

"It's not you I am unhappy to see!"

"Except it is, Michael Pilgrim."

"Here. Yes. Of course. Can you blame me?"

"I could not abandon my people. Just as you could not forsake your own."

Bright ribbons of galaxies looked down at them through a gaping hole in the roof.

"You have come to believe our cause is hopeless, haven't you?" she said, quietly.

He looked round to see if anyone overheard.

"Aye."

"And you blame yourself for all those who have lost their lives?"

"I suppose that I do."

"You do yourself a wrong, Michael."

A lone voice disturbed the night. A bright, clear tenor, charged with longing.

Sing me a song of a soul that is gone,
Say, could that soul be I?
Merry of soul he sails on a day
Over the sea to sky.
Billow and breeze, islands and seas,
Mountains of rain and sun,
All that is good, all that is fair,
All that is me is sun.

It brought to Michael's mind the struggles they had shared. How he was almost cut in two by a City-sword to save Iona from burning as a witch. They survived constant dangers back then. Perhaps all was not lost now.

Certainly, the reinforcements more than made up for their losses. Among them were companies of hillmen and reivers, formidable warriors. In fact, folk from all over the North were still heeding the call to arms. Yesterday a small band even joined them from down London way. Word of the Pilgrimage was spreading, swift as plague.

"I see you came with Aggie Brown from Malton," he said. "And that brain-addled rogue, Baxter. Both were Crusaders with me and Tom. Shame we can't drop Aggie into Albion with those butchers' knives she's so fond of. It'd all be over before breakfast."

Iona held him a little tighter. "I sensed terrible cruelty in her soul."

"The Crusades seeded and watered bloody tastes in Aggie. It would be a great irony if she paid them back to the City. But isn't that true of everyone here? We have grown too used to fighting. To the apparent worthlessness of life. The City has never allowed us to trust in peace. I always dreamt defeating them would allow humanity a second chance. And that, this time around, mankind might get it right."

She squeezed his hand. "That is a dream worth preserving."

"How did you persuade King Adair of Fife to send so many warriors?"

he asked. "And led by his eldest son, no less?"

"It was your work," she said.

"I sent them no summons."

"No, I did that much. But you spared Adair's life when he believed it lost at Lindisfarne. In exchange, you asked only for a vow of peace. And that he would provide help when needed."

"I never expected him to honour that promise."

"People are better than you allow."

"Well, I suppose you haggis-eating Scots are famous for your prickly sense of honour."

She laughed. "As are you pie-eating Tykes."

"Ah, for a mutton pie!"

More light talk might have healed his heart a little. But Michael Pilgrim's fate tended in other directions. A messenger appeared at the entrance of the overgrown supermarket.

"Where is the Protector of the North? He must come at once. Something has happened."

* * *

Something turned out to be someone given up for dead weeks earlier.

Michael, Tom Higginbottom and Iona hurried over to the hotel where Lady Veil held court. Here, a basement had been converted into a makeshift control room, complete with table and maps. Other commanders of the small army were present, mostly expecting a plan to lead them home.

Michael frowned at the sight of Blair Gover on a stool in the corner. His hands bound together with leather twine. A fresh welt across his face suggested the generous application of a riding crop.

All this, he took in at a glance. What made him step forward, a glad cry on his lips, were three shabby travellers: Seth Pilgrim, Hurdy-

FOURTEEN

Gurdy and a young man he did not recognise.

"Seth! We thought you were . . ."

No need to say what.

"But you're here, Seth, that's what matters."

When the lad met his eye, Michael had an odd sense his dead brother, James, was looking at him.

Hurdy-Gurdy bowed with a flourish. He seemed thin as famine.

"You will not guess what is in *my* pocketses," he said. "I have a little trinket. A bauble. A sparkly-warkly, tinselly-winselly thing."

Hurdy-Gurdy bowed ironically to Blair Gover.

"What an honour! Noble, puissant Bertrand Du Guesclin!"

Gover's mouth twitched with contempt. "Still playing the tedious clown, O'Hara."

"I can play other games. Guessing games. What does Doctor Gover guess we have in our pocketses?"

"Clearly not sanity."

"Ho ho! Do take a look at this."

Hurdy-Gurdy pulled out an object familiar to Michael since boyhood.

"How the hell did you get your hands on the Baytown Jewel?" he asked.

Hurdy-Gurdy's yellow-tinged eyes did not leave Gover's face. Abruptly, he crooned:

"Once I had a sprig of thyme,
It grew both night and day,
Till the false young man came a-courting to me
And he stole all my thyme away."

As he sang, he flipped open the locket, extracting a pea-sized, translucent pearl. It glowed in the candlelight.

The effect on Gover was instantaneous. He lurched to his feet, reaching out bound hands.

"Give it to me!"

Hurdy-Gurdy raised the pearl between finger and thumb.

"Finders keepers, losers weepers."

Gover's feverish gaze did not shift from the pearl.

"How did you come by it?"

"Why not tell them, Seth?" said Hurdy. "Yes, you can be old Gurdy's glamorous assistant for this command performance. The credit belongs to you, not me."

Michael listened with amazed pride as his nephew told the tale of Helen Devereux and the drone attack at King's Lynn. How his young friend – introduced as Cutty Smart – rescued them when they were stranded on the salt marshes. How Seth had recruited a sizable number of strangelings to assist in their fight against the City. How, more incredibly still, Helen Devereux and Averil had appeared in a vast hologram projected over Albion. The packed room of leaders from all over the North and Midlands listened to the tale in respectful silence. If only James could see his wastrel, wayward son now!

"Well bugger me sideways," Tom Higginbottom muttered. "You've done right well, lad. First time ever."

Seth flushed with pride. Although he was not aware of it, his shoulders went back a notch.

"Gover," said Michael. "Several times you've asked after the Baytown Jewel. Did you hide this pearl, or whatever it is, inside the locket for safekeeping? And leave it in the Baytown Museum, where none of your enemies would ever suspect?"

Dozens of eyes were upon the City-renegade.

"I can confirm it is my property, Pilgrim. Therefore, I insist upon its immediate return." He held out his hands.

Hurdy-Gurdy waved the pearl. "Jump, boy! Jump, Rover!" he urged.

"What does it do?" asked Michael.

"Hurdy knows, sir!" cried the old holotainer, thrusting up his hand like an eager schoolboy. "Gurdy knows, sir! Can he have a merit, sir?"

FOURTEEN

Gover exhaled slowly. "It seems I must beg for what belongs to me. Know this, Pilgrim. It is nothing. Such toys are used in Albion to store data. You would not understand, of course. Suffice to say, it contains trifles I value for personal reasons."

Lady Veil's hands moved, though not in sign language. She planted herself before Gover, and struck him viciously.

"Give him a chance to answer first," Michael warned.

Gover touched his bleeding lip.

"I have told you what you need to know."

Lady Veil drew back her arm to strike again then thought better of it. She gestured to her interpreter.

"She says, 'He is lying, of course. We need to know exactly what data is stored in the info-pearl. I will torture him with fire to find out.'"

Given the peril of their situation, Michael could hardly prevent her. Drones might return any moment. If there were the slightest chance of this pearl aiding them, it must be taken.

Then he had a sudden thought. Why else would Gover risk entering Albion through a tunnel that might easily have been guarded? Why, for that matter, hide something so valuable in the Baytown Museum, far from the City? Michael's suspicion became a certainty.

"No need for torture," he said.

Iona nodded approvingly. "There's never a need for *that*."

Not yet, thought Michael.

"I believe that I have the answer." He turned to Gover. "This little thing is what you were hoping to find in Albion, isn't it? Or something exactly like it. Its twin, as it were. Am I right?"

Gover considered. "Perhaps."

"So, I am right."

"Very well, yes, yes, yes. Good for you, Pilgrim. What a clever boy you are turning out to be."

Michael felt a stab of excitement. The City-man had promised to shut down all power in Albion with this jewel. Deactivate and render harmless the drones and security systems. Incredible as it seemed, this little globe was a key of some kind. But tiny keys could open apparently impregnable doors.

As quickly as hope flared, it died. Unless they gained entry into Albion, the pearl was useless. Gover had made it clear he needed machines contained within that venomous hive's walls to bring the place to a juddering halt.

Michael sighed. "We still don't know how to get inside the City. Unless we find a way in, we are no nearer success than when we did not have the pearl."

"Now that ain't entirely the case, 'bor," spoke up Cutty.

The Fen Man's accent was strange to Michael's ears, even a little comical.

"I'm a-thinkin'," added Cutty, 'there's a crazy girl back in Ely who might help if you asked nicely."

"What he means, Uncle," said Seth, "is that the Fen Folk have discovered a way to get in and out of Albion."

Stunned silence. Michael Pilgrim took out a knife and sawed through the leather twine binding Gover's hands.

"If at first you don't succeed . . ." he said, grimly. "Welcome back to the party, Gover. Looks like we'll be sight-seeing in Albion, after all."

FIFTEEN

Averil Pilgrim recovered swiftly from the Caesarean birth. Youth helped, as did the City's medical technology, diligently applied by Dr Wakuki.

For days she lay unconscious in a bath of amniotic fluid, the neat excisions below her stomach healing. Baby entered her dreams like a whale floating through dark waters. Nothing felt real, except constant unease.

Then Averil was released from her coma-like state. She opened her eyes to find Dora and Dr Wakuki watching her. Holograms displayed information about her bodily functions, manipulated by Wakuki's skilful fingers. He hummed softly as numbers rolled and images of her vital organs flashed.

Smiling, Dora took Averil's hand. "Welcome back," said the plump, motherly woman.

"Where . . . where is Baby? Is he well?"

Dr Wakuki pursed his lips. Averil realised he was troubled.

"As well as can be expected," he said. "First, you must eat, rest, begin courses of exercise. Your readings are very encouraging. You are a strong girl, Averil. I suspect that is what kept you alive during the latter stages of your pregnancy."

Averil's alarm flared. "Please tell me, is Baby deformed?"

When he attempted an encouraging smile his face looked strange.

"I want you to always remember that *deformed* is a matter of perspective," he said. "Whatever happens, you have done well, Averil. You have fulfilled all that was expected of you. As a reward, I have insisted you are given a free choice."

"I don't want no choice. I want to see my baby."

"You will see him . . . her . . . *them*."

"What do you mean, *them*? Did I have twins? It was so heavy in my womb, so full."

A hypo-syringe was applied. Averil span back into murky dreams.

* * *

The next day, she was again woken by Dora and Wakuki. Her first sensation: breasts uncomfortably overcharged with milk. This time, she was encouraged to dress in a suit of grey silk. Although the cut across her womb ached a little, she felt remarkably active.

Going over to the plasti-glass window, currently set to opaque, she adjusted it to transparent.

It revealed a great drop. Her room was a dozen storeys high, right on the perimeter of Albion's central cluster of large, interconnected tower blocks. A bright summer morning provided clear views. Pleasure parks stretched to the dark line of the boundary walls, six or seven miles distant. In between, lakes glittered between manmade hills.

Splendid pavilions and pleasure facilities dotted the green sward. Many clustered round the River Great Ouse, flowing through a series of shallow lakes. Flocks of swans and geese were visible on the water. Of people, there were few. With the population of Albion so reduced, Beautifuls used to leisure were forced into long hours of daily work.

Averil recalled Dr Wakuki saying she had fulfilled all expected of her. What did that mean? Something to do with a choice. And where was Baby? The child he referred to as *them*?

FIFTEEN

She turned from the window. The object of her thoughts had entered, quiet as a cat.

"Albion is beautiful, is it not?" said Wakuki. "And safe enough, if you follow the rules." An idea seemed to disturb him. "Though that is not what Mughalia and the people in the other Cities found true."

He glanced round furtively, aware the word Mughalia would have triggered surveillance. "That was . . . regrettable but unavoidable," he added.

Averil wondered what lay beneath his words. Wakuki remained, as always, a mystery.

"In a few minutes you must make a simple decision," he said. "No one can make it for you. Follow me."

He led her from the bare room with its austere bed and equipment, a place she would never visit again save in memories and dreams. An elevator whisked them to the thirteenth floor.

Here, lay a suite of offices, mostly unvisited except by cleaning drones. Dora and Wakuki conducted Averil to a heavy, padded chair in the middle of an empty conference room.

"Sit," said Wakuki. "Lay your arms on the rests."

She did so. Automated bands snaked from the chair, trapping her arms and wrists. Averil squealed.

"Why?" she cried. "I've done nothing wrong! Where's Baby? I want to see my baby."

"You shall," said Wakuki.

"Why have you tied me up?"

"Because we don't know how you will react to Baby."

Apprehension became certainty. Baby was deformed, monstrous. Just like when they exposed her son on the beach. Only more hideous. Why else would they think she might harm her own child?

"Now is the time for your choice," said Wakuki.

* * *

Dora left quietly. Minutes passed. Neither Averil nor Wakuki spoke.

Her chair faced a large window, whether deliberately or by accident. She could see a boulevard flanked by more tower blocks with extravagant garden balconies and landing facilities on their roofs. These megaliths marched down to Albion's core, the Double Helix Statue. Her heart beat uncomfortably.

Behind her, the door opened. Instantly, she detected a smell both familiar and strange. She struggled against her bindings to look behind her. There was no need. Dora appeared, guiding a drone cot on wheels, complete with monitoring devices, feeding nipples, temperature regulators. On the cot, visible through transparent sides, lay a naked baby. Her baby!

But Averil was seeing things. She shook her head. Closed her eyes to clear the blur. Except, when she opened them, the same. It must be the medicine she was taking, a delusion. Where was Baby? This was not Baby.

"It is real," said Wakuki, softly. "Or *they* are."

She mewed with nausea. She strained to escape the straps pinning her. She appealed to Dora, who hovered by the mobile cot, twisting a pair of surgical gloves.

Then Averil risked looking again. And hyperventilated.

In essential respects, it was a normal infant. Two legs and feet kicking feebly. Two arms and tiny hands twitching. Its skin, however, was maggoty pale rather than healthy pink. It was grotesquely large for a week-old child, as though its organs and flesh were over-ripe.

Such features did not make Averil gasp for air. No, the child was unlike any other. Could never be like other children. Nor was it designed to be. Instead of a single head, it had been engineered to have two.

Averil detected recognisable faces on the different heads, the shapes of chins and noses, eye colour. Absurd – and revolting – the heads reminded her of two particular people. The right, a female, Merle Brubacher. The left, a square-jawed male, Marvin Brubacher.

Her gaze shifted instinctively to the creature's genitalia. A tiny penis hung above what was clearly a vagina, so that – like the heads – one could not say whether the child was male or female.

Air gathered in her lungs to scream. She looked round for Dora, for any friend. Tears glistened on the meditech's plump cheeks. Yet Averil's scream became a whoop of controlled, exhaled breath. No, she would not scream. Here, before her, was the choice Wakuki promised. She must not appear weak. Weren't many of the new Angels equally grotesque? She understood the monstrous child not as a choice, but as a test.

"What did you do to my real baby?" she asked.

Wakuki seemed to quiver: unless it was an involuntary twitch of the eye. He stepped over to the cot, then looked out of the window.

"If you promise to listen calmly, I will explain," he said. "Can you do that?"

Averil nodded.

"First, you must understand one thing very clearly. This . . ." He hesitated. "This child – or hybrid – is not yours. Your genes are not in it. Do you understand?"

Another nod.

"When you came to Albion I was given clear instructions. Instructions I could not refuse. Your natural child was aborted, this one replacing it in your womb. Your body has been hosting an astonishing experiment."

His voice gathered confidence as he droned out a series of technical details. Averil only half heard. All she knew was this: they had scoured Baby from her womb. A memory came to her. A cuckoo singing in the graveyard of Holy Innocents Church back in Hob Vale. Uncle Michael had explained how it laid an egg in the nest of a blackbird. How the chick hatched first and lifted the rival eggs onto its back when the blackbird parents were away foraging. It then rolled them out of the nest, to break and stain the headstone beneath with shell fragments and slimy yolk.

She became aware of Wakuki's voice.

"You perhaps see why the child was designed to be so unusual. When the Joint-Presidents learned of my discovery, they squabbled fiercely whose genes would be the first to create a child. Their passion was understandable. It is a miracle worthy of history. Ever since gene-renewal we have all been sterile. Here, at last, was a solution, building upon Dr Guy Price's remarkable work to create Angels. For once, I could help create new life, rather than taking it away. In your case, I . . . I had explicit instructions I could not ignore." He licked his thin lips. "Even though I might wish to have done so."

Averil felt only numbness. Baby was gone. Murdered, like the blackbird chicks. Why did she not feel angry? She had raged when they exposed her son on the beach at Ravenscar. Why not now?

"I come now to your choice, Averil," said Dr Wakuki.

Dora stepped forward with a cry of concern. "Has she not suffered enough?"

"Silence!"

The meditech shrank back.

"What is my choice?" whispered Averil.

"To stay in Albion as part of my team. To help rear this first experiment. If so, I shall ensure you become a Beautiful, living as we must, forever. Or – and this is not to be rejected lightly – I have extracted a firm undertaking from the Brubachers. You shall be returned to your primitive home, entirely unharmed, and with great wealth in City things. Think wisely, Averil. Remember, the Five Cities no longer exist. They have been turned to ash. There is just Albion now. Just Albion."

The way he uttered that name made Dora look at him in surprise.

Still, Averil wondered why she was not angry. They had lied and lied. They had tricked and abused her. They had killed Baby – though perhaps Baby would have died anyway. Only Beautifuls did not die.

She gazed the full length of the boulevard visible outside the window with its miraculous mansions. An aircar descended, lights flashing.

Then she turned to Wakuki.

"Yes," she said. "Yes."

* * *

That same afternoon, Averil was conducted to Marvin and Merle Brubacher's palace. The Joint-Presidents shared a large tower with scores of hangers-on. This coterie, protected by drones and Guardian Angels, all muscle, claw and scaly hide, formed Albion's new elite, the Perfects.

Most Beautifuls strove for Perfection through obedient service, rebuilding a fraction of their incalculable losses – losses it was Discordia to even mention. Nevertheless, compensations were imminent. Britain and Ireland, as well as selected zones of Northern France, would be divided into personal fiefdoms, allocated by the Ruling Council.

"Ah, there you are," said Marvin Brubacher, as Averil entered the rooftop garden where they dined.

Merle Brubacher sat beside him. As usual, her exquisitely sculpted face suggested discontent. She waved a hand. "Come! I want a closer look at it."

Dora and Averil conducted the mobile cot to the table.

The Joint-Presidents leaned forward curiously. The child lay on its back, twitching occasionally.

"What do you think?" asked Marvin, popping lobster into his mouth.

"Mmm."

"Quite."

"Quite what?"

"Ugly little girl, isn't she?" he said.

"You mean ugly *boy*."

He waved his fork and chuckled. "I mean, it's neither fish nor fowl."

"True," said Merle.

"It's certainly less pleasing on the eye than I expected. Wakuki has disappointed me this time."

"Wakuki's *compromise*, as the good doctor called it, was yet another miscalculation on his part," said Merle. "I am beginning to wonder if his heart is in his work."

"It was you who insisted the firstborn of his new process should represent us both," said Marvin.

"You forget, darling. I do believe it was *you* who agreed to the two heads thing."

Merle examined the child again. She seemed to feel no urge to touch her progeny.

"Don't be too hard on Wakuki," said Marvin. "He has demonstrated incubation works. It is his other delays that concern me."

"Indeed."

He turned to Dora and Averil, who bowed low.

"Ensure it lives as long as possible. At a minimum, until the Great Assignation. We may wish to display it."

Merle's face softened. "Do you breastfeed it?" she asked.

"Yes, ma'am."

"Good, good. Breast is best," she said, retrieving the phrase from a great depth. "They always used to tell new mothers that. Marvin, my love, do you know, I even tried breastfeeding you, my darling boy. Think of it!"

Marvin smiled back. Yet his eyes were as drained of warmth as his mother's.

"Did you? I'm surprised. It doesn't sound your style."

"Well, I did give it a go. It was expected of proper mummies back then."

Marvin extracted some white flesh from a langoustine. Merle's face reverted to her usual wary coldness.

"Take it away," she said. "And remember, breast is best."

* * *

Averil learned a whole new anxiety. If the monstrous child died, and didn't look exactly bonny, who would be blamed?

No journey to Honeycomb for her then, no renewal of her cells when her skin dried out like last year's rose petals. No possibility of outliving frailty in her own mini-kingdom.

Rumours of the Great Assignation, as it was known, flooded Albion's holostreams. Every Beautiful was commanded to attend on pain of Discordia. There, all would learn what land had been granted to them and their future descendants, unborn children incubated using Dr Wakuki's new method.

With so much at stake, little wonder Averil feared being judged useless by the Ruling Council. Over the coming centuries, vast labours lay ahead for true humanity. Only those fit for the task would be allowed a role. Calls for volunteers to develop specialist knowledge were broadcast daily. Facilities to acquire minerals and metals and oil must be rebuilt for the manufacture of drones. The existing capacity for Angel-nurturing must increase tenfold, a hundredfold, if the demand for obedient labour was to be met. Enormous scientific obstacles remained, especially as the Five Cities' best brains had perished in a white glare of fusion bombs. Not to mention those lost to gene sickness, or expelled from Albion.

Yet a new optimism coursed through the City, stirring minds jaded by endless leisure. Change itself had been reborn. Was not humanity made for competition and change? And the world was limitless, a blank sheet, entirely vacant save for adaptable flora and fauna. Evolution itself was now the servant of mankind.

Advances might be slow, even faltering, but millennia lay ahead. No more torpor and sameness. One's precious life could begin in earnest.

So it was discussed on official holocasts from the Ruling Council masquerading as news. The Great Assignation would commence this brave new world. Those who dared to doubt kept their opinions very quiet.

* * *

Dr Wakuki summoned Averil to his apartment, a labyrinth of high-ceilinged rooms and corridors.

Wakuki motioned Averil to sit. He seemed weary of spirit. She was reminded of his tears when the Five Cities ended in blinding flashes and clouds of dust. She listened in silence as he described the task he had been given, to find a new strain of plague to resolve the primitive problem forever.

"It is a question of two dilemmas," he said, as though thinking aloud. "Easy in theory. But *they* have no idea how dangerous – and probably impossible – it would be to avoid cross-contamination. There are always survivors. Always. I learned that in my work culling primitive-swarms on the Chinese mainland, when I lived in Han City. *They* refuse to see that."

"You mean Marvin and Merle, don't you?" she said. "They want you to do this thing?"

He did not reply.

FIFTEEN

"Could you invent such a plague?" she whispered.

He looked at her steadily. "I believe that I already have. Though once released it would soon mutate beyond all control, whatever *they* think."

Averil rubbed her mouth. Nothing seemed beyond his miraculous powers.

"I have seen what the plague does to people," she said. "It is terrible."

"Of course." He looked into her eyes steadily. "Does what I have created disgust you? I have devised a means to wipe out every person you ever met among the primitives. Do you think me a monster?"

"No, no."

"Perhaps you should."

Averil suspected another test.

"You . . . you must save the Beautiful Life, that is what matters." she said. One of her uncle's favourite words came to her. "That is your duty."

Sadness crossed his face. He exhaled slowly.

"A good answer," he said. "You will go far in Albion. Now run along."

Averil almost clasped his hand with relief, sure she had passed his test. Perhaps it was time to mention to Marvin and Merle which fief she hoped to gain from the Great Assignation.

As she rose to leave, he activated long lines of holoscript data. His gaze was oddly unfocused. He hummed a strange song. Had she known such things, she would have recognised it as a lullaby.

* * *

Dazed by the implications of Dr Wakuki's words, Averil wandered into the centre of Albion. With the gene sickness at last cured, Beautifuls mingled freely, gathering in cafes to be served dwindling supplies of now exotic coffee and tea; more importantly, to be seen and acknowledged. All were in competition. The prize on offer presented itself to Averil as she entered the Double Helix Plaza.

At the foot of the towering statue, an area had been converted into a three-dimensional, glowing relief map of Britain, including rivers and mountains to scale. Ireland, Brittany and Northern France were also presented. Around the map were holoconsoles to zoom in on specific areas. The Greater Britain on display contained thousands of distinct, glowing scales, each scale a separate fiefdom. Some were large, evidently intended for those judged most worthy by the Ruling Council; others were relative specks, destined for Beautifuls without particular status.

Averil noticed how tiny filaments of glowing lines connected each fiefdom to Albion. However large the fiefdom, it would always be dependent on Albion for fresh supplies of Angels or drones. Likewise, for technology and produce from the new colonia being established to replace those destroyed. In effect, the Ruling Council based in Albion would retain absolute control while granting apparent independence to each mini-kingdom. No doubt, only limited weapons, sufficient to guarantee one's personal protection would be allowed. It was already public knowledge that acts of Discordia would result in the re-assignment of one's fief.

A familiar figure could be seen inspecting the map. Yet Dora, as a meditech, could never hope to qualify for the Great Assignation. Averil motioned her over.

"Dora! What fief do you think I should ask for?"

The older woman met Averil's eye.

"Do you want to be a queen now?"

Unwelcome memories of Queen Morrighan touched Averil. Power had turned that petty, scheming woman into a tyrannical brute. How inevitably her fall flowed from the transformation.

FIFTEEN

"I deserve something for bearing that hideous child."

"Yes, something."

"Well, my mind is made up," declared Averil. "I shall ask for Baytown at the Assignation. And as much of the area around it as possible. That way, I can keep safe the people I have known."

"If any are left alive," said Dora, "you can have the pleasure of being worshipped. First, it is time to feed the child. Remember, breast is best."

As they summoned a drone-taxi to whisk them to the Presidential Palace, mobile tiers of seating began to arrive for the ceremony. It occurred to Averil almost everything – apart from organic servants like Angels or technicians like Dora – relied on electronic signals from a central system to function. It would have appalled her to learn that others, less than thirty miles away, pinned desperate hopes on the same fact.

SIXTEEN

"What do you mean it's the wrong kind of barge?" Already several barges had passed along the River Great Ouse from King's Lynn. Michael Pilgrim's question was addressed to a diminutive young woman, wiry as an elver. Each time, she shook her head and fingered a mobile phone from the Before Times, her personal lucky charm.

"Got to be patient, 'bor," advised Cutty. "And trust Young Ell here."

They hid in a dense stand of weeping willows, watching the barge glide slowly towards Albion. The city's towers rose, fabulous in the distance.

Patience was a virtue Michael had practised hard over the last fortnight. Finalising the Fool's Plan, as everyone called their mad, last-ditch attempt to bring down the City. Gathering troops and dividing them into new units called Hundreds. Scouting out lands around Albion and access points through its boundary wall. Persuading those inclined to flee they could yet succeed, nay, must succeed.

"What's the right kind of barge going to look like?"

Ell's grin revealed as many black teeth as grey.

"She'll know when it comes," interpreted Cutty.

Michael recollected his grandfather saying, "For trust to exist, Michael, first one must risk trust." Certainly, faith in folk's better nature had worked for Reverend Oliver Pilgrim when preserving

SIXTEEN

Baytown. Why not now?

"I'll make sure everyone is ready," he said, backing out of the undergrowth.

He followed an ancient pipe for draining the low-lying land. Its shadow concealed folk as restless as their leader.

Michael had selected the raiding party with great care. The qualities he needed most: reliability, courage, stealth, resourcefulness, pluck in a fight and willingness to die. Not much to ask for then. Michael would love to possess such qualities himself. Either way, he had chosen Tom Higginbottom, Cutty Smart and Hurdy-Gurdy.

Young Ell, of course, was the person the whole venture depended on. At least, for the apparently impossible task of sneaking into Albion. Once inside, the Fool's Plan relied upon one man alone. Without Blair Gover's unique knowledge of the info-pearl, they might as well scurry home like whipped dogs.

The final member of the party was definitely not of his choosing. At the last minute, Lady Veil had insisted one of her black-uniformed fanatics join them, a cold-eyed creature he had yet to observe smile. He suspected the only thing capable of lifting the corners of Captain Ariana's mouth was a dead City-man.

"We could be here a while longer," he advised. "But we need to be ready to move in an instant."

Gover pulled back the cowl concealing his face. He had gained a new, brooding intensity over the previous days. Michael wanted to interpret it as a sign of determination to make the Fool's Plan succeed. Yet he suffered from an agony of distrust.

"I do not share your confidence in these swamp dwellers," declared Gover.

"They're tough as eels," pointed out Michael. "And can squeeze through narrow places. Gaps conceited heads get stuck."

Cutty's face poked through the undergrowth.

"Time to get a-jumping. Ell has spotted a fair one."

* * *

They grabbed laden backpacks and slung their guns, hastening to pre-assigned places. Four tall scaffolds, spaced out along the straight bank of the Great Ouse, concealed among trees. Each bore a hinged gantry jutting out over the water. The contraptions looked uncomfortably like gallows to Michael.

No orders were needed. The party divided into pairs, save for Ell, the first to go. Michael ensured Gover accompanied him: whatever happened, their fate would be the same. They climbed up a stepladder to a small wooden platform where a rope dangled.

Doubts assailed Michael. Would Gover really destroy the thing he had spent his whole life building? As so often, lines from his grandfather's beloved Shakespeare entered his mind: *I pall in resolution, and begin to doubt the equivocation of the fiend, that lies like truth* . . . Which character had said that? A villain, Michael seemed to remember. And Gover was certainly one of those. Well, there was no turning back now. If resolution waned – and the City-man's promises turned out black lies – courage alone must serve.

A surge of recklessness banished Michael's fears.

"Come on then!"

Gover stepped gingerly onto a small wooden platform attached to the end of the rope. They embraced each other, wrapping their arms round the thick line. The dull waters of the river rippled below.

"Here it comes," said Michael.

A large drone barge slowly advanced, bearing just one rectangular container. Lots of clear deck around it. Lacking a crew, it possessed no cabin.

He could feel Gover tremble. On came the barge. Now it was passing the abandoned drainage pipe, where the first gantry poked through. Michael realised he had stopped breathing. He drew in a big lungful to steady himself. Gover's eyes were inches from his own, staring wildly.

The girl had assured them barges carried no alarm system, except for sensors on the hull to avoid collisions. Clambering up and boarding via the hull, might conceivably trigger some warning, and alert a curious security drone. Hence, the method she had devised.

It had worked well enough before. Maybe the City believed no one was mad enough to stowaway on their transports. Even all-powerful Albion could blunder.

Then the time for doubt was past. A slender figure swung out from the trees on her hinged gantry. Young Ell, gripping a long rope, perched on a small wooden platform like their own. The distance she had to travel no more than thirty feet at this point of the waterway. To Michael it seemed an impassable gulf. Like a trapeze artist the girl arced until, at the furthest limit of the rope, she hung over the barge. At that critical moment, she released her hold, and jumped, landing nimbly on a clear section of deck.

"See how it's done," Michael told Gover. "When I say, let go, bloody well let go."

The barge drew near to where they crouched. They tensed. No time to think. Nearer. Nearer. *Now.* They jumped, solid ground became water beneath them. Wind rushed. Then the barge loomed.

"Let go!"

Seconds later, a jolt as he landed; Michael was surprised how easily. More like stepping across a stream than a leap across a gully. The sides of the barge were low and deck spongy to prevent containers sliding around. And Gover was beside him, steadied by Young Ell.

"Get out the way!" she hissed.

Just in time. Hurdy-Gurdy and Tom Higginbottom swung out and joined them on the deck, Hurdy-Gurdy turning a nimble somersault with the vainglorious cry, "Look at me! Look at me!"

Captain Ariana came last.

"Aargh!" she cried, letting go of the rope too soon and landing in the water at the side of the barge. Before she could be sucked under by bubbling hydrojets, quick hands dragged her aboard.

* * *

Young Ell led them straight to one of the containers, looking for a door. Though previous experience suggested no one was watching, they felt horribly exposed on the barge's open deck. Not least because Ariana's clumsiness might have triggered an alarm. Ell located a hatch and lever on the side bearing the legend: *Manual Entry*.

"Is it alarmed?" asked Michael, nodding at the lever.

She flashed him her black-toothed grin. Pulled it down. A pneumatic hiss followed. The door opened. She motioned them inside.

The container reminded Michael of similar relics from the Before Times. Except this was uncorroded, clean, chilly as a January morning. He played his rechargeable torch round the narrow space and was surprised by huge bunches of a green fruit like curved baby marrows. Some had turned yellow. They hung from hooks or were piled in plastic crates. The beam caught a few spider webs; so they were not the only stowaways.

"What are these vegetables?" he asked, pointing at the marrow-like things.

"Strange fruit," said Hurdy-Gurdy. Then he sang in a mocking voice:
"*Yes, we have some bananas,*
We have some bananas today . . ."

His voice was loud in the confined space.

"Your incessant attention-seeking is pitiful," said Gover. "You are worse than a child."

SIXTEEN

"And you, sirrah," said Gurdy, plucking and peeling a banana, "would be a more pleasant fellow if you remembered the child you once were." He draped the banana skin on his head, gobbling pale mush until his cheeks bulged. Everyone except Gover – and Captain Ariana – could not help smiling.

The fanatical woman was wet and shivering. Michael ordered her to strip and dry herself. Fortunately, Young Ell had insisted they bring blankets.

"What do we do now?" asked Tom Higginbottom.

"We wait, 'bor," said Cutty. "Try to stay warm and quiet. No lights from now on. Ain't that right, Ell?"

She was too busy puzzling how to peel a banana to reply.

Long hours followed. The darkness in the container absolute. Sound became the sole means to judge the world outside. The barge's engines rumbled faintly. Sometimes echoes made everyone freeze or reach instinctively for weapons. After a few hours, the engine noise ceased. A profound silence commenced.

Michael calculated they had boarded the barge late afternoon. Therefore, it must be early evening. He knew the River Great Ouse flowed through heavily monitored water gates to form a large basin for barges to load and unload. He had spent hours examining through binoculars the immense warehouse beside the basin. Perhaps they were in the warehouse.

He risked a thin beam from his torch and picked out Ell's face. She raised a finger to her lips.

More minutes passed. No voices outside. Why should there be? Ell had spoken of drones that seemed not to notice her. When she sneaked round the warehouse, not a single human. It said much for her unusual pluck that the drones did not terrify her. He was learning the Fen Folk were full of surprises. Still, he dreaded the container door opening.

Discovery followed by quick deaths. A compulsion to escape this dark, airless place gripped him. From their restless movements, others in the company seemed to feel the same.

"Hush!" breathed Ell.

The sides of the container clanged. Some giant's hand had gripped it. The floor lurched and Michael felt themselves hoisted. A judder passed through the floor as the container reconnected with solid ground.

Suddenly, there came a slight jolt and noise of motors. They were being carried, surely away from the barge and water basin where it must have docked. Carried heaven knows where.

Michael risked his torch. When its beam found their guide's face, her lopsided grin had gone.

"It didn't do this afore," she whispered. "We was just taken into a big hall full o' boxes like this one."

Michael sought out Gover with the torch. "Any idea where we're going?"

"Straight to hell, like as not," muttered Tom Higginbottom.

SEVENTEEN

While the party of raiders cowered, Averil Pilgrim was led to an echoing, underground hall beneath the Double Helix Statue.

Hard to stay confident amidst so much bustling indifference. Let alone the perpetual smile required for a proper display of Accordia. Hundreds of Beautifuls were donning ceremonial gear, taking up pre-determined positions for the grand procession.

The costumes had been chosen by Merle Brubacher herself, it was whispered. Long, capacious white gowns capped by hoods with duraplastic, moulded face masks, each identical, each entirely blank. The symbolism deliberate, for the time approached when all who wore the mask would be reborn, granted a new face to turn towards eternity.

Averil's excitement at her costume wavered as she remembered Dora reporting a rumour among the technicians. Namely, the simplicity of the design stemmed from a chronic shortage of cloth and dyes; that the wasteful, extravagant economy of Albion was floundering. Of course, it meant nothing, just Dora being Dora.

Stately music filtered from outside into the chamber. Up in the plaza surrounding the Double Helix Statue, tens of thousands would be gathering, all who had survived the calamitous destruction of the Five Cities, less than a tenth of the original population. Averil suppressed the implications. She smiled still harder. So close to her dream, she must not risk disloyal thoughts.

She looked round for a friendly face, finding only featureless white masks, eyes barely visible through slits. No one conferred or gossiped with their rivals in the Great Assignment. Quite suddenly, Averil wondered what old neighbours and friends in Baytown were doing on this summer night. Dancing at the Puzzle Well Inn, perhaps, for it was a Saturday, and folk loved to dance.

It came as a relief when familiar figures arrived at the numbered zone she had been designated. She quickly removed her mask.

"Dora! Wakuki! Are we to walk together in the procession?"

Dora guided Baby's mobile cot. In her functional medi-tech's uniform, she looked out of place. Dr Wakuki, too, wore his usual self-sanitising plasti-suit rather than white robes. A porter-drone beside him carried a large, transparent plasti-steel case. It contained numerous thin vials. Averil frowned. Behind trundled a security drone, as well as two men armed with small pistols. She recognised the pair from banquets and receptions as intimates of the Joint-Presidents.

Wakuki bore livid bruises on his cheek and round his eyes. His lower lip was split. The nervous, slender man flinched when his escort jabbed him forward.

"Doctor! What is happening?"

She sensed something appalling, and inexplicable.

"It seems, Averil, I am guilty of Discordia."

"Rubbish! That's not possible."

"But it is."

"I'm sure there's been a mistake. I'll talk to Marvin and Merle myself. They cannot know about this."

He hesitated then said, "No mistake. My actions might very well be considered Discordia. You see, I refused to share my work on the virus meant to settle the primitive problem once and for all. How strange it ends this way. Yet I am glad I will not have that crime tormenting me."

SEVENTEEN

He quivered. Tears glistened in the corners of his eyes.

"They instructed one of their Angels to beat me," he whispered. "When I still refused to give them the virus and antidote, they applied instruments. I had to give them what they wanted in the end. My pathetic protest was in vain. But I am glad to die with an easier conscience."

The Beautifuls guarding him shifted awkwardly.

"Now, Wakuki," said one, "you're actually a very useful fellow to the Ruling Council. If you beg for clemency, you might yet be shown mercy."

Wakuki pointed at the big box of vials being carried by the porter-drone. "Where is the clemency for humanity in there?" He turned to Averil. "Good luck with the Beautiful Life, my dear. It all passes in a blur, you know. However long you live, in the end it is only just a mysterious blur."

He was led to a few rows behind Averil, accompanied by his escort. There, other criminals in manacles huddled.

Dora brought over the mobile cot. She reached inside for the child it contained. Baby looked pale and sick, despite cosmetics applied liberally to both its heads. As long as the child lived long enough for the ceremony, Averil did not care. She found it increasingly hard to conceal her repugnance for the cuckoo-creature.

All around, the procession prepared to move off, hundreds of white-robed supplicants destined for Assignation, flanked by Angels and security drones. Averil felt a rush of power. At last she belonged. Nothing could rob her of the place she had earned. If only Queen Morrighan was still alive to abase herself! But the past was dead. Soon a new fiefdom would be hers, one she would rule with her father's compassion and, to ingrates foolish enough to oppose her, Queen Morrighan's ruthlessness.

"Do I look like a queen, Dora? Do I?"

The medi-tech flinched as music boomed, fanfares edged with dissonance, madness. The whites of her eyes became visible. The procession commenced in measured, stately steps.

*　*　*

Perhaps some gothic extravaganza from the Before Times inspired the Brubachers. Or a two-dimensional movie from their youths depicting mighty emperors or pharaohs. Perhaps they wanted a ceremony to end all ceremonies. Except pomp is never satisfied. Power depends on appearance.

The white-robed crowd held up screens set to searchlight. Individual holograms were projected into the night sky depicting recordings of the Brubachers. King and Queen. Emperor and Empress. Each hologram a clip specially chosen, a message of loyalty monitored for irony through central systems.

Kneel in your mind, if not physically. Kneel before limitless wealth, before the chances and choices that granted the Presidents of the Ruling Council pre-eminence. Kneel to offer them whatever they crave. Kneel to be what Big Jacko once dismissed as a *Yesser*, finding it easier, safer to obey than question. Kneel and receive your due.

Up a ramp into dimmed lights stepped the procession in white robes, shiny white masks glinting off so much spilt light. Voices rose in a great roar. Drones flew over crowded terraces, spraying joy-chemicals for all to inhale.

Witness! Admire! Weep in ecstasy at the vision of the Joint-Presidents' aircar descending from the heavens, to bless and disburse.

As if spontaneously, a slow, solemn chant began: *Beautiful Life! Life Perfected!* Over and over, as the years must bloom and repeat until the sun burnt itself out.

Joy spray tickling her upturned face like dew, Averil breathed deep.

SEVENTEEN

She forgot Dora cowering with the mobile cot by her side. Or Wakuki, hands bound like an ignoble bonder. Doubt and time fell away. Just the chants and cries of the crowd awaiting Assignation, the purity of white robes, blank-faced masks glowing faintly, awaiting gifts more precious than love or spring or fragile seasons . . .

Dazed, Averil barely realised when it came her turn to climb up the pyramid steps at the base of the Double Helix Statue, where Marvin and Merle Brubacher floated on separate air-thrones, dressed entirely in cloth of gold, faces concealed beneath golden masks.

Here, as she had been instructed, Averil held up the two-headed child for all to see, the blessed Janus-child linking past and future. Fresh roars hailed its immense image projected into the sky. Proof that even parenthood now lay in the gift of the Ruling Council. Hail the Ruling Council! Hail its all-wise Presidents!

Then Averil was led to one side, the child handed to Dora, who slipped away.

Next came Wakuki, bearing another offering. The transparent case contained numerous vials of liquid, some blood-red, others white as milk. A voice declared momentous news. Soon the lands will be cleansed of all but true humanity! Tens of thousands of intoxicated voices rose in gladness.

No more would primitives trouble paradise. Hail the Joint-Presidents who held the power of life and death! Hail! Hail!

The holo-image showed Wakuki's awe as he grovelled at the feet of the floating thrones. Then he was dragged off, a clear warning to all. Even the most favoured could fall if the Joint-Presidents chose.

Now to the serious business. The night sky filled with a three-dimensional map of Britain, Ireland and Northern France divided into fiefs. Beautifuls were summoned to receive personalised info-pearls containing details of the lands assigned to them. In homage, each knelt and placed their heads into the gaping mouths of machines for circuits to be injected into their skulls, similar to those used for the retirement of technicians or Angels. No one questioned what function the implants might play.

The night progressed like a happy dream. When people tired, aerial drones circulated, spraying yet more stimulants. Midnight came. Averil clutched tight her own info-pearl. At dawn, they would be allowed to activate the pearl and learn what bounty they had been Assigned.

If only those who had mocked and abused plain Averil Pilgrim could see me now, she thought, if only.

EIGHTEEN

The container vibrated, a sensation carrying Michael straight back to troop transports during the Crusades. What sorrows the City inflicted when they conscripted him and Tom – and so many others – to wage genocidal war against their own kind. Their own brothers and sisters. Not to mention the children, big-eyed and starving.

Did Tom Higginbottom feel the same? The old friends slumped on the floor together. As though reading his thought, Tom whispered, "You ready, Michael?"

"As I'll ever be. Somehow I got thinking about Syria. What we did."

A pause. "Queer that, so were I."

"Should we really do here, what we did to those poor fuckers back then?"

"There'd be some justice in it."

"And yet they are still people."

"Some of 'em."

"It is possible to break an enemy's power without slaughtering them all."

A harsh voice broke in from the darkness, its mantra all too familiar to Michael from York and the long march south with the Pilgrimage of Fools. A prayer belonging to a cult of hate, much like the Floggers' cruel anthem:

"City men aren't men," recited Captain Ariana. "City-women aren't women. Every devil must die. Every building burn. Every scrap of devil-knowledge must perish in the cleansing fire."

Michael was aware Gover must be listening, likewise Hurdy-Gurdy, and assessing their own prospects of survival.

"Quiet," Cutty cautioned. "We ain't out o' the bog yet."

Minutes passed. They rattled along. Where to? Michael guessed some processing or storage facility. Maps of Albion drawn up by Gover, Lady Veil and Hurdy-Gurdy, aided by prisoners from the City, indicated the northern third of Albion's circle was a starkly functional zone, visited only when necessary. Otherwise, its factories and warehouses, food-processing units and laboratories, were the preserve of drones and a lesser breed known as technicians – the same class of ex-primitives who once served as Deregulators.

Michael touched the **F** for Felon lasered onto his cheek by just such a City-servant, an old schoolfellow, Will Birch, one-time Deregulator of Whitby.

The vibrations in the container ceased. Stillness descended. They had arrived. A distinctive click indicated someone – Ariana, no doubt – had cocked a pistol.

"No guns, you fool," hissed Michael. "Uncock it right now."

Another echoing thud as something seized the container. As before, he had the sensation of being carried and gently set down. Silence. Half an hour passed. Michael ordered everyone to switch on torches.

"Time to get changed," he said.

Outer clothes were removed to reveal black, functional overalls, the closest recreation of technicians' uniforms they could manage, based on Hurdy-Gurdy and Gover's recollections. A disguise likely to win mere moments of respite. Moments their entire, mad venture might depend on.

With a faint hiss of blade from scabbard, Michael drew the City-

EIGHTEEN

sword, its plasti-steel edge sharp enough to carve a hole in the container walls given time. He pointed at Tom, who went over to the exit.

"Now," murmured Michael.

The lever went down. The door opened smoothly. Michael, blinded by glaring arclights, stuck out his head.

A warehouse lay beyond, greater than any cathedral nave or castle keep. Its girdered roof rose high above. Hundreds of containers were stacked on racks, watched over by enormous crane-drones like metal storks. Lifelessness lay heavy across its many aisles. Not a soul to be seen.

Michael slid through the door and crouched, sword in hand. A moment later, Gover joined him, strictly against orders. They exchanged glances.

"Any idea where we are?"

"Just where I might have expected. A storage facility near the Travel Hub. What your bloodthirsty friend back in the container . . ."

"Captain Ariana?"

"Yes, her. What she might call, in her melodramatic fashion, the belly of the beast. Or part of its digestive system. By the way, Pilgrim, do keep that crazy lunatic away from me. I rather suspect she has instructions to collect my head."

Gover's customary cockiness was back. Michael wondered what it meant.

"Where do we go next?" he asked. "You have spoken of needing what you call a *master control console*. Would there be such a thing here?"

"Do you hear that?" asked Gover.

Michael listened carefully. He detected a distant echo of music and massed voices.

"Whatever it is," he said, "it sounds a few miles off. Do we need to go where those voices are coming from?"

"The very opposite direction," replied Gover. He pointed at a brightly lit exit on the far side of the huge warehouse. "Chop, chop, Pilgrim. Over there."

* * *

They walked in a line down long aisles of containers. Most were empty, confirming Gurdy's speculation Albion was running short of supplies.

Near the entrance, Michael and Tom moved forward to scout.

Beyond lay a pavementless road running between more warehouses and factories. It was evening, the sky darkening towards midnight. Stars should be visible to grant wonder and humility to mankind. They were obscured by grotesque holograms filling the sky.

"Fuck's sake," breathed Michael.

The images depicted a procession of ghosts in white robes, faces pale as death, and as featureless. The music clear now, along with an echo of collective chanting. Abruptly, the sky filled with an aerial platform bearing two thrones. Golden figures occupied the chairs, also masked. Except these glittering masks were sculpted to recreate recognisable faces, a man and woman.

"I reckon they're all mad," said Tom. "Too much power and time on their hands has sent the bastards crazy as snakes."

"Maybe we're the mad ones for being here," said Michael.

Hurdy-Gurdy's head appeared between them.

"Oh! Oh! Oh!"

They looked round, seeking enemies. The City-renegade pointed a stiff finger at the hologram.

"What does it mean?" asked Michael.

"I see my fate in two faces," declared Gurdy. "My, oh my. 'Let he that hath the steerage of my course direct my sail! On, lusty gentlemen!'"

EIGHTEEN

"Pull yourself together," snapped Michael.

Back with the others, Hurdy-Gurdy explained that nearly all Albion seemed to have gathered in the city centre for a ceremony or rite. A lucky occurrence, as roads and buildings in the industrial zone would be deserted.

"What if drones spot us?" asked Tom Higginbottom.

The threat on everyone's minds.

Gover stirred. "They are not programmed to hurt or kill within the City's boundaries, unless specifically instructed. Even then, overrides from a member of the Ruling Council must be issued. A precaution against fatal mistakes, you understand."

"Were there mistakes?" asked Tom, doubtfully. "In the past."

"In the early days, yes. And very fatal ones. I would go so far as to characterise them as massacres. You know what a fully armed battle drone is capable of. Hence, the linkage of all drones – and even hand-operated automatic weapons – to a master control system."

The raiders considered this news. Michael just hoped it was true. With Gover, there were always nuances.

"Right then," he said, "where's this master control console?" He lifted the Baytown Jewel concealed beneath his tunic, releasing the locket's catch to reveal the precious info-pearl. "I'm ready when you are."

Blair Gover licked his lips. He was sweating visibly.

"To reach one, I need a screen. Yes, very badly." His voice took on the faintest edge of hysteria. "Is that too much to ask? I am nothing in Albion until I have a screen! Nothing!"

Hurdy-Gurdy leaned forward; Gover recoiled from his rank breath. "Hurting, are we, my dear?"

The whine of an approaching electric motor reached them.

Hide, gestured Michael, grabbing Gover's arm. They ducked between a narrow row of containers. Just in time. A small, wheeled vehicle rolled into the warehouse, bearing two men in black uniforms. They halted and climbed out.

The tallest of the pair consulted his screen. "Bananas for their banquet in the morning," he read out. "Do you know this is the first consignment in six months?"

"So one of the plantations survived the grand fuck up?"

"Shhh. Careful."

"There's no eyes and ears here."

"Still, can't be too careful. They want Angels to replace us low-levellers anyway. Don't want to give them an excuse to retire us early. Come on now, better get the bananas."

"Do you mean, while we're still useful?"

"Something like that."

Michael felt a familiar indecision. Capture rather than kill? Dare he risk it, with so much at stake? One thing was certain: they had screens.

He sought Tom's eye; the latter dragged a finger across his throat. Michael shook his head, holding out both hands to denote manacles. Both drew the precious City-swords won during his nightmarish escape from Scotland. The blades had come home.

"Dock 64, according to the manifest," said the tallest. "Knowing our luck the fruit will be spoiled and we'll get the blame."

As they turned to climb back into the vehicle, two figures slipped from behind the containers, swords hidden behind their backs. At that moment the tall technician noticed them. He was fooled by their uniforms for no more than an instant.

"Hey!"

The man made a grab for his screen. Michael bounded forward, pressing the tip of his sword to the man's throat.

"It's really not worth it," he said. "Drop the screen."

It fell with a clatter.

Looking round, he discovered the second man with raised hands,

EIGHTEEN

staring into the barrel of Tom Higginbottom's pistol.

The technicians quaked as Gover examined their screens. Whatever he found did not please him.

"Too limited access," he muttered. "These wretches have the lowest clearance. Still, there are always ways round..."

He activated a holopad to tap floating symbols with astonishing rapidity. What message he sent, Michael could not guess. *For trust to exist, first one must risk trust*, he told himself.

Finally, the City-scientist raised the screen to its former owner's eyes. He forced the man's fingers over its flat face. A hologram projected as Gover repeated the same procedure for his own eyes and hands.

"Done," he said. "You may dispose of the fools now."

Michael ignored the implication. "What next? We must get moving. You've got your precious toy."

Gover's fingers flew over the holopad.

"We're not going anywhere."

"No?"

"We wait."

"What for?"

"To travel in style," said Gover.

* * *

While they waited, the two prisoners were bound and gagged. Captain Ariana volunteered to lock them in an empty container. Afterwards, Michael wondered why he allowed it. As far back as the Council of the North, it had been obvious how the Grow People intended to manure the earth. On her return, he noticed blood on her face and the pommel of her knife.

"You've killed them," he said, simply.

Triumph mingled with excitement in her smirk. She produced a wooden device with three wheels. Each wheel bore ten numbers. Michael recognised it as a counting device. When she held it up, the counter read **002**.

"Are you Growers insane?" he asked, in disgust.

Tom Higginbottom placed a restraining hand on his arm.

"Take care you don't end up my number three, City-devil," said Ariana, showing the counter to Gover. "I'm watching you."

He continued to consult his new screen. Michael found his utter absorption suspicious. High time to keep a tighter rein on the City-man. He sought out Hurdy-Gurdy's eye.

Just then, a long vehicle with rows of comfortable seats appeared at the entrance to the warehouse.

"A special treat for you primitives, Pilgrim," smiled Gover. "Your very own horseless carriage."

Hurdy-Gurdy skipped over. "Ooh, a charabanc! Let's get cosy, Baby Blair." He leered. "Feely-touchy chums from now on? Kissy-wissy? Where's my love-locket?"

A blur of movements handcuffed Gover's wrist to his own.

"Get this madman off me, Pilgrim! I'm warning you."

"Shut up, Gover," said Michael.

Hurdy-Gurdy led the shackled man into the waiting transport, chattering gaily. Once all were aboard, he instructed the windows to darken, so no one could see in. Yet the world remained visible outside. Another City-miracle, Michael realised, they sought to expunge from the world.

"Where should it take us?" he asked their guide. "And please, for your sake, no games."

Blair Gover sighed. "Always threats. How tedious you have become." He consulted the screen. Busy fingers moved. "Off we go."

EIGHTEEN

The transport rolled into the night, gaining speed. Michael stared in awe at the buildings they passed, constructed according to a single vision of functional architecture, shiny white, unadorned. No vegetation spoiled the perfection. Here, man truly was the measure of all things. Shadows and dark corners banished by banks of unfailing lights, blurring day with night, night with day.

A steep, mathematically conical hill rose to their right, conifers marching in neat rows up its sides. At the top squatted a wide circular building, like a shining mushroom.

"What is that place?" Michael asked.

Gover glanced up from the screen. "Warboys Hill. Once there was a quaint village called Warboys. Its rubble now forms the hill. Upon which rests a fusion plant, sufficient to power all Albion."

"Is that where we are going? So we can use the pearl to stop it?"

"No, Pilgrim, that facility is sure to be manned. Besides, the City has a range of alternative power sources. Neutralising that particular one would achieve nothing."

"Where then?"

Something flickered behind Gover's irony; something hot with suppressed rage.

"You might say we are travelling to change itself," he said. "Look, we are nearly at our destination."

The transport joined a large boulevard. Monorail tracks led the same way. The only vehicle they encountered was a drone truck bearing supplies to the City-centre. Holograms still filled the sky with images and sheets of light.

Gover tensed as they drove beneath a ceremonial arch. Then the Travel Hub of Albion stretched before them.

* * *

It was known as the Gateway of Gateways. Before the Five Cities' destruction, frequent transports landed here, bearing supplies and, more importantly, streams of Beautifuls. From here, a monorail track ferried thousands to Honeycomb for cell renewal, until civil strife, quarantine and gene sickness halted all traffic. It was many months since a shuttle left Albion for the island of Anglesey, where Honeycomb lay. Once, trains had run back and forth daily.

Michael felt fresh awe at the sheer scale of this place – and what it said of the City's astonishing power. Miles of airstrips led to the boundary walls, visible in the distance. Pitiless lights cast long shadows. A passenger terminal large enough to process tens of thousands was surrounded by numerous other buildings: hangars, warehouses, fusion-charging facilities, and in one corner, the glittering monorail station leading to Honeycomb and eternal life. This diamond-crusted pyramid shimmered with all colours of the spectrum.

Hurdy-Gurdy pointed at it. "Behold, the Gates of Perdition! The apex of that pyramid is woe and damnation!"

"You are hysterical, as usual," sniffed Gover. "Honeycomb is the ultimate expression of evolution."

"Do not believe him," moaned Gurdy.

Michael felt a moment's confusion. He had to confess Gover seemed the saner of the pair.

The transport veered between long lines of stationary drone aircraft. Some were big-bellied, capable of carrying hundreds of passengers or tons of materials. Others smaller and more specialised. Few seemed in use. Like the containers in the vast, echoing warehouse when they arrived, most of Albion's prodigious potential lay idle.

"Ah, *nous arrivons*," said Gover. His hands were trembling. "There may be a technician or two inside. They must not be allowed to raise the alarm."

The transport rolled to the entrance of a circular tower with plasti-glass walls, three storeys high. Through the transparent walls, banks of computers were visible. A small, red glow flickered on the topmost level. Someone was up there.

"Just me and Gurdy this time," said Michael. "When we give the okay, follow us in."

"Are we going out to play?" asked the dishevelled holotainer. "Oh goody gumdrops. What is to be my part?"

A few minutes later, two technicians stepped from the transport. Both wore black coveralls. One, unusually burly, carried a long bag; the other smoothed back his dishevelled hair, his expression bland, pedantic, subservient. In short, the model City-servant, focussed solely on his duties and indifferent to independent thought.

A few steps brought them to the doors, which swished open. The ground floor of the control tower was deserted. Low consoles glowed with lights. Michael's nose wrinkled at a smell he did not recognise until he realised the place had no smell. An elevator rose through the centre of the building, surrounded by a staircase winding up.

Ignoring the elevator, Michael and Gurdy took the stairs up to the middle floor. This, too, was deserted, leaving just the topmost level. Before leaving the stairwell, Michael drew one of the City-swords from the bag and passed it to Gurdy. He met his companion's bloodshot eyes. Nothing needed explanation. Then he drew his own sword from the bag, along with a two-barrelled pistol. They concealed the weapons beneath coats draped over their arms.

Gurdy activated the door from the stairwell; it opened silently.

Within lay a control room crammed with devices and monitors. Beyond the floor-to-ceiling glass windows, the Gateway spread for miles. Though a dozen workstations suggested that when the travel hub was in full use it kept many operators busy, right now, a single man sat at a console, reading holo-data with a peevish air. He was dressed in the dazzling clothes of a Beautiful.

Gurdy stepped inside and bowed low, as befitted his status.

"Here to relieve you, sir."

The man frowned, the very picture of plump, youthful arrogance.

"About time. I still might miss my turn at the Assignation. No thanks to you." He peered closely at Gurdy. "Why, you are the spitting image of Declan O'Hara."

Suspicion crossed his face. Recollection, perhaps, of Declan O'Hara's ignominious banishment for rebellion and Discordia. The man reached for his screen.

Michael rushed forward. He need not have bothered. Hurdy-Gurdy threw aside the coat concealing his sword and lunged with astonishing speed, plucking the screen from the man's startled grip, while holding the sword's razor edge against his soft, white throat.

"Care to give head?" he purred.

Resistance slumped from the terrified Beautiful. The control tower was theirs.

NINETEEN

Seth Pilgrim lay on his front, too close to a stinging nettle for comfort. Around him, he sensed rather than saw the men and women of North Column, hiding as best they could. Not that a drone would have difficulty picking them out – or off. So far, not a single aerial menace had flown overhead, unless you were a mouse fearing owls.

He wriggled forward to find the officers of Yellow Hundred at the edge of the copse. Seth had been assigned to a North Yorkshire hundred, led by Aggie Brown and another of Uncle Michael's old Crusader comrades, Corporal Baxter. Of the two commanders, he preferred Baxter. Not because he inspired confidence, but because Aggie plain scared him.

Although his fellow soldiers hailed from Baytown, Scarborough, Pickering and Malton – in other words, his supposed home turf – there wasn't a friendly face among them. Small wonder at that. Dour North Yorkshire folk prided themselves on long memories of a man's misdeeds. It was evident he was with Yellow Hundred so a strict eye could be kept on Big Jacko's former stooge. A bullet in the back wouldn't exactly have surprised Seth. Only his position as the Protector of the North's nephew and saviour of the Baytown Jewel, along with its precious contents, kept itchy fingers off triggers. Maybe, too, his role as go-between with the company of strangelings haunting the army's rim.

Seth hoped those inducements would be enough to persuade Aggie from reaching for her collection of butchers' knives.

"Any signs?" he asked.

Baxter and Aggie were peering through a lilac bush at the high walls of Albion, particularly the wide steel gate assigned to North Column.

They had positioned themselves just over two miles from the walls, in line with Lady Veil's instructions. Any nearer might stir the interest of security drones. To their left, the ground dipped to form fenland, reed-filled peaty water and islands of trees from which bitterns boomed at regular intervals. It was here that Bella Lyons – or what remained of her – was lurking with the other strangelings.

"See that?" breathed Baxter. "Dementia!"

An immense hologram cast palettes of light, colour and motion across the sky. As they watched, masked figures with spectre-white robes and faces marched towards a towering statue. Seth reckoned a good twelve miles lay between their hiding place and the procession. Three hours brisk march, seeing the ground was so flat – and assuming the steel gates opened.

"What you want?" grunted Aggie.

A long speech for her. Seth played his one card straight off. With Aggie, it didn't pay to hang around.

"Wondered how it's going. So I can tell the strangelings."

Baxter's pinched, ratty face took on a furtive look. Seth felt pretty much the same way about the humanimals assembled to punish their cruel creators.

"Keep those freaks away from us, guy," advised Baxter. "They got no right to exist."

Aggie snorted. Seth took it to be agreement.

"They're part of Lady Veil's big plan," he pointed out.

"Them monsters aren't part of any good plan," said Baxter,

earnestly. "I mean, *she's* a fucking freak herself. Freaky enough to freak me out."

Aggie inspected a large cleaver. It glowed in the sickly light spilling from Albion.

"Dementia," agreed Seth, weakly.

* * *

The weeks before Michael Pilgrim rode a barge into Albion had passed in a rush of preparations. Haste was necessary. After the drone attack on the motorway, no one could say when the City might swat the Pilgrimage of Fools. Luckily, Lady Veil slept just four hours out of twenty-four and no essential detail was beneath her notice.

With the Pilgrimage reinforced, she divided the army into three columns, each roughly two thousand strong. These were further divided into Hundreds, units intended to operate independently once inside Albion.

Seth watched their training from the sidelines. The main emphasis of Lady Veil's drill seemed to be starting efficient fires, slitting throats and leaving no prisoners. He noticed the soldiers from York, dominated by Lady Veil's black-uniformed Grow People, were particularly zealous. So eager to get killing, in fact, joining Aggie and Baxter's Yellow Hundred felt a lucky break.

Close companionship with Hurdy-Gurdy meant he accompanied him to several important meetings. In Lady Veil's headquarters at the old station hotel in Peterborough, the air hazy with tobacco smoke, she explained her big plan through an interpreter.

"She says, 'If the monster Blair Gover fails to shut down Albion's systems, there can be no attack. If he is successful – as his life depends on – then we will not gather as one large, concentrated force. We shall position three loose columns called North, Middle and South opposite the three gates in the boundary wall adjoining the Travel Hub. There will be roughly five miles space between each column. When the gates open and the drones are deactivated, we shall pour separately into Albion. Better to spread out there in smaller units, eliminating resistance wherever we find it."

Lady Veil's hands took on an intensity reflected in the interpreter's eager voice. "She says, 'Like prides of hungry lions, each Hundred must show no mercy to its prey. Strike then leave the carcase where it lies. Move on to the next and the next. Remember, they outnumber us many times over, just as defenceless sheep outnumber the wolves devouring them. Their blood shall fertilise the land. Then we shall be free to plant and grow again!"

The Grow People present rose to applaud, breaking into their chant of "City-men aren't men. City-women aren't women. Every devil must die! Every building burn! Every scrap of devil-knowledge must perish in the cleansing fire."

Seth laid a protective hand on Gurdy's shoulder. They would have to get past *him* to cleanse this City-man, and he'd like to see the crazy fuckers try.

Iona of Skye, the fair young woman Seth heard was carrying his uncle's unborn bairn, interrupted. Not everyone in the Pilgrimage was quite so set on wholesale massacre.

"Will there be much resistance if we get inside?" she'd asked in her clear, soft, lilting Highland voice. "There's more ways to tame a wild cat than skinning its fur."

Lady Veil examined the Nuager Priestess as she might a foolish child. Her hands moved.

"She says, 'If Gover succeeds and the lights dim, all Albion will panic. These are people entirely unused to danger. There will be little resistance so long as they are not given time to regroup and rearm. That is the most important thing: ruthless speed. Remember, they

NINETEEN

have relied on drones to wage war for over a hundred years. When the drones cease to work we must seize our one chance. Kill, I say. Then kill again!"

One of Lady Veil's most trusted officers, Captain Ariana, had risen, face flushed with fervour.

"They will be easy meat," she declared. "And good meat deserves a nice hot roasting!"

The assembled Grow People applauded. Once more Iona struggled to make herself heard.

"Do you plan to burn them alive as witches? Are we to become like savages, nay, the heartless devils you condemn, in the name of winning civilisation?"

Questions which received no answer, for she was ignored. Perhaps it was too late for niceties and scruples. Even Uncle Michael kept silent, his face a picture of inner conflict.

Attention turned to a large map of Albion. Lady Veil detailed entry points into the City and how they would gather at a place called Travel Hub, a wide concrete field, before dispersing and advancing on the centre. It all sounded simple enough, until Seth recalled Big Jacko's fatal over-confidence before the Battle of Pickering.

"How shall we know when to attack?" asked one of the commanders. "If we are spread out, miles apart and well back from the wall, there will be long delays as messengers ride to and fro."

Lady Veil's interpreter responded. "She says, 'We shall know easily by a sign in the sky. Everything is anticipated.'"

* * *

Out on the fen edge where Yellow Hundred skulked, glimmers of summer sunset turned the deep blue of a star-speckled night. They had been promised a clear sign when it was time to advance. Any mistake would provoke drones like wasps defending their nests.

In the likely event of disaster, Seth did not doubt his feeble cover of ferns and copse would prove useless. His private plan was to immerse himself in mud then make for Ely. Cutty had told how Young Ell's intrepid father found this tactic confused a drone's sensors – until he'd been torn apart, of course.

The thought of wise, funny Cutty was uncomfortable. Seth had urged his friend not to join the suicidal raiders entering Albion with Uncle Michael. Why not send someone better suited to the grim business of killing? Cutty's knack was for finding agreement, just as water finds ways to flow where it will. He was loyal, resourceful and dogged in fending for his people, not fending off pitiless enemies.

But the Fen Man had laughed, embracing Seth when there was no one to disturb them, in the way they both liked. He couldn't let Young Ell go in alone, he'd said, without a single one of her own people for a friend. And the notion of using her as a guide into that rat hole was his idea. Simple fairness required him to 'toggle along with her".

And so Cutty was gone, and might never hold Seth again.

"What time on the clock is it?" he asked Baxter.

The clock was an hourglass full of sand and a stick for notching when it turned. By that reckoning, they were two hours off midnight.

The hologram still hovered over the city, though the ceremony it depicted was repetitive. Every few minutes, a fresh wave of white-robed figures knelt before their king and queen on the floating golden throne. The details grew hazy as high clouds blew in.

"What the fuck are they up to?" he asked Baxter. The former Crusader had more experience of City-oddities than most.

"Search me," admitted the twitchy man. "But they're taking it damn seriously."

Seth wondered how the thousands of folk hiding round Albion felt, clutching crude weapons and fearing what craziness brought them here. If his own gut was a guide, like puking. The masked people seemed more like magical demons than flesh and blood, creatures fellable with blow or blade or bullet.

Aggie Brown stirred impatiently: she couldn't wait to test her cleaver on the bastards. Baxter filled a pipe with tobacco and *stuff*, producing a flint-wheel lighter.

"You mad?" Seth reached out to grab his hand. "Remember the orders. No flames or lights."

Baxter nodded, the whites of his eyes lit by a sudden flare of the holoshow.

"You're right," he muttered. "Got to set a good example. Michael told me that. And I promised to be good."

Examining his lump of stuff mournfully, Baxter's face brightened. He nibbled off a chunk, chewing like a hungry squirrel.

Time passed. Then Seth noticed something streak up from behind the walls, straight from what he assumed to be Travel Hub. Two more in quick succession. They exploded into flowers of distant sparks.

"The signal rockets!" he cried. "Did you see?"

Aggie Brown and Baxter were already on their feet, blowing whistles to assemble Yellow Hundred. A standard-bearer hastily rolled out a yellow banner. All around, men and women pulled on yellow armbands. An appropriate enough colour for me, Seth thought, donning his own.

It took longer than expected to line them up from their hiding places. Taking a roll call took even longer. All the while, Baxter trained his binoculars on the border wall, still brightly lit.

"I mean, what the fuck's going on? No sign of that gate opening. I mean, are we meant to walk right up and knock? Shit."

Aggie did not waste useless words. She hauled a young lad with a drum into position, indicating what she wanted with a cuff to his head. The lad began an urgent tattoo.

All along the green lands opposite the wall, other flags and Hundreds were forming up. Several already advanced on Albion, two miles distant.

"But the lights are still showing," protested Baxter. "The gates are closed. Maybe them rockets are wrong."

Too late now. Seth readied his own weapons and blew on a special birdcall whistle to alert the strangelings lurking in the nearby reed bed they must follow. It had been decided Yellow Hundred wouldn't enter Albion alone, however much Baxter wished it otherwise. Scores of strangelings appeared from the darkness. Grotesque were-creatures from tales to scare folk on a winter's night. Lolloping, flapping, set on acts Seth preferred not to contemplate.

Still the lights burned bright. The gates stayed shut.

"Fuck's sake!" called out Baxter, focussing his binoculars. "There's drones coming up now."

Seth could see lights on sleek, dark shapes rising from a large tower. No doubt to investigate the movement and noise opposite their zone of wall.

"Is this it?" he thought.

Understanding came to him in a rush, wisdom perhaps, the same finality visited upon his father when he died alone, unwept for by his only son. Seth saw how his own debts were about to be paid. For his neglect to Father and betrayal of Baytown, for poor Old Marley's murder and others he tried not to remember. Seth saw exactly how it must be, stood among old neighbours, farmers and fishermen grasping silly weapons, preparing to embrace night or day. If those lights in Albion did not go out very soon, it would be black night for sure. The endless night where Jojo waited, and Mother, and Father.

"Tykes! Tykes! We're fucking Tykes! What you going to do about it, yer bastards!" Seth bellowed, adding his voice to the taunts started by Aggie Brown, cleaver raised in a ham-like fist. An enormous blunderbuss waved in the other.

NINETEEN

After everything Seth had lived through and done, he was almost home. Not to Yorkshire, but the greedy earth waiting to consume him. To reassemble his dust in the form of a plant stem, or the flesh of a new born animal, or even plain, honest soil. But he wasn't dead yet. The bastards needed to get him first.

TWENTY

"The signal rockets are up," said Tom Higginbottom, emerging onto the top floor of the control tower. He added under his breath, "Let's just hope we bloody well know what we're doing."

As the rockets scattered petals of light over the Travel Hub, Gover had taken up position in a large swivel chair, surrounded on three sides by consoles. He explained that a dozen Node Points like this were spread out across Albion, each capable of controlling the city's entire interlinked systems if managed by the requisite codes.

"Can this truly be so?" asked Michael Pilgrim.

It seemed inconceivable the myriad devices and drones and machines and systems in Albion wove together like a vast, single tree's roots. Could one man control such a tangle, as he had once seen a clever puppet master at a fair, jerking the strings of his numerous toys?

Michael knew every creature bore some share of free will. The tamest-seeming horse might decide to kick its owner; seeds broadcast by the wind chose whether to germinate, sometimes resting in the earth long years until they judged the time right for life's battle. How then, could so many mechanical wills – and even drones possessed some autonomy – be mastered entirely by one man? Unless, of course, it was another of Gover's elaborate games.

Yet Gover had explained the mystery several times. Just as all living creatures were activated by shared traces of historic DNA, so for the systems evolved by himself and Dr Guy Price when they established the Five Cities. Master codes buried deep within all other codes, intended as the ultimate failsafe.

Perhaps, Michael reasoned, it was logical. The very conception of Albion was founded on expecting only the worst from people. Gover and his pals had created a society designed to nurture the worst: selfishness, vanity, limitless self-indulgence, idleness, pleasurable cruelty, the elevation of trivia over truth. Above all, wilful irresponsibility – except for one's narrow self-interests. And if you feared everyone, trusted no one, except as potential enemies, it made sense to devise an ultimate means of controlling them.

These thoughts flashed through Michael's mind as he glanced round the control tower. Everything seemed safe enough. Their Beautiful prisoner trussed tight as a spatchcock in a chair. Ariana by the stairs and lift, gun primed. Cutty and Ell had been ordered outside, watching for movement in the Travel Hub. Most important of all, Tom and Hurdy-Gurdy stood near Gover, pistols and blades ready for the first sign of betrayal.

"Well then, mister," he said, meeting Gover's bloodshot eyes. "Who'd've expected this?"

"What, Pilgrim?"

"You doing the right thing for once."

"Ah. The right thing. That, as philosopher's have pointed out, is a moveable feast." He smiled. "Let's begin, shall we?"

He held out his hand expectantly. Michael produced the Baytown Jewel from his pocket. He found the catch then opened the locket, extracting the fat info-pearl between finger and thumb. Still, he hesitated.

"Use this power well," he said.

Gover licked his lips as he took the pearl. Turning to the console, he ordered up a holo-keyboard, tapped out codes. From the top of the central console, a tiny metal cup on a rod rose. He gently placed the pearl into the holder, tapping out more codes.

He sat back. The info-pearl glowed a metallic blue. Holo-data appeared in the air around him, numbers and symbols dancing, shifting. He remained impassive.

Michael found he could scarcely breathe. After a few minutes, Gover leaned forward to a manual button on the console. A tray emerged bearing a flat, blank screen, the size of a thin book. This he activated. Triumph mingled with wonder touched his face. Patterns of vivid colour from the data streams filled the air.

He met Michael's eye. "It's time to start in earnest, Pilgrim."

"Do it."

"Sure?"

"Yes."

"If you insist."

Gover touched his screen. Instantaneously, a circular perma-glass shield slammed down from the ceiling, encasing him. All around the control tower, blast shields slid into place, sealing off windows and doors from attack. At exactly the same moment, two hatches in the ceiling opened. A brace of small aerial drones fell, propellers activating until they hovered.

"Kill him!" The scream came from Captain Ariana.

Bang. Her musket flashed. The bullet ricocheted off the protective plasti-glass case behind which Gover tapped out codes.

His voice boomed through loudspeakers, so loud all present covered their ears. "I advise you to drop your weapons. *All* your weapons, including the concealed ones. By the way, the scan of your bodies I am now conducting reveals them clearly."

The drones pointed cannon barrels.

"Do exactly as he says," mumbled Michael. His mouth tasted of

TWENTY

vomit.

Guns and blades fell to the floor.

Gover pointed. "Kill mode. Avoid mess. That one. And, yes, that one."

The aerial drones swivelled. Stubby barrels found targets. Two crumps of cannon. The foreheads of Ariana and the Beautiful prisoner exploded.

"Paralysis mode. Non-fatal. That one and that one."

Flashes of blue lightning lanced at Hurdy-Gurdy and Tom Higginbottom from the drones. They were hurled to the floor, twitching convulsively. Michael alone remained unharmed.

"Don't worry, Pilgrim, I have other plans for you," said Gover. "In the meantime, collect every gun or edged weapon. Place them in the lift. Then wave your hand over the red console to the left of the sliding doors. If you resist, or conceal anything more deadly than a toothpick, I shall kill your friend Tom Higginbottom."

Gover resumed tapping while Michael hurried to collect the weapons. An aerial drone followed him round the room. Finally, he sent the lift down to the ground floor with its cargo.

Still Gover did not pause in his work. Michael went over to Tom and Gurdy, who both lay gasping. Thank God they were both alive. For now.

Gover cried out, "Hah! Blair, you really are a clever boy!"

He settled back in the swivel chair, hands behind his head.

* * *

The holo-data flowed on, streams of numbers and symbols floating like a cascade of molten jewels. Slumped beside Tom and Gurdy, Michael watched Gover behind his impregnable shell. He seemed to be recording a message into his screen.

How diligently Gover had anticipated this moment, luring his naive companions like a skilful angler. Despair filled Michael's gut. *Fool*, he told himself, *utter fool*. What vanity on his part to imagine this man, this undoubted genius, creator of Albion's wonders, would ever bring about its destruction! In time, Gover would send out drones to scatter his erstwhile allies, the Pilgrimage of Fools. First, he must remove more important enemies in the City.

Tom moaned. When Michael looked up from laying a cool hand on his forehead, the protective screen had risen silently back into the ceiling. The drones still hovered, cannons trained on him.

"I would strongly advise you to avoid sudden movements," said Gover, chewing the side of his thumb.

Michael noticed the info-pearl on its little cup had begun to pulse with yellow light. Gover followed his gaze.

"It will take a while for the codes to run," he said. "A very delicate operation." He sniffed nervously. "Actually, the consequences of interrupting the process would be catastrophic."

They examined each other, silently assessing.

"Still, that same process," said Gover, "gives us time for a necessary *tête-à-tête*. What I have to say may surprise you."

"Oh, you've done that already."

"True. First, you may be wondering why I did not incapacitate you along with your friends. And what choice friends you keep, *n'est-ce-pas?*"

A giggle burst from him. Lurking hysteria behind the chuckle. Michael realised that whatever his successes so far, Blair Gover still faced vast challenges. Easy to make a mistake under such pressure. A sliver of ice in Michael's soul, one that never quite melted, whatever the danger, grew alert.

"Tom's not a bad sort," he said, affably. "Especially after a few ales at the Puzzle Well Inn."

TWENTY

"I shall take your word for it, Pilgrim. It is an establishment I'll never patronise. But to answer my own question, I did not stun or kill you because I wish to offer you a chance. An opportunity, let us call it, to *do the right thing*."

Again he chuckled. Michael waited. Codes flashed and whirled.

"You'll be astounded to hear," said Gover, "I have come to respect you. In fact, more than anyone I have met in a very long time."

This did surprise Michael.

"I'm flattered."

"Don't let it go to your head. Time is short, so I will explain what will happen when the codes have run sufficiently. Note, I say *sufficiently*, because it will take several hours for them to run fully."

"What is this choice?"

"One you have been offered before," said Gover. His voice rose in barely suppressed rage. "Before I was treacherously attacked and forced to trek as a hunted fugitive through . . . through that bestial Highland wilderness. Let alone suffer a wound still causing me pain. Before, I say, my enemies pressed heedlessly on with experiments to new life forms that led – oh, I warned them, how I warned them! – to gene sickness. Before, in some deranged desire to cling to power, they destroyed the Five Cities – my precious creation – like hideously cruel children trampling exquisite flowerbeds."

He paused to draw breath. Abruptly, he calmed.

"You see, Pilgrim, with the loss of Mughalia, Mitopia, Neo Rio and Han City, I have new, unanticipated problems. Indeed, they may be called humanity's next great dilemma. That is where you come in."

* * *

As he told his tale, Gover kept an anxious eye on the unfurling codes.

First, he confessed his time among the primitives had transformed his vision of their potential. Rather than the bloodthirsty imbeciles assumed by the City and, indeed, by its founders, Gover had discovered little people full of possibilities, not least, when it came to co-operative endeavours. As a result – once he assumed complete authority in Albion, an imminent event – he would commence by granting dispensations to them.

Initially, he would use the Pilgrimage of Fools as an unlikely resource. Over time, however, once the situation was normalised, Albion would reinstate regular examinations to recruit large numbers of technicians.

"Why do you think this is necessary, Pilgrim?" he asked, darkly.

Michael shrugged. "You find us little people amusing?"

"No, I do not find you amusing. Or pleasant. Or *nice*." He emphasised the word as though it tasted sour. "One thing you must learn to refute is puerile sentimentality of the kind that labels anyone *nice*. It muddles your thought processes and makes you less useful to me. The reality is that no one is ever *nice*, except for themselves."

"I can think of endless examples that contradict you, Gover. Your cynicism, which you consider so clever, is in fact like a child simplifying its world."

"Oh, I am too old to qualify as a child. Far too long in the tooth."

"So why exactly do you want to help us?"

"You are not listening. I do not want to help you. You must help me. And, by so doing, help yourselves. You see, by destroying the Five Cities, my opponents reduced the current population of Beautifuls to unviable levels. I intend – slowly and cautiously – to allow small numbers of technicians to earn elevation to the status of Beautiful. In this way, over time, we shall re-establish other cities beyond Albion."

Michael could not help but marvel.

"Here you are, one man surrounded by enemies, and already you're planning a grand future."

"Several hundred years into the future," replied Gover, smugly.

TWENTY

"You mentioned my friends massing outside the walls of Albion," said Michael. "How do they fit in?"

A series of shrill beeps distracted Gover. For a while he watched in tense silence as the data shimmered. Finally, he relaxed.

"Where was I? Ah, yes. I wish to give you a choice. An astonishing choice. To serve me as a sort of client-king of primitives, ensuring your people are compliant. In return, you earn at the end of your natural life, something precious."

"What might that be?"

"To live forever."

"Me?" asked Michael, astounded.

Gover coughed. "I know, I know. Do not thank me."

"What's the less astonishing choice?"

"Why, to die, of course. Just to die."

* * *

Gover threw up his hands in mock resignation.

"Knowing you, as I do, I'm sure you are considering my proposal through your usual moral lens. A spectrum discerning only good and bad, black and white. For once, I advise you to consider the benefits of *grey*. Think wisely, Pilgrim. When these codes are more embedded, I shall have no more leisure for you."

He resumed close monitoring of the holo-displays, forgetful of Michael's existence. Occasionally, he tapped floating symbols and assessed the results. Beads of sweat on his forehead caught the multi-coloured, shifting light. The security drones hovered.

Michael sat between Hurdy-Gurdy and Tom Higginbottom, afraid to move. He entered a maze of doubts, so immense were the implications of Gover's offer.

To live forever! Wasn't that to be a god, with all a god's potential?

To possess eternal youth, countless seasons for heedless pleasure and knowledge? One might plant an acorn and watch it grow from shoot to sapling to winter-defying oak. Was that not a prospect worthy of sacrifice? The books to be read, undreamt places visited, foods and wines tasted, conversations with friends and strangers as shifting tableaux of humanity blew like cycles of leaves past the mirror of one's mind and senses.

To live forever! Nothing to fear except fear itself. Sickness would not touch him, nor the slow, inevitable rot of flesh and teeth and faculties. Instead, growth eternal, not decided by indifferent biology but free will. What good he could accomplish. What monuments construct.

Only a fool would turn down such an offer. The City was sure to win anyway. Why throw away his life? He had suffered enough for a dozen lifetimes. All he need do was compromise. Accept Gover's grey blur between white and black, dark and light, as the ultimate reality. Cease struggling in vain.

After all, it was not just for himself. Gover was offering a chance for his people, or a lucky few of them. Serve the City and be rewarded with its greatest glory. Simple reason indicated that over time, more and more primitives would become Beautiful, building new cities that made the ones destroyed resemble thatched hamlets. Throughout that process, he, Michael Pilgrim, would supervise benignly, no longer Protector of the North but Protector of Primitives, ensuring justice and compassion prevailed, banishing brute ignorance.

But as Michael slumped on the floor, mind afire with visions, he knew it could not be. The grey world Gover proposed would soon become dyed crimson with the blood of innocents. If just a few were blessed with freedom, the vast majority must be oppressed. Those lessons were old as power. Old as rich and poor. Old as weak and strong.

He did not trust Gover when it came to so-called primitives. Slaves do not always wear manacles and chains. Sometimes they carry a chip in their heads for convenient retirement. Sometimes they wear explosive wristbands, as he had done during the Crusades, to punish the slightest impudence with arms blown clean off.

There was more. To live forever, an endless repetition of days, and only so many ways a human being can conceive of filling them. Because time would no longer be precious. Love itself would fail in the face of endless repetition. Because living forever would kill all humanity inside him, leaving an incurious drone of flesh and electronic impulses, jaded, tired, eager but afraid to die.

Such was Gover's marvellous choice. Inevitably – for Michael never thought alone, invisible teachers, people and books, whispered advice and encouragement – he recalled Grandfather's stern yet kindly voice, his beloved Shakespeare, "for both pleasure and wisdom, Michael, the two are not contradictory."

"Tomorrow and tomorrow and tomorrow," he muttered to himself, as some might a prayer. "Creeps in this petty pace from day to day, to the last syllable of recorded time . . . Life's but a walking shadow, a poor player, that struts and frets his hour upon the stage, and then is heard no more."

The words gave him courage to be contented; to be no more – or less – than a plain, time-bound man.

Michael stirred from his reverie. For a long while Gover monitored the codes. Then he glanced his way.

"Soon I will be ready," he said. "Well, Pilgrim? Decided?"

It seemed he had no doubt of Michael's choice.

"I have decided to be free," he said. "I may not be much, Gover, but I shall stay true to myself, the story I want my life to leave."

"You must realise I will have no choice but to neutralise you and your friends."

"Everyone dies in the end."

"So that is the end of the tale you choose?"

For once there was no sneer.

"I will die free."

"As you wish."

Gover turned to issue a fatal command to the drones. Then he paused. Perhaps he recollected the dangerous journey they had shared through Scotland. How easily the man he condemned now could have abandoned or disposed of his prisoner. How easily he could have pretended to agree with him to save his own skin.

"Of course, I really should kill you," he said. "God knows, you are dangerous and persistent. However, I am a good man. Everything I do is done from necessity. Everything. Therefore, I'm giving you five minutes to get you and your friends out of here. Leave Albion. Soon things will begin that you do not want to be caught up in."

With a last, dismissive wave, Gover turned back to the holo-displays, code unravelling into code.

Michael needed no encouragement. He dragged Tom Higginbottom, still unconscious, to the lift, summoning it as he returned for Hurdy-Gurdy. As the door opened, he almost tossed them inside, on top of the weapons placed there earlier. The lift descended to the ground floor.

Five minutes! He hauled his friends to the front entrance. It opened obligingly. Michael cast a glance back at the weapons in the lift. Dare he risk being trapped here by fetching them?

Cutty Stone appeared.

"What's been going on, 'bor?"

"Get Hurdy and Tom out!"

Together they manhandled the unconscious men outside. Instantly, the sliding door clicked shut behind them. The blast shields fell into position. Michael gaped at the brightly lit Travel Hub. A hand shook his shoulder.

"Where is she?"

"Who?"

TWENTY

"Young Ell."

"She's with you."

"No, she ain't."

"I thought she was here with you, Cutty."

Both looked instinctively at the sealed control tower. No one was getting out of there.

Just then, a dozen gunship drones, a full squadron, rose from silos in Albion's walls. With a roar of jets, the drones turned.

* * *

Inside the topmost storey of the control tower, a willow-thin girl crouched deep in shadow beneath a workstation. Though her heart beat fast, Ell understood this much: somehow she'd escaped not just the City-man's notice, but that of his wicked drones.

The slightest noise might betray her. Wiry and slippery as the eels she'd been named after, she eased to rest her back against a solid panel. Then she went still, as only fisherfolk or hunters know how. The way taught by her father, before a drone caught him: a different sort of devil-machine from those hovering in the centre of the room, propellers swishing, but just as cruel. Ell cursed herself for not trying to get out when Michael Pilgrim had been told to leave. Somehow she hadn't been able to unlock her frozen limbs. Too late now.

Meantime, the boss man at the console talked to himself like a loon or simple.

"Ha! Well, you've done it, Blair, old chum. Ha! Knew you wouldn't let me down. And now... Oh, yes... *le framboise sur le gateau!*"

Holo-data strips glowed red across his face. His hands worked and he spoke sharp commands to the machine.

"Almost there. Almost there. Come to me, my beauty. Ah! *Voila! Nous arrivons.*"

A three-dimensional map of Albion appeared beside him. Its lights depicted districts within the circle of the boundary walls. Towering buildings and plainer, functional constructions. Hills amidst parkland and ornamental gardens, lakes, woodland. Simultaneously, a second holo-image appeared, one Ell recognised from projections into the night sky, thousands of folks dressed like ghoulies, worshipping a golden king and queen on floating thrones.

"Well, well," crowed the City-man, "if it isn't Marvin and Merle. So sorry to interrupt your fun. But every good party needs a gate crasher, *n'est-ce-pas?*"

TWENTY-ONE

Seven or eight miles south-east of the Travel Hub, the Double Helix Statue rose. On the statue's wide plaza, the Great Assignation progressed towards bliss for the chosen ones. Helen Devereux considered it unlikely they would enjoy it for long. Most Beautifuls were congenitally dissatisfied. The concept of *enough* viewed with suspicion by the City's plutocratic founders, even before the plagues released them from natural restraints. Inevitable they would descend into jealous squabbling over who had the best fiefdom. In the City, the more things changed, the more they grew deranged.

Helen knelt with other rebels by the side of the colossal statue. Security drones surrounded them, along with a few blank-faced Angels bearing long curved blades.

A fresh wave of white-robed and masked Beautifuls came forward for info-pearls detailing their future fiefs. In return, they offered their heads for the injection of a control chip. Helen wondered how they could surrender their liberty, even free will, so happily. Joy-sprays intoxicated them, true, lulling doubt, but still . . . Perhaps such Faustian bargains underpinned any society with distinctions of high and low. Right now, she was several rungs beneath low.

Helen turned to the slender man kneeling alongside her. His presence was as great a surprise as the fact she was still alive. Here was Dr Wakuki himself, the man famed for concocting plague viruses to keep the hordes of South East Asian primitives at manageable levels. How the mighty had fallen.

The little man quivered as another prisoner was led away by Angels. In a *jeux d'esprit*, Marvin Brubacher had devised a novel form of execution. Stripped naked, the wretch was placed in a deep circular pit. Powerful jets of water rose, bearing its terrified cargo a hundred feet in the air, at which point the water died back – and gravity brought the suspended victim tumbling back to hard earth. Already a dozen twisted bodies lay around the fountain pit.

"Why are you here?" she whispered to Wakuki.

He stared straight ahead. "We must get it off them," he murmured.

"What?"

"The box I was forced to give them."

Helen recollected the transparent case of vials.

"Will you help me, if we get a chance?" he pleaded.

"I do not understand."

When Wakuki explained what exactly was in the box, a horror gripped her, so intense she felt dizzy.

"Of course," she said, trembling. What help she might offer was unclear.

Up went the fountain, bearing a twisting, struggling woman. Down went the water, followed by a spinning body that landed with a crump of flesh.

It's no use, thought Helen, there's nothing we can do.

Through fanfares and flourishes of heroic music, Helen heard a coarser noise. Jet engines. She turned instinctively to the north-east, the direction of the Travel Hub.

* * *

Averil Pilgrim clutched the small box containing her own info-pearl,

TWENTY-ONE

tears of gratitude stinging her cheeks. She took a sniff of joy-spray then burst into spontaneous applause.

Never had the world seemed so perfect. No sense of loneliness now among the white-robed Beautifuls. They were one happy family! And the loving, kind, generous parents protecting them floated above their thousands of children in the great plaza.

Averil reached up in supplication and adoration – and she was not alone. The golden couple's own emotions were unreadable behind their masks. All the better then to supply one's own.

She marvelled to remember how the Brubachers had favoured her in horrid Mughalia. Oh, how wise they had been to destroy that place, along with all the other ungrateful Cities! Everything would be better because of that. How lucky, too, she had been chosen to carry Baby.

The thought of Baby brought unease soon banished by a sniff of joy-spray.

Look at that jolly fountain! Up it went, water catching the light like diamonds. Another stupid, nasty, ungrateful person carried up then down like a soggy leaf. Like Humpty Dumpty tumbling from his wall. Averil giggled naughtily. Whoosh! Up then down you go! Even as she laughed, something inside felt tearful.

But she was a good girl. Nothing like that could happen to her. She would always have a magnificent apartment with sparkling clothes and fine views of the City. Jewellery and perfume and astonishing food and drones to service her every wish. Yes, and Angels, in time, her very own to adore her. She wasn't the kind to bite the hand that fed her, not like crazy Helen Devereux or Dr Wakuki . . .

Another unpleasant thought. Her head span, heart beat fast.

Marvin and Merle were so kind! So funny, almost.

Averil smiled in surprise. A new entertainment had arrived. She looked up as the ground echoed to the sound of unmuffled engines. No one had expected this!

Yet the rumbling provoked an instinctive wariness. It reminded her of the attack on Hob Hall. Of a large drone carrier that had disgorged monsters setting her home ablaze,

Louder and louder, roared the jets until she covered her ears. Suddenly, a dozen large battle drones were floating low over the crowd, lights flashing, drifting towards the Double Helix Statue where the Joint-Presidents had risen from their aerial thrones.

She looked round. How queer! Every other drone in the square had slumped, as though deactivated. Only the ones in the sky seemed to work. Then the triumphant music stopped. The holograms in the sky faded as the engines of the battle drones hushed to a low whine. A new, expectant stillness filled the square. So sudden it felt loud. Averil heard the panting breaths of the crowd around her. Still the drones hovered, lights flashing rhythmically.

The enormous hologram reappeared, zooming on the faces of the Joint-Presidents. Both had removed their masks and were shouting panicked commands into their screens, trying to make the flying thrones descend.

One of the drones glided over until directly over the golden-robed figures. Two mechanical arms projected from the drone's belly, designed to seize prisoners. Grabbing claws fastened round the man and woman; close-ups presented their agonies.

Waves of panic swept the crowd. At that moment, a huge head appeared in the sky, alongside the writhing Joint-Presidents. Averil recognised the man at once. It was him! The same man who had visited Helen Devereux in Baytown. Blair Gover, who the Brubachers sought with such energy and determination.

In the silence, his voice boomed out, faintly effeminate, shadowed by a lisp, yet icy.

"My friends," echoed the voice, "as you see, I am back. And just in time, it would seem."

TWENTY-ONE

Moans greeted his words.

"Fellow Beautifuls!" he declaimed. "Do not be afraid. Be reassured. I have full control of every system in Albion. All drones, all life services, all energy sources, all communications. You are quite, quite safe. From this moment forth, the Beautiful Life that traitors have squandered shall resume its former, natural course."

Silence in the crowd. Perhaps those implicated in the Brubachers' Life Perfected imagined punishments. It seemed Blair Gover anticipated their thought.

"Do not fear," he said. "Reason and science shall replace the pomp and barbarity of my recent predecessors, the usurpers of power, the murderers of over four hundred thousand Beautifuls. Therefore, I say, be comforted. All who revert promptly to the Beautiful Life have nothing to fear from Blair Gover."

He sighed regretfully. The noise, amplified many times, was like a great wind of change.

"But not all will see sense. Some must be destroyed for everyone's good." His voice took on a hard edge. "You get to choose once, and once only. The chips now in so many of your skulls allow me to retire unreliables at any time. Moreover, those who voluntarily renounce the Beautiful Life may leave Albion whenever they wish. Blair Gover is no tyrant!"

The word echoed round the plaza.

"But take note, those who leave Albion will be delivered to my allies for safekeeping."

Holograms of armed primitives waving barbarous flags and advancing towards the boundary walls appeared. Fresh terrors dispelled what shreds remained of the Great Assignation's joy. To fall into the clutches of primitives was a destiny avoided for more than a century.

Blair Gover's enormous head coughed. His mouth and teeth resembled a dark, wet cavern.

"That leaves those guilty of crimes I can never forgive."

Again, Marvin and Merle Brubacher's faces filled the sky. Both were straining against the grip of the drone's mechanical hands.

"You and you," said Blair Gover, "shall have your names deleted from every record, so you might never have existed. The new life forms you so recklessly created – against my express warnings of gene sickness – shall be rounded up and incinerated. Every last one." He paused. "I considered you friends, allies, people I trusted. That is what grieves me most. Still, you have always been inseparable, so I will grant you one last favour. It is time you got even closer."

The drone's arms slowly brought together the heads of Merle and Marvin Brubacher, mother and son, until they touched. Then, with slowly increasing force, pressed skull against skull. Eyes opened wide in agony. Keening cries of pain became gurgling moans. Until, as the skulls cracked, blood and grey brains oozed like slime. The drone's claws opened, dropping their limp bodies to the ground.

Averil buried her face in her sleeve.

"Disperse now in an orderly fashion to your homes," boomed the terrifying voice. "Remember you have nothing to fear. Return calmly to your homes and stay there to await further instructions."

* * *

If not for Wakuki, the case laden with plague vials might have been forgotten. But when the security drones guarding the prisoners deactivated, he tensed like a cat. His nervous glance flickered round the crowd. His hand shot out to grab Helen Devereux's arm.

"I need your help to get the virus to safety," he said.

Around them, Beautifuls were tearing off white robes and masks, hurrying to escape the plaza. The entourage of the Joint-Presidents, intimates who had eased Marvin and Merle Brubacher to prominence,

TWENTY-ONE

were among the swiftest to disperse. Helen knew them well enough to anticipate their schemes to win over Blair Gover. Hypocrisy loves power, as power loves hypocrisy.

Most of all, Helen was in deep shock. So he was alive. Blair Gover was alive. Her heart had always retained that suspicion. Seeing him should have flooded her with hope. Now she would survive, even influence his policies towards the so-called primitives. Yet the intensity of his magnified face filled her with foreboding.

"We must hide until things grow calm," she said. "Where can we go?"

Wakuki did not reply. Still gripping her arm, he half dragged Helen to the seating occupied by the Brubachers' hangers-on. People shoved past blindly. Some still wore masks in the hope of remaining incognito.

"Where is it?" he wailed. "We must find it."

His eye fell on a Perfect young man. One of the guards who had escorted him here. In his hand, the heavy case of plague vials. With a cry, Wakuki blocked his path.

"Give it to me! Do you not realise what it contains? Have you gone mad?"

The young man pulled out his pistol. His hand jerked as he pulled the trigger. Nothing happened. Gover had deactivated Albion's guns along with the security drones. Every firearm, save antiques, could be contacted via monitoring devices attached to Albion's central processors – so preventing abuses.

The Perfect looked down stupidly at the useless gun. Before he could react, Helen jumped forward. Years of living among primitives had hardened her baser skills. Without hesitation, she punched him hard. A lucky upward blow to his Adam's apple. Clutching his throat, the man dropped case and gun.

Seizing the case, they ran, pushing through jostling streams. Most of the people surrounding them were too dazed to protest. Yet small knots gathered to mutter and argue, clutching precious boxes of infopearls, the keys to lost fiefs. If not for the circling battle drones, engines roaring, perhaps some might have resisted. Against such overwhelming force, only the suicidal dared disobey Gover's command, repeated on a loop: "Disperse to your homes. You will be quite safe... Disperse to your homes..."

* * *

As a Baytown lass, Averil Pilgrim knew the value of havens in a sudden storm at sea. Away from the Double Helix plaza, the crowd thinned. She cast anxious glances back at the low-flying drones. Where to go? Her own apartment was in the same block as Wakuki's laboratory.

Averil sensed her best protection lay not in places but people. The brutal, calamitous fall of the Brubachers still seemed unreal, a disaster from a dream. Their deaths changed everything. Now she was forced to confront how few real friends she possessed in Albion: just Dora, and maybe Wakuki, and Helen Devereux. But she had left them awaiting execution, possibly already dead. They must surely hate her.

On she hastened. No one noticed her, too concerned with their own safety. Public transport was still functioning, choked with people competing for quick routes home. More battle drones kept appearing in the sky. She realised some master intelligence was slowly comprehending the city's unified systems, finding ways to deploy its resources. Yet the progression was not entirely smooth. She passed a large tram packed with people banging its doors and windows, crying out to be released. Its motors had failed, doors automatically sealed.

No one stopped to help. Little surprise, perhaps. The vast majority of Beautifuls were indifferent to their peers, except as adjuncts and props for their lives. When she first arrived in the City, this aloof quest for status had seemed a strength, like Queen Morrighan's ruthlessness.

TWENTY-ONE

Now Averil prayed they would come together to restore normality.

After half an hour's walk, she reached the entrance to her block. A small crowd besieged the main entrance.

"What is happening?" she asked.

"The door keeps opening and closing by itself," said a woman. "Things are breaking down!"

As if in confirmation, along the wide boulevard of immense buildings lights flickered. Knots of people shoved and cursed into the lobby whenever the doors slid apart. Wriggling between shoulders and elbows, Averil forced her own way to the front, at last pushing inside.

There, some instinct told her to avoid the elevators. She located the emergency stairs and hurried upward, counting floors. At the thirteenth, out of breath, she found the corridor to Wakuki's laboratory and private apartments. Dora might be hiding there.

Lights flashed erratically in the long, windowless corridor. Averil knew she must not get trapped in darkness. Wakuki's door, however, stood ajar. She peeped inside and called out, "Is anyone there?"

* * *

Averil Pilgrim sidled into Wakuki's apartment. The passageways to the laboratory and Dora's modest quarters were familiar. When she passed a tall window, Averil paused to look out. Drones still circled, unmuffled engines agitating the night. Far below, in the well-lit streets, small dots of people hurried home to their towers. At a crossroads, several drone vehicles had collided.

"Is anyone there?"

No one replied. Some sense told Averil she was not alone.

"Dora? Are you there?"

The sliding double doors to the laboratory were open. Then she went still. Were those faint voices beyond? Suddenly, a young man stepped from a side room. She recognised him as an intimate of the Brubachers. The last time they met he had carried a pistol and was conducting Wakuki to humble himself at the Great Assignation.

Gone was the man's mocking insouciance, likewise his pistol. In their stead he carried a desperate air and a long, sharp kitchen knife.

Averil backed away. She became aware of a looming figure behind her: a tall, broad-chested Angel wearing body armour and spiked boots. It carried a halberd tipped with a curved cleaver. One of the Brubachers' specially engineered bodyguards.

The young Beautiful motioned to her. "This way," he said.

She had no choice but to follow.

"I was only looking for Dora," she protested. "She's a medi-tech, you know, quite harmless. Is Dora here? Oh!"

They had entered Wakuki's inner laboratory, a sanctum lined with benches and machines. The lights dimmed then brightened.

"My God!" she cried, a hand flying to her mouth.

A small knot of people stood round a large, open plasti-glass carrying case; it was empty. Dr Wakuki cringed, as though recently struck. A second bodyguard Angel held a horny, clawed hand tight round the little man's neck. Nearby, knelt Helen Devereux and Dora, their hands bound.

What made Averil cry out were two ghosts. People whose gruesome deaths she had witnessed a mere hour earlier. Merle and Marvin Brubacher.

The rulers of Albion no longer wore gold and diamonds. Their outfits were plain, practical.

"You are too late!" squealed Wakuki to his captors. "I told you. I vaporised the entire batch as soon as I got here. And scrambled its formula from all devices. It has gone. Until someone is crazed enough to rediscover it. That person will never be Wakuki!"

Merle Brubacher wrung her hands in anguish.

TWENTY-ONE

"There's no more point, darling," she pleaded to Marvin. "He showed us the melted vials."

"I still don't believe him," said Marvin.

The young man escorting Averil cleared his throat. "Look who I found outside."

Everyone turned. Merle waved an impatient hand at the newcomer and hissed in frustration to Marvin.

"We are being distracted by these fools! We should go. Find a way out."

"You know every aircar has been disabled," said Marvin. "That bastard Gover has the master codes. I always wanted to believe they were a fable. Our one hope is getting some leverage on him. Wakuki's plague-virus is just the thing. Oh, and her." He nodded at Helen. "I'm sure he will want to keep her alive."

Averil still did not believe her senses. She had seen the Brubachers' heads ground together.

"How?" she spluttered. "You died."

The young man laughed.

"The Joint-Presidents always use facially modified doubles for really long and dull ceremonies where they do not need to speak. As the Great Assignation was scheduled for a good twelve hours, proxies wore their costumes and masks."

Marvin's full attention was back on Wakuki. "Listen, you little pixie. I know, and you know, there is a master copy of your virus somewhere in here. If you do not produce it, you shall suffer unimaginable pain."

The slender man choked as the Angel's hand tightened round his throat.

"Simply tell me and you get to live."

"No!" cried Helen. "Don't give them such power. They are mad enough to destroy all humanity out of spite."

Averil listened in confusion. Yet the Brubachers' survival told its own tale. They seemed indestructible.

Abruptly, Wakuki sagged. "Yes!" he gasped. "I give in."

"We must go right now!" wailed Merle.

"Do shut up, Mother dearest. Release him."

The Angel seemed to struggle to understand. It kept choking Wakuki until Marvin gestured to show what he wanted. The Angel dropped the limp figure from its grip. He collapsed in a heap, grovelling and snivelling.

Then the diminutive man found an improbable strength. With a mingled snarl and shriek, he launched himself up at Marvin Brubacher. The bodyguard Angel grabbed as he lunged, obeying its conditioning. With a neat twist and discernible crack, it broke Wakuki's neck. He twitched a few times then hung limp.

At that precise moment, the lights of Albion went out.

TWENTY-TWO

In the isolated control tower of Albion's Travel Hub, holo-data glowed angry red, strips cascading through the air round Blair Gover. Hunched on his swivel chair, he reached out constantly to steady or speed the flow. His work was reaching a critical stage.

City technology always seemed devil's work to Ell, beyond natural understanding. Not the way she instinctively read the sky's moods or sensed the best spot to fish. Even so, she guessed from the sheen on the City-man's forehead and intensity of his gaze, from muffled curses and exclamations, things were not going to plan.

The large, three-dimensional map of Albion floating in the centre of the room had taken on new, pulsating colours as he weaved his sorcery. Ell sensed each new colour somehow meant another aspect of the City under his control. Too much, surely, for a single man's brain to master. The info-pearl glowed on its raised cup like a pulsing full moon.

One thing was dead certain: he had complete control over the hated drones. The two evil wasp-things that killed Captain Ariana were currently hovering near the entrance to the room, Ell's only way to safety. Outside, beyond the steel shutters that had closed to protect the tower, she heard the faint rumble of drone engines overhead.

Flexing her leg muscles, Ell suppressed a dangerous tremble. How long before she made a noise and they detected her? She didn't care to guess. Still Gover's attention was fixed on the columns of light.

"Counter those anomalies for goodness sake, Blair!" he admonished himself. "Spare the over-ride . . . Damn you, Guy Price! I suppose you added *that* code just to spite me. Well, we'll see about your little tricks . . . No, no, you don't! . . Better. Good. Yes. Oh, that's much better."

He reminded her of a man on a wobbly roof-ridge, steadying himself – and his nerves – to avoid tumbling to hard ground. The same was true for herself. The need to stretch aching limbs was growing unbearable.

After an hour, Gover chuckled and activated a flying drone's view of an immense crowd dressed in white. Ell watched in terrified wonder as he spoke in his crisp, oddly womanish way: "Do not fear. Reason and science are restored . . ." For long minutes he rattled on until she wondered if he was mad. Like a malignant child, he wriggled with pleasure when one of the drones crushed a couple of City-folk on fancy flying chairs.

Another hour passed. The drones went off to explore the rest of the tower. She silently stretched and flexed, each movement infinitesimally slow. So far so good.

Gover manipulated the holo-data until images appeared of the land beyond Albion. Now Ell almost betrayed her hiding place. Those were her own people advancing in lines, flags raised, guns and pikes shouldered. There, on a white horse, was the City-exile called Lady Veil. As the holo-image magnified her, Gover muttered.

"My. My. Not slapping me around now, are we? I think a salutary lesson is in order."

With a faint whine of motors, the blast shutters around the control tower retracted. On cue, the flying drones returned and rose to the ceiling where a door slid open to reveal starlit sky. Like wasps emerging from the nest, they slipped outside. One hovered near the control tower, scanning for enemies. The other powered up its propellers, sweeping towards the boundary walls of Albion: toward the Pilgrimage of Fools and its veiled leader.

TWENTY-TWO

Ell knew what she must do. And without a second's delay. But now the opportunity had come – brief as a moth's wing beat – she could hardly breathe. His back was towards her. Drones temporarily gone. Now, now she must strike, as the fisherman hauls up his rod when the float sinks deep. With agonising slowness, she crept from the dark space beneath the consoles, drawing her knife.

Instantly, a sixth sense of danger alerted him. He reeled, jabbing at his screen. But she was lunging, just as the drone surged back into the wide, circular room. A cannon crack. The knife flew from her hand. The impact of the shell threw her limp body towards the control console, where she struck the pulsing info-pearl on its flimsy rod and cup, sending it flying. The transparent globe struck a corner of metal. Cracked. And went dim.

Even as Ell felt consciousness slip away to darkness, the endless dark, she heard a wail of terminal despair. Of utter disbelief and grief. Then the lights went out.

* * *

When the lights faded in Albion, hungry night asserted itself. Four hours remained until dawn.

So many lights of every intensity and hue, burning like miniature suns for decade after decade. The city had feared darkness as it loathed death. Now, right across the twenty-mile diameter of Albion's circle, the only glimmer came from starlight reflected on its pleasure lakes and waterways, or faintly silvered windows.

Albion's great fusion generators shut down with astonishing speed. Flying drones obeyed the command to deactivate, plunging to the ground or smashing into the sides of buildings. Interwoven command and monitoring systems malfunctioned, triggered by codes at the heart of their digital DNA. How appropriate, then, that the Double Helix

Statue, symbol of the Five Cities, should go black as a crow. Buildings ceased to function: elevators, lights, water pumps, domestic systems and appliances, everything except for the most primitive designs. All transport froze, resembling the stranded cars out on the desolate ghost roads. Freezers and fridges crammed with delicacies ceased to chill. Fans to circulate air. In the industrial zones north of Albion's central pleasure and residential core, fully automated factories ceased production. To the south, in drone-maintained agricultural facilities, animals smelt change, even as they fed and shat. Automated doors and gates behaved wilfully: some flew forever open, others locked, a few decided on gaps between the two.

When the lights failed and hungry night resumed its ancient sway over the petty defiance of mankind, all Albion drew its collective breath. A vast lungful of change. Air fated to be released in one long howl.

* * *

After fleeing the control tower, Michael Pilgrim hid beneath the wings of a large aerial drone. Beside him, Tom Higginbottom and Hurdy-Gurdy were reviving. Cutty Stone skulked near the Control Tower's sealed entrance, in the hope of rescuing Ell.

For an agonising time, nothing happened in the Travel Hub. All they could do was wait. Then two small aerial drones rose from the top of the control tower – the same pair protecting Gover. One took up position on the roof, the other winging off towards the boundary wall, visible a few miles away beneath pitiless lights. He heard the crack of a cannon firing. A faint cry. Then, like a cloud-shadow flowing over the land, the lights of Albion dimmed, flickered, and went dark.

A sudden, deep silence descended. Michael leapt up, seeking tricks and traps. Wherever he turned, north, south, every point of the compass, shadows and silhouettes of buildings appeared stark against

TWENTY-TWO

the star-speckled, blue-black sky. A sliver of moon hung between enormous towers to the south-east.

"Tom! Hurdy! What the fuck's happened?"

Hurdy-Gurdy tottered to his feet. Though still twitchy from the electric shock, new vigour flowed into him from the darkness.

"Night," he whispered. "Pure, unpolluted night."

He raised clenched fists and declaimed, "Come, thick night, and pall thee in the dunnest smoke of hell!"

Tom Higginbottom was also on his feet.

"Them drones just fell from the sky," he said, also gaining boldness. "Them evil, bastard drones are dead!"

Michael was not so sure. What was switched off could surely be reactivated. Further minutes passed. No machine moved or flew. Nothing glimmered in the darkness.

"Let's find Gover," he said. "Make sure he's out of action, too."

They hurried to the control tower. There came the flash and crack of a musket. Followed by another gunshot. Michael raced forward, though he was unarmed. Outside the entrance, he found Cutty reloading, peering out across the airfield.

"That were our good friend, Doctor Gover," said the Fen Man. "The doors opened all by 'emsleves. Out he pops like a rabbit fleeing his burrow, and off he scarpers."

Michael pulled out his rechargeable torch.

"Let's look for Ell," he said.

First, they recovered their weapons from the elevator. Having warily climbed the stairs, they found the brave girl who guided them into Albion. Her chest was torn open and burned. Nearby, the aerial drone lay lifeless on its side.

"I reckon she hid and jumped Gover," said Cutty. "An' somehow caused his little game to end."

Michael knelt by the body to close her staring eyes.

"Can Gover do more mischief?" he asked Hurdy-Gurdy.

The City-renegade was searching around the control console. With a cry, he stooped and plucked up what remained of the precious info-pearl. Cracked, it looked like a child's marble.

"I believe the destruction of this pearl interrupted the master-codes at a decisive moment, aborting the entire system. Ha! Indeed, just before it was under Gover's control. Ha!"

"I wouldn't crow too loud," said Tom Higginbottom. "There's still thousands and thousands of the bastards out there. And they won't be happy. Folk'll risk anything to save their necks."

He pointed through the high windows at the silhouetted skyline of Albion's immense buildings.

"Then let's make sure our own friends find us," said Michael.

* * *

They built a line of bonfires near the control tower and waited. Although there was little wood around, machines and padded furniture burned bright when piled up on the tarmac. As they worked, the survivors of the raiding party scanned the runways, guns primed.

An hour brought the drum of hoofbeats. Soon, a large mass of cavalry rode from the darkness. Michael cried out with relief.

The horses were sweating as they cantered up. At their head, Lady Veil and squadrons of black-uniformed Grow People. The less disciplined men and women following broke into a wild cheer. The Growers stayed grim and silent. Nothing would satisfy them until their bloody work began in earnest.

"You got through the gates easily enough then," said Michael, standing by Lady Veil's stirrups. She glanced down at him, eyes bright with expectation, hands moving. Her faithful interpreter spoke.

"She says, 'The boundary gates opened when the City's systems

TWENTY-TWO

failed. We shall wait here until the foot soldiers join us. Then we shall advance immediately on the centre."'

She wheeled her horse to examine the tower blocks a few miles away. Again she gestured.

"She says, 'I have longed for this moment, Michael Pilgrim. Yet nothing is achieved until everything is achieved. We must build more fires to gather the army. Only when we are as one can the cleansing begin. The Hundreds must not become mingled or they will dissolve into confusion. Position each unit no less than ten yards apart."

Michael nodded. "I'll see it is done."

Lady Veil ordered a party of riders to search the enormous terminal building for potential resistance. Little was expected that night. They knew Albion's population was concentrated in the centre for the Great Assignation. The morrow would decide everything.

When the scouts returned, it was with a few technicians and a handful of captured Beautifuls. Most had fled into the darkness at the horsemen's approach. The prisoners were paraded before Lady Veil while they waited for the infantry. Michael made sure he kept close. Here was the first test whether she would demonstrate the restraint towards prisoners they had agreed at York.

"Remember," he warned, "those who willingly surrender or refuse to take up arms against us must be spared."

Lady Veil ordered the binding of the prisoners' hands then gestured with her own.

"She says," intoned the interpreter, "'These technicians may be useful later. Let's hope so, for their sake.'"

No stronger commitment was forthcoming. It hardly reassured Michael.

Two hours before daybreak. The Pilgrimage of Fools massed on the runway. Acrid bonfires lit faces pinched by hardship and hunger.

As chief general, Lady Veil decided the disposition of the forces. A third of the army led by the Protector of the North, would secure the northern area of Albion's enclosed circle, namely, its industrial zones. The remainder, including all the Grow People, as well as fierce companies of Reivers and Jocks, would strike deep into the heart of the City.

Michael agreed without enthusiasm. Questioning the prisoners had revealed few Beautifuls visited the industrial zone at the best of times. He noted the force he led included many of the less martial Nuagers, as well as farmers and Fen Men.

"Remember our agreement," he said to Lady Veil. "Where we can, show restraint."

But she had no more time for quibbles. Already dawn glimmered on the eastern horizon. She was determined to be in the centre by daybreak, a brisk march of six or seven miles.

Companies of Grow People led off the column, following monorail tracks south-east, directly through a small corner of the industrial zone then a strip of woodland and park, to where the first of the great tower blocks rose, plasti-glass walls touched by pink as dawn hardened.

TWENTY-THREE

Stillness across Albion. Birdsong in the green parks and woodlands surrounding its compact centre. Waterfowl raised droplets of silver as they rose in flight from artificial lakes.

On this day, this last day, the wide boulevards empty of motion. No miraculous aircars defied gravity. No transports or automated vehicles threaded patient journeys. No twenty-four hour, drone-tended cafes and stores and entertainment places showed light or life. Not a single Beautiful, walking off a revel, or technician hurrying to fulfil arcane duties.

How many dawns had the people of Albion greeted? Thankful, perhaps, for life when the world that raised them was a vast charnel-house, a memorial to mutability. How many days taken for granted, as the young see only a limitless future for themselves, dazzled by summer. How many days piled upon days, for filling with pleasure and meaning, as best one could? This day was different.

In tower blocks and high-ceilinged duplex apartments, tens of thousands greeted sunlight with relief. All power in their homes faded not long after midnight. Every button or scanner or sensor grew disobedient to commands. Even screens became inert.

They waited, numbed by disasters unimaginable mere hours before. To lack a screen! Comforting holo-displays for instant responses. Streams of gossip and images to comment upon, made personal in line with fashion and the strict dictates of Accordia. Faces and clothes to compare oneself against. Four-dimensional images of activities one should be doing, lest one fall behind. Above all, constant connection, a sense of belonging to life. This deprivation alone paralysed many.

All over Albion, Beautifuls adopted foetal positions to stay calm. Some resorted to cuddling pillows like children. For decade after decade, every need answered, no question of discomfort unless one was foolish enough to dabble in Discordia. Few had sympathy for *that*. A century of rich reward for passivity, not questioning, simply sitting pretty, for perfectly timed, gracious *bon mots*, for suppressing awkward doubts and ambitions.

Impossible that the power would not resume any moment. The drones reactivate. Aircars hum and rise. They waited as sunlight brought morning. Some realised they were hungry or thirsty for the first time they could remember – not even drinking taps worked, and most apartments lacked food supplies, meals or snacks or tipples being summoned from endless choices of dishes prepared by drone-chefs. Some tried to leave their large, airy apartments, only to discover the sliding doors had frozen, trapping them inside. Some peered through windows or stepped out onto balconies, then shrank back in horror.

* * *

Lady Veil's back was straight as any barbarian conqueror riding into Rome. Behind her, companies of Grow People gaped in astonishment at the rectangular mountains of glass and plasti-concrete. How vast was Hell! Yet the devils remained out of sight, hiding and no doubt watching, waiting to issue forth. Certainly they caught glimpses of faces behind windows.

Not far into the City, they came across a large group of dazed men and women conferring together. A few devils still wore the strange white robes from last night's sky pictures; most were garbed in bright fabrics, bizarre suits or dresses. None appeared to carry weapons.

For a long moment, the two sides hesitated. Regarded one another. A moment that would decide Albion's fate.

Folk from village and farm clutched smith-forged guns and blades. Was it possible that harming these gods – so young and blessed with grace, more divine than mortal – would not awaken the drones scattered all around?

Perhaps Lady Veil had anticipated this moment of doubt. Perhaps this was why she had taught the Grow People how the world must be cleansed. She rose on her stirrups and pointed at the huddled, cowed gods and goddesses. Her interpreter screamed out the command.

"Kill and cleanse! Kill and cleanse!"

Still the black-uniformed soldiers hesitated. A few musket barrels lifted. Smoke and flame spat out. The first Beautifuls fell, swept aside.

"Kill and cleanse! Kill and cleanse!" echoed the battle cry.

* * *

A few miles away. Michael Pilgrim led a smaller column from the Travel Hub. His orders were surprisingly vague by the methods he applied as a general, based on exact dispositions and timings to surprise the enemy's weak points. Lady Veil had merely called on his troops to secure the industrial zones, a scattered hotchpotch of plants and facilities in the northern half of Albion's circle. A task proving so easy Michael suspected a trap or ambush. Hardly a human being could be found amidst the cavernous warehouses and factories. Those people that were there – almost exclusively technicians – either fled or surrendered without resistance. They were amazed not to be slaughtered. As for drones, there were endless numbers, frozen like grotesque statues when the City went dark.

For a few hours they marched round in vain, scouts fanning out to explore the area. They returned without any indication that a sizable force of the enemy was waiting to confront them. Michael grew convinced they had only been sent here to allow Lady Veil a free hand in the city centre. Confirmation of his doubt occurred later in the morning.

Scouts had climbed to the top of Warboys Hill, where Albion's main fusion facility stood, for a better view, Michael and Tom Higginbottom amongst them. With binoculars, they scoured the industrial zones for signs of life. Nothing except occasional birds. In the direction of the Travel Hub, a single trail of smoke rose near the cavernous, empty terminal. It was here Iona of Skye had insisted on establishing a makeshift hospital. He calculated the smoke denoted cooking rather than hostilities.

But when Michael looked south towards the towers of Albion, his mouth went dry.

"See what I see?" he asked.

Tom Higginbottom followed Michael's gaze, training his own binoculars.

"Aye," he said. "The madwoman is getting her way down there."

"Damn her! I should have anticipated this. We must get into the centre."

They examined the southern horizon again. Their elevated position placed them on the level of the tallest tower blocks. Smoke was rising on all sides of the City. Black smoke billowed from burning buildings.

"I reckon many of those fires were lit almost simultaneously," said Tom. "She trained them Growers for this moment well. You can't fault Lady Veil for looking ahead."

"I don't want a massacre on our hands," said Michael. "She knows that well enough."

"And you've always known she craves the opposite."

TWENTY-THREE

"I'll not be party to her vendettas, Tom. If we plant mankind's new future badly, it'll grow badly."

Michael prepared to turn his horse to gallop down the hill. To his surprise, a strong grip fastened on his arm, holding him back. He met his friend's tired eyes.

"How did you expect this to end?" asked Tom. "With us all shaking nice clean hands and agreeing to differ?"

Unexpected tears pricked Michael's eyes. He almost heard Grandfather's voice. "Remember, the quality of mercy is not strained, Michael. It droppeth as the gentle rain from heaven. It blesseth him that gives and him that takes. Preserve. Preserve. Preserve."

Was this burning – what the Grow People called a cleansing fire – his precious new hope in human decency? Was the new age to be ushered in by barbarity? Old fears started up like mocking voices, that human beings were unreformable brutes, daft and cruel enough to torch the whole world for a brief advantage.

"What about civilisation, Tom?" His voice was small.

"Maybe it'll come later, maybe it won't," said Tom. "For today, let's get stuck in and finish off this bastard place whatever happens."

"Yes, you're right."

"And I'm right curious what's cooking down there," said Tom.

An apt turn of phrase: the plumes of black smoke were thickening fast.

* * *

In Wakuki's apartment, Averil Pilgrim fidgeted on a sofa. All morning, there had been gunshots and screams from the boulevards below. Bands of primitives were visible like packs of feral dogs seeking prey, some on horses, most afoot. Averil wondered whether anyone she knew might be among the savages.

Savages! Momentary guilt followed her contempt for former neighbours, even friends. But what else were they? All you need do was compare their filthy hovels to the palaces surrounding them to see that. No doubt they were murdering anyone they came across. What stronger proof of savagery?

Merle Brubacher could not settle, alternating between fury and complaints. Where were efficient servants when she needed them? She was cursed with incompetents, cowards and traitors hoping to steal her place. Oh, there would be a harsh accounting when normality returned.

Averil listened miserably. How long it was taking to restore power. It was all anyone could think about this morning. That and how quickly the primitives would be eliminated when the drones came back to life. No one doubted loyal teams of technicians and Beautifuls were heroically repairing fusion flow and algo-networks across Albion.

As for Blair Gover – who everyone blamed for this temporary crisis – Merle alternated between outlining hideous acts of revenge and silent tears.

Only Marvin Brubacher kept his head. Realising most Beautifuls were hiding in their apartments, if they weren't already trapped by faulty doors, he had gone from floor to floor, gathering those capable of resistance and arming them with motley weapons. Knives, swords meant as ornaments yet with edges sharp enough to dismember, clubs, even a few antique firearms still functioning from the Before Times. As for the digitally controlled guns that would have rendered swift corpses of the savages, these had shut down along with the screens and every other system.

Upon noticing smoke rising from neighbouring tower blocks, he had returned to Wakuki's laboratory. The fires changed everything. Although the City was designed with peerless fire control systems – sprinklers, flame suppressant gases, fleets of firefighter drones – none were operative.

"I've got together a few hundred of us," he advised Merle. "And we have our bodyguard-Angels. It's time to get out there and start clearing the City. The fires will bring more of our people out on the street. We must outnumber those scum many times over. Through sheer force of numbers, we can drive the primitives back to their dens."

Averil realised it was a long time since he had used the words *we* and *our* so emphatically. Where was his usual *I* and *my* now? Perhaps this attack would bring the Beautifuls together. If so, the primitives in their roving bands wouldn't stand a chance.

Quivering, Merle Brubacher listened to her son. "You go. I don't feel well, darling. Oh, how did it come to this? I will stay here until power returns."

"You must come, Mother! For all we know it could take days to get the fusion stations operating again. If all else fails, I'm going to break through to the Travel Hub. Remember my steam train? It is entirely mechanical. We could escape to Honeycomb and rebuild there. Don't you see? Gover has somehow used a code to disable everything on the universal network. Do you remember, we always suspected he and Guy Price had a trick like that up their sleeves? Those were rumours we were fools to ignore. If only Guy was here now!"

The young woman who was his aged mother wept, still refusing to quit the security of the apartment.

"Mother dear," he pleaded, 'do come with me. We haven't been apart for so many, many years. For so very long. Do not force me to leave you here alone."

But Merle could not stop shaking.

"I'm safer here with my Angels, darling." The blank-faced creatures stood patiently by the door, halberd in hand. "Oh, Marvin, come back to Mummy when everything is safe!"

He threw up his hands in despair.

"I must go, Mother. Already it might be too late. I will return for you if I can."

Averil left with him, along with Helen Devereux, her hands tied, in case she proved a useful hostage when Blair Gover surfaced. With the banks of elevators broken, hundreds of Beautifuls made tentative progress down unlit stairwells to gather outside.

On the boulevard, no primitives were visible. The acrid stink of burning made Averil cough. As she watched, large groups of Beautifuls emerged from their hiding places. Here were the boldest of them, those determined to fight and risk their precious lives. Those willing to hazard eternity for the paradise of the City. Averil realised she must choose now: flee and hope for mercy from her own people, or march alongside these strangers, wherever the road led.

She noticed her reflection in a glass door. After surgery and other improvements, she closely resembled the models of human perfection around her: sleek and unblemished, all oddly alike, their clothes equally sumptuous. If she was captured by a group of savages, would they even recognise her as one of her own?

"To me!" called out Marvin Brubacher. "Assemble our people! We shall march to the Double Helix Statue."

Averil felt confidence return. So many Beautifuls were appearing on the street, a human tide to wash away the little bands of savages. Someone passed her a gold-plated steel rod from a light fitting as a staff – and vicious club. Averil almost laughed hysterically. In Holy Innocents Church, far away in Hob Vale, there had been a carving of a pilgrim, leaning on his staff. *Oh, Father*, she thought, *forgive me, but I must be a different Pilgrim to you.*

* * *

Seth Pilgrim and the Yellow Hundred found themselves in a vast plaza

TWENTY-THREE

dominated by the twisted statue from last night's sky display. Close up, it was colossal.

Their company had spent the morning prowling round a single, long boulevard, Bella's strangelings in tow. Aggie Brown ensured any Cityfolk they chanced upon – not many – met unpleasant ends. Now and then, excited trigger fingers shot up at windows, knocking crazed holes in the plasti-glass until Aggie ordered them to save their powder for living targets.

Following instructions issued by Lady Veil's staff officers, diehard Growers in uniforms black as ravens, Yellow Hundred had set fire to several mountainous buildings. At first, the flames took slowly, needing encouragement from furniture and wall-hangings, even a few small drones, but once the bonfires got hot enough in elevator shafts and lobbies big as the nave of York Minster, the flames licked plasti-concrete floors and walls – and liked what they tasted. Whatever systems had once been in place to stifle fires were no longer working, along with everything else.

So far, Yellow Hundred had suffered a single casualty. A chair launched from a high balcony struck a lad from Pickering too daft to scurry out of range.

With noon well behind them, they needed rest. Noxious traces in the smoke-tainted air parched their throats. Fortunately, pools of clear water surrounded the big, ugly statue. Though it was peculiar in taste, without a trace of earth, Yellow Hundred drank like thirsty horses.

As they rested, chewing dry husks of bread and salt meat, Seth noticed other Hundreds entering the wide plaza. Some were running, as though in retreat. His eyes stung from the bitter smoke. Beside him, Baxter puffed hungrily on a pipe of *stuff*. Aggie Brown, however, was on her feet.

"Shut the fuck up!" she commanded, though no one had said a word.

Gunshots echoed off canyons of buildings; Seth detected a growing buzz of voices, like angry wasps.

"Do you hear that?" she growled.

"What the fuck is it?"

A slow smile spread across Aggie's ugly fat face.

"Line 'em," she grunted, knocking Baxter's pipe from his mouth.

Drums beating, Yellow Hundred formed a row two deep, facing the source of the swelling noise. Other Hundreds were doing the same, marshalled by Lady Veil on her charger. Several companies of Grow People formed the centre of the line.

Yet when the first ranks of the City-people appeared through the drifting smoke, Seth almost turned tail. Lady Veil's plan was literally misfiring. By setting ablaze so many tower blocks at one time, she had driven thousands of those hiding inside out onto the streets. There they had regrouped, arming themselves as best they could. Amongst them were blank-faced creatures modelled on humans – not many, but enough to make Seth wonder if Hell itself was being loosed to clear the Pilgrimage of Fools from Albion. He realised, too, the bulk of their own army was scattered across the city, igniting more buildings and therefore forcing out more enemies. As it was, less than a thousand stood in line by the Double Helix Statue to counter a force already many times their number.

"Pikes and spears at the front!" came the command. "Shooters behind!"

Seth was just glad to carry a musket and pistols, qualifying him for the dubious safety of the second rank.

Into the plaza pushed the mob of City-folk, waving knives and improvised weapons. By a cruel irony, the primitives' weapons were technologically superior now. Yet there were so many out there! All well-fed and fit. Maddened and with little left to lose as their world burned around them.

"Aim low!" cried the officers of the Hundreds. "Aim low!"

Round lead shot from the guns would skip along the hard flagstones if it struck the ground, almost always finding a target to cripple amongst the mass of bodies confronting them.

A few light cannon and rocket tubes were also rolled into position, their crews frantically laying out fresh charges for further salvos.

"Fire!"

A ragged explosion of flashes, bangs, puffs of sulphurous, stinking smoke. Seth's musket recoiled against his shoulder.

"Load! Load!"

Not that he needed encouragement. Shouldering his gun to peer through the smoke, all hope faded that the volley would stop the mob running towards them. Weapons waved. Voices shrieked out fresh hate. The City-folk trampled their fallen, grabbed weapons from wounded men and women, eager to engage close up.

Another crash of guns, everyone firing at their own pace now. A hundred feet from the line, the front of the surging mass paused. Then countless people jostling behind forced them on. Roaring, they dashed forward, preparing to grapple their tormentors with bare hands if need be.

Beside him, Aggie Brown levelled a blunderbuss big enough to bring down a bull. She was grinning.

* * *

Michael Pilgrim urged on his column. They were in the heart of Albion now, the industrial zone left behind. Ahead, rose a chaotic noise of battle he knew too well. Gunshots, screams, the bedlam of massed voices like clashing waves.

A clatter of hooves on concrete heralded Tom Higginbottom with his party of scouts.

"Is it like it sounds?" asked Michael.

"Worse. You'll love this."

Tom reported they had ridden to the entrance of a great square dominated by a statue. It seemed Michael's worst doubts about Lady Veil's hate-filled strategy might be coming true. Hundreds of their people were surrounded, using the massive podium of the statue as an elevated place to defend. As many appeared to have fallen.

"There's thousands and thousands of the City-bastards out there," said Tom, "mad as hornets. And they're winning, I reckon, despite piles of bodies."

Michael pondered.

"Remember Pickering, Tom? We were badly outnumbered in the market square. Outnumbered and surrounded. Let's do what we did back then. The thing is not to stop or break into a charge. Keep pushing steadily, whatever happens."

Tom licked lips stung by toxic plastic in the smoke.

"Whatever we do, we haven't got long."

Frantic minutes followed. Their Hundreds formed into a broad rectangle, with double rows of spears, halberds and pikes at the front and sides. Why had Lady Veil not drilled the army in this obvious formation, Michael lamented inwardly. Too obsessed with individual throat-cutting and burning, too confident the City-folk were incapable of putting up a fight. Tom had made it clear their enemy consisted of a huge, enraged mob. But collective rage could turn to dismay if a dragon shoved its fire-breathing snout and bristling fangs deep into their midst.

When everyone was in position, he rode to the front and drew his sword. His instinct: order an immediate advance. Then, looking at their faces, he understood the frayed nerves of the farmers and fisherfolk clutching unfamiliar weapons. Many gazed round in awe, intimidated by the sheer size of the buildings, if nothing else. Stationary drones frightened them equally. Who was to say they would not come alive at any moment? The column might not even advance, let alone maintain a strict formation, when it saw the numbers massed against them.

He stood in his stirrups, his deep voice reaching to the back rank of the column.

"This is a good day, friends! The bastards we're up against don't even have proper weapons. We have guns for close and long-range work. Pike and sword, sharp as fresh-whetted scythes! Know what? We bloody well know how to mow, too. Right to the end of the field. Don't we, friends?"

Hundreds had fought with him at Pickering and Lindisfarne. They knew his meaning and cheered. Emboldened, he pressed on.

"Justice, sweet and pure, is on our side. This is our one chance to win it. Our single chance. To be free, I'll fight! And die, if need be. What about you, friends? Are you with me?"

Muttering and angry oaths greeted his question. More cheers.

"Every one of them little monsters we've met so far was soft as butter. Take away their toys, they're like scared bairns. The moment we get those fuckers running, they won't stop this side of London!"

The fabled old capital was a byword for a flooded hellhole, peopled with cannibals.

"That's one city they can keep!" called out a gruff Yorkshire voice. Soldiers laughed and clapped.

"That's right!" pressed on Michael. "Most of all, friends, remember this. Don't stop moving forward. If we stop, they get the edge. Advance when the drums beat. Fire low when the drums stop. Load. Advance when you hear drums again. Let's hit the fuckers like a hammerhead! For freedom and justice! For civilisation!"

A lone cry rose from the ranks. Soon others took up the chant. "A Pilgrim! A Pilgrim!"

Were they not the Pilgrimage of Fools?

Drums beating a tattoo, the column advanced into the great plaza. And just in time.

* * *

Seth Pilgrim pulled the trigger. He could hardly miss. That wasn't the point. The question was whether his trembling fingers and muscles would manage to reload.

The incensed madness of the massed Beautifuls had soon driven them back. Without the haven of the statue's grand podium, they would have been swept away. Already he'd seen Baxter dragged down by a pack of silk-robed young men and women. Bellowing triumphantly, possessed by fury, they tore at his eyes and face, trampling and beating him with clubs and stones until the once affable, twitchy fox of a man lay inert.

Aggie Brown grunted as she swung her enormous cleaver, clearing spaces even the most crazed City-folk were reluctant to fill. A circle of bodies surrounded her before she slipped on fresh blood. Then the mob was over her. She died the same way as Baxter, snarling to the end.

Elsewhere, comrades from Yellow Hundred fought back-to-back. Like floating islands they edged to the statue's podium, hauling themselves up, away from the reach of grasping fingers.

From his elevated position, Seth saw more Beautifuls run into the square. For every one of the bastards they felled, another four or five appeared through the fog of smoke. The air reeked of strange chemicals as Albion burned. A vile stench, like rotten tilth and old bones on a bonfire. Through the haze, he could make out a small group of the enemy gathered at the rear, urging the rest forward. Even amidst the wails and gunshots and madness, someone was still in command.

Then Seth heard a distant chant.

TWENTY-THREE

"A Pilgrim! A Pilgrim!"

He risked taking his eye off the enemy to see a column advancing through the smoke. Familiar flags waved. Drums beat. The phalanx shuffled forward, maintaining a tight formation, stopping every twenty paces to fire off a volley of muskets, pistols, rifles and crossbow bolts, before ranks of spears and halberds closed up again. The deadly spikes bristled and jabbed to allow the men behind to reload. Seth recalled the merciless carnage in the market square at Pickering. There he had faced this same brutal tactic from the other side. Perhaps that was why he hesitated before calling out, his voice squeaky: "A Pilgrim! A Pilgrim!"

The column's tattoo recommenced. They advanced, forcing back mobs of panicking City-folk. A few bold groups charged the lines and were speared or slashed down. After twenty yards, the drums stopped. Spearmen parted to allow shooters forward and the murderous cycle replayed.

Trained, disciplined soldiers might have formed up, fought back. But the Beautifuls of Albion were a pack of individuals forced together by shared peril. Their strength lay only in numbers. One by one, then in groups, they turned and fled. Trapped between two forces, the plaza choked with smoke and bodies, their courage broke. They scattered for shelter. Even the group in charge disappeared into the fog of musket smoke and sooty fumes.

* * *

Many, many hundreds lay dead or dying all around. Wounded Beautifuls groaned in agony or screamed for help or water. No one offered them aid.

Hurdy-Gurdy knelt by a woman's corpse. Her uniform torn, forehead caved in by a heavy implement. Her face's lower half was hideously deformed by modification. He covered it with a blood-stained veil.

When he looked up, Seth and Cutty Stone were watching. The two friends' hands entwined. Neither had words to utter.

"She was not always mad, you know," said Hurdy-Gurdy, clowning forgotten. "Not always vile. They destroyed what was good in her. She became a creature of pure revenge." He sighed. "Perhaps it is fitting then that revenge consumed her. Ironic, my young friends, as well."

"How's that, Gurdy?" asked Seth.

He seemed not to hear. Hurdy-Gurdy stroked her blood-soaked hair. "Farewell, my dear. We both did terrible, terrible wrongs then tried to do right. Perhaps too late, we tried to do right." He sighed. "When we are born, we cry that we are come upon this great stage of fools. My own exit will follow yours soon. But the stage shall not be left bare. It never needed us, my dear, not really. And that is the best show of all."

Hoofbeats and jingling harness brought over Michael Pilgrim and Tom Higginbottom. They leaned down from their saddles to examine Lady Veil's corpse. Michael's face bore marks of deep exhaustion. He nodded to his wayward nephew.

"Good to see you, Seth. Thank God you made it. And if it isn't Masters Gurdy and Stone."

Hurdy-Gurdy remained on his knees beside the dead woman.

"There are too many of our fallen to bury today," said Michael. "Even Lady Veil. May her spirit be at rest."

He gestured at the buildings hemming them. Smoke billowed from windows melting in the heat. "The city's on fire all over. Even though I've assumed command now that Lady Veil is dead, we hear the Grow People have spread out to set ablaze anything already not burning. They call Albion the martyr's funeral pyre. Drones, vehicles, houses, buildings, everything. All must burn, so they say."

"But you are their general, General," said Hurdy. "Have you no sway?"

Michael laughed bitterly. "There will be scant discipline tonight. The night that's coming is one for wild, vengeful bands not disciplined soldiers. And it is not one to find us in the city centre. We'll withdraw to the parklands. There's water there, if nothing else. In the morning we can regroup and see how things stand."

"I fear a rough night," said Hurdy-Gurdy, rising to his feet.

"Then help us find a good place to spend it. As you see, many Hundreds are still loyal to my command. In the morning, we shall reassemble the army in the Travel Hub. Meanwhile, we need your knowledge of this place to find a safe camp for tonight."

An hour later, a straggling column that included numerous wounded, marched from the city centre, guided to the east by Hurdy-Gurdy. He led them to a large, shallow pleasure lake encompassing several square miles; it was dotted with manmade islands for pavilions and gardens, linked by ornate, arched bridges.

"This is Holywell Lake," he said, "an appropriate enough place for a Pilgrimage of Fools."

They camped on its shore, at the foot of a large, conical hill, a couple of miles from the outskirts of the city. The old holotainer explained the hill was all that remained of St Ives, a populous town in its day. A sly expression crossed his face as he crooned out a song, watching soldiers strip and bathe in the lake water to wash away sweat, soot and blood:

As I was going to St. Ives,
I met a man with seven knives,
Each knife had seven sacks,
Each sack held seven heads,
Each head bled and bled:
Blood, heads, sacks, and knives,
How many were left alive?

* * *

From the top of St Ives Hill, Michael was granted visions of Albion worthy of nightmare. Visions with a dream's powerlessness to intervene. Tower blocks and lesser buildings blazed in the darkness, flames fanned by a fierce wind blowing in from the east. Fortunately, Gurdy had chosen their campsite well. The smoke was carried away from them, otherwise they would have coughed through a long night.

Michael Pilgrim paced on the crest of the hill, fascinated by the inferno.

Should he not rejoice? Hated Albion was on its way to becoming a pile of ash, its defenders scattered like chaff, fleeing the city in all directions. Was it his fault the Grow People's fanaticism would write itself in chaos and massacre? Yet victory tasted acrid as the tainted air. He was the leader now, and must establish his authority for the good of all. Fires were springing up not just in the city centre, but the industrial zone. Hurdy-Gurdy, graver by the hour, warned of chemicals and poison gases being released. Already, several explosions had cast fireballs into the sky.

As they conferred, staring through clouds of smoke and ominous, dazzling flashes, Tom Higginbottom pointed north. The massive fusion plant on Warboys Hill, almost ten miles away, was ablaze. Chemicals and arsenals of ammunition for the security drones were bad enough. If the fusion plant exploded, no one wished to contemplate the consequences.

"We must anticipate the worst," Michael told his officers. "Keep St Ives Hill between us and the fires to the north. I am tempted to retreat from Albion altogether but the troops are too exhausted."

At the southern foot of the hill, Holywell Lake's waters shimmered with fiery reflections. Bodies floated where despairing Beautifuls had waded into deep water to drown themselves. Shadowy groups escaping into the countryside flitted through the eerie, semi-darkness like ghosts. A few, dazed beyond fear, staggered over to the huddled primitives they had dreaded only hours earlier, begging for a little food and protection.

Michael remained on the crest of the hill with a squadron of cavalry. His anxious thoughts drifted to the Travel Hub where Iona and other Nuagers had established the hospital and safe haven for wounded folk of both sides. Although Michael knew the Nuagers were well-armed and far from defenceless when provoked, City-folk might gather in sufficient force to overrun them. A good fifteen miles of hostile ground, much of it burning out of control, lay between Michael and his lover, heavy with their child. If anything happened to her, he would blame himself until his last breath.

In the early hours, he woke from a fitful doze with his back against a tree. A boom, followed by waves of percussive rumbling, flares of incandescence, pulsing flashes, shook the earth for miles around. A silo of munitions going up, he reckoned. Nor did the explosions stop there. The fusion plant on Warboys Hill tore itself apart soon after, forming a pillar of fire visible far, far across the flat Fenlands, tinting their silty waters crimson. Shards of plasti-concrete and metal showered like glowing sparks over Albion, some reaching as far as St Ives Hill.

As Michael cowered behind a tree, praying no debris would hit him, Hurdy-Gurdy appeared with a red and white striped umbrella held above his head.

"This is the way the world ends," said the madman. "Not with a whimper but a bang."

* * *

Between parklands surrounding the centre of Albion and its starkly functional industrial zone, an extensive buffer of scenic woodlands had been cultivated. Paths of yellow brick parquet wound through artfully selected trees and scented shrubberies, waterfalls, rock formations. A delightful arcadia for loitering and trysting serenaded by holograms of nightingales or twittering charms of finches. Not now.

Smoke obscured the path as the woman stumbled deeper into the woods. She coughed and coughed. Billows of hot air parted the black shroud over the city. She stared up through a gap in the trees at an immense tower block illuminated by flames.

Tiny dots were falling like soot from the topmost storeys, a steady rain of plunging figures. Thousands upon thousands of trapped Beautifuls had retreated to the highest storeys to escape the smoke and flames spreading inexorably upwards. Thousands more dosed themselves with sprays and cocktails of the strongest intoxicants until they raved, wept tears of incoherent joy, then slumped unconscious.

Those still capable of decision smashed floor-to-ceiling windows. Buffeted by hot winds, they gazed down into trenches of fire and smoke far below. Perhaps they wondered at the miracle of their lives: so much seen and touched and felt. So much time rubbed between ever-renewed fingers of self until – here, now – it must blow away like dust. And so they blew away, falling, twisting, vanishing into the pall below.

The woman in the woods watched with an unaccustomed fear – and such was her nature – a residue of scorn. She would not jump and die. Not her. Nor did she flee the doomed City alone. Two tall, broad creatures with featureless faces and wickedly curved halberds accompanied her. Oh no, she would not jump from frying pan to fire. She knew her brave son would be making his way to the Travel Hub under the cover of darkness, to find his precious toy train that once seemed a mere indulgence. It would bear them to Honeycomb, where an unprecedented justice would be hatched against their enemies. First, she must find him.

Merle Brubacher pushed through the trees, coughing, choking. One

TWENTY-THREE

guardian Angel went ahead, the second behind. When they came across other refugees from the carnage, slumped or gulping from trickling waterfalls that no longer gushed, their pumps out of action, the Angels chopped them aside.

She reached a clearing within a swathe of tall gingko trees. Had such things ever interested Merle Brubacher, she would have known the trees were survivors, not unlike her precious self. Its species had endured 270 million years.

In the clearing stood an ornamental pagoda, transplanted from the gardens of Japanese Emperors deposed by time. There, a man struggled to adjust the saddle on his skittish horse. The beast whinnied, unsettled by waves of heat and sparks in the wind.

Merle Brubacher halted. Disbelief became sudden, vindictive elation. Yes, here was confirmation of her triumphant destiny! The man had been known to her for more than a hundred and fifty years. First, as a pampered employee, then ally, then equal, then mortal enemy.

"Blair Gover!" she cried.

Her immediate instinct was to order the Angels to dissect him with their halberds. Then she wondered if he could still prove useful. She imagined presenting him to Marvin as a gift. Her cowardice in Wakuki's apartment seemed an unforgivable lapse now; it left her without her son's protection, and made her seem weak. And Merle Brubacher swore never to be weak.

Oh, for a drone! The Angels that had seemed so ripe with potential were stupid and unsubtle. One could not trust this pair to manage a prisoner without reverting to their primary function and killing him.

Blair Gover's astonishment matched her own. Yet it was he who spoke first.

"My God, you are still alive!"

"I will always be alive. Did you think Marvin and I have no doubles?"

He paused to reflect. "I should have anticipated that." Gover averted his eyes from the burning towers behind her. A sudden scream in the near distance was drowned out by the bark of a dog or fox. Or was it the harsh caw of a triumphant crow, followed by a cry of, "No! Get away from me! No!" Menacing silence returned to the clearing.

"What have you done, Merle? Why did you turn against me?"

Merle Brubacher shook her head.

"What have I done? I *evolved*, you fool."

"We had everything. We ruled the whole world. Was that not enough?"

"Enough?" Her voice was shrill.

"Think what we have lost," he said. "When we wished to travel we flew faster than sound. When we hungered, the whole world's fruits were there for our choosing. Biting cold or burning sun, they did not trouble us. If we wanted to please our minds, endless entertainments were a word away. If sad, the subtlest stimulants adjusted our moods exactly as we wished. Was that not enough?"

"I reject the very word *enough*," she cried. "Or *too much*. That is for the little people who cannot compete. You knew that, Gover. Yet you went soft. You broke the rules of power."

He shook his head. "Perhaps we deserve this. For our hubris. For our blindness. "

Merle Brubacher turned to the Angels. "Hold him! But do not kill! No kill! Understand?"

Gover woke abruptly from his horrified daze. He scrambled to mount the horse. A hopeless attempt. Even as he placed a foot in the stirrup, the Angels lunged forward. Before they could reach him, down came a hurtling whoosh of feathers and claws.

From the trees swooped a creature, half small man, half owl. It tore with wicked claws at the blank faces of the guardian Angels, the gashes releasing a thick, black ichor. The Angels stumbled back, waving to fend it off.

TWENTY-THREE

Moments later, other horrors surrounded Merle Brubacher. She screamed, looking for a means of escape. A humanoid fox lunged. Was that upright creature a slavering dog or a teenage boy? And there, a girl-hare, its fur spotted with blood, claws curled.

Merle screeched at the Angels. "Don't just stand there! To me! Kill them! Kill them all!"

But the empty faces of the Angels – though designed without the capacity to express emotion – somehow suggested wonder. They stared rapt at the pack of strangelings. It was as though they recognised distant kin.

"I ordered you to kill them! To me! To *me*!"

The guardian-Angels stood rooted, weapons dangling.

Bella Lyons moved forward. Something about the young woman kneeling and shouting was familiar. She squealed to her comrades and they paused, surrounding the woman, licking lips, hooting, sniffing or snuffling, according to characteristics melded through their flesh.

Then, as sometimes it would, like the waking pictures behind her open eyes, a memory came to Bella Lyons.

After the City-folk and drones carried her and Abbie away from Fylingdales in the great air machine, its hold full of sobbing young people like themselves, they had been paraded like prize pigs for salting . . . Faces cold and watchful, none listening as Bella broke from the terrified huddle of kids to confront them, to beg they be taken home, where they were loved by parents and friends and relatives, folk who would weep forever that they'd been stolen.

Only one woman bothered to reply. A hard-faced woman neither old nor young, clearly used to command. She stood beside a handsome man with one eye brown, the other brilliant blue. The woman had laughed, saying, "We'll see how much spirit you have left, my dear, once we've improved you. Won't we, Guy?"

"Yes," he had said, "though we do like a bit of spirit. It shows a strong survival instinct. They will need that to perform the full gamut of tests once re-released in the wild."

"Oh, *spirit*," the woman had replied, scornfully. "It always amazes me how the little people before the plagues were so proud of their precious *spirit*. As though *spirit* made them somehow unique. Or worthy of preservation. Naturally, these primitives are no better. One day we will need to dampen their spirits forever."

Spirit, that was their word. And now, in this wood, this clearing, the same woman begged for her life. The same woman who had laughed about wanting to *improve* her.

Bella's memory pictures flashed a different way. Now she was a little girl, Abbie beside her, going through the magic tunnel back in Fountains with Jojo in the lead. "Don't be afraid," he had urged them. "I'll be a wizard when we get back out in the sun. An' I'll cast a spell so the whole world is like it was before the Dyings. There'll be families having picnics on the grass. And they'll share food with us from the Before Times. Just like in the picture book, food and drink no one knows how to make no more. Cake and fizz and sugar! An' all the machines will be our friends, not like drones, they'll help not hurt. Everyone will be happy and safe, you'll see. Come on, Abbie! Come on, Bella! Let's go back there together!"

The girl-hare had been allowed no tear ducts. Else she would have wept to remember kind, earnest, noble Jojo. To remember their childish dreams of the Before Times that could never return.

She hopped closer to the young woman who long ago, in the old life, the good life, taunted her with *spirit*. Her hare's tongue worked at the syllables.

"S-s-s-pi-pi-t-t-t."

She could not voice it. Speech and the power to explain her feelings had been stolen, along with everything else.

TWENTY-THREE

Merle looked up in terror at the hybrid creature – one of Dr Guy Price's organic toys, that much was clear – until the hare-girl squeaked. Moments later, breath was crushed from her lungs by biting, kicking, tugging monsters.

When Bella Lyons restored order, the man and horse were gone. The two blank-faced creatures had stumbled away, razor-sharp halberds abandoned. The mangled body of the woman lay on its back, staring up sightlessly into the foliage of a ginkgo tree. The pack of strangelings moved off in search of fresh vengeance – and encountered plenty.

* * *

Averil Pilgrim waited in darkness. Towards dusk, Marvin Brubacher led his party through the empty streets of the industrial zone, even as the great towers of Albion took fire in earnest. They numbered two hundred now, increasingly well-armed, with more picked up on the way. Yet no one wanted a fresh confrontation with the primitives. The battle before the Double Helix Statue, which Averil had watched, standing beside Marvin, proved their superiority. Only with drones could the Beautifuls hope to regain what was theirs.

Averil found it easier not to consider such things. Nor feel. She was quite numb, her joy-spray fully used up to win a little calm. Everything was dreamlike: the smoke billowing, air alive with pretty sparks like fireflies, the people around her, their bright silks soiled with soot and blood and grime. Helen Devereux, too, arms bound in front, prodded along like a reluctant cow.

As night took firm hold, Marvin ordered a halt at the edge of the Travel Hub. An area of plasti-concrete and occasional patches of grass stretched for miles. Hundreds of drone aircraft parked in neat parallel lines around fuelling and control centres. The scene was lifeless as tombstones, not a single light except for reflections of the burning city.

Marvin sent out a few reliable Beautifuls to search for primitives but the whole area was abandoned. Little surprise with the savages rampaging and looting in the city centre. Yet Averil's sharp young eyes noticed a glimmer of lamps in the enormous glass terminal building that had so astonished her when she first landed in Albion. The returning scouts reported a sizable number of primitives tending the wounded. Makeshift beds had been laid out. Bright flags depicted whales, suns, moons and stars. A dozen armed men kept guard.

Even in her haze, Averil realised she could be useful.

"Marvin," she said, pointing at the terminal. "They must be Nuagers. They prefer peace to war. I'm sure they won't attack unless we attack them."

He laughed harshly. Yet his strange face bore no trace of mirth. "How kind of them."

"They're soft. If you wanted to attack *them*, they might not even fight back. You could steal their guns."

He glanced speculatively at the lamps in the distance. Averil became aware Helen Devereux was staring at her, a strange look on her silly cow face.

"An interesting proposition," he said. "But no, let them enjoy themselves while they can. We shall find better weapons in Honeycomb. I cannot afford the slightest delay in escaping."

Marvin Brubacher turned to address his bedraggled followers. For a long moment, Averil detected weariness, more of soul than body, in his gaunt expression. He drew himself straight, looking boldly from face to face. The whites of his eyes took on a red tinge from the conflagration.

"What a fine party this is!" he cried.

Stifled sobs greeted his words.

"Tears won't put out the fire behind us," he said. "Don't try, or you'll be trying my patience. And that I would not advise. It has worn mighty thin." Again he paused. "But when we get to Honeycomb, we'll find all is not lost. Blair Gover might have brought this ruin on us, but he can't take away Honeycomb. *There* we will find drones, fusion plants, the means to renew our cells. Honeycomb shall be our new Albion until we decide how to regain what seems lost to us now. What is a day, a year, when we shall have forever to live like gods?"

No one sobbed now. New courage settled on the motley crowd of survivors.

"An unconquerable will! That's what we must show going forward. Remember, the whole world was made just for us. For our precious lives. Now follow me. And if you fall behind, look after yourselves."

Commanding everyone to stay low, he picked a stealthy route, a good distance from the Nuagers, hurrying from the shelter of one large drone aircraft to the next. Averil kept her gaze averted from the fires behind them. Honeycomb, she told herself, everything would be sweet and safe and perfect in Honeycomb. Marvin knew. He thought of everything. She trusted him absolutely as she would trust – but Averil did not dare to think how few people there were left on this earth to rely upon.

At last, they reached the engine depot at the edge of the runways where Marvin Brubacher's favourite new toy, his steam train was maintained. He hurried into the high-roofed shed, directing the ugly machine to be fed with fuel.

How clever, thought Averil, the steam engine relied on not a spark of electricity or any code. It would fly to Honeycomb and no one could stop them!

She felt a tug on her arm, and turned to find Helen Devereux.

The former curator of the Baytown Museum, once adored by her naïve assistant, had never appeared so haggard to Averil. Yes, an old wrinkled hag. Even in her drugged state, Averil felt an almost physical disgust at Helen's blackening teeth. So different from the lovely, brave young men and women rushing to load the train with spare coals and whatever food and drink could be found. They seemed a higher species.

"Averil!" hissed Helen. "Now is the time to run. No one is watching. We must go!"

She shrank back as though from a diseased beggar. Go? But they were going to Honeycomb.

"We must warn your people over at the terminal. Marvin Brubacher must not reach Honeycomb."

Then she understood. Clarity washed away her haze. Helen wanted her to give up the Beautiful Life, as though Honeycomb should not exist. She was jealous, the same old story ever since their arrival at Mughalia. But Averil was never going back to the pigsties of Baytown. Back to the certainty of dying, not just physically, but in her heart. Never would she risk falling into the hands of another Queen Morrighan. *She* would be like a queen after the Beautifuls gathered and pitted their wits against darkness, after they triumphed. Thousands upon thousands must have survived. Most would find their way to Honeycomb in time, a great army for rebuilding then revenge. Oh, Averil knew where the safety of power lay – and was prepared to risk everything to secure it.

"We must go," urged Helen. "While we still can."

Averil seized her. Here was how she could please Marvin!

"What are you doing?" hissed Helen.

"The prisoner is trying to get away! Stop her! Help me someone! "

Then Helen Devereux did a thing Averil would never have imagined possible from her. She pulled back her head, and slammed it against Averil's nose. The girl staggered back, clutching her face, and in that moment Helen was running, running. She vanished behind a long drone aircarrier.

Steam was up in the laden locomotive. Averil pulled herself aboard, even as it chuffed and puffed and clanked from a siding onto the main monorail track to Honeycomb. A few minutes later, they were pushing

TWENTY-THREE

through the boundary gate into the darkness of wild, open country. Not once did Averil look back. She did not dare.

If she had, she might have noticed a child-size, airborne creature, half-human, half-owl, pursuing the train for a few miles then banking back towards the inferno of Albion.

TWENTY-FOUR

It had been a hard winter but now spring was awakening.
One dawn, when frost and mists defied the sun's growing confidence, a large company of horsemen prepared to debouch from a derelict motorway service station where they had spent the night. All were armed as if for imminent battle.

Along an ancient dual carriageway, picking trails between rusted vehicle hulks and saplings, they came to a work of mankind undismayed by time. It was a steep embankment of earth, reinforced with City plastibrick. Six month's neglect had already encouraged a few plants to burrow into its smooth sides. On top, two parallel monorail tracks ran upon a thick plasti-concrete bed.

Michael reined his horse at the foot of the bank. Sweat was visible on man and beast. He glanced down. Mangy white sticks poked through autumn's leaf litter. Bones were a familiar enough sight but these were recent.

"Tom," he said. "Why not take a look up there."

The iron-shod hooves of Tom Higginbottom's horse clumped up the embankment. He was forced to cling tight to its neck.

"Nothing to worry about here," he called down. "Here's hoping."

The company joined him, spreading out to form a long column, two abreast. To their right, the sea at high tide roiled and moved, grey beneath a slate sky. To their left, mountain slopes clad with young

TWENTY-FOUR

woodland. The monorail track followed this undulating strip between mountains and sea.

As they travelled, Michael noticed ever more bones scattered around the embankment, along with plastic clothes and boots. Confirmation, perhaps, of Hurdy-Gurdy's theory that the great mass of Beautifuls fled this way when Albion tumbled. Summer back then: autumn and winter lay between, and no one knew how those months had been used by the refugees. Hence this expedition beyond the ruins of Liverpool to North Wales.

The weeks following the City's cataclysm had been busy for the Pilgrimage of Fools. The necessity of returning home to prepare for winter pressed heavy on the volunteer army. Already, too much valuable time had been lost. What use vanquishing the hated City if you and your kin starved? Still, some precautions to ensure their enemy never recovered its strength could not be neglected.

Fires burned on and off for weeks, fanned by dry weather and the fanatical ministrations of the Grow People. Their thoroughness as arsonists applied to practical buildings, equipment, boats, and exquisite palaces alike. In short, almost anything combustible.

At first, Michael tried to restrain them. A futile endeavour. Besides, a thorough razing of Albion's terrifying technology comforted an ever-present fear.

His special concern became the thousands of drones and weapons all over the City. In this work, he received unexpected assistance. Iona's hospital and safe haven in the Travel Hub – a sanctuary for all who needed it, regardless which side they belonged to – attracted hundreds of useful prisoners. Strictly supervised, the technicians and even a few willing Beautifuls proved skilful at locating and disabling drones. Michael used their knowledge to identify arsenals of weapons and ammunition. Initially, he considered keeping some back for the defence of the Commonwealth of the North. But the Crusades, along with too many bloody conflicts, had taught him blades too easily turn against their wielders. Every weapon and military drone they found was rendered useless.

Albion's fall attracted hordes of scavengers from all over the South Country and beyond. Such was the Grow People's destructive zeal, the loot left for the marauders diminished day by day.

Some spoils of war took a human form. Iona was distressed to hear of survivors wandering in the countryside rounded up as slaves. Impractical and effete for heavy work, their godlike beauty attracted baser, bestial attentions.

"A cruel way to begin a better age," Iona sighed to Michael. "Can we no protect them? Remember, I was bonder to the Prince O' Ness. I ken such sorrows."

He shrugged helplessly. Short of patrolling the countryside to liberate the slaves, there was nothing to be done.

Sometimes he turned scavenger himself, mindful of his Grandfather's stern injunction to *preserve, preserve, preserve*. Although the Five Cities had long discarded paper as their chosen medium for written communication, relying on diverse holo-projections (what Michael called writing on air) he did discover a large library of books from the Before Times, unscorched by the Growers' flames. This treasure house gained an instant armed guard. Indeed, he commandeered it as his headquarters to put off potential looters.

"We shall establish a great library and university in York Minster," he told Iona, his earnestness making her smile. "Think of it! The core of a new learning, the property of all mankind. In time, freshly penned books shall join these old tomes. And some of the world's wonders shall be preserved."

The bump of her pregnancy was unmistakable now. She held her stomach as he talked; Michael sensed her thoughts were on their baby,

TWENTY-FOUR

not musty, dusty paper covered with often incomprehensible words, symbols, stories and voices. Nor could he disapprove. Every person's flesh is a book, a dialogue with time, a conversation between soul and world. Their child in Iona's womb was writing its own prologue even as it formed.

* * *

A long day's ride brought the company to the Menai Straits between Anglesey and the mainland. Again, the tide was high, waves cresting in the wind. Only a single bridge stood intact, an imposing affair of City construction; others had been reduced to enormous piles of debris in the wide sea channel. Likewise, all buildings for half a mile on each side of the monorail track had been flattened.

To find shelter that night, Michael ordered a detour into the ruins of a town overlooking the straits. According to his map from the Before Times, it had been called Bangor.

As they camped, cold, stiff, hungry and weary, he sought out Hurdy-Gurdy. The old holotainer sat before a large fire tended by Seth. Michael watched from the shadows as his nephew placed a blanket round the grizzled City-man's shoulders. Over the previous months, Gurdy had aged visibly. The magic keeping him hale and strong was dimming.

"This'll warm you, you old devil." Seth passed over a porridge of oats, dried mushrooms, walnuts and strips of salt pork.

Michael cleared his throat and met his nephew's eye. Both tensed.

"May I join you?"

"Uncle," said Seth.

As warm a welcome as he was likely to get. Another bowl was found for him, Seth eating straight from the cooking pot. No one spoke for a while. As he chewed the tough pork, Hurdy hummed a keening melody, concluding each verse with a belch.

"Thanks," said Michael, laying aside his empty bowl. "Right welcome, that was. Now Master Gurdy, I want to ask what we can expect on yon island tomorrow." He gestured in the direction of Anglesey. "You're the only one among us who has been there."

"Ah, travellers' tales!" Cunning eyes flashed in the firelight. "Be not afeard! The isle is full of noises. As for me, I must sleep. Hurdy is tired of the clouds."

"No time for sleep yet," said Michael.

"But poor Hurdy is a-weary of this world. He is ready to sleep and wake no more."

"You're just tired from the ride," broke in Seth.

Michael produced his ancient map of the area.

"I don't imagine much of this is still here," he said, illuminating it with his torch.

Gurdy did not even bother to look at the faded paper. "The shape of the land is still there," he said. "The rivers and hills. The streams and beaches."

He explained how the Five Cities banned all primitives from setting foot on Anglesey when they built Honeycomb, exterminating those foolish enough to hang around. Moreover, constant drone patrols had enforced the rule ever since.

"That must require a fair number of drones. What if they've managed to get some working again?"

Gurdy leered. "Then all the king's horses and all the king's men won't glue our gullets together again."

"Reassuring. What about those refugees from the City that Helen Devereux told us about? You reckoned thousands upon thousands would have tried to reach here. By the number of bones around the monorail, a great many perished on the way."

"Desperate feet find ways to stumble on," said Gurdy. "I predict a

TWENTY-FOUR

great many will have completed the journey."

"Even more reassuring. Well, I'll bid you both good night. Looks like tomorrow will be a big day."

"Tomorrow is today and yesterday," declared Hurdy-Gurdy, addicted as ever to the last word. "Breakfast, lunch and supper. Not necessarily in that order."

"What the fuck do you ever mean?" asked Seth.

"Buzzzzz," was Hurdy's reply.

* * *

Daybreak found them beside their horses, examining the suspension bridge over a wide channel of seawater. Visible on towers by its entrance were automated cannon emplacements, as well as a dozen stationary aerial drones on platforms, poised like hawks. On the far side of the bridge, Anglesey stretched away into a haze of tree-covered hills. The wind sighed, stirring branches still bare of leaves.

"Only one way to find out if them drones work," said Tom.

Michael's instinct was to volunteer himself. But leadership can make an apparent coward of the bravest man. He must preserve himself for the common good.

Tom shook his head. "Not this time. Better me than you, I reckon."

Before he could set off, a horseman trotted forward.

"I'll go with you."

Tom examined Seth Pilgrim with surprise then distaste.

"I prefer someone reliable at me back."

Seth's flush of shame became anger.

"Then you watch *my* back, Tom Higginbottom. Yah!"

Urging on his mount, Seth cantered down the smooth plasticoncrete surface of the monorail track as it sloped to join the bridge. Tom seemed inclined to spur after him: the poised aerial drones persuaded him otherwise.

The company watched as Seth rode alone to the entrance of the bridge. No drones moved. No cannons swivelled. Slowing, he trotted over the wide strait to the far side, before riding back again.

The clouds that had brooded for days opened and a shaft of sunlight brightened the grey channel. Though generally scornful of superstition, Michael was a man of his time, and took it as proof his dear brother watched from the grave – and approved his son's reformation.

On they rode, following the monorail track across the island. No other roads existed, save the trails of deer or wild boar. All buildings and traces of humanity lay in mounds beneath vegetation. Crows and rooks cawed indifferently as they rode. Bones remained plentiful on the way, and Michael did not doubt carrion birds and feral dogs were the fatter for it.

Around midday, they came across a broken-down steam train and several carriages. It stood abandoned on the track. The plant and moss suggested it halted there some time in the previous summer. Presumably, its passengers completed their journey on foot.

Helen Devereux had described this exact train; and how Averil chose to join it. Michael thought it better to say nothing in case Seth's hopes were raised that she might yet be alive.

The monorail tracks continued over a saltmarsh then through boggy, lichen-hung woodland, rendered eerie by mist and the calls of unfamiliar birds. It was dusk before they reached another long, elevated bridge over a wide, shallow sea channel.

Beyond, in the dwindling light, a small island rose dramatically. Michael's old map named it Holy Island. All traces of a town called Holyhead and its satellite industrial districts had vanished, presumably demolished, the rubble removed. Hurdy-Gurdy pointed excitedly at a low mountain.

TWENTY-FOUR

"Behold!"

Seth sighed. Hurdy had been in one of *those* moods for days.

"Fiddle-dee-dee! Ah, me! Behold the wellspring of the Five Cities' power and depravity. That mound of granite and limestone conceals a masterstroke against nature."

It looked natural enough to Seth.

"Within that cradle of earth and stone a monstrous child was spawned." Gurdy paused for maximum effect. "Can you guess its name?"

Seth waited.

"Well, what was it?" he asked, finally.

"Buzzzz."

"I had a feeling you might say that."

Then Hurdy murmured, "Honeycomb."

* * *

Seth sat swathed in blankets, Hurdy-Gurdy beside him. Day was driving back night but he retained a lingering bad dream. He poked the embers of their fire, more for illumination than warmth.

"We'll be breaking camp soon," he said. "What do you reckon we'll find?"

"Be-a-ut-if-i-ca-tion," said Gurdy with relish.

"Is that something to worry about?"

"Looking at you, darling, I would say not. Ha! Ha!" His tone became pedantic. "It refers to the cellular process by which renewal rejuvenates human tissue and organs, rendering them – assuming repeated treatments – effectively sempiternal. *That* was Honeycomb's special racket."

"Right you are," said Seth, none the wiser.

Dawn came, horses were saddled. Seth's breakfast of gravelly oatcake tasted like mould. As he chewed, men and horse's breath clouded the frosty air.

Michael Pilgrim led the first ranks along the monorail track to a stretch of sandy sea channel between Anglesey and Holy Island. An elevated causeway bridge connected the two, though at low tide it might have been possible to wade or swim across.

Their horse's hoofs clip-clopped as they cantered over the causeway. Weapons were kept to hand: all were acutely aware of their vulnerability. No one challenged or opposed them. Back on land, they spread out across landing fields dotted with abandoned flying drones – a smaller version of Albion's Travel Hub. Here the monorail ended in a large glass terminal building.

One grim difference between the two places was obvious and pungent. A grisly detritus littered the plasti-concrete surface: yet more piles of bones and the clothes that formerly warmed their owners. Some appeared to have been burned in a feeble attempt at public hygiene. A sickening stench rose from more recent bodies. It seemed no attempt had been made to bury them. Rats scurried and a large pack of feral dogs prowled, alarmed by the horses and armed men. Crows and other carrion birds strutted among the bones.

"What the fuck happened?" Seth muttered. "There's so many."

Gurdy declaimed, "For God's sake, let us sit upon the ground. And tell sad stories of the death of kings."

Tom Higginbottom and a dozen men were sent over to the terminus building. Numerous drones stood inert. Grotesque, menacing statues, evidence – Seth prayed – the survivors never restored Honeycomb's fusion capacity.

He peered through the morning mist at Holyhead Mountain, rising steeply a couple of miles to the west. Limestone crags climbed above furze and bracken at its foot. Gulls haunted the cliffs on its seaward side with circling white shapes. A lone road ran from the monorail terminus, up the hill to a monumental, arched entrance near the mountaintop. This, Gurdy told him, was the sole way into Honeycomb, an underground warren carved from living rock.

Seth looked numbly at the piles of skeletons. Perhaps Averil lay among them, dishonoured and unmourned.

A single gunshot echoed from the terminus. Minutes later, a procession emerged through its glass doors. Gaunt figures dressed in multiple layers of once gaudy robes, skirts, cloaks, trousers, anything to fend off the cold. Many stumbled along with the aid of sticks. Seth counted fifty or so, no more. Behind, chivvying them but keeping their distance, were Tom Higginbottom and his men.

"Surely there must be more survivors," said Seth. He could not see Averil among the assembly of scarecrows.

Hurdy-Gurdy sang softly as he watched a rat the size of a fat puppy scurry past:

Three blind mice, three blind mice,
They cut off their tails with a carving knife,
Just three blind mice.

* * *

Fires were lit and stew pots set to bubble while Michael Pilgrim questioned the prisoners in the terminus building. Hurdy-Gurdy listened to confirm their tales bore a semblance of truth. As usual, Seth accompanied him. He felt safer with his remarkable friend to hand.

The Beautifuls were wretched and malnourished, eyes over bright, bellies distended. Starvation had brought on a host of other illnesses. Most had rasping, strained breath. Some, it was clear, had little time left on this earth, fallen, immortal angels banished to Hell.

A scribe from the Council of the North recorded their testimonies, piecing together the chain of events.

Marvin Brubacher's steam train had chugged slowly along the monorail track where shuttles once sped at two hundred miles an hour, ferrying Beautifuls back and forth between Albion and Honeycomb.

A stunned, interminable journey for the ex-President of the Ruling Council and his followers. If the locomotive built as a toy broke down, they would be stranded in savage country. Yet the machine was well-built: it lasted nearly all the way, breaking down just ten miles from its destination.

The survivors reached Honeycomb, footsore, hungry, thirsty, exhausted and stricken by grief, where they found a skeleton staff of Beautifuls and technicians struggling in vain to restore the facility's capability. Due to gene sickness, Honeycomb had been closed to Beautification for many months, but it welcomed the survivors with plenty of preserved food and spare blankets. Those among them with engineering skills tried to reactivate machines so complex it became obvious only other machines could affect the repair.

Nevertheless, morale steadily improved in those early days. If nothing else, they were very much alive and active. In that brief, hopeful time, a primitive-born girl attached to Marvin's inner circle rose to prominence. She possessed precious knowledge how to hunt fresh game and fish; also what edibles to scavenge from the surrounding woodlands.

It was possible Brubacher's company could have survived the winter with tightened belts, using rations stored in the terminus building and the labyrinth of Honeycomb itself. Unfortunately, the freezers loaded with food had failed along with everything else, their contents spoiling. For the first time in many of their lives – most had been extravagantly rich even before the Great Dyings – eating became the

TWENTY-FOUR

issue on everyone's minds.

Marvin Brubacher himself showed strength of will and organisation to survive, swearing they would regain all they had lost.

Then, two weeks after their arrival, the first large group of refugees from Albion appeared on the causeway bridge to Holy Island, bearing tales of their exodus from the stricken City.

The journey along the monorail tracks – hundreds of interminable miles through the wilderness – had been plagued from the start. Though they travelled in large groups, countless fell behind, prey to weariness and despair. The trail north from Albion was marked by suicides swinging from tree boughs. Worse, rumours became certainty that hunters followed. Bizarre creatures, part human, part animal, prototype Angels determined to feast on stragglers. It was whispered at night round campfires these monsters sought vengeance for the gene experiments everyone now condemned as foolish and unwise.

Still, the strongest slogged on, feeding on whatever they could find. Sometimes they encountered small primitive villages or isolated farms. Driven by hunger, they overwhelmed their occupants, stripping every shred of food or useful equipment. Thousands more Beautifuls were trudging behind them along the monorail track. They must keep ahead or risk finding the land emptied by others as needy as themselves.

That first day a hundred new refugees arrived in Honeycomb. Another hundred appeared the next. Two hundred the day after, all starving, all armed and ready to fight for the means of life. Within a week, several thousand had gathered, filling every available building, even the cabins of drones. Many were forced to sleep in cold, lightless Beautification cells within the mountain itself.

Marvin Brubacher maintained his authority to begin with, but not for long. Within weeks all food stores had been plundered. Individual fights broke out daily that escalated into mass brawls. Rival groups and leaderships advocated different ways to survive. A sizable group left Holy Island, seeking a place to settle in the interior of Anglesey. Most soon returned, complaining of wild beasts and no shelter, a land of marsh and bog, inhospitable and bare. They also reported that the humanimal monsters which plagued their hellish journey from Albion were in the woods all around, watching, awaiting an opportunity.

Autumn brought cold, worsening the famine with sickness, something they had believed happened only to primitives. Parties of hunters scoured the lands for miles around, finding little enough. Even the birds were flying south. Folk used to delicacies from all over the globe dined on grubs and berries and called it a feast.

By midwinter, thousands had already perished. A proportion of them climbed Holyhead Mountain to leap off the high cliffs into the sea. As snow fell thick and settled, cannibalism ceased to be taboo.

One evening, tensions boiled over. A mob stormed the terminus building Marvin Brubacher claimed as his fief, dragging him out then beating him to death. Those few of his close followers still alive fled into the dark corridors of Honeycomb. And never emerged from the mountain again.

"What of the primitive girl?" Seth broke in. "What happened to her?"

The starving wretches claimed not to know. When pressed, a few assumed she had gone to die among the maze of cells in the mountain. "In the Beehive," one called it.

The rest of their story was predictable. The number of Beautifuls dwindled until all that remained were the few stricken ghosts before them.

After they had finished, Michael Pilgrim sighed. "We will grant you what you scarcely cared to grant us," he said. "The means for life. Give them some stew. Hardly any, at first, or it will kill them."

* * *

TWENTY-FOUR

That afternoon, Seth and Hurdy-Gurdy followed the road up Holyhead Mountain to Honeycomb's imposing entrance. A black perma-steel arch gave access to a cavernous reception and processing area. The aesthetic was austere and functional. Their footsteps echoed in the silence. Scores of registration booths lined the walls. In the centre stood a circular desk for a handful of human receptionists, otherwise every aspect of the place had been automated.

Their torches lit small patches of the enormous hexagonal room. Already it smelt of mould and neglect. A few corpses slumped by a wide exit leading into the interior of the mountain. Disturbed by intruders, rats stared and sniffed, whiskers twitching.

"I expected Honeycomb to be like a god's palace," said Seth. "Somewhere worthy of eternal life. All jewels and gold and fountains. But it's just bare and ugly."

For once, Hurdy-Gurdy remained grave.

"Young Nuncle should know that Honeycomb was never intended as a pleasant destination in itself. Merely the means to endless destinations. Oh yes, a certain lack of comfort reminded one of the stakes of passing through here. We thought of it as a purging of impurities. And so, the physical and the moral became blurred."

Seth grimaced. "I hate it. It's strange, but once all I wanted was to be powerful as City-folk. As though that would make life good forever. But look at what's left of their terrible power. A few fucking rats. And even they won't hang around once the meat is used up."

"Is Young Nuncle really sure he wishes to see more?"

"I have to try to find her. I have to."

His voice echoed.

"Then we shall go a-roving into the night."

"Have you been here before, Gurdy?"

"Of course. I came to Honeycomb, oh, eight or nine times. We would stay for three or four days to drink our nectar. It was fed into us by tubes along with drugs to keep us stupefied. Then, all refreshed and dandy as young bees, we would buzz back to Albion or one of the other Five Cities, until our yellow and black stripes grew frayed, our wings ragged. Then *buzzzz*, back we came for more."

Seth listened with a troubled mind. Was it for the miraculous process Gurdy described that Averil stuck it out with the Beautifuls, even when Albion fell? Perhaps she had been afraid of going home, that folk would hate her as a traitor. He knew all about that. He longed to be able to reassure her, convince her she was safe from harm, that loving arms awaited her back in Baytown.

"Let's look for my sister," he said. "I'd dearly like to find a trace of her."

Torches bright, they left the reception area. A long corridor stretched, giving access to offices and private quarters, stores for equipment and feeding systems, laboratories, ventilation generators, drone workshops and mini-fusion plants, everything needed to service the levels below. All had been ransacked for anything edible. Honeycomb was designed like a huge beehive with twenty levels descending deep into the bedrock of the mountain. In its heyday, Beautifuls had accessed individual cells via banks of elevators, conducted by drones.

When Hurdy-Gurdy and Seth reached the elevators the doors were sealed. A putrid aroma, sweet and reminiscent of old meat, escaped from the lift shafts. Faint noises suggested movement. Unless it was water dripping, or echoes of wind circulating through passageways.

"You wish to go further, Young Nuncle?"

"I must."

"This way then."

Gurdy led him to double doors marked *Emergency Access Only*. Beyond, a pitch-black stairwell descended. Cheeping, scurrying rats fled their lights. It became necessary to tread carefully: more bones lay on

TWENTY-FOUR

the stairs. One corpse was relatively fresh, forming a dark, noxious sludge round his or her skeleton. Perfect white teeth grinned at them from its skull.

As they descended, Hurdy-Gurdy crooned, his voice pure as a choirboy's:

My precious life, endless as oceans
Circling the Earth.
My precious life, a line unbroken
Birth to rebirth.
Oh, my precious life!
Oh, my precious life!
This whole world made just for me,
All I ever want to be.

"For fuck's sake!" snapped Seth, edging round two skeletons apparently embracing. "There's a time and a place, you know."

Hurdy gripped his arm, staring into his eyes with savage intensity.

"No! There is only ever *this* moment. *This* place. Remember that, learn from it, and you will live better than I did. You might learn then that the only precious life is one lived for others."

Seth shook himself free. They carried on down the stairs to another entrance. The doors opened to deepest night. Each level mimicked the pattern of hexagonal cells in a honeycomb, with corridors dividing the walls, a maze of identical routes to identically proportioned rooms.

The depth of the darkness intimidated Seth, yet he called out, "Averil! It's me! I've come to bring you home! Averil!"

Driven by hysteria, the sense that this was his one chance to find her, he plunged down a random corridor. Soon, awareness of direction was lost: as was Hurdy-Gurdy.

"Averil! Averil!"

The doors were mostly closed, but some lay open. Each cell was the same as the next, small and stark. A bed occupied one side, along with monitoring equipment. Tubes and wires ran from a control panel on the wall. Through these tubes, the cell-renewal elixir had flowed from a central reservoir, creating the possibility of cross-contamination that led in time to gene sickness. A toilet and shower made up the rest of the furnishings.

Some cells contained skeletons, as though starving people had come here to die, returning to the place where they once sought eternal life. Other cells were sealed from the inside; Seth did not care to explore what they concealed.

"Averil! It's me, Seth! You can come out now. I'm here to take you home."

On he rushed, slowing until he slumped in the dark, exhausted and utterly lost. Despair made him clutch his head.

In this position, Hurdy-Gurdy found him, after a long search. He hauled Seth to his feet.

"Wakey, wakey, Young Nuncle. Time for you to be reborn. To be a Beautiful." He added with a flourish, "Exeunt omnes. Pursued by a bear."

* * *

Michael Pilgrim knew he must escape this cursed place. Weeks of destroying drones and scouring the maze of Honeycomb for survivors had left him longing for home. But, at last, the diligent work was accomplished. Stairwells and elevators in the mountain blown up, using munitions scavenged from battle drones, until choked with rubble. Emergency exit tunnels demolished by the same means. The reception area and entrance had been detonated by piling up missiles and cannon shells and lighting a slow fire around them. The resulting explosion – witnessed from a safe distance – brought down a large landslide of limestone boulders, concealing the arched gateway.

TWENTY-FOUR

The next day, the company planned to depart. All were eager to leave the desolate field of bones, not least the surviving City-folk. Michael had guaranteed them allocations of land and assistance to establish themselves if they travelled to Yorkshire. There was no shortage of unploughed pasture available. A small number declined such a future of toil, preferring to dwindle and die after marvellous, elongated lives. The rest begged for protection from the creatures lurking in the dark woods they must travel through. This Michael felt inclined to refuse. The refugees from Albion deserved to find their own way through the harsh world their greed had created. But he knew damn well what his Grandfather would have done. Better to end this well, he thought, than be nagged from the grave by the old man's nice conscience.

Towards the end of that last afternoon on Holy Island, Michael walked round Holyhead Mountain to a derelict lighthouse on a promontory of bare rock. The door stood ajar and he climbed warily, pistol to hand. But no one lingered in its stark chambers, just the ghosts of former keepers and of ships crossing continents. At the top was a low balcony surrounding the old light mechanism. Here, he leant on the rail, his long hair stirred by the sea breeze.

From this vantage he gazed west, along a path of gold laid by the sun across the placid waves. A clear spring twilight, clouds elsewhere. On the horizon's edge lay Ireland and, further north, the Isle of Man. Places he would never visit, amongst all the others in this vast, teeming world.

For a while he watched seabirds wheel. At the foot of the cliffs, dolphins broke the water. On rocks, a large seal basked. The repetitive roll and break of waves stirred him. He stood on the rim of the cold sea, looking out, breathing. Like every human being since time's dawn, he stood in the company of myriad life.

How strange is this existence, he thought, how beautiful the world's music, for all its dissonances and meandering codas. How sad then, people seemed incapable of treasuring the world's harmonies.

At the thought of human weakness, familiar doubts troubled him. Doubts that questioned the purpose of mankind. What insane destroyers people could be! Himself included. The cruellest of species, foolish, revelling in ignorance, wanton children without kindness – unless it came to rewarding themselves or their own genes – happy to torch the whole world for the sake of shadows.

Truly, it would be better if they had never evolved to plague the planet. By that reasoning, his Grandfather's injunction to *preserve, preserve, preserve* was worthy of contempt. Perhaps even just another example of mankind's monstrous selfishness. Preserve what exactly? And why? Humanity itself scarcely deserved preservation. Only the Great Dyings stopped his miserable kind from poisoning the entire planet. Perhaps the devastating plagues had been nature's way of saving itself. If so, good riddance.

Maybe the Grow People were right. Only nature was pure, and until folk lived in accordance with its ways, they had no right to keep spoiling and choking what it gave.

He recalled the Modified Man's warning before he died: *Remember their arrogance will destroy them one day.*

For a while, he stood on the rock's edge, head bowed, listening to wind and gull cries, the waves breaking. Unexpected tears trickled down his grizzled cheeks. Tears, in truth, of self-pity. He was sick of struggling in vain to make the world better. He had done enough – too much – and was weary to the bone.

He wept also to think of old grief and guilt from the Crusades. Not to mention all his other bloody battles and skirmishes. How many men had he consigned to the cold grave through violence? He should know that number exactly, reproach himself with it daily, yet he could not even remember them all. How could he not remember so important a number? His stubborn pilgrimage against the Five Cities had been a

TWENTY-FOUR

harvest of wasted lives.

He wept, too, to think how poor a father he had been to his son, George, always distracted by cares, too clumsy to show proper love. Perhaps he did not know how to love, not truly. Perhaps he did not deserve love. And now he and Iona had brought a new bairn into the world, a bonny baby daughter, born at Christmas. Was he to neglect her, like George, or raise her to happy womanhood?

Recollections of loved ones made him look up. The horizons both daunted and drew him to their vastness. In all directions of the compass, continents large enough to sustain every creature, if used with moderation, viewed with care. Were not the souls and bodies of those he loved wide as continents, and deserving the same consideration? We all can change, he told himself; I must change.

Such thoughts reminded him of Amar back in Hob Hall, striving to ensure a bumper harvest. God knew they needed one. The Pilgrimage of Fools stole much labour from the land last year. And the land had repaid their neglect with scanty crops. Many in Baytown went hungry during the exceptionally cold winter just gone, a dearth he was determined should not be repeated.

Then Michael Pilgrim wiped his eyes. Purpose resumed at facing down the necessity of feeding family and community. Well, a fasting belly may never be merry, or so wise tongues claimed in Baytown. And if they worked together, all might yet eat well come the Winter Solstice and Christmas. It was a purpose to share, if nothing else. For no one really stood alone on the rim of the cold sea. Part of each other dwelled in every human heart and mind, a gift of connection.

"We can change," he whispered to the sea.

It whispered back in endless motion, not *preserve, preserve, preserve*, but *change, change, change*.

EPILOGUE: HARVEST

"One in, one out, I suppose."

Michael Pilgrim looked up sharply. This time, the words came not from his long lost pal, Charlie Gudwallah – indeed, could not, this side of the grave – but from Charlie's daughter, now running the Puzzle Well Inn in Baytown, alongside her fisherman husband, Ben Higginbottom, Tom's eldest.

Nor did the young woman's words refer to the death of a baby child, as Charlie's had, another world ago, or so it felt. She referred to the ancient inn bursting its seams with thirsty revellers in advance of the Harvest Fair at sundown on the beach.

"Well, there's only so much room for bodies," Michael conceded, jammed against the bar, his favourite clay tankard awaiting a recharge.

There was no shortage of folk in Baytown eager to stand him a drink. Michael Pilgrim was always guaranteed a respectful circle of faces at the Puzzle Well. Sometimes it made him uncomfortable: memories of past glories don't necessarily appeal to a man who suffered great heartache and hardship to earn them. He contented himself with a swift ale before pushing through the scrum into late September's soft, lulling light.

He climbed the steep road from the jetty, greeting busy folk. Packhorses and donkeys laden for the fair gathered on the beach as the tide turned, their owners jostling for the best space to raise temporary stalls or set out their wares on blankets.

At the crest of the hill, he passed new houses constructed from salvaged bricks and stones: easier sometimes to start afresh than repair the work of previous generations. Baytown's population was swelling steadily, likewise its confidence, along with that of the entire region.

His path followed the cliff edge, until he reached the ancient Youth Hostel at Hob Hole, an inlet in the cliffs at the foot of Hob Vale. It, too, had been renovated, home to a commune of Nuagers active as traders up and down the coast, far north as Lindisfarne and even Scotland, and far south as the Fen Country.

This meant more neighbours for Michael to greet on his way. Children flew kites or ran on the beach, giddy at the prospect of tonight's jollities. A fat harvest was safely home in barns and storerooms. As anyone sensible knows, work must serve leisure or there's a famine of joy.

Up the muddy road he climbed. Near home, he reached the Baytown Museum, perched amidst the grass-covered mounds of a deserted medieval village. Near the gateway to its former car park, stood a man with a peculiar face, neither young nor old, though progressing rapidly towards the latter. Grey streaked his hair and eyebrows. Lines etched his forehead.

Michael grew wary. A feeling shared by his neighbour. The man was a relative newcomer to Baytown, supervising a small hospital based in the Museum. The rest of the large building served as a school and academy for science and engineering. The latter was also overseen by the brooding figure at the gate.

"Afternoon," said Michael. "Are we to expect you and Miss Devereux at the festivities?"

The man's smile was a mite lopsided. His eyes did not smile at all. "You refer to tonight's fertility rite? Perhaps I should offer my services as resident witch doctor in case of alcohol-induced injuries. Would my presence add to the general juju, Pilgrim?"

Michael considered the offer. "No, Gover. We can be sure of that."

Blair Gover had limped into Baytown a year after the fall of Albion, starved and ill-shod, expecting no greater courtesy than a lynching. A last fond farewell with his former love, Helen Devereux, drew him – or so he claimed. In truth, he had nowhere left to go.

Michael's instinct had been to launch him over the cliffs then celebrate with free drinks all round at the Puzzle Well Inn. But revenge can be a wasteful, self-defeating luxury, especially when needs press hard. It so happened Gover's arrival that winter coincided with a plague – not the worst kind, but bad enough – rumoured to be heading their way from Lake Country.

Michael's last act as Protector of the North had been to declare a general amnesty for crimes committed by both sides in the long struggle against the City. Even as he bunched his fists and glared at Gover, he could almost hear his Grandfather's voice: "True justice, Michael, requires absolute consistency from the law. Remember the power of mercy, lest you be judged in your turn!"

Which was why, after consulting Baytown's council and Helen Devereux, he made Gover a reluctant offer, hoping it would be turned down. "We've had no decent medicine hereabouts since Dr Macdonald died – a finer person than you or I will ever be. And I do believe you might prove handy in other ways. We badly need to generate power through wind and wave if we are to have electric light. Not to mention more efficient agriculture, so we don't risk hunger every other year."

"Simple innovations can increase general health and productivity," agreed Gover.

"And we were thinking – it was Miss Devereux's suggestion – you could teach useful science to our young 'uns."

"Your generous offer," said Gover, "sounds suspiciously like drudgery. In short, I am given a choice between slavery and death."

Michael refrained from mentioning that Gover once offered him the same.

"No, not death," he said.

"What then?"

"Just my boot up your backside. And a sincere prayer I never see you again."

"No worse?"

"Just my boot. And my blessing."

"I see."

A dark look crossed Gover's face. "Humanity is a constant disappointment to me, Pilgrim, always was. Always will be. Apart from Helen, of course. Actually, even her."

"Still, it's no fun dying alone," pointed out Michael. "Or being lonely when you're old and you call out for help. You'd be glad of humanity then. And we badly need a doctor. I'll say no more."

That bargain had been struck five winters earlier. Since then, Gover proved a skilful doctor indeed, apart from a repellent bedside manner. As for his work as professor, astonishing knowledge and ingenuity taught his pupils how to manufacture and maintain wind and water generators for lights, as well as miraculous steam-powered hauling machines on wheels, for ploughing and carting, their boilers fashioned from salvaged metal and stoked with plastic *tilth*.

Michael left Gover to contemplate the twilight heading his way, and headed up the lane towards Hob Hall.

First, he reached Holy Innocents Church, now given over to Nuagers and their cosmic spirit voyages. There, he encountered Iona, with their six-year-old daughter, Averil, both clutching – for reasons he did not choose to explore – willow wands plaited with seagull feathers, dried witch hazel, and disturbingly phallic balloons made from a pig's bladder.

"Daddy!" cried Averil. "Look at this!"

She waved the totem blithely so that the balloons quivered.

"Mummy said I should make one for you, too!" added the little girl. "It's lucky."

"How kind of Mummy," he said.

That afternoon a solemn service of thanks to the Lucky Stars had been held at the ancient church, led by Iona in magnificent Nuager Priestwoman robes. A service which partly explained why he had wandered off to the less spiritual environs of the Puzzle Well Inn.

Iona took his arm as they headed for Hob Hall

"Are they all drunk at the Puzzle Well?" she asked, pushing back her thick black hair, which was starting to show silver threads.

Averil giggled behind a hand at such a notion. She waved her lucky wand. "Naughty Daddy!"

"Everyone sober as stones," he said. "In any case, it's only right to finish off last year's ale and cider before you brew more. Same goes for the wine."

"There's common sense for you," laughed Iona. "What a practical man you are, Michael Pilgrim."

"Someone has to be round here. Anyway, doesn't wasting earth's bounty displease the stars?"

"So it does." Her gay, lilting brogue drew him as always. "I might well help with the work myself later," she added.

"I shall look forward to that."

She bobbed up to kiss his cheek. The excitement of leading a ceremony generally stirred her affections.

"So I might," she said, archly.

They strolled back to Hob Hall, arm-in-arm, Averil running around them with her wand, spraying good luck at the invisible Faery o' the

Vale. She believed wholeheartedly in that magical creature, and who could disprove her faith?

After he had dressed into clothes fit for a notable occasion, Michael left Iona naked and still drowsing on their wide old bed.

The ancient corridors and staircases of Hob Hall, with their varnished black wooden boards, had barely changed in three hundred years. He hoped they would outlast his children's children.

That afternoon, there was a tendency among the Hall's diverse residents for ribaldry. Fifteen orphans living in the attic rooms made much noise. Plague and war had created too many homeless waifs thereabouts, and it was the Pilgrim family custom to take them in. Michael paused at the sound of running feet and excited shrieks. Let them enjoy today, he thought, aware of their yesterdays' hard edges, and the uncertainty of their tomorrows. Who did not face the same fate?

Passing the back door to the cobbled farmyard, surrounded on three sides by outhouses and living quarters for labourers, he glimpsed purposeful activity. Amar was supervising the loading of handcarts with cider and ale barrels, baskets of bread and meats of all kinds, as well as cheeses, fruit pies, honey-stewed apples and pears from Pilgrim orchards in Hob Vale, prepared as a treat for the children.

Despite so much plenty, Amar's expression was lined by melancholy. Even five years later, he still took Averil's loss hard, blaming himself. Not all casualties of war bear wounds written on the body. Yet he remained steadfast in efficiency and kindness, supervising the labourers and skilled workers who supported their families through work at Hob Hall. Increasingly, they were claiming empty land of their own, restoring farmhouses round the vale.

A crowd was gathering in the yard. Folk of all ages excited as bairns. Michael knew them well enough to predict the kind of hangover usually described thereabouts as "skull-cracking".

He stole away to his favourite retreat, the old library, once his bedchamber. Although hundreds of precious volumes had been loaned to the new school at the Baytown Museum, he retained beloved companions on the sturdy wooden shelves.

With a sigh, Michael settled in his favourite chair for a peaceful pipe. His faithful old sheepdog, Bess, shaggy and smelly, a canine Methuselah, limped from the kitchen where she snoozed away her last days, conveniently close to fire and food bowl. The scent of his tobacco drew her.

"Why, old lady," he said, scratching her head.

Michael fell to musing as he smoked. Soon he would be forty years old, a decent enough age by Baytown reckoning. With luck he had two good decades ahead, maybe three. How swiftly time must flee. It seemed a mere moment since he was small boy on the beach by Hob Hole, playing cricket with his big brother James. How to fill that remaining time glowed in his mind like the tobacco in his pipe, always burning away.

Some things he knew for sure. If nature willed it, he and Iona would have more children, though he feared to lose her through childbirth. Then again, he had learned to delight in passing pleasures. Good food and books and friends and music and conversation connect happy days. No more would he travel far from home or be a leader of men. All his offices save Baytown councillor had been resigned.

Tobacco smoke rose in ribbons as he pondered. Bess laid her greying head on his boot, until a clanging bell from the farmyard disturbed them.

The first shadows of twilight found a procession of Hob Valers walking along the beach to Baytown.

Michael and his family led the way in clean, brushed clothes, wearing ribbons and badges of woven corn to honour the harvest. He made sure his son, George, was at his right side, and tried hard to engage the lad – now more gangly youth than boy – in a man's conversation. But George was shy with the father who'd been absent through crucial years of his childhood. It seemed to Michael he would never break down that distrust.

Beside them walked Helen Devereux, conversing with Amar about the school, her special domain. Age was an advancing tide across her wrinkled face; she stooped a little as she walked. Though Gover might scorn a rustic fair, Helen had dressed in her brightest clothes, wearing the Baytown Jewel for all to see. The talisman was an object of awe, its magic fabled to have set free all those oppressed by the City. Helen wore it with pride, a pride earned many times over.

Dozens of other folk dwelling in the Vale followed, lads and lasses sporting crowns of bright flowers. Last came handcarts bearing food and drink, along with a few musical instruments, including Michael's violin. The Baytown orchestra created by Dr Macdonald had revived of late.

Their footsteps quickened as they approached the fair on the beach. Bonfires flickered in the fading light. Hundreds had already gathered, mainly in family groups, or huddles defined by farm or hamlet or even whole villages. Separate bands of fiddlers and guitarists and singers competed for rings of dancers.

The start of the fair delivered a much-anticipated cargo. A small flotilla led by Tom Higginbottom's trading boat was days overdue from a trip south to the Fen Folk, exchanging Yorkshire wool for salt. All day, Tom's wife and children had kept an anxious eye on the sea. At last, just as the fair warmed its toes, familiar sails were spotted.

When Tom's large coble was dragged ashore, it carried more than just salt. An old man with crazy white hair and wild, bloodshot eyes somersaulted from the prow to land, a little wobbly, on the shingle, arms spread wide to receive applause.

"Hurdy does love a crowd!" he declared.

After him, came two young men. One beamed at the prospect of pleasures ahead; the second, his friend, glanced round nervously, inclined to retreat back to the boat.

"Seth! Seth!"

Tears pricked Michael's eyes at the sight of his nephew. He knew well what courage it had taken to return to Baytown, amnesty or no amnesty. Old resentments and black looks showed in faces concealing bitter memories. He hastened forward for an embrace. Then he turned to the crowd, a hard edge in his voice.

"Friends, we all see folk here tonight who have done this community wrong in the past. I could point my finger at a good dozen from where I'm standing." He sought out faces in the crowd. A few looked away uneasily. "So let's have no more hate or nonsense. Tonight of all nights. Tonight we thank nature for her bounty. Most of all, we come together as good friends and neighbours. Let nobody forget, our best strength lies in each other."

For a moment frowns lingered. The mood against Seth might have turned either way. But Helen Devereux stepped forward to greet the bold rescuer of the Baytown Jewel at King's Lynn, seconded by a less enthusiastic Tom Higginbottom.

Gaiety was restored when Hurdy-Gurdy delighted the crowd with an outrageous song, dance and acrobatics routine, accompanying himself upon a borrowed guitar and tambourine.

"Look at me!" he cried gleefully. "All the world's a stage, and all the men and women merely players. Look at me, damn you!"

And the humble audience did look at Hurdy-Gurdy, clapping and laughing, until his own sorrows and regrets were set aside – for a while, at least.

EPILOGUE: HARVEST

"I thought, Uncle," Seth explained later, as stars formed ribbons across a cloudless sky. They were toasting absent friends with shots of apple brandy beside the Pilgrim family bonfire. Most of all, Seth raised his glass for Averil. Her loss felt an unhealable wound. "I would pay my belated respects at Father and Mother's graves. And lay a headstone for Averil, though her body was never found."

"That would do her honour," said Michael, softly.

They watched Iona dance hand in hand with little Averil, singing a childish rhyme together. Iona's long hair brushed her daughter's head as they capered.

"Of course, she chose the wrong side," said Seth. "But I've learned how easy it is for the world and those who seem powerful to fool us into doing wrong. Even bright, brave Averil."

Michael stirred. "We shouldn't be too hard on her. She was afraid for her unborn child, and was never quite the same after Big Jacko and his Queen abused her sorely. The City offered her a pearl beyond imagining. Little wonder if she wavered. I have no doubt she'd have seen sense in time, if allowed a longer life. Let's choose to remember her as she was before the drones came to Hob Hall, all those years ago. Let's remember the best of her, and hope others will do the same for ourselves."

For a while neither spoke. The burning driftwood pulsed faintly. Sparks rose from the fire. Seth hesitated then said. "I came back, too, because I thought, if I don't face the folk I wronged now, I never shall. I don't want to live afraid of the past no more."

Michael remembered how the Crusades blighted his happiness. "You do right," he said. "You've found your own wisdom. Your mother and father would be right glad."

"Maybe," said Seth, rubbing his eyes.

"And I see you've not just found wisdom. Look yonder at your special friend. Cutty has been making eyes to dance for a while, I notice. Which is why I might very well tune up my violin."

Round bonfires lit like beacons to summon good fortune, the folk of Baytown danced and drank. Ribbons of sunrise appeared over the eastern horizon of the sea. Cold winter felt easy to forget that night. Waves broke a murmuring song against the beloved land. The froth created by land and sea's eternal embrace glowed faintly, lit by the stars, and the plump, grinning face of a red harvest moon.

Acknowledgement

I would like to thank the following people for their generous support for the Pilgrim Trilogy:

Everyone at Cloud Lodge Books, but especially William Campos and Orlando Ortega-Medina. Orlando has been the perfect editor.

A big thank you to the wonderful people at York Literature Festival and York Explore. Rob O'Connor and Wendy Kent are owed particular gratitude.

Special thanks to Jo Caruth for sharing invaluable information about the early Fenlands of East Anglia. Jo and David Gill also took me for an inspiring walk round Flag Fen in Norfolk.

Many thanks to the 'early readers' who commented on *Pilgrim Tale*: Sara Bowland, Jane Collins, Richard Gray, Bob Horne, Dori Murgatroyd, Anna Perrett, and Craig Smith. Their thoughts really helped me create my dystopian world.

Flight Lieutenant Rick Weeks for arranging a fantastic visit to RAF Fylingdales.

Many thanks, too, to "late readers" whose enjoyment of the series encouraged me to press on, especially Helen Harrison, Richard Murgatroyd, Andrew Field and Kate Vernon-Rees.

Lastly, a big thank you as ever to Ruth Murgatroyd for supporting my writing and just being herself.

A few words about writing dystopian fiction in a time of dystopia. The recent COVID pandemic has demonstrated how fragile societies are in the face of unexpected shocks. Also, how ineffective and venal self-serving elites can be in the face of a crisis. At the same time, we have witnessed wonderful courage and self-sacrifice from ordinary people in extraordinary times. I very much hope positivity about human nature shines through the dystopian world of the Pilgrim Trilogy. The moment we lose our faith in the power of human goodness and co-operation, we are lost.

With that in mind, I also hope readers of the trilogy consider the reckless nature of humanity's current inaction when it comes to meaningful remedies for the environmental disaster brewing around us. Otherwise, who knows when clouds of deadly *tilth* could be blowing our way . . .

Tim Murgatroyd
12th February 2021

About the Author

Tim Murgatroyd was brought up in Yorkshire. He read English at Hertford College, Oxford University, and now lives with his family in York. He is the author of several novels of historical fiction. Pilgrim City is the concluding volume of the Pilgrim Trilogy, following on from Book 1: Pilgrim Tale and Book 2: Pilgrim Lost.